# I Hope You Dance

*"Heart-warming, charming, and funny,
I Hope You Dance offers the hope of second chances in
both love and life. A lovely and satisfying book."*

– Katharine Swartz

# I Hope You Dance

## BETH MORAN

LION FICTION

Published by Lion Fiction
an imprint of
**Lion Hudson plc**
Wilkinson House, Jordan Hill Road
Oxford OX2 8DR, England
www.lionhudson.com/fiction

ISBN 978 1 78264 170 4
e-ISBN 978 1 78264 171 1

First edition 2015

A catalogue record for this book is available from the British Library

Printed and bound in the UK, August 2015, LH26

*For more about Beth visit:* www.bethmoran.org

*For Ciara —*
*who, given the choice,*
*never sits it out if she can dance*

# Acknowledgments

Huge thanks to Jessica Tinker, for her fantastic enthusiasm and much needed insight. I am so grateful to be working with an editor who shares my vision. Also to Julie Frederick – it was a genuine pleasure to work with you – and all those at Lion Hudson who helped put the book together.

Thanks to Robyn Neild for another beautiful cover and Phil Bowell at 18two Design, who took my vague thoughts about a website and created exactly what I wanted.

Dewi Hughes at Silverlock Tenders – your encouragement and practical support has been inspirational. Vicky, Pearl, Alison and all those awesome Free Range Chicks – I couldn't have got here without you. And again, big, big thanks to my King's Church family for cheering me on. Ruth Humphries – it's so good to run alongside you, sister!

Thanks also to Duncan Lyon for talking through some of the legal elements in the story. The wonderful Robbins family – for keeping my feet on the ground while giving me the confidence to aim high. Ciara, Joseph, and Dominic, who make it all worthwhile – I'm so blessed to have you. And to George – I can't thank you enough for helping me get out there and dance.

# Chapter One

My mother always told me I had lousy timing.

This afternoon, in front of my boss, my boss's boss and a whole load of his most lucrative clients, I proved her right.

Of course, she was talking about the Viennese waltz, the Argentinian tango and the foxtrot.

"Come on now, darling; you have to feel the beat. Embrace the rhythm of the music. Feel it. One, two, three. One, two, three. Da, dum, dum. No, *feel it*. FEEL IT!"

My current timing issue involved five Chinese businessmen and a psychological breakdown.

I had managed to quite successfully assume my usual role of note-taker, head-nodder and occasional bland comment-maker from the corner of the table. However, my delightful boss, Cramer Spence, then asked me a question.

"What do you think, Ruth?"

I looked up from the sketch of a great-crested newt I had been doodling onto my notepad. The newt clawed frantically at the sides of a compost bin, trying to scrabble its way out, its black tongue dangling out of one side of its mouth. Sliding against the bin, slick with rotting vegetable juices, the newt slipped deeper into the mush of month-old carrot peelings and banana skins. Cramer raised one plucked eyebrow at me. He did this a lot, the eyebrow raise. It was, according to Alice, his signature move. Alice was the twenty-one-year-old temp he had been sleeping with until he fired her, a month ago.

I lowered my eyes back to the pad. What I thought was this: I wanted to take the pencil waggling about in Cramer Spence's grubby fingers and jab it into his eye. The one beneath the signature-move eyebrow. I am not a violent person. That this thought didn't horrify me, horrified me.

Cramer Spence coughed. I could hear the impatience in his voice. "Ruth?"

I stared at the newt. At the way its tiny, webbed feet clung to the plastic surface in a desperate attempt to escape the decomposing mess it was drowning in. I remembered the feel of Cramer Spence's fingers as they had slithered and slimed their way down my spine in the staff kitchen only two hours earlier. I felt again his hot, damp breath as he murmured how he really loved the way my chest looked in the top I was wearing, and how about popping a button undone to make the Chinese clients feel happy? My hand subconsciously pressed to the top of my high-necked blouse, sagging where my flesh had wittered and worried away until my collar bone poked out like a scrawny chicken carcass. Something inside my brain exploded into a million pieces.

The newt was me.

"I think that when you groped my backside last week your hand felt like a plastic bag full of sausages so old and rancid they started squiggling about inside the bag."

Cramer choked. His boss sat up straighter in his chair and for the first time looked interested.

"And I think that when you whined at me to stop being so uptight your breath smelt like you'd been eating slugs."

The Chinese businessmen clients frowned. Their interpreter, a long-legged Asian woman with glossy lipstick and thick, swingy hair, snorted.

I stood up, carefully tucking my chair back under the conference table. How professional! Even in the middle of a personal breakdown I attended to company policy on health and safety. "I also think that I no longer want to work for someone whose eyebrows make them appear like a very ugly woman in drag."

# CHAPTER ONE

I picked up my bottle of water, swung my nine pound ninety-nine handbag over my shoulder and marched out of the room. I made it down all three flights of stairs to the lobby, and out onto the deserted street, before breaking down into the kind of hysterical, juddering sobs that sounded more as though they came from my fourteen-year-old daughter.

Slumped against the concrete wall of the adjacent building, out of sight of the office windows, I marvelled at the sheer awfulness of what I had just said and done. During the bus ride home to Woolton, the suburb in South Liverpool where I lived, I ignored the stares of the other bus passengers, tried to get a grip on myself and trawled through my current problems to find a bright side. No job. A pile of unopened bills. A teenage daughter who *needed* to dye her hair and wear Dr Martens. A dead partner who had left no will, no life insurance and no way to pay the upkeep on our four-bedroomed detached house with ensuite bathroom, double garage and serious negative equity. No way out. Except one.

I was going to have to call my mother.

Fraser had been killed in a car accident eighteen months earlier. Having known great loss once before, I expected to feel the anger, shock, despair, physical pain like a vice compressing my heart until I couldn't breathe. I knew I would get through it, that there was another side to the thick, black swamp of grief. I knew our daughter, Maggie, would survive, although the scars would mark her heart and shape her spirit for the rest of her life. I fretted and at times panicked about how I would find the strength to put the bin out, deal with the car when it broke down, handle Fraser's mother.

But it never crossed my mind to worry about coping financially. Maggie's father had been rich. *We* had been rich. Then I started opening bank statements. And bills. And answering the phone. And out of the secret shadows of Fraser's man cave crawled a great, writhing debt monster that grew bigger and uglier with every menacing step.

My job, obsessive penny-counting and tactical delays with creditors kept the monster from eating us alive. Until Cramer Spence decided it would be fun to launch a campaign of seduction aimed at the tragic widow. I was out of control, out of my mind with worry and out of options.

Most of all, I was furious. Not at Fraser, or Cramer Spence. At myself.

I couldn't fight it any more. We were going home.

Three weeks later, the van I had hired to ferry the remains of our stuff from Liverpool to Southwell, a small market town in Nottinghamshire, slunk around the corner into the cul-de-sac where I had been born and raised. Our house sat at the end of the row of five 1970s detached boxes lining one side of the street. On the opposite side, five nearly identical houses faced them. I hunched lower in the van, eyes sweeping both rows, searching for signs of life. It had been eight years. Nothing much seemed to have changed. Me included. This felt a long way from the victorious, I-showed-them, hero's return I'd dreamt about. Quite the contrary. Everything the neighbours, old friends, school reports and postman had predicted would happen, had.

I didn't look at the house at the end of the street, the only one to stand apart from the box-sets, the one everyone called the Big House. Not yet.

Inching so reluctantly up the shallow slope of my parents' driveway that the van stalled, I switched off the engine, took a moment to breathe. My eyes welling up for the squillionth time that day, the first sight my mother had of me as she yanked open the front door and marched down the path was her youngest daughter wiping a dribble of snot on her sleeve while keening like a baby.

Did I mention I was an emotional wreck? I thanked God, yet again, that Mum had the good sense to arrange for Maggie to spend a week with her paternal grandmother while I sorted things out in Southwell.

# CHAPTER ONE

Mum stepped up into the van, handed me a neatly ironed handkerchief and gripped hold of my hand tightly. With her other hand she gently turned my face towards hers, boring deep into my eyes and, beyond that, to my splintered soul.

"Welcome home, my darling girl. Welcome home! Now. I'm going to put the kettle on. Take a moment to remember this is not a step down, a step backwards or a step into a pit of deadly snakes. This is a stride onwards and upwards! Things have been tough. I have ground my teeth down to the bone in sympathy for the toughness of your tragedy. But now you are home. No more tears today. We are celebrating. Our girl is home!"

She skipped her lithe dancer's frame back into the house to make tea, her white ponytail the only hint she carried a free bus pass. I knew Mum would have laid out one of the best china plates with home-made cookies and my favourite chocolate slices; dug out the green mug with blue spots that my eldest sister, Esther, gave me for my sixteenth birthday. The tablecloth would be ironed, and fresh flowers in colours that I loved – reds, purples and blues – arranged in a vase on the table. I did not doubt for one second that my mother had willed me home with the unbreakable force of her love for me. Even stronger than my many attempts to shut it out.

I sat in the hub of the van and took a moment. I looked at the garden, at the bright green baby fruit nesting in the Bramley apple trees. I pretended to be absorbed in the geraniums, the dahlias and palest pink clematis blooming on the fence. I examined carefully the front of the house, the large bay windows and Victorian lamp beside the door, slowly moving my eyes along to the gate dividing the front from the back garden. Then carried on, across to the left, an inch of view at a time. I forced myself to breathe slowly, to relax my hands on the steering wheel, to not make this a big deal. Prepared myself to find it gone, or changed, or dead. But there it was. In front of the Big House. In front of David's house. The willow tree. From the driver's seat of the van, I drank it in.

I had left the best chunk of my heart under the boughs of that willow tree, right beside where my initials were carved, RH, underneath David's DC. I could tell what month it was from the size and the colour of the leaves. Guess the hour of the day by lying underneath and watching how the sun dappled through the branches and where its shadows fell. I sat there, and like a peek inside a stolen treasure box, or someone else's diary, I let myself remember. And in doing so, I found the strength to stick on a smile, pull my shoulders into a posture fitting of a champion ballroom dancer's daughter, and step back into the house I once swore I would never enter again.

Four hours later, I slouched at the kitchen table drinking tea, waiting to get the next hurdle over with. The front door slamming had announced Dad's return. Mum, icing cakes at the kitchen counter for one of the many "causes" she took upon herself, bustled into the hall. To give her some credit, she tried to whisper.

"Gil! Where have you *been*? I told you Ruth would be here at one. It's nearly five o'clock. We had to unload the van by ourselves!" There was an indistinguishable mumble. "She's in the kitchen. Please be welcoming."

Dad came into the kitchen. He looked old. His hair was still a thick mop roosting on the top of his head, and he stood, like my mother, as if he had a broom up his shirt. But his energy had clearly faded, like a torch running out of battery. Maybe due to my presence in his kitchen. Or the fact that, temporarily, it was my kitchen now too.

"Hi, Dad."

He nodded. "Ruth" – his eyes flickered everywhere except at me – "you got here."

"Yes, thanks."

"Coffee?"

"I already have tea."

"Right. Well. I've got some papers to sort out. I'll be in my office."

He opened the door, pausing with his hand on the knob. I could picture Mum gesticulating at him from the hallway. He coughed. "Anyway. It's nice to see you. Glad you could come and stay."

He left. *Oh, Dad*, I thought. *Really? "Nice"?*

I tried not to mind. Not to feel as though he'd slam-dunked my heart into the kitchen bin. I knew we were both to blame. But I was weak, and tired, and lost and afraid. *Nice?*

To take my mind off the limp welcome, I gazed into the bottom of my teacup, pondering the offhand comment Mum had made about unloading the van. Mum had not only tried to make Dad feel guilty – unusual enough in itself – but I couldn't remember hearing her lie before.

We hadn't unloaded the van by ourselves. By the time Mum and I unrolled the door to the hold, an enormous tropical bird had flown out of the Big House and flapped across to join us. The tropical bird's name was Ana Luisa. She was in fact a young Brazilian woman disguised behind a rainbow coloured, feathered and fringed sun dress, with a matching scarf wrapped around her head, and huge red-rimmed sunglasses that she pushed up to reveal chocolate pools for eyes and skin like butterscotch. She had the body of an Amazon underneath that fluffy dress, with the strength to accompany it. She never stopped smiling, never broke a sweat or became short of breath and emptied boxes faster than Mum and I put together.

"Oh, yes, I have to be strong to clean that big, dusty house for Mr Arnold. When Mr David is home he tidies up after himself, not a problem, but Mr Arnold – my, my! He is so much in the world of his studies and his important research, and planning lectures or writing the next chapter of his book, he doesn't even notice the gas left on or a pair of shoes right in the hallway where he will trip and smash his head on the flagstones. I am telling you, if I was not here to take care of him I don't know what would become of him. He would starve to death sitting in that office thinking of some old scroll with an Egyptian lady's shopping list from ten thousand years ago written on it…"

I had stopped processing at *when Mr David is home*. Mr David still called the Big House home? Why wasn't he married to some gorgeous television producer who followed him around the world filming his kids' wildlife programme, renting out penthouse apartments in between shows? Why didn't he have some rambling farmhouse where a rosy-cheeked wife who thought nothing of castrating a few bulls before breakfast waited to greet him with home-made ice-cream and a back rub? Where were his blond-haired, grey-eyed children, waiting for Daddy to bring back treasures from his travels? Why didn't he spend his time off taking them camping in the woods, climbing mountains, teaching them how to fish and start a fire with a bunch of dead leaves?

And if David sometimes came home, was he home now? Was he home soon? This year? This month? And how could I ask without my voice betraying me, my head spinning and my legs giving way?

I lay in bed watching the moon glimmering through the gap in my old curtains as the clock ticked off those strange hours that dwell in the middle of a sleepless night. Everything felt the same. The same bed, same pale blue walls. It was all clean and fresh, but under the scent of freesias wafting from a vase on my dressing table, it still smelt exactly the same. Pencil shavings. Rose-scented drawer linings and the faintest whiff of the nail polish remover I used to scrub away my enforced dance-show prettiness. In the moonlight I could trace the outline of the pictures covering the far wall. My sketches and paintings of animals, reptiles and birds. One or two insects. All drawn from real-life observation, all scientifically accurate and annotated with David's facts about the species, habitat, eating habits and other information he deemed relevant.

Every picture recounted a story, a quest, an adventure. A memory. I felt some comfort there, in the dreams and sunny days of my childhood. I had once found a way to be happy here. To survive.

I had known who I was, then. Could I do it again? Eventually, sleep came, the animals racing with me through my dreams. Fast and urgent, we ran. Running to escape the darkness that hunted us. Desperate for safety. For home.

# Chapter Two

The following morning, I dragged myself out of bed to deal with the man picking up the hire van. Figuring that while I was up I might as well make coffee, I shuffled into the kitchen in my pyjamas and found a note propped on the kitchen table. Written on stiff card, with my mother's initials inscribed on the top corner, it said:

> *At the day centre supervising bingo. Back around 12.37. Please drop the cake off at the specified address. M xx*
>
> *p.s. It is so wonderful to have you home! You are as utterly beautiful as ever (although worryingly scrawny).*

My first thought was to crumple up the note and toss it into the bin. Or go back to bed and pretend I hadn't seen it. Then the familiar creak of my dad's footsteps on the stairs changed my mind. A day at home trying to avoid each other, swimming through a sea of simmering disappointment, felt more tiring than throwing on a pair of jeans and walking a cake down a few streets. I finished my coffee upstairs, pulling on clean clothes then shoving my dark mass of split ends into a ponytail and hastily brushing the caffeine from my teeth before preparing to run the small-town gauntlet.

One of the hardest things about going to Liverpool University had been the sheer volume of human beings. More than that, the endless supply of *different* people. The chance of bumping into a familiar face outside of the university campus or halls of residence was minute; the never ending stream of strangers, intimidating. In Southwell, even with a growing population of ten thousand, it had been impossible to walk anywhere without seeing people you knew. Every child in the town (bar the handful educated privately) attended the same school. On my last visit for my sister Lydia's wedding eight years earlier most of the shop workers still recognized me (helped, of course, by the bride's semi-celebrity status).

I briefly debated using Mum's parrot headscarf as a disguise, wrapping it elegantly around my head, Audrey Hepburn style. Was I delusional? Wearing a headscarf through the streets of Southwell in twenty-five degree heat to avoid being recognized? That would be ridiculous. Only a complete loser would contemplate going to such extreme lengths to avoid being seen.

So, scarf firmly wrapped around my head, secured in place with a pair of original 80s sunglasses I had found in a kitchen drawer, I scuttled through my home town.

I knew the name of the street the cake was destined for, but hadn't ever ventured onto it. The Nook turned out to be a tiny lane off one of the roads cutting down the far side of the hill. I huffed my way over the top, scurrying past the houses of old school mates, the bungalow where a retired cleaner from my parents' dance academy lived, and the huge cottage where I used to babysit, quietly cursing my mum's goodwill.

The kitchen had always been her second "studio", so to speak – the place she was guaranteed to be if not dancing. And it was not mere food that came out of Mum's oven: it was an expression of herself, each stew or roast or biscuit carefully concocted to be as life-affirming, invigorating, heart-warming as possible. But what she called her "Christian duty" was an understatement. It seemed that in the last twenty-four hours she had iced more cupcakes than one church – let alone one family – could stomach. As if all her energy once spent twirling and tapping on the dance floor was now funnelled into measuring and mixing, sifting and slicing. I had felt exhausted simply watching her, without having to join her too.

Bramley House was a ramshackle cottage set back from the road, surrounded by rambling gardens. Children's bikes and skateboards littered the brick path leading up to the red front door. A greenhouse stood to one side, along with two dishevelled vegetable patches. Assorted pots and planters lined the front of the house and several pairs of mud-encrusted wellies lay discarded beside the welcome mat.

Amazed and relieved to manage a ten-minute walk and only see one other pedestrian (an elderly dog-walker who unsurprisingly crossed to the other side of the road), I made my way up the drive.

Awkwardly balancing the cake box in one arm, I reached up to remove the sunglasses. At that moment, an ear-piecing screech split the air from several directions. I caught a glimpse of what appeared to be a blue-skinned goblin swinging towards me at head height from the corner of one eye and half a second later was karate-chopped in the back of both knees, one after the other in quick succession.

My legs buckled, sending me tumbling forward onto the ground, just slow enough for the goblin to catch me smack in the side of my face with his Spiderman trainers. I landed on top of the cake box with a graceless "oof", forearms scraping painfully across the rough stone path as they landed beneath my chest. Something heavy bounced onto my back, squeezing out what minuscule amount of air remained in my lungs, while another weight pinned down my legs. A sharp pointy object pressed tightly against my neck as I tried to lift it up off the exploded cake box.

"Freeze in the name of the law!" The voice sounded reassuringly like that of a small child rather than a knee-sized ninja warrior. My relief lessened somewhat when the scarf was unwound from where it had fallen over my eyes, revealing the blue-faced goblin child's wild, staring eyes boring into mine from three inches away.

I tried to reposition myself, in order to suck some air back into my desperate lungs. The pressure increased on the back of my neck.

"Who goes there?" The goblin bared his teeth at me.

Struggling to find enough breath to answer, I forced out a strangled wheeze. Whoever, or whatever, was straddling my ankles began hitting my thighs repeatedly with what felt like a mallet. Or perhaps a sledge-hammer. "'Oo there. 'Oo there. 'Oo there," they cried out, in time to the pummels.

I managed a mangled cry of "Help", causing the goblin in the Spiderman trainers to try pushing the scarf into my open mouth. He shook his head, eyebrows knotted into a menacing frown. "Right, that's it!" Pulling out a small plastic spade from his back pocket, he waved it carelessly over his head.

"Get him!" the someone, or something, on my back cried. "Get the baddie!" They jabbed the pointy object I now suspected was a sword, or a pair of shears, or a machete, harder into the back of my neck.

The pummelling on my thighs increased in speed and intensity: "Get baddie! Get baddie!"

The goblin roared, "This is your last chance to confess everything before I pluck out your eyes, intruder!" Just as I began wondering if I was actually going to end up maimed, if not dead, a large hand swept out of the sky and snatched the spade out of the goblin's grasp.

The weight quickly lifted from my back and ankles, and above the roar of blood galloping through my veins I heard three children getting ordered inside in no uncertain terms.

Gingerly, stiffly rolling onto my back on the garden path, elbows grazed, gagging on a parrot, I wiped away the smear of cream-cheese icing obscuring my vision and sucked in some much needed oxygen.

A face loomed in front of me, causing me to groan with disbelief as I contemplated winding the scarf back around my head and diving for the bushes. It was no good. My body wasn't budging.

"Meat Harris. I should have guessed."

Meat Harris squinted. He tilted his still-meaty frame forward and offered me his hand. I declined, pretending to ignore the pain as I heaved myself into a sitting position. The last time he had offered me that hand it had been in the form of what he liked to call a "meat sandwich". He crouched down next to me on the path instead, thigh muscles bulging under his cargo shorts, and shook his head a little.

"I am so sorry. This is totally embarrassing. Last time I saw them they were happily building a clothes horse fortress round the back. I only went to check the cricket scores for a moment…" He looked at me again: the blood, the dirt, the cake, the rip in the knee of my jeans…

"She's going to kill me." He stood back up, this time reaching his hands out and pulling me up without waiting for permission. "Come inside. I need to deal with the kids first but if you wait a minute we can get you cleaned up. I'll put on the kettle, make some tea."

*Urrr – no thanks.*

"No. I'm fine."

He looked at me again, more carefully this time. "Ruth? Ruth Henderson?"

*Yes, it is me. The victim of your merciless bullying for the many joyful years we were at school together.*

I nodded, feebly. "I brought a cake from my mum." We looked at the mush of carrot cake on the path, already attracting a neat line of black ants. "Right. I'm going to go, then." I bent down to pick up the sunglasses, now missing one lens, an arm hanging off.

"No way. You're coming in. I'm not letting you go like that."

"With all due respect…" My voice began to tremble. It took a lot less than a random attack from a gang of child savages to make me cry these days. "I really just want to go home."

"Ruth. No. Look. Hang on a second. I need to speak to my kids, but… " He jogged over to the front door, pushing it open and shouting, "Sweetpea? Can you come here a minute?"

Okay, that just about did it. What kind of woman let Meat Harris call her sweetpea? There had been girls at school who fell prey to his Neanderthal charm. Who enjoyed being associated with the kind of boy most people were too scared to argue with, or say no to. Those who tittered while he shoved weaker kids down the school bank into the dyke, batted their eyelashes at his continual putdowns and made him feel clever for hiding dog poo in other girls' PE trainers.

Kerry Long? Simone Jackson? I did not want to see those girls on my best day, let alone with cake in my hair, blood running down my arms or the imprint of a shoe on my face.

That they appeared to have produced more than one mini-Meat sent shudders down my spine. How was he not in prison by now?

He pointed one finger at me. "Don't move." And disappeared inside. I sidled half way down the garden path, my legs reluctant to accept my brain's command to march out of there before he came back. When the front door opened again, Lois Finch, my second best (and only other) childhood friend, fellow victim of many of Meat's hideous pranks, launched herself down the path like a tiny rocket and flung herself at me, seemingly oblivious to cake, dirt or bodily fluids.

"Oh, Ruth. It's so good to see you. Your mum said you were coming home. I can't believe it. We've missed you so much. How are you? How's Maggie? How are things?"

I disentangled myself and stood, shuffling from foot to foot, looking anywhere but at Lois.

"Hi, Lois."

*Um, excuse me, but Lois? Lois was Meat's sweetpea?*

She gasped, taking in my dishevelled state, before narrowing her eyes and glancing back over her shoulder towards the house. "A blue elf, a white knight and a camel in a swimming costume?"

I shrugged. I hadn't seen the knight or the camel, but it sounded as plausible as anything else that had happened to me in the past fifteen minutes.

"I am so sorry. I asked him to watch them for five minutes while I changed Teagan's nappy. Connor's been learning about stranger danger at school, and they've got a bit obsessed. I never would have thought they'd launch the attack squad on someone bearing cake, though. Not unless they looked suspicious…"

I tucked the headscarf discreetly into my back pocket.

"Well, come on in. We'll get you cleaned up and then we can fill each other in on the past fifteen years. I would offer you some carrot cake, but I think we'll leave that to my darling husband to sort out. Once he's finished his little chat with the three musketeers."

*Husband? Darling? What!?*

Lois smiled at me before reaching up to flick a large crumb off my ear. "It really *is* good to see you. You haven't changed a bit."

I may not have changed that much, but she had. Her frumpy curtain of colourless hair now shone with highlights, and had been cut in a feathered bob showing up brilliant blue eyes. The purple smudges, a permanent feature underneath her eyes while growing up, had gone. She was still thin, but healthy thin, not close-to-snapping skinny, and she sparkled. A far cry from the ghost of a girl I once sat next to in English. And could Lois Finch really have become Lois Harris?

We had hung around together out of necessity – I had probably been Lois's only friend, and I liked her, but was so wrapped up in David I spared little time for anyone else outside lessons. We wrote once or twice from our respective universities, but once pregnant, I dropped all contact. We hadn't spoken since. I fought the urge to turn and run. Pride wanted me to avoid this, but my pride was squished into the garden path among the cake. I swallowed, and looked sideways at her.

"Meat Harris?" I shook my head, and frowned. "*Meat Harris?* How on earth did that happen?"

Lois burst out laughing. "Come inside for a cup of tea and I'll tell you."

"I think it might take something stronger than tea to drag me across the threshold of Meat Harris's front door. Seriously. *Meat?*"

Lois grabbed hold of my arm and started trying to pull me down the path. "No alcohol, I'm afraid. But I could rustle up a couple of pain-killers." Freakishly strong for someone so minuscule, Lois barrelled me into the hallway before I knew it.

A voice called out from somewhere towards the rear of the cottage. "And these days most people call me Matt."

"That was mean. And calculated. And manipulative." I rubbed my arms, the grazes still stinging.

I found Mum pruning her rose bushes when I finally extricated myself from Lois, Matt and the four of their six foster kids who weren't at summer activities (I did bring with me an exuberant collage made out of leaves and flowers by way of an apology). She tilted back her straw hat and peered thoughtfully at a flower head. "I don't think so, darling."

"What? That's the second lie you've told in twenty-four hours."

At that, I had her attention. She straightened up smoothly and placed her rainbow secateurs inside her gardener's apron pouch. "Mean? Manipulative? *Calculated*? Humph! It was done with only your best interests at heart. Why would you object to seeing your best friend again?"

"Lois isn't my best friend. I haven't spoken to her in fourteen years. That made it a bit awkward. And for goodness' sake, Mum. Meat Harris? Have you forgotten he put an eyeball in my lunchbox?"

Mum bristled. "Ruth Henderson, you know better than to judge a man for his past transgressions."

"Well, maybe if you'd told me he'd found God before we were nose to nose on his doorstep I could have thought about something other than the time he smeared chocolate on the back of my skirt and told the rest of the class I'd had diarrhoea."

"I have mentioned Pastor Matt many times. You know your father and I consider him to be a man of integrity and uncommon kindness. We hold him in deep respect and high esteem."

"And I was supposed to guess the new minister was *Meat Harris*?"

I shook my head, prepared to go. "Just don't do anything like that again. Please. I can't cope with your schemes right now."

If Mum sniffed any harder she would have sucked the secateurs right out of the apron pocket and into her nasal cavity.

I sighed. "I'm going to unpack."

An expert in having the last word, she waited until my hand grasped the back door knob before retorting, "If I had told you Lois lived there you wouldn't have gone. You may not have spoken in years, but she is still the best, and only, friend you have."

I carefully closed the back door behind me. Not slamming it like a teenager at all. Hardly at all.

Stomping upstairs, I ignored the pile of unpacked boxes and bags and flopped onto my bed. My thoughts tried to get to grips with the day's events. Meat and Lois, a bully and a wisp of a girl, now a preacher and a mother raising six foster children. I thought about the young woman who had stared at this same patch of ceiling so many times before – her hopes and dreams, her plans and promises. I thought about David.

That evening, Mum lured me downstairs with the aroma of lasagne, scooping a generous "curve-regenerating" portion onto my plate before insisting we talk about money, my current absolute least favourite topic for dinner table conversation. Or anywhere conversation.

"Really, Mum? Couldn't we talk about herpes, or landmines, or the prime minister's underwear, instead?"

"No. No wriggling out of this. How much do you need?" She picked up her cheque-book and flapped it in my face.

"Nothing."

Dad sat at the other end of the table, carefully grinding pepper over his lasagne. Slowly, slowly, barely twisting the wooden knob, hoping that before he over-peppered his meal we finished discussing such taboo matters and he could commence his pasta in peace.

"Don't be ridiculous, Ruth. You have no money and no income. How are you going to pay off all these hideous debts if you don't let us help you? You can't possibly expect us to sit back and watch our family flail about like fish."

"Relax. I'm going to get a job. I'll chip in what I can towards the bills. And as soon as possible we'll be out of here."

"STOP TALKING!" Mum stood up from the table so quickly her chair toppled over. "I will not hear any more. Not another word!" She pointed one long finger at me, steady enough to perform brain surgery. Her voice quietened to previously unheard of levels of hushness.

"You are our daughter. I carried you, bore you and cared for you. And you tell me to *relax* while you cry yourself to sleep at night and drift about the house a shadow of the girl I raised, trying to gather up all the broken dreams and scattered fragments of your life and wondering how to start putting them back together? *Relax*? You *must* let us help you! I cannot mend your broken heart, as much as it near kills me, but I can do this. You have to let me take care of the money situation."

I sighed. How could I explain that Fraser taking care of the money situation meant Fraser controlling it, lying about it and messing it all up? How could I explain that rejecting their offer didn't mean I didn't trust them, but that I needed to know I could take care of things myself for the first time in my life?

"What if it was Maggie?"

"What?" I looked at my dad. His head was turned, staring out of the window. The evening sun reflected off the silver in his hair.

"If this was Maggie, and you could help."

I would rip off my own arm to ensure Maggie's happiness. Any mother would.

Oh.

"Okay, I get it. But understand that if I let you help me, *take care of it*, it won't really be helping me. I relied on Fraser the whole time we were together." I couldn't say the truth. I had become a token girlfriend to Fraser, a pleasant accessory to complete his fantasy lifestyle.

Mum nodded her head. "I understand. You feel childlike, vulnerable and useless, and you need to earn your keep in order to become empowered. Right. That's settled then."

*Is it? How? When? What?*

"Stay here as long as you need, and once you are working contribute as and when you can. If you happen to drive our car and it's low on petrol, fill it up. If you use the last of the mayonnaise, buy a new jar. If you notice the bathroom is a mess, clean it up. Any spare money after paying for Maggie's hairdressing fees you can use to pay off your debts. Good. Now, I don't wish to be rude but I have to take this clean washing over to Camilla Mattersey."

Dad and I finished our tea, both staring out of the window now. We knew the truth. The car would always be full of petrol and a new jar of mayonnaise would appear in the cupboard before the old one was half empty. The bathroom, however, would be frequently allowed to fall into a state of disarray. I was going to be spending a lot of time in rubber gloves.

Later that evening, while Mum walked a spaniel whose owner had a broken ankle, I sat in the garden and watched the sun set over the crest of trees on the ridge behind our house. Dad waited until the garden lay cast in shadow before coming out and standing next to the wicker chair I had dragged onto the patio.

He handed me an envelope.

"What's this?"

Dad coughed. "A birthday present."

"Dad, my birthday is in November. Lydia's is August."

"No." His eyes flickered on the flagstones, the pots full of tumbling flowers, the fence posts, the compost bin. "The other birthdays."

"Didn't you already give me something?"

"Your mother gave you something. I didn't argue with her about it."

"Shall I open it now?"

He shrugged at the rose trellis. The trellis didn't know either.

I carefully opened the envelope. Inside was a cheque. For five thousand pounds.

"Dad. Thank you. But I can't accept this."

"Right. Well. Keep hold of it. You might change your mind."

He shuffled his feet. I said nothing more, just tucked the cheque back inside the envelope and tried to breathe through the giant lump constricting my throat. He went inside.

I clutched the envelope until the last breath of summer heat faded away, night chills raising goosebumps on my bare skin. Nearer to the house, glints of golden light peeked through the cracks at the edges of the windows and French doors. The pipistrelle bats that roosted in the eaves of our neighbour's summer house swooped above my head. The scent of warm earth mingled with the honeysuckle growing on the back fence and the faint whiff of a barbecue from a distant yard.

The night brought with it the memories of a thousand nights before: childhood campouts, my sisters sending me, the wild one, out of the tent to check on a strange noise. Sneaking through the shadows to go badger spotting in the Spinney with David. That one July night, when I squeezed myself into the dusty hole beside the shed, buried my head into the shiny satin party dress covering my knees, and cried until my dad found me, gently tugged me out of the hole and carried me up to bed.

I remembered that I had been looked for, held, treasured, once. I clutched the envelope carrying the promise that despite a bridge burnt fourteen years ago, I could know that love again. This evening had been the longest conversation Dad had allowed me since, still a child myself, more terrified than I had ever been and desperately needful of a father's reassurance and protection, I confessed my pregnancy by a boy I had met only weeks previously – and with it my wanton transformation into *one of those girls.* In doing so, I had also slammed a hammer onto the final nail in the coffin of my relationship with my father. The death certificate read "Cause of death: disappointment".

## CHAPTER TWO

Feelings squashed away in a battered old filing cabinet deep in the recesses of my brain surfaced. The filing cabinet, labelled "broken lumps of heart", existed long before Fraser's death. The truth is, I couldn't blame my partner for loving me so half-heartedly. I had only had half a heart with which to love him back. I heaved my leaden body out of the wicker chair and went to bed. And stayed there.

# Chapter Three

$\mathcal{I}$ spent five days clarifying to myself that, yes, I was the useless appendix of the family, by sleeping, crying, staring at the wall, sleeping, eating cheesy crisps, sleeping, drinking cold coffee. One day the doorbell rang as I shuffled back to bed having emptied my bladder. A young woman pushing triplets in a three-seater buggy greeted me, having come to return Mum's casserole dish. Her husband had left two weeks earlier to serve in Sierra Leone. She looked fresher, more energized, happier and like she was taking better care of herself than me.

Ugh. I had to pull myself together.

I just needed to sleep for a few more years first.

On the seventh day, Mum woke me up by yanking off my duvet and smacking my fuzzy pyjama-clad bottom with a hair brush.

"Wake up! Maggie comes home this afternoon! I will not let her come home to a useless pile of soggy dishrags for a mother. I will not let her find you looking and smelling like a week-old omelette!"

"Mum!"

"Well, it's true and if I can't say it, who will?"

"I'm not a teenager any more. This is never going to work if you keep telling me what to do."

"I will treat you like a teenager if you act like one. And I'll tell you what to do until you decide for yourself to make your own decisions."

"Fine. I decide to continue my emotional breakdown. Now don't you have some blind, lame leper with sixteen children and a husband on death row to make soup for?"

She did go. And came back a minute later with a broom. *A broom*. And began trying to sweep me off the bed.

I swore, a lot, and clambered over to the far side of the room, beside the window seat.

"What are you doing?" I growled like a polecat.

Mum grabbed one of the suitcases dumped with the rest of my stuff in the corner of the room and unzipped it. She began tossing the contents all over the honey-coloured carpet.

"Do you *want* to be here for the rest of your life?"

"I don't want to be here at all."

"Well, you can either lie about like a skinny slug, or you can get up and do something constructive!" She reached for another suitcase. I tried to intercept her and we ended up frantically wrestling for the handle.

"I have given you seven days to feel sorry for yourself. Now it is time to *woman up*! To drag yourself out of the mire of pity and start learning how to live again. Yes – you are grieving. Yes – you have some huge, mountainous money problems. Yes – you have no job, no social life and overgrown eyebrows. But! *But...* You have you, and me, and for mercy's sake, Ruth, you must have hope. You cannot live without it. I've made you a pot of tea. Don't let it stew."

She waited until I had sipped my slightly stewed tea, slumped in a pair of faded jogging bottoms and a ratty T-shirt, before telling me the real reason she wanted me to *woman up*.

"Esther's coming over today to see Maggie. And you, of course."

"What? Why didn't you tell me this earlier?"

Esther was the eldest, and most sistery, of my three sisters. Sistery, not sisterly. It would be wrong to call them the three witches – no pointy hats or warts to speak of – but they had a sixth sense when it came to pushing my buttons.

"I'm sure I must have mentioned it. Perhaps you couldn't hear me over the rustle of your crisp packet."

"What time is she coming?"

"Her last Zumba class ends at two-thirty. She will be here by three, I should imagine."

"Just her, then?"

"She's bringing Arianna and Timothy. Max is on a stag weekend in Blackpool."

The thought of Maximilian Brownstone-Pilkington tramping the streets of Blackpool in a T-shirt bearing a crude message heartened my spirits enough to go and have a shower.

My sisters weren't terrible people, but the truth was, they had never got me. When I tramped mud on their sequinned skirts, or left my stuff on the floor, tripping them up during a Lindy Hop routine, they hissed and called me "The accident". When younger I would run crying to Mum, who hushed me before rapping her wooden spoon on the kitchen table and announcing that God does not make accidents, and an unexpected gift is better than those asked for. When I realized what my sisters really meant I stopped running to Mum. At ten years old, clumsy, usually filthy, certainly graceless, I felt like the family accident. If God had planned me, why did he put me with a family of dancing angels? He could at least have made me a boy. Not that I wanted to be a boy.

I wanted to be a kick-butt girl. Who kicked boy's butts when they laughed at her for wanting to climb trees, build dens and shoot bows and arrows with them. The glitz and glamour of the ballroom that so entranced my sisters bore no comparison for me to the allure of a day spent exploring nature's playground, with the only boy who didn't laugh me away.

Hair brushed but not styled, face clean of both dirt and make-up, I was unpacking in my room when the tinkling sound of Esther's family burst up the stairs. Allowing myself one long, deep sigh, I went to say hello.

I hadn't seen my sister since Fraser's funeral. She wore a few new wrinkles, but her hair was the same shade of platinum, still noticeably lighter than her skin. A pair of skinny jeans and a silk vest top showed off her Zumba-teacher's body. Taking after Mum, she stood six foot one in her heels, and didn't we know it.

"Ruth!" She stooped, slightly further than was necessary, and kissed me on both cheeks. "It's good to see you, although" – she stepped back and pulled a sorrowful smile – "look at you. You must be feeling dreadful. Oh, darling. What can I do?"

"I'm fine, thanks. You look lovely, too." I grinned. Part of me enjoyed playing up to Esther's belief that I was a scruffy, boorish, hopeless baby sister. The other part wanted to use my overgrown nails to pluck that patronizing look off her face.

Mum intervened with afternoon tea in the garden. Arianna and Timothy, now six and eight respectively, nibbled on roasted pepper sandwiches and chatted to their grandma about cello lessons and their new mandarin Chinese tutor. They didn't want any cake, asking for dried fruit instead. Both my sister and mother seemed to think this was normal.

"Soooo. What are your plans, Ruth? I suppose you'll be needing a job, what with Fraser's" – here her voice lowered – "*secret debt problem.*"

"Whispering doesn't make it any less of a problem. Or a secret."

"Oh yes, of course. But really, Ruth, you are thirty-four years old –"

"Thirty-three."

"You can't just pack in your job, come home and expect to sponge off Mummy and Daddy. No one's denying you've been through an awful time, but grief isn't an excuse to slob around in cheap leggings for the rest of your life watching scripted reality shows."

"*Esther.*" Mum's tone stopped me tipping my scalding hot drink over the top of my sibling's artfully messed-up bun.

"Sorry, Ruth. I didn't mean it. I'm just worried about you." She reached a hand across the table and squeezed mine.

"Don't be. I'm fine," I replied, pulling it away.

"Oh, darling." Mum shook her head. "That is precisely the problem! We don't want you to be fine. No Henderson has ever settled for fine. We want you to be fabulous! To shoot for the stars and catch them. To follow your heart, come up fighting, savour every moment, explore the mysteries of the universe, let life take your breath away, live passionately and fearlessly and with wide open arms…"

"Mum! Cliché overload! For goodness' sake, give me a break."

Timothy piped up: "Grandma, do you have any quinoa salad, and why is there a witch in your garden?"

At that point, Arianna, upon sighting the witch, screamed and fell off her chair, dragging the blue and red striped tablecloth with her. The three-tiered cake-stand toppled over the edge, carrying with it like carbohydrate lemmings four pieces of lemon sponge, two lavishly creamed scones and more vegetable sandwiches than even the most organically minded, health-crazed, additive-free kids could stomach. Fortunately, my great-grandmother's tea set didn't join them.

Esther scooped up her distraught daughter, now covered in evil cake. To see the way the two of them, mother and daughter, daintily handled each crumb of sponge, meticulously picking off every last morsel with napkin after napkin, squealing with disgust, it was as though centipedes crawled on them. I couldn't resist scooping up a finger-full of cream from Arianna's knee and eating it with a louder than necessary smack of the lips. The tiniest ghost of a smile hinted at the corner of Timothy's pale mouth.

I turned to the witch and took in her electric blue hair and the thick, black eyeliner rimming her pale green eyes. With a baggy grey dress hanging over red and black striped tights, a scowl as deep and dark as a cauldron, I could quite easily see how the visitor had been mistaken for someone who muttered dark spells under the full moon.

"Hello, Maggie."

I rose to give my daughter a stiff hug (making a mental note that Maggie was still angry with me) and spied the towering frame of the Scottish Dragon behind her. Mum, who had been scooping up the cake-ridden napkins, wiped her fingers clean and daintily kissed the dragon's cheek. I did not do this. My kiss would not have been so graciously received.

Instead, I sat back down, assuming the fake all-is-well-and-my-daughter-doesn't-hate-me-and-I-don't-care-what-Fraser's-mother-thinks smile. Experience had taught me the best way to deal with the Scottish Dragon was to sit up, shut up, and sing "Nothing's Gonna Stop Us Now" by Starship in my head.

By the way, if calling the mother of my deceased partner, and grandmother of my only child, the Scottish Dragon sounds disrespectful, I agree, it probably is. But after multiple disastrous, hideous, esteem-crushing visits to her castle in Scotland, I needed some mechanism of survival that would enable me to withstand her bullying without hyperventilating, screaming or requiring medication. To reduce her from a terrifying, mean old woman to a funny, slightly silly caricature I could feel sorry for helped. A bit.

And, believe me, Scottish Dragon was the least disrespectful of the names I came up with. What is a suitable name for someone who refused to believe you were allergic to asparagus, sneakily asking her cook to blend some into your soup to prove a point? What a drama queen, going into anaphylactic shock over a vegetable. Or someone who "misplaced" your Christmas present, three years running, even though you had been emotionally blackmailed into spending every single Christmas at her house?

Or, the kind of person who demands a christening for her granddaughter at the family chapel, invites a hundred guests, ninety-nine of whom you don't know, none of whom include your own family and friends, and then turns up in black and spends the day dabbing her eyes with a lace handkerchief at the disgrace of it all?

Was it terrible that I considered an upside of Fraser's death that this woman no longer had any control over me, my child or my life? Any guilt I may have felt at the dreadful state of our relationship evaporated when I asked Margaret (yes, I was also steamrollered into naming my daughter after her) to help us out financially after Fraser died, leaving us broke and in danger of losing our home.

I was not her family, she had coolly replied down the phone. I had ensnared her son, dragged him down to my low level of existence, kept him miles away from his own mother, gleefully spent all his hard-earned wages and now had the cheek to expect her to fund my shallow, self-indulgent lifestyle instead. All that, after bringing shame on her family name.

I hung up, reminded myself she was an old woman grieving her only son, poured myself a very large glass of wine and breathed a sigh of relief that I never officially became her daughter-in-law. Some people are fire-breathing dragons. They burn to a frazzle anyone and anything around them. We are better off keeping these people out of our lives.

Except, here she was.

She hobbled, scraping her black stick across the paving slabs, over to where Mum had pulled out a chair. "Please, do take a seat, Margaret. We had no idea you would be coming all this way, too. You must be exhausted."

"Don't be ridiculous. How is sitting in the back of a car exhausting?"

"Grandma's on her way to London to visit her sister." Maggie had taken a seat next to Timothy, kicked off her Dr Martens and grabbed a handful of sandwiches. "Where do I sleep?"

"Is anybody going to offer Brown a cup of tea?" the dragon snapped, referring to her driver. "Or will I have to fetch it myself?"

"No, of course not," Mum smiled. "We were just about to ask. Ruth?"

I spent as long as possible taking tea to Margaret's driver, dropping off a cup with Maggie, now lying on her new bed with headphones on, then killed more time reassembling some fresh cakes and sandwiches.

"Would you like something to eat, Margaret?" Mum genuinely believed all it took was a few kind words and the dragon would morph into a bunny rabbit. "I made them myself. Or a cup of Earl Grey? Peppermint?"

Margaret sniffed. "No. I do not. Hasn't Brown finished that tea yet?"

She left, not a second later than her driver's allotted break allowed for, and the waistband on my trousers expanded to fit me again.

Dinner was at six. It did not turn out, I am guessing, quite as my mother had hoped. She had really tried, too.

"Did you have a lovely time in Scotland, Maggie?"

"All right." Maggie stabbed a piece of carrot with her fork, eyes on her plate.

"The grounds there are spectacular, aren't they? Did you go for any walks?"

"No." She jabbed at a pea, sending it bouncing onto the table top.

"Was it nice and sunny?"

"No."

Mum pushed on, relentless, only pausing to top up her youngest grandchildrens' water glasses. "Oh dear. I suppose that's why you didn't walk then. Did you meet any Scottish relatives while you were there?"

"No." A flick at her mashed potato this time.

"Oh. What did you do then?"

"Not a lot."

End of conversation.

Arianna cried because, well, she always cried, and Timothy refused to eat the pastry on his chicken pie because it wasn't wholemeal. Esther gritted her teeth as she tried to make herself feel better by having digs at me about jobs, money, clothes and general life choices compared to hers for the past twenty years. She had a *hilarious* story about when I got sacked from the bakery in Southwell after a monstrous nose bleed contaminated the cream cakes. *Hilarious!* Every sixteen-year-old girl thinks it is funny to leak blood all over a crowded shop, including a load of kids from her school, one of them being Meat Harris.

By the time we started on the ice-cream, I actually missed Dad.

"Where *is* Dad?" I had to ask this three times before Mum stopped pretending she couldn't hear me.

"Out."

Timothy looked confused. "Didn't he know Maggie would be here?"

Everybody froze. Except Maggie.

"No, little cousin. He knew I would be here, which is why he isn't. Haven't you heard? Pop can't stand to be in the same room as me because I'm a bastard, and the irrefutable evidence that Auntie Ruth had sexual intercourse outside marriage and is therefore a fallen woman."

"MAGGIE!" I dropped my spoon with a clatter.

"What's a bastard?" Timothy smirked.

"What's sexual intcourse?" Arianna stopped crying, and tried to prize Esther's hands off her ears.

"Why did Auntie Ruth fall down?"

"Timothy. Enough." Esther gave him *that look*, and he squiggled down lower on his chair, delightfully watching to see what would happen next.

Mum slammed the ice-cream scoop decorated with four tiny red hearts onto the table top. It was somewhat muffled by the tablecloth, tablecloth liner and two-inch-thick heat-resistant mat, but the force of her slam made up for it.

"Maggie. How could you possibly say – how could you possibly *think* – such a terrible thing?" She shook her head, distraught. "Pop loves you. We were sorry and sad you lost your dad. Devastated you had to leave your lovely big house. But this is a wonderful blessing to us, to have you here. To have you home!" She waved her hands at the rest of us, blinking back her tears. "We love you, Maggie. Pop loves you. He has a prior engagement tonight, that's all."

"Yeah. He's had a lot of those in the past fourteen years." Maggie got up from the table and walked over to the door of the dining room. "Thanks for dinner, Nanny. I don't want any ice-cream."

I followed her upstairs. She let me sit on the bed and put my arm around her. But really, what could I say? She was right.

"You know Nanny's telling the truth. If Pop has issues, they're with me, and they are wrong, and it's because of me he stayed away, not you."

"What's with him, anyway? Hardly anybody gets married these days."

"Oh, Maggie, it's not really about that. It's way, way more complicated. One day I'll tell you, but not tonight when we're tired, and Nanny is upset, and Esther has to try and explain what a fallen woman is to her over-protected six-year-old, who already thinks you're a witch."

*And when I can maybe get the words out past the huge lump of broken glass wedged in my chest.*

"Why don't you come and teach them how to play poker?"

Maggie blew the hair out of her eyes. "That would be cool. To have a witch teach you poker. Plus, it would really annoy Auntie Esther."

I grinned. "Esther will just be glad to see you getting along. Uncle Max – he'll blow the roof off when he finds out."

I left the kids in the sitting room practising their poker faces in the gilded mirror above the mantelpiece. Esther was helping Mum clean up the kitchen.

"So, what's with Maggie's hair? Are they going to allow that at school? Doesn't colouring it like that wreck the condition? What will the other kids make of her with hair like that? Won't they think she's weird?"

"I wouldn't lose sleep over it. It will probably look totally different by the start of term." I started rummaging in drawers for something to wrap the leftovers up in.

"But why would you allow it? Next thing, she'll be having a tattoo, or one of those things in her ear that stretches a hole until it swings about near her shoulders." She wiggled her hands underneath her ears to demonstrate where Maggie's lobes could end up.

"No, she won't. She's promised to do nothing permanent until she turns eighteen. And, by the way, how I raise my daughter is none of your business. I am a young mum, not a stupid one." I slammed a drawer shut. Tried another one, yanked out the food wrap and banged it closed with my hip. "When Arianna is fourteen I'm going to have so much fun watching you go nuts. She'll be eating McDonald's, watching videos of half-naked pop stars on YouTube and saying 'innit' and there'll be nothing you can do. Grow up."

I took a deep breath and stepped outside. I could blame my emotional state for taking control of my mouth and letting these things come out, but I still hated myself for it. The truth was, Maggie's hair had nothing to do with teenage rebellion, or even bad taste in hair fashion. It was a message to the world. A message that she was hurting, bruised and bereft. And it killed me that I couldn't make the hurt go away.

A few weeks after her father's death, I signed Maggie up for bereavement counselling. The first signs of Fraser's financial betrayal had surfaced. I was floundering. I managed to get up each day and function – smile at Maggie, check she'd done her homework. But trying to hide the extent of my own grief from my daughter left me no strength to deal with hers, so I found someone else to be the emotional rock I thought she needed right then.

I *thought* it helped. When people asked me how Maggie was coping, the honest truth was I had no idea. What was coping for a fourteen-year-old? Wasn't it enough simply to cope with puberty, getting through school and that boy you have been obsessing about for weeks asking out your best friend?

With the sudden jolt into a single-parent family, a lost, broke, barely-holding-it-together-parent family, a new house, new town, new school – wouldn't anyone scream at their mum, stop doing their homework and shoplift a few bottles of nail varnish?

As far as I knew, Maggie didn't smoke, drink or mess about with boys. I wanted to believe she coped okay. But part of this involved electric blue hair. Or, I should say, blood red, Shrek green, zebra striped, flame orange, curly, choppy, extended, back-combed hair. Maggie's counsellor had asked her to find a creative way to express her emotions. I suggested writing poems. Rapping. Learning the trumpet. Sculpting. Baking cakes. Gardening. Building furniture... Maggie wanted to express herself through creative hair. I advised she write a journal. Maggie: hair. I proposed synchronized swimming. Maggie: hair. Dressmaking? Jewellery? Nail art? No. Hair. So black dreadlocks announced her grief. Red extensions symbolized her growing, writhing anger. The yellow fluff ball demonstrated the thrill of her first concert.

Electric blue? To her it meant: "I want to shock my snobby, stone-hearted grandmother, my sophisticated, stylish nanny and my snotty aunt with a stonking great 'up yours'. And if I make my weird, wimpy cousins afraid of me, so much the better."

What did my uncut, rarely washed, frizzy brown ponytail say? I was too darn tired to care any more.

Esther took the kids home to bed soon after dinner, before they had time to move on from poker faces to actual poker. Mum got straight to work in the kitchen, kneading bread dough. I sat at the kitchen table with a piece of paper and a pen, sketching a family of swans. The female swan wore a flowery apron. She span in a frantic circle, balancing a three-tiered cake stand on one wing.

"Where was Dad this evening?"

"Out."

I looked at Mum, my eyebrows raised in question. For forty-eight years, my parents' marriage had been a Viennese waltz, a close-hold, eye to eye, in perfect synchrony. I suspected that selling the studio had ended the dance.

Mum paused in her work to fling a leaflet at me.

"What's this?" The leaflet was for an organization called U3A. The University of the Third Age. "He's gone to university?"

She continued kneading, pummelling the bread so hard I thought the counter would crack. I flicked through the leaflet. The

U3A was an organization for retired people who wanted to "keep learning, develop new skills and broaden their interests". It seemed to be about older people getting together and having some fun. I approved.

"Which class is he doing?"

Mum snorted. "Which *isn't* he doing? I don't know. It started with photography. Then Italian. Architecture. Theatre. Whatever."

"Why don't you go along with him?"

"*Go along with him*? Because I am far too busy. I am not ready to while away my days at a geriatric singles club indulging my hobbies when there are people in this town needing my help. It is a pointless little group. Why would I want to learn Italian?" She started punching the dough with rapid jabs, one fist after the other.

"You might go to Italy."

"Then I'll get a CD out of the library. Not join some club." Pummelling complete, she pulled the stretchy dough off the work surface, squished it into a ball and slammed it back down again with such force I almost felt sorry for it.

I didn't point out that my mum's entire career, the business she had given her life to, the hours spent sewing sequins, perfecting turns, pinning hair in buns, could very easily be described in a similar way. Mum knew life needed art, and beauty, and a chance for human beings to connect via a common goal. That learning a new skill, particularly with others, fed our souls.

I suspected the truth was more complicated. She didn't want to feel old and useless. She chose to fill up the hole of retirement by making herself *needed*, and was sulking that Dad preferred a different dance.

# Chapter Four

Sunday, Maggie stayed in bed while my parents went to church. At least they still did something together. I thought about cooking Sunday dinner. Then decided even thinking about it was enough of a step forward for one week, so continued lying on the sofa staring at the ceiling until they came home.

Maggie had met Pop only twice before – at Lydia's wedding, when she was six, and Fraser's funeral, when I don't think they even spoke. While we lived in Liverpool, Mum came to see us once a year, during the dance school breaks. Dad had been catching up on paperwork, in the middle of decorating, attending urgent meetings – making rubbish excuses for every single one of those visits. I had no idea how to nurture a relationship between a man who had built a wall that high and the child who believed he disapproved of her very existence.

Of course, my mother had been scheming about it for weeks.

After a very late lunch of garlic chicken, roast potatoes, parsnips, sweet potato mash, caramelized baby carrots, minted peas, roasted leeks, two varieties of homemade stuffing, chipolata sausages, cauliflower cheese, cabbage and French beans picked that morning, cranberry sauce and gravy, Mum folded her napkin and announced that Maggie and Pop would be washing up, seeing as I had helped cook the dinner. This wasn't quite a lie. Once Mum got back from church and the house began to fill with cooking smells I did find the energy to mash the sweet potato.

"What?" Maggie looked disgusted. Translate: scared.

"Grand Prix is on," Dad added, confused.

"*Gilbert!*" Mum said with such piercing intensity Dad jolted in his seat.

"I can watch the highlights later," he muttered, getting the point.

He stacked up the empty plates and disappeared into the kitchen. Maggie slunk in after him.

Mum and I sat in silence for a moment, listening to the clink of crockery and the scraping of plates.

"You've just made them both feel really awkward," I said.

Mum began folding the napkins into quarters. She kept her eyes on the job but I could see them sparkle. "Yes. For the first time they actually have something in common. Don't you dare set one foot into that kitchen."

Over the next few days we fell into some sort of rhythm. Mum rushed about bringing sunshine into the lives of the gloomier residents of Southwell. Dad learned Italian, studied wild flowers and hid behind his newspaper. Maggie scowled, picked at her nails, vented her fury on the internet and was dragged along behind my mother on various act-of-mercy outings designed to show her that "things could be a lot worse".

I slept. Cried a couple of times. Stared at the reptile drawings on my wall. Wished I could be like the red-eared terrapin, carrying a rock-solid home all to himself that no bank could take away; hibernating through the harsher months in the quiet solace at the bottom of a pond. I occasionally wondered, in an abstract sort of way, what on earth I was going to do. Did I think about David? What a pointless, heart-wrenching waste of time that would have been.

By Friday, Mum's patience had reached its limit. Me scrabbling off the sofa and pretending to be searching for jobs on Dad's computer as soon as she came in the door fooled no one. It had taken an initial few hours on Monday to search for jobs in the area, followed by a ten-minute check each morning to confirm that no, there were still no jobs requiring the first year of a maths degree, six years of higgledy-piggledy temp work followed by eight months pushing paper for a pervert, no references and a mini-meltdown.

She arrived back from taking an elderly friend to the doctor's just after ten, sweeping in with a blast of vanilla. "Is that computer even on? The time has come to stop this imaginary job search. There are obviously no pretend jobs that are suitable. Therefore, I have taken matters into my far more capable hands. You start on Tuesday."

I muffled my scream using a green gingham sofa cushion.

She ignored me. "And to celebrate I have a fun afternoon lined up. It's the final day of the holiday club at Oak Hill and Eloise Mumford has a dreadful bout of her dicky tummy. Your offer to save the day by filling her place has been graciously and enthusiastically accepted."

My head remained in the cushion until she twirled out of the room. I know she twirled, as I could hear her pointy heels clicking out the quickstep on the wooden floor.

I heaved myself off the sofa and slumped into the kitchen, as she knew I would.

"Go on, tell me about it then. And don't miss out any details. I am too tired for your schemes."

"Vanessa Jacobs. You remember Vanessa? She was kept behind a year at school. Lived in that orange puffa coat and had a dad who dressed up as David Bowie. Well, she runs a clothes shop in town and needs a new assistant. Twenty hours a week. It will be a breeze for a genius like you, Ruth. And she doesn't care if you have no retail experience; she is prepared to give a hard worker with a great attitude a go."

"Really? Vanessa Jacobs is prepared to give me a go?" Oh, yes. I remembered Vanessa Jacobs. Half the girls in the school had copied her and bought puffa coats, but nobody else ever managed to find an orange one. We had not been close, maintaining a mutual mild dislike from a distance. Until I found her arms around the neck of the boy I was in love with.

"I have been cutting Granny Jacobs' toenails for the past three months while she languishes on the chiropodist's waiting list. Vanessa owes me one."

"Mum. I know nothing about working in a shop and the thought of having to greet people, smile and say 'That looks wonderful, madam. How about this matching scarf?' all day is too much. I can't do it. I need something simple, no pressure, safe. No interaction with the general public. Or preferably anyone else." Especially if they happen to have stomped on my heart and laughed about it.

Mum sat down at the table, pushing out another chair with her foot to indicate I should join her.

"Ruth. You need a job. This is two and a half days a week, a fifteen-minute walk away. Vanessa schmoozes the customers. She's looking for someone to sweep the back room and count the stock. You are a mathematical wizard. This is no pressure and as safe as you're going to get. Why not try it until you find something better? It'll be something to put on a CV. And a chance for a good reference. All I'm asking is that you try it."

"Fine. I'll give it a go. But you are not allowed to nag or moan at me if I can't hack it." I breathed out a long sigh at the thought of working for Vanessa Jacobs. "When do I start?"

"Your interview is Tuesday at half-ten, so you've plenty of time to settle Maggie in at school first."

"Interview! I don't even have the job? Mum, I cannot have a job interview with Vanessa Jacobs."

"Oh, give over, Ruth. The interview is a mere formality. Vanessa Jacobs is not the sort of woman to be left trimming her grandmother's toenails! Now, do you think a top without quite so many holes in would be more appropriate for the holiday club this afternoon?"

The Oak Hill Centre grew out of the church my family had attended for over four decades. My parents had been among the founding members back in their twenties, when a bunch of hippy Christians got frustrated with the constraints of organized religion and decided to try something different. If the photographs from back then are anything to go by, "different" included replacing the organ with a rainbow-strapped guitar and tambourines, preachers wearing shorts with socks and sandals, and baptizing new members in the River Trent. Praise the Lord, and they certainly did, things had de-cheesed slightly over the years.

I didn't want to help out at the holiday club that afternoon. I was too tired, too weak, too depressed to smile and chat and sing happy-clappy songs in a room full of hyperactive children. I hadn't been a regular at church since I left Southwell. As a young girl, I had believed in God. I just preferred exploring the wonders of his creation to singing about them.

Then I got pregnant, which in 1998, in the older, middle-class congregation of Oak Hill, was still pretty scandalous for an unmarried teenager. Although the church members were amazing – they knitted baby clothes, sent over changing mats, baby baths, blankets and even a brand new pram – I felt their pity, and their dismay, real or imagined. At nineteen you haven't yet realized that no adult has led a smooth, trouble-free life, with no mistakes or regrets. That pretty much everyone understands how easy it is to drink a few too many glasses of vodka at a party and do something stupid with a charming boy you hardly know.

I felt exposed, embarrassed, ashamed. A lot of students get drunk and have sex with near-strangers at parties. Not a lot of them have their parents' friends, their Sunday school teachers and half the town know this for a great big, round-bellied fact. I was still me, Ruth Henderson, but to them I must be Ruth: teenaged single mother, estranged from her dad, living in a bedsit with no money. Maths prodigy turned wasted opportunity, government statistic and source of much parental anguish.

Many, many times I had imagined leaving Liverpool and coming home. I wanted to show my old friends, my family, and the women who had babysat me, prayed for me and given me thousands of toffees, that I had not become the cliché. I was a good mother, with a good man, living a great life, a successful one. I had never done this, because deep inside I didn't believe it. Yet here I found myself walking up the steps into the Oak Hill Centre's main hall.

I was here for one reason: Maggie. She had decided to punish me by spending time with Nanny, following her to the club and agreeing with everything she said and did. She even wore the cardigan Nanny knitted her in pale purple wool. It had worked. I was jealous. So I came.

Oak Hill had grown out of the original building twice in the past fifteen years. Currently, they were in their new-new premises, a spacious glass and wood construction on the site of Southwell's old secondary school. Tastefully decorated in soft colours, the large entrance hall had bright sofas lining one wall, with contemporary posters adding warmth and an informal feel. A water cooler stood beside a simple reception desk, notice boards highlighted the many events going on in the building, and a table bore neat rows of leaflets and a large vase filled with red gerberas.

Through glass double doors I could see a café area, stocked with modern coffee-makers, a chiller containing cakes, cookies, sandwiches and fruit, and several farmhouse-style wooden tables with soft padded chairs. There were more sofas, stripy ones this time, lower coffee tables and vases full of flowers. Along the walls hung dozens of prints painted by children, depicting all the things kids care about: football matches, dogs and dinosaurs, ballerinas, castles and space rockets.

What had happened to stewed tea in mismatched cups served with custard creams? Where were the old, straight-backed chairs and tiny windows? This building was full of air, and light, and life. If I wasn't so stressed I would actually find this a pleasant place to have a cup of coffee.

"Come on, Ruth; stop gawping. The children will be arriving soon."

Mum shooed me into the main hall. At the far end was a stage rigged up with lights and speakers. On this stood a drum kit, several guitars propped up on stands and a range of microphones – all set against a huge curtained backdrop emblazoned with the words "SUPERHEROES CAMP" in graffiti-style letters. The rest of the hall split into different zones – creative zone, sport zone, challenge zone, chill zone. What struck me most was the room's massive size.

"You have your services in here?"

Mum nodded, pretending to be nonchalant, but unable to hide her slight smugness. "Yes."

"You could fit half of Southwell in here. How many people come?"

"About four hundred."

Four hundred? When I used to come to the old building on Oak Hill Road, we were lucky to get more than forty. Where did all these people come from? Why?

Mum preened a little. "I told you Pastor Matt had done a good job."

A good job? This was a miracle.

A perky girl in her early twenties wearing a "supergirl" costume pressed a blue sticker onto my chest and waved her clipboard in the direction of the creative zone.

In the half-hour before the kids arrived, I hovered under the gazebo that marked my zone and watched dozens of helpers rush about doing things – setting up games, filling the gunge tank, practising dance moves. The team ranged from young helpers like Maggie, counting out biscuits in the energy zone, right up to Mrs Messenger, the creaky cleaner who had seemed at least a hundred when she dusted the Bibles a lifetime ago. She now manned the registration desk with a heavily pierced man dressed as a hobbit.

Ten minutes before we were due to start, Lois blew in with five of her foster kids. Poppy, whose disability required one-to-one supervision, had stayed at home. She took the two-year-old, Martha, and her four-year-old sister Freya, to the mini-heroes zone ("small but mighty") and left the eight-year-old boy with batman in the gold zone. The eldest of her children, Seth Callahan, who had been with the Harris's for only a few weeks, sprawled on a sofa in one corner, engrossed in his phone.

I watched Maggie glance over at Seth, then flip her head back to the biscuits. Five seconds later she looked over again. Engrossed in his screen, he didn't appear to notice. I could understand her second peek. Seth had thick, ebony hair several weeks past needing a cut and dark eyes, the lids slightly hooded. His features would have been almost feminine if not for the brooding scowl. He wore a battered jacket and slim-fitting jeans over heavy boots. He looked like the kind of boy girls like Maggie scorned in public and dreamt about in private. The kind of boy that drove daddies to sit on the front porch with a shotgun on their lap. Lois had told me nothing about Seth Callahan other than that he was fifteen but was retaking year ten after missing most of his schooling during the past few months.

He would be in Maggie's school year. I felt a prickle of anxiety at the prospect of this gorgeous, dangerous-looking boy becoming another wound in my precious daughter's heart.

"Ruth!" Lois gave me a hug, the round ball of baby strapped to her front making it impossible for her to reach properly. "You're the answer to my prayers. You've no idea what it would do to me running this zone alone. That sign is a mistake. I made a more accurate one."

She pointed to the back of the "creative zone" sign, where it hung down below the gazebo edge. Written in thick black marker pen, this side read "clothes wrecking chaos I don't know what I'm doing migraine zone".

"I think I might have suddenly remembered an urgent appointment somewhere else. Far, far away..." I turned, ready to bolt.

Lois grabbed onto my arm with her tiny, impossibly strong hands. "I don't think so." She grinned. "Look." She waved at a painting that some primary-aged child must have drawn. "Which one of the Harris family do you think *created* that?"

"Um. Freya?" I guessed it was probably the eight-year-old, but I couldn't remember his name.

"What? Not even Connor?" That was it – Connor. "Me, Ruth. I did it."

I tried to hide my smile.

"And with Eloise ill, I'm left in charge. The kids saw through me in about ten seconds. They kept asking me to demonstrate art techniques and help them out and then pretended to be upset when I ruined their craft. Yesterday they waited until both my hands were stuck to an egg carton and then had a paint fight. No wonder Eloise's stomach couldn't take it."

"I'm not sure what you expect me to do, Lois. I find one child a handful."

"I expect you to wow the kids with your legendary art skills into respecting the creative zone again. I'll do the rest."

The next two hours passed in a gluey, paint-splattered, clay-encrusted whirlwind. I sketched tigers, fashioned elephants from milk cartons, butterflies from pipe-cleaners, caterpillars from clay, and ended up wearing so much paint I felt like a walking, talking canvas. The sign was true. My clothes were wrecked, I had no idea what I was doing and yes, I did feel a migraine pecking at the back of my eyeballs. But, boy. For two hours I forgot about poverty, homelessness, irritating parents, estranged parents, Vanessa Jacobs' dress shop, grief, deep, dark loneliness and crawling back to Southwell with my tail between my legs. I had a ball.

When was the last time I had done that?

For the final section of the afternoon we had a short talk by the perky woman about how Jesus loves to help us out with all our problems. She asked the kids if they had any problems they wanted Jesus to help them with.

One little girl was worried about her hamster, which had been flushed down the toilet by her elder brother. Another one felt anxious she might not get a pink and purple sparkly princess fairy ballerina mermaid castle cake for her birthday next week. A boy put his hand up. He needed some help finding worms to put in Casey Jones's lunchbox. Someone else wanted Jesus to make her ill on

Saturday so she didn't have to wear that stupid bridesmaid's dress to her auntie's wedding. A tiny, frail little girl asked if Jesus could help her mummy not die from her really bad cough because she would miss her mummy if she couldn't see her ever again. A hush fell on the crowd as every person in that room thought about the sweet, small girl never seeing her mummy again. The woman at the front looked at her. "Would it be okay if we asked Jesus to help your mummy get better?"

Yes, that would be okay.

They asked Jesus. The little girl said thank you very much and the band leader tried three times before he managed to choke out the going home song.

By the time the kids left, the zones were dismantled, and four hundred chairs were being set out ready for the church service on Sunday, it was nearly six. Matt had arrived earlier to help clear up before taking his younger children home, leaving Lois and Seth to finish off. I watched Maggie try to surreptitiously work her way closer to Seth's section as they moved back and forth putting chairs out. Seth had his earphones on, head down and frown in place as he quickly and mechanically filled up the rows.

*Oh, Maggie. Be careful.*

Lois came over to congratulate me for the hundredth time on saving the creative zone. "You're a natural. Those kids loved you. You should come and help us out on Sundays."

I concentrated on lining up the chair in my hands with the rest of the row.

"Thanks."

"Will you at least think about it?"

"Okay." *There, I've thought about it. Sundays? Church days? My answer is no.*

"So, first Friday of the month is girls' night. This month I'm celebrating surviving a whole six weeks with no school. Don't get me wrong – I love having the kids around all day, and lazing in our pyjamas until lunchtime if we want to – but I am so tired, my eyeballs feel as though they're filled with sand. We're meeting at mine at eight for a Chinese. You're coming, aren't you?"

"I don't know. I wasn't really… Mum has probably already cooked something. Maybe next time?"

Lois began to say something, then a light popped on in her head. She leaned in closer. "Please come. You really helped me out today. Please let me buy you a take-away as a thank you. I owe you big time."

"No you don't. I enjoyed myself, honestly. But I'm really tired. I don't think so."

Seth sauntered across. "The chairs are done. Are you nearly finished, or shall I walk back?"

"One minute, honey." Lois furrowed her brow. "The girls are really friendly. They'd love to meet you. Can't you come just for a bit?"

Friendly women? That was precisely the problem. *What brings you to Southwell, Ruth? Where are you staying? What do you do?*

I couldn't bear pity, or trying to bridge those awkward moments when I told people my partner had died and no one knew what to say. The attempts at optimism: *I'm sure something will turn up!* Or encouragement: *Wow, you are so brave!* So I would be left either dodging questions all night, or committing social suicide by talking about the taboo "girls' night" topics of death, debt and desperation. I was, quite frankly, too exhausted to deal with it.

"I'll come another time, I promise."

Lois conceded defeat. "Well, have a nice evening. I'll see you soon. And thanks again."

# Chapter Five

So how come, two hours later, I found myself once again loitering on Lois's cluttered front path, clutching a bottle of flavoured spring water and trying to work myself up to ringing her doorbell?

My mother. How else? I was only a thirty-three-year-old woman. I couldn't possibly be left alone to control my own social life, could I? Or any other part of my life, it would seem…

I should have sussed that Lois had given in too easily. That sneaky pastor's wife had phoned Mum.

I had been standing wrapped in a towel following a long shower when my bedroom door crashed open.

"Seriously, Mum?"

"Sorry, Ruth. But I am too exasperated for formalities like privacy. I am reaching near dangerous levels of frustration and bewilderment. How can someone so impressively intelligent make such consistently stupid decisions?"

I sighed. "Lois called."

"YES, LOIS CALLED!"

"I can run my own life, Mum. Please back off before I flip out and stab you in your sleep one night with your Harrods letter opener. I'm somewhat unstable at the moment."

"Precisely. You are all inside out and twisted up and out of time. You need help. Get dressed in your least hideous outfit, brush your hair and go and make some friends."

"Just stop it! Didn't you hear me? I spent all afternoon doing what you wanted, making friends with Lois, talking to people. I am really tired. I'm having something to eat and then reading a book in bed."

Mum pointed her elegant finger at me. "You are not tired, my darling. You are bored, and lonely, and lost. No one can live without friends. You in particular need them to heal, and to grow, and to find yourself again. These women are good women. They will be those kinds of friends."

"I have friends."

"No, you do not. You know what a true friend is, and that zero plus zero equals no friends."

"That is rubbish! You have no idea who my friends were in Liverpool." I grabbed another towel and started rubbing at my hair with it.

"Name one."

"Louisa." I threw the towel on my bed and instead turned on my hairdryer to maximum power.

"Work colleague." Mum, refusing to take the hint, shouted over the noise.

"So? I can be friends with my colleagues. What about Susanna?" I gestured the appliance wildly.

"How often did you see them out of the office?"

"At least once a month." *So there*, I muttered in my head.

"At a non-work-related do?" She reached down and flicked the dryer off at the socket. Silence.

"How many times have they texted since you left work? Phoned? Offered to help pack, dropped by with flowers or a box of chocolates to cheer you up, politely hinted that you need a haircut or given you a hug?" She banged her fist into my bedroom door, her point well and truly proven. "It is a horrible, heart-wrenching fact, but is still a true one. You have no friends, Ruth. And by golly how you need some!"

One day, someday, hopefully before my hair is completely grey and I have lost the majority of my marbles, I will finally surrender to the truth that my strange mother is always – *one hundred per cent of the time* – right. I hate it. But I love her. I got dressed in my least embarrassing clothes, brushed my hair and went.

Lois opened the front door. "Stop lingering on the doorstep, Ruth. I'm paranoid you're judging the state of my garden." She gestured behind her. "Come through – we're in the back."

Lois led me through the house, past discarded transformer toys, piles of folded laundry and the reams of paraphernalia that affix themselves like barnacles to large families. The dining room contained a formal oak table barely visible underneath piles of papers, books, a dismantled computer and more clothes. At the far end a pair of French doors opened up onto a flagstone patio. Here stood another wooden table, this time laden with a Chinese take-away feast set around two silver candelabras. The rest of the garden consisted of a huge lawn, with a football goal at one end, an enormous tree with a tree house, a trampoline and a swing. Nearer to the patio was a sand pit, a saggy looking paddling pool and more of life's clutter.

Around the table sat four other women. I recognized one, Ana Luisa, the Brazilian housekeeper from the Big House. She jumped up and kissed me on both cheeks, engulfing me in tropical perfume that wafted out from the folds of her bright maxi dress. The others Lois introduced and they smiled and said hi. Lois then said grace.

"Hi God. Thanks for tonight. Thanks for great food and the chance to eat it with women who chew with their mouths closed, don't empty their bowl onto their own – or anybody else's – head, and break wind discreetly, not with a prior announcement. It is wonderfully refreshing, and I am already blessed. Thanks especially that Ruth was able to join us. Please help her to find this evening restorative and fun. Amen."

The other women said Amen and started to pass around the plates and load them up with food. One of the women, Emily, lifted every container that Lois passed her up close to her nose and examined it, before either scooping some onto her plate or passing it straight on to me. She used careful, deft movements and it was only when she spoke to me I realized why.

"Is this chicken or pork?"

"Um…" I leaned in. The light was beginning to fade and we were in the shadow of the cottage wall. "I think it's chicken."

"Is the pepper red or green?"

"There's both. Red and green."

"Could you pick me out some red, and some meat?"

I lifted some onto her plate.

"Thanks, Ruth. I hate green peppers. I don't understand why anyone eats them. Aren't they just unripe red peppers? We don't eat green bananas or green strawberries. Or green tomatoes. Except for in that film. Which was a great film, don't get me wrong, I sobbed like a pregnant woman, but it was wrong about the green tomatoes. Don't you think green peppers are just a big con? I reckon it's a whole emperor's new clothes situation and the supermarkets are laughing their heads off at us while banking on nobody ever saying anything. Well, I'm not fooled. I'm not playing their game. Only ripe vegetables pass these lips."

Ellie, a forty-ish woman with a man's haircut and dressed as though she expected to be riding a bucking bronco before the night was over, hollered across the table, "Is she going on about peppers again? Let it go, woman! Give it a rest! Ruth does not need to spend her first evening with us being hit over the head with your pepper speech. You need to find yourself a life."

"I have a life!"

"Well, you need to look for a better one."

"That's offensive." Emily folded her arms in mock outrage. "You just told a partially sighted woman she has a poor quality of life, and then taunted her about how she can remedy her miserable situation. What are you going to do next? Pass me nasty notes I can't read? Maybe Ruth would rather discuss peppers with me than listen to a cowgirl bullying a person about their disability." Emily pointed her fork in Ellie's direction. "I need to get a life? And that from a woman whose best friend is a horse."

"I love you, Em," Ellie shouted back.

"Love you too, sister. If you were a pepper you'd be totally scarlet."

As the light faded and the shadows crept further across the lawn, bringing with them the evening insects, the guests continued to shout, laugh, mock each other, throw advice across the table – welcome and unwelcome – eat more than a fireman after a double shift, tell stories and share the honest ups and downs of their up-and-down lives.

I listened to Emily tell us about how she had barged in on a strange man in a restaurant toilet cubicle when her kids sent her into the men's for a joke, laughing so hard she choked on a prawn cracker. I watched Ellie and Ana Luisa hold their friend Rupa's hands as she cried because another round of IVF had failed and she was broke, and felt broken, and was trying so hard not to grow bitter. Lois told us how between Connor's nightmares, Poppy's medical needs, an eight-month-old baby and a teenager who sometimes stayed out past two doing who knows what, she and Matt were surviving on three hours of sleep a night, and still an ungainly hunk of the four hundred Oak Hill members thought that Pastor Matt and his unpaid wife should be there twenty-four hours a day, seven days a week to sort out their problems, dry their tears, pick up the pieces of their bad decisions and listen to them harp on about how tough their lives were.

"Don't get me wrong – some of them do have genuine problems, and need our help. And we love to help them. But less than one per cent of those problems are emergencies needing to be dealt with during our off-time, half of them should and are being dealt with by the pastoral team, and the rest are nothing that with a bit of common sense and effort these flabby-bottomed people couldn't solve themselves. A tiny, yet misguided, proportion call us at idiotic times of the day because they want to feel important. They think their problem is worse than everybody else's and quite frankly they're too selfish to care that we are so, so tired we haven't had a decent romantic evening together in four months and thirteen days. Yes, I am counting. And yes the word 'romantic' is a euphemism. I'm on the brink of yelling it out in the middle of Sunday's service. Ruth, I'm presuming you've worked out these evenings are confidential."

I listened, and laughed, and cried a little bit, and did not feel for one second pitied, or a loser, or anything less than a normal human being who gets up every morning and lives and breathes and simply tries to do the best she can to take the muck life throws at her and build a nest with it.

Somewhere around eleven, Lois went inside to make coffee. I cleared my throat, snuck a glance back inside the house and spoke.

"Could we maybe do something for Lois?"

Everybody leaned forward and listened.

"I was thinking. Between us, maybe we could take care of the kids for a night so she could go away with Matt?"

Rupa shook her head. "I don't think it's that simple. They're foster kids, so aren't allowed to be left with just anyone."

"Surely we could find some way round that. Have them go away, without actually going away?"

We considered this. "I wouldn't mind coming over and sleeping on the sofa, getting up in the night to see to the children," Ana Luisa said. "But I don't think this is very romantic to hear Connor's nightmares through the wall, and listen to someone else try to comfort him."

Ellie tapped her fork against her glass. "They need to be near enough to make it legal and appropriate, but far enough away to pretend they aren't." She looked around. "What about the tree house?"

"Or a caravan?" Rupa asked. "Is that romantic? I've never stayed in one."

"What about one of those VW camper vans? They're cute. I bet you can hire them. We could park it in the garden." Ellie mimed driving a camper van.

"No, no, no!" Ana Luisa waved her hands about to emphasize her point. "Too small. And can you imagine what the bed is like? Not good for romance! You might as well bring your horse box, Ellie."

"A tent would be bigger." Ellie looked at Ana Luisa. "But it would be freezing at night now that we're heading into autumn. And air beds are definite passion killers. Almost as bad as a water bed."

"Ouch, Ellie." Emily winced. "I do not want to know how you acquired that information."

"Ignore her!" Ana Luisa purred. "Tell us everything!"

I was still thinking about other ways to sleep in the garden in relative comfort.

"What about a yurt? I've seen pictures of them. You can get them with four-poster beds, rugs and things to make them really luxurious. We could put a coffee table and cushions in there; leave them a lovely meal and some chocolates."

"Oooh." Ana Luisa's eyes shone. "Like an Arab prince and his beautiful bride. This is a wonderful idea, Ruth! I can picture this… it looks good!"

Emily clutched my hand. "Yes. With millions of flowers in there. And candles."

"Candles in a tent? Isn't that a fire hazard? They could get all excited and knock one over, and then that would be the end of that." Ellie mimed getting excited and knocking over a candle.

"Stop miming; I can't see you in the dark. It's rude," Emily huffed.

"I'm getting excited and knocking a candle over. You can imagine it in your head. Now I'm putting out the flames with the sheet." Ellie pretended to choke on the smoke.

"If candles are no good, we could string up loads of fairy lights."

"And we would need some sort of heater, and a little cool box filled with treats like strawberries and cream." I considered what else. "They'd have to use the bathroom in the house – that's the only thing."

"Sorry, Ruth. Has no one told you where the bathroom is?" Lois had crept up behind me with a tray of drinks. "Rupa, can you grab those mints you brought while I show Ruth to the loo?"

I followed Lois inside to the downstairs bathroom, which also contained a shower cubicle. Problem solved. We would just make that area of the house off limits to the children for the night.

By unspoken agreement, we said nothing about our yurt plans to Lois. I sat back in my chair and sipped my coffee, watching the easy conversation between these possible new friends and feeling a tiny spark of something strange and wonderful mixed up in my belly among the noodles and black bean chicken. I named it hope.

Saturday was a sharp jolt back into reality. I took Maggie school uniform shopping in Nottingham, trying not to let her see how much it cost me, mentally and in pounds and pence, to kit her out for the new term. I wanted her to fit in, to feel confident and look good, but that came at a price. It was a whole extra type of grief, having to scour shops for sale items, say no to a thirty pound school bag, try to balance shoes that would last the year with the scant pennies in my purse. Two years ago all this had been of little or no consideration. I tried to push down the anger I felt towards Fraser for leaving his daughter in this situation. Tried to hide from Maggie how much it hurt to have to say no. Thought about the cheque from Dad, hidden in a shoe-box at the back of my wardrobe.

By late afternoon, we were about done. Maggie, who had been cooperative but uncommunicative, suggested we stop and have a drink.

I shook my head, my hands beginning to tremble. Two cups of coffee seemed like a ludicrous waste of non-existent money.

"Why don't we go home and I'll make us one there?"

Clang. The shutter in front of Maggie's face slammed down. She turned away, her offer of forgiveness spurned, and began clomping back towards the car park.

Rats. I resisted the urge to start pulling out my hair. I hated this. Hated having to scrimp and worry and scuttle about the shops with hunched shoulders, always, always, always thinking about money.

"All right." I hurried after Maggie and stopped in front of her. "I would love to have a drink with you. Here. In town. You pick somewhere."

The cost of half an hour chatting with my daughter, without her checking her phone once? Priceless.

# Chapter Six

When the alarm went off on Tuesday morning, it felt as though a bear was sitting on my chest. I lay there for a long time, ignoring the ticking of the clock, my eyes squinched tightly shut against the beams of sunlight poking at me from the edge of my curtains. I could hear my parents rattling about in the kitchen, the faint sounds of another argument drifting up the stairs. Maggie was in the shower, next to my room, the water making spattering sounds on the wall beside my bed.

This was it. My summer of hiding and indulging my despondent emotions was over. Time to set off on the road to recovery. Today was going to be a good day. Maggie would have a great start at her new school, I would get myself a job and then cook us dinner to celebrate. I pushed off the bear with the strength of my forced optimism, clambered out of bed and went to get on with my new life.

"Ruth Henderson?" Vanessa Jacobs stopped straightening cardigans on the rack in front of her and peered at me through chunky-framed glasses. "Wow. You'd better come into the back."

I followed her through the shop, the sign of which said "Couture" in simple, thin lettering on a plum background, down a long, slim space lined with uncluttered rows of boutique-style fashion. At the far end stood a glass counter containing a couple of displays featuring accessories, including locally made jewellery and designer handbags. It was tasteful, elegant and about five zillion miles from the nearest orange puffa jacket. Vanessa Jacobs had come a long way.

She offered me a low stool in front of a full-length mirror, set among piles of boxes.

Ah. Now this could be a problem. I had sold all my decent clothes, bought using Fraser's secret debt mountain, for pitiful and desperate amounts on internet auctions. My mother declared that my few remaining items, worn to death over the previous couple of years, were in no way suitable for an interview with Southwell's queen of fashion. Ever prepared, Mum triumphantly produced a chocolate coloured shift dress, the label still attached.

"I mentioned your wardrobe deficiency to Lois, and she gave me this! She bought it for a conference and then found it was too small for her."

A dress too small for five-foot-nothing, tiny Lois. Yes, I contained about as much fat as a diet yoghurt at that point, but I stood several inches taller than Lois, and shared my father's sturdy frame. Squeezing the dress on, I managed to wrestle the zip all the way up to the top with a little help from an empty stomach and Maggie. I had not, however, yet managed to successfully take more than the shallowest of breaths, sit down properly or bend my body further than about two inches in any direction.

I looked at the stool. "Actually, I'm fine standing."

Vanessa raised one perfectly plucked eyebrow at me. She waved her hand at the piles of cardboard boxes and cellophane-wrapped outfits hanging from the ceiling all around us.

"There's not enough room for both of us to stand. Please sit."

Oh dear. Gingerly, apprehensively, with as much care as Neil Armstrong landing Apollo 11 on the moon, I lowered myself the long, long distance down to the stool, wondering if my backside would ever reach the shiny black seat.

*Come on, Ruth. You can do it. Take it steady now.*

The dress material began to stretch and strain impossibly taut around my hips and back as the angle forced my body forward in order to avoid toppling over. My knees began jutting up higher than my hips as I closed the gap an agonizing fraction at a time. I grabbed onto a nearby clothes rail for balance, smiling valiantly at Vanessa as I descended the last few inches. She watched me, her expression blank, as I finally hit the wooden surface. At that moment, in the clumsy silence, was a distinct *rrriiiiippp*.

Vanessa took a tiny step back, her eyes widening in horror and surprise. I felt a gentle waft of cool air on my back, right above the top of my faded knickers – a noticeable contrast to my face, burning with mortification.

I took a deep, rallying breath – *rriiippp*. Squared my shoulders – *rriiippp*.

*Fine, this is okay; this is salvageable. She doesn't know what's causing the ripping sound. Maybe it's just my stomach gurgling with interview nerves. Or a mouse scrabbling about behind the skirting board. Or a ghost… Just sit absolutely still, do not move a SINGLE MUSCLE below your neck, and get through the next few minutes.*

Vanessa narrowed her eyes. "Is there a problem?"

"Nope. No. Not a problem. I'm great. It's great to be here. This is great. Isn't it? I love job interviews…" My voice trailed off into one of those weak, embarrassed laughs. Vanessa perched herself on the edge of a normal-sized metal chair a few feet away, and smoothed out her black silk skirt. The mass of frizzy curls that had spent the nineties in a pineapple ponytail were now sleek, chestnut ringlets. She pursed glossed-up (and I suspected plumped-up) lips and stuck out her large, pointy chest.

"Well, you've certainly embraced the size zero look. Half my customers would pay to show that much skeleton."

*Yes, Vanessa. I should write a book. "The Bereavement Diet: How Losing Your Partner Can Lose You Those Pounds!" Or "The Poverty Plan to a Slimmer You: If You Can't Buy, You Can't Eat!"*

"Um, thanks. You look, um, great. The shop too. That's… great." I squeaked that last word at a pitch I suspected was undetectable to human ears.

Vanessa raised one eyebrow. "Yes. Perfect exam results might get you a nice certificate, but they can't teach you how to succeed in the real world. Business acumen is what matters, not being able to complete a quadratic equation."

I was further impressed. I couldn't remember Vanessa ever turning up to a maths lesson, let alone listening enough to pick up words like "quadratic". Or "equation".

"So. Tell me about yourself. What have you been up to since leaving Southwell? Didn't you go to university?"

"Yes. I went to Liverpool, to study maths. But only completed my first year."

"Really?" Vanessa's two-inch fingernails tapped away on her iPad screen. "What happened?"

"I had a baby." Vanessa Jacobs knew this, of course. She knew that I knew she knew. This was about establishing the pecking order. As if it needed to be established. I remained frozen, sitting bolt upright, trying not to be distracted by the breeze tickling my spine.

"Yes, I heard a few rumours. We all presumed it must be David Carrington's. But then, if it was, you wouldn't be needing a job, would you?"

I said nothing. The prickles of heat intensified across my chest and neck. There was no way on this earth I was going to let Vanessa Jacobs see how his name affected me. See how the memory of her smirking over his shoulder as she wrapped herself around him still punched me in the gut.

"Your boyfriend died?"

"My partner. Yes."

"Sorry to hear that. It must be depressing finding yourself alone at your age." Vanessa swiped a hand across the screen of her pad. She did not look sorry. "Work experience?"

"I've worked in various office jobs. Temping, admin stuff, some accounts."

"CV?"

"Yes."

She looked up, waiting.

"It's in my bag." Squeak.

"Well, can you please get it out of your bag so I can see it?"

*No! I can't actually. This preposterous dress designed for an underfed child pixie will not allow me to do that.*

She tapped her pointy shoes a few times on the wooden floor.

As slowly as if either trying to hide the fact I was drunk, or missing several of my vital faculties, I leaned forward and reached the corner of my bag with the tips of two fingers. Quickly coughing to smother the sounds of the further destruction of the pixie dress – *rriiippp!* – I yanked the bag close enough to open it and remove my CV while still on the stool. As I attempted to lift it out, it got caught on the bag's zip. I could feel the sweat dripping at the edge of my hairline, and prayed it wouldn't cause my foundation to run. After what seemed, both to me and I'm sure to Vanessa, like several hours, I managed to wrestle the document free and hand it over with minimal movement. My potential boss scanned it.

"No retail?"

"No. But I'm a quick learner, and prepared to work really hard. I could do a probationary period…" Yuck. I was grovelling. To Vanessa Jacobs. In a dress with a gaping hole down the back. I wanted to slap myself.

She held up one hand, like a stop sign. "You see, Ruth. My problem is this. We have a certain *image* to uphold at Couture." She was rolling her words around her mouth, enjoying this, treating me like an idiot. "We are very proud of our clientele." Who was the "we"? Mum said she worked by herself. Did she include her fake boobs as a separate person? "Our ladies expect a certain standard. A visit to Couture is not simply a shopping trip, but an experience. An event. We provide a complete service, including image enhancement, capsule wardrobes and personal styling. For that, the staff need to project Couture's three 'c's – competence, confidence and chic."

She looked me up and down over the top of her glasses. Squinted at my ill-fitting outfit, my sensible work shoes and flushed, blotchy complexion. "You don't have any of those things."

She sat back, and waited. I stared at the floor, remembering when Maggie brought home the African land snail from her infant school and Fraser trod on it. I considered my bank balance, added to that Maggie, and the image of day after day after day of living with my parents. Then took a deep breath.

"What about if I got some new clothes? I'd be happy to stay in the back, clean up, sort stock. I am great at accounts. That would leave you more time with the customers. The clientele." I paused for a couple of seconds. "I know your grandmother needs quite a lot of looking after these days. I could help free up some time for you to be with her."

She stared at me, confirming that yes, I was making a veiled threat referring to her grandmother's toenails.

"New hair. New make-up. New shoes. New attitude. If you come back tomorrow looking reasonable I'll let you have a couple of sample outfits from the shop at a discount. You can pay for them out of your wages. But I am serious about the attitude. No one wants to buy clothes from a failure. And you stink of failure."

"Um. Would it be possible to take a jacket now? A long one?"

What I should have done then, I suppose, was stop in at the hairdresser's to book myself an appointment for that afternoon, before going home to raid my mother's shoe closet. But like any sane woman in my situation, I instead called in at the delicatessen and bought myself the largest cheesecake in the display case – a caramel baked mud cake with cappuccino flakes and extra whipped cream. I ignored the spasm of guilt at breaking into the emergency ten pound note hidden in the side pocket of my purse. The green and pink zebra-striped coat Vanessa had grudgingly lent me screamed "emergency".

As I rounded the corner into the cul-de-sac, my mobile rang. It was the school secretary. Could I please come in and have a chat with the headmaster about Maggie's first day? As soon as possible.

No, I wasn't to worry. Nothing bad had happened to her. But she was in big trouble.

To my great relief, Mum's car was in the drive when I huffed up the road to drop the cheesecake off before heading over to the school. I let myself in, took a couple of minutes to change, hide the ruined dress under my bed, brush my hair (for the second time that day!), blow my nose and restore my make-up, then snagged the car keys from the wooden love-heart pegs by the front door.

I decided to take the cheesecake with me, eating a third of it sitting in the school car park, figuring I would need the energy boost before facing yet another headmaster's office. At least there was a new headmaster, new school building and therefore new office since I had donned the Southwell Minster school uniform, which slightly helped me to remember that I was the parent here, not the naughty school girl.

The headmaster seemed like a nice, if slightly world-weary, bloke. He hadn't wanted to suspend Maggie on her first day, despite this being the standard procedure for grabbing another girl by her ponytail and slamming her head into a locker, then wrestling her to the ground in some sort of rolling around cat fight.

Maggie wielded her sympathy card with skill and expertise.

"She disrespected my hair. Said my alcho mum had cut it."

Currently, her hair was mostly short and black, to represent being severed from her old school, her friends and her house. A white fringe hung down past her nose, signifying the part of her that wanted to hide. One blue streak remained tucked behind her ear, as somewhere behind all the fear and sadness was a strand of hope that felt excited and optimistic to be starting a new school (I wondered if a boy in a battered black jacket had anything to do with this).

"And that my druggie dad dyed it." Oh dear. "Someone told her about my dad, so she shoved her face right up into my personal space and laughed. She said that explains it."

Maggie looked straight at Mr Hay. "Sir, are your parents still alive?"

"We're not talking about me, Maggie."

"Sir, if someone said your dad, who had died, had coloured your hair, wouldn't you get mad? Wouldn't a normal, rational, human reaction be to slam their head into the nearest hard object? I'm fourteen. The nerve synapses to my pre-frontal cortex are breaking down, I am pumped full of crazy teenage chemicals and there isn't a single other person in this whole school who's got my back. If I had let that comment slide, I would have been done for."

"In situations like this one, the best course of action is to talk to a member of staff."

"Get real, sir. You know in situations like this one talking to a teacher is a suicidal course of action. Sir – *she brought my dad into it.*"

We agreed to an after-school detention and a promise to work on controlling her behaviour. Maggie returned to class, and I went back to the cheesecake. Back in the car, as I contemplated whether my churning insides could handle another piece, the passenger door opened, startling me into jerking the cake box off my lap.

"Careful with that! I'm commandeering it for emergency relief." Lois slid into the passenger seat and grabbed the box.

"Half a Delilicious cheesecake gone. I'm guessing a visit with Mr Hay." Lois stabbed the plastic fork into the rich brown caramel swirls and shovelled a monster piece into her mouth, proceeding to talk around the food. "I'm up next. See that broken window? Seth threw a chair through it. I'm supposed to be taking Freya for a check-up this afternoon. Matt is having to miss a meeting with his regional minister buddies to take her. Is it okay that I'm a pastor's wife but sometimes I want to throw Seth's parents through a window for managing to so spectacularly screw that boy up? Right, I'm done." She wiped her fingers on a napkin and fluffed her hair in the mirror. "I'm already ten minutes late, but if you want to chat about why you're sitting in the school car park with a six thousand calorie dessert, call me later. Or even better, come round. Bring the remains of the cake. We can swap war stories about how we are failing our wayward teens."

She hopped out of the car and marched towards the school entrance with the efficiency of a mother of six on the case. I watched her go and wondered how the girl I sat next to in English had transformed into this strong, loving, impressive woman. And how I, according to the business acumen of Vanessa Jacobs, stank of failure. Well, at least now I stank of failure and caramel mud cake.

When I got home, I found a letter waiting for me in the hand-crafted Fairtrade letter rack. Apparently a credit card account, held in my name, had racked up debt to the tune of five figures. The monthly interest alone would swallow up most of my wages from Couture if I got the job. The address on the account was Fraser's old company. Someone in his office had finally got around to forwarding the letter to our house in Liverpool, and the new owners had sent it on.

I crawled up to my room, stuffed the letter in my tampon box where my post-menopausal mother wouldn't find it, and buried myself deep underneath the duvet of denial, where I planned to stay for a very long time. I couldn't even think about Dad's cheque still loitering in the shoebox. Was it okay to cash in five-thousand pounds' worth of guilt money, if the person was right to feel guilty? If you took the money, did that mean the debt was paid, they were forgiven, and you couldn't feel mad at them any more?

I couldn't even wallow in peace. Mum returned home in a jolly whirl of enthusiasm and hope, wanting to hear all the details of the job interview, bellowing up the stairs, wondering where I was. I lay there, sweaty from the heat of the duvet, and listened to her rattling pots in the kitchen, hoping to lure me out like a chicken from under a bush. I threw back the bedding (quietly) and slowly slid my bedroom window open. With the practised ease of every female who has survived an overly smothering mother, I nimbly lowered myself onto the conservatory roof and slithered down to the window ledge behind the bookcase, out of sight from the kitchen. I had done this a thousand times before, in another life. Although those times I wore trainers, and no holly bush grew underneath the window.

# I Hope You Dance

With scraped feet and grazed elbows from crash-landing onto the patio, I scuttled around the side of the house to the car, before remembering the car keys were in my bag, and my bag was in the house.

Right. Regroup. I could give up and go back inside. But I was a long sob-fest away from facing Mum. I had no shoes, no phone, no purse. And the unmistakable smooth figure of Dad now rounded the corner at the bottom of the cul-de-sac.

*Quick, Ruth: think. Where can I go to stress, cry, wait things out and figure out where I'm going to get new shoes, new hair, new make-up and a new attitude before nine o'clock tomorrow morning?*

I went to the only place. The place I had always gone. It was cool and dark. The summer's growth had brought the heavy boughs of the willow tree low enough to brush the grass in front of the Big House. The leaves were layered thick and deep, allowing only a few faint chinks of light through the canopy of arching branches. I burrowed in, shuffling back along the mossy ground until my back hit the trunk in the centre. The tree stood only six feet or so tall, the circle of branches just broad enough for me to lay down without my toes poking out of the edge. It was like being enclosed in a magical tent, with walls in constant flickering motion.

I leaned back into the rough bark, inhaling the scent of dank earth and crisp late summer leaves, and began to focus on the rustling of the boughs and the soft, murky atmosphere. As the distant rumble of cars, the sounds and sights of life and all its confusion and difficulties, faded into the tender gloom beneath the willow tree, I faded with it, into the stillness. The tangled web of thoughts inside my head gradually eased, as I continued to breathe deep and slow with the rhythm of the old tree. The brain-buzzing stopped, the permanent crick in my shoulders unfolded a little. I stretched out on the brown grass, melting into my surroundings, and stared at a caterpillar dangling from a branch above my head. And for a short while, for the first time in several eons, I just was. I was me.

For about half an hour I daydreamed about previous days and nights spent under the willow, playing with the insects there, having picnics, talking, laughing, making plans, being with David. Allowing myself this indulgence as compensation for a bad day. Half asleep, I recalled the last time I heard David's voice, which had led to a mammoth fortnight of similar indulgences, leaving me riddled with guilt and spiralling into six months of depression.

Maggie was five. I hadn't seen David since that awful night. The jagged pain of missing him had gradually faded to a dull, background ache I had grown accustomed to but could always find if I looked for it. I had known, and loved, David for almost as long as I had known myself. Like two trees sprouting from seeds planted close together, we grew up each of us entwined in the other, and the damage done when we ripped apart had snapped off parts of me that would take a long, long time to grow back.

I was eighteen when I left him. My family thought that, given time, distance and the perspective of maturity, I would see my feelings for David to be nothing more than teenage infatuation. A crush to smile wistfully about in years to come as I fondly recalled my obsession with the boy next door.

No one questions a child loving their mother or father, grandparents, siblings, a nanny – a dog! – with fullness of heart, true intensity and utter devotion. That to lose them at any age can cause deep sorrow and anguish, changing them forever. That they would always feel that loss. David was not dead. But I had loved him this way. I had loved him and then lost him.

So, when Maggie was home from school with tonsillitis, spending the day curled up on the sofa watching kids' TV, at first I thought I was imagining it, that I must be coming down with a bug too.

I was in the kitchen, scooping ice-cream into a bowl to soothe her raw throat, when I heard his voice. Gentle, strong, warm. With trembling fingers I put down the spoon and clutched hold of the worktop, straining my ears above the sudden roar of adrenaline. It was him. *It was him.*

David had a way of speaking that smiled, even in those rare moments when he was angry, or scared, or sad. I could feel him, helping me over the fence at the back of the farm where we tracked foxes. Grabbing on to me, hands trembling, before opening his acceptance letter to study Zoology at Bristol University. Tucking my hair back behind my ears as I ranted about the one million ways my family had upset me. I could see him. His hair, peppered with streaks of blond from endless hours spent outside, eyes watchful as he examined another specimen, then dancing like quicksilver as he recounted to me his latest discovery.

I walked into the living room and lowered myself onto a chair. Maggie had fallen asleep so couldn't see my legs shaking, hear my heart hammering to get out of my chest, back to him, to where it belonged. The television screen displayed a rainforest, and there, in the centre of the screen, stood David. Talking to the camera about snakes, he wore dark green trousers and a light green T-shirt with a knapsack slung over his shoulders. He grinned, stuck his tongue out to demonstrate a snake smelling his environment. He looked a little broader across the shoulders, his face showed the weathering of a life spent outdoors, but it was David. Still that same generous ease of movement. Still so alive and awake and aware. He spoke to every child watching as if only to them, as if they were as fascinated, delighted and inspired by boa constrictors as he was. And just as he had done for me in the wilds of Nottinghamshire so long ago, he couldn't help but draw the viewer into his world, to see it as he did: a remarkable, miraculous, spectacular feast of discovery and wonder.

I reached for the remote control, eyes never leaving the screen. When the camera moved to a close-up of a python I searched the TV guide for the name of the programme – *Whole Wild World*, on every weekday at eleven o'clock, and again at four. I found a blank DVD and set the player up to record.

The ice-cream melted into a puddle on the worktop.

For the next two weeks I watched every episode. Many, many times. Maggie had gone back to school, and Fraser went on a conference for a week. The house fell into chaos, we lived on junk food and ready meals, and I only turned the TV off for the few hours every day between Maggie coming home and her going to bed. Once Fraser was back, he still spent so much time out of the house working or playing football that things weren't much better. I walked around in a trance, like an addict on a fix, my head, my heart, my dreams full of David. Riddled with guilt. Knowing I was cheating on Fraser as surely as if I had invited another man into my bed. I had moments of crippling awareness about how I would feel if Fraser thought this way about another woman. But I had opened a door and, like any addict, it was always one more episode, a promise that tomorrow I would leave it behind and get on with the life I had chosen.

Eventually, after a particularly bad couple of days, Fraser noticed. It says a lot about how things were between us – it took him weeks to become aware that while my body remained in the house, in every other way I was no longer present. We weren't having sex, which was unusual, but not unheard of at that point in our relationship. I had been sleeping badly, growing increasingly anxious, scared I would say David's name in my sleep. Yet, like so many who keep secrets, something in me hoped I would; that Fraser would find the DVDs; that I would be discovered, because I wasn't sure how to stop myself and I knew this behaviour was killing me. Killing us.

Having observed my twitchiness, my bad temper, my lack of interest in anything, he confronted me over an Indian take-away.

"What's going on, Ruth?"

I choked on my naan bread, coughing then drinking some water as I scrabbled for composure. "What?"

"I want to know what's going on. You've been on edge all weekend. And you look terrible."

"Nothing's going on. I've been feeling under the weather. I think I'm fighting a bug, that's all."

"Maggie told me she's seen you crying. More than once."

Maggie had seen me.

"I said I've not been feeling great. And I always get weepy this time of the month."

"Did something happen when I was away?"

This was how Fraser dealt with me. He didn't bother to argue or discuss. He asked until I answered.

"No! I haven't been feeling great."

"Did you meet somebody?"

I pushed back the chair and stood to my feet, hoping he would interpret my anger as righteous rather than guilty.

"Seriously, Fraser. Are you accusing me of having an affair? When I have to look after Maggie all day?"

"Sit down. Don't pretend you don't have ample opportunity when she's at school. It's not as if you do anything else."

I was crying now. Crying that I was explaining myself with practical evidence; that my love for my partner couldn't stand up on its own. "If I was having an affair, wouldn't I be happy and excited? Not looking terrible!"

Fraser shook his head, his features softening slightly. We were twenty-five, trying to transform a relationship born out of obligation, necessity and a smattering of lust into love for the sake of our daughter. Trying to build a foundation of commitment, and respect, and trust. My *Whole Wild World* binge had led to this conversation – one which threatened to smash that foundation like a pneumatic drill attacking concrete. But it had been a long time coming.

"Sit down, Ruth. Please. And try not to wake Maggie up. I'm sorry you're upset, but I'm watching my girlfriend fall apart. You can't blame me for wondering why."

I sat back down, then took another drink of water with unsteady hands. Neither of us said anything for a while. Our food congealed into stodgy lumps in the cartons.

"I promise you, Fraser, I haven't gone near anyone else. I've barely spoken to anybody this past couple of weeks, except for Maggie and the woman at the library. Maybe that's the problem. I don't know what to do all day now Maggie's at school. I clean the house, which I detest, and do the gardening. I shop, and cook, and read a bit. I feel like a servant. I'm lonely. And so bored I could scratch my own face off. I know I don't need to work, that it gets complicated with school holidays and everything else, and I don't have a clue what job I could do, but honestly, Fraser, if I don't do something I'm going to go mad."

He let out a huge sigh of built-up tension. Here was a problem he could fix. He found me an office job through one of his contacts. I got a chance to use my brain again and feel slightly better than a tapeworm, as well as meet some people who seemed to quite like me. I snapped the DVDs in half and locked David back into the deepest, darkest dungeon of my mind. I never told Fraser that I spent the rest of the year on anti-depressants.

Half asleep underneath the willow tree, having binged on David memories, when I first heard his voice drifting through the leaves I again blamed my imagination. It rumbled, warm and deep, with a slight croak from tiredness, or lack of use perhaps. He laughed, and my soul danced. Then I heard a car door slam, followed by the clack of heels running on the driveway, and I froze. This was no dream.

"Mr David!" Ana Luisa's voice sounded muffled, as if she was burying her head in his shoulder.

He laughed again as he replied, "Steady on, Ana. I'm weak from hunger; you'll have me on the floor."

"You are hungry? That is no good, Mr David! Come inside and I will fix you a nice big bowl of my grandmother's feijoada. Fresh this morning, in your honour, Mr David. Come, come inside."

"Ana Luisa, you have made my year. I have dreamt about your grandmother's cooking for weeks. Let me grab my bags and I'm there."

"Okay, see you inside. Hurry now!"

*Shoot. I don't know what to do. I'm stuck under the tree. David is here. I don't know what to do.*

I heard David open the boot of his car.

*I have to see him. No, no I can't see him yet, not like this. But how can I not see him? He's here. He's actually here. I can't believe it! David. He's here.*

*I can't suddenly appear from under the tree. That would be crazy. He'd think I was crazy, hiding under his tree. Can I crawl close enough to peep through the leaves? At least then I've seen him. But what if he saw me spying on him? Oh, man. This is bad. I don't know what to do.*

Ana Luisa tapped back out of the door. "Come on, this is waiting for you. This cooking you have been dreaming about. I want to hear all your adventures."

I shuffled forward enough to glimpse a flash of her through the branches. She wore a figure-hugging peacock blue dress, with a tiny silver cardigan covered in shimmering feathers and metallic-heeled sandals. Her hair was a black mane, and in the afternoon sunlight Ana Luisa's skin was deep, silken honey.

It hit me like a piano from a three-storey window. Ana Luisa. David. *Ana Luisa and David!* They had probably met when he was filming the rainforest snake episode. And she invited him to her house to sample her grandmother's cooking. How could I have assumed she was simply the housekeeper? A magnificent woman like that?

Grabbing the top of my head with both hands, I screwed up my eyes. I was done. I felt like a foolish little girl, and wished I could be anywhere else than under that stupid tree. I just wanted David to go in the house so I could get away. It took forever for him to unload three bags and carry them ten feet down the path to his front door. The whole time Ana Luisa hovered and smiled and made flappy bird movements with her hands to encourage him inside. Finally, she disappeared after him. I counted to a hundred before creeping over to the far side of the willow, building myself up to the great escape.

"Ruth? I have brought you a glass of freshly squeezed orange juice. I didn't know if you wanted to come out from under the tree, or drink it in there."

"Ana Luisa! You scared me. I…"

"Oh, Ruth. You do not have to explain yourself to me. It is a lovely tree, a fine place to cool down and grab a few moments of serenity on a day like this one. Shall I leave the juice here?" She bent down, placing the drink on the grass underneath the tree. I caught sight of her impressively curvaceous cleavage as she did, and promptly burst into tears.

"Oh, Ruth! Oh dear!" Ana Luisa fluttered about on the edge of the branches.

My nose started to run, and I fumbled about for something to wipe it on.

"Here." She held out a tissue, trying to reach me from her position outside the tree. "Oh. This is no good. Can I come inside? Would you mind?"

I nodded, unable to speak. Ana Luisa ducked under the canopy and knelt down beside me. Even her knees were lovely. She took hold of my hand, and murmured what I assumed were Portuguese words of comfort as I sobbed.

A while later, I managed to pull myself together somewhat. "I'm so sorry. This is really embarrassing. I just had an exceptionally bad day, and the willow was the place I always came when I needed to feel better. It, it…"

I started off again. Ana Luisa pointed to the initials carved on the tree. "This is you. You and Mr David."

I nodded.

"This is a very special place for you. I understand. When I was a little girl I used to hide in the back of my mao's closet. She had a fur coat she kept in there. Not a real one, a pretend only, but it was so soft and cosy, and it smelt so like her. After the men came and took my sister, I used to hide there a lot. Oh –" she took hold of my tissue and wiped her own eyes – "I miss her so much. And my mother. She is a beautiful woman. She taught me everything I know.

"But" – she shook off the memories with a huge smile – "we are not talking about me. Tell me about your exceptionally bad day,

Ruth. One thing Mao taught me is that a problem shared is half way better."

"I'm being silly. It's no big deal. I needed a bit of a cry and didn't want Mum to see and get worried. It was really kind of you to bring me a drink. I'll finish it, and then get back home. Maggie will be back from her first day soon."

"Very good. So while you drink your juice you can tell me why you needed a cry. Otherwise I have to start on Mr David's bag of tropical washing, and I want to put opening that smelly suitcase off for as long as possible. You do me a favour, and we become better friends."

I sipped the juice. Ana Luisa waited. I took a deep breath.

"Maggie got in trouble at school today for fighting. Which is another reminder of how angry and hurt she still is after losing her dad. How hard it is for her to have to start again in a new place. I feel like I'm failing her because I don't know how to make that better."

"Yes. That is hard. And you are angry and hurting too."

"And then I had a letter today from Fraser's work with some really bad news in it. I don't know how to deal with that either."

She nodded, her brown eyes wide and gentle. "And you wish Fraser was here to share this problem, so you can deal with it together. This makes you even sadder."

*Not quite, but close. If Fraser was here I would leave all the sorting out to him.*

"Yes. And part of sorting out the mess is finding a job. So I went and had an interview at Couture this morning."

"Couture?" Ana Luisa actually hissed. Not when she said the name. Afterwards. She hissed like a panther.

"Yes, I'm desperate. But according to Vanessa Jacobs, who is probably right, I stink of failure. And obviously she can't have me contaminating her boutique with my stench. So, if I want the job, which I absolutely don't but right now I have no other options, I need to turn up tomorrow with new shoes, hair, make-up and attitude."

I looked down at my crumpled clothes and bare feet, waved a hand at my tear-streaked blotchy complexion, my awful, awful hair.

"And the only way I can get new shoes in time is to call my superior sister. Mum is two sizes bigger than me and Maggie only wears Dr Martens. Esther makes me feel like a drab, pathetic, feeble disaster at the best of times. I'm not sure I can face her condescension on top of everything else."

I didn't mention the worst part of my day, as it directly involved Ana Luisa, and besides, I couldn't have spoken the words if I tried.

She clapped her hands together lots of times. "This is not a problem. I will cut your hair!" Untucking one foot from under her, she waggled it next to mine. "Six and a half?"

"Yes."

"Ah ha! My whole life I have questioned why God would give me such a troublesome shoe size, trusting that in his mysterious wisdom he had a reason. And today we find the reason! I have shoes that would shove Vanessa Jacobs' snotty attitude right back up her nose where it belongs. You will be transformed! Oh, this is so much fun, Ruth. I am so glad you came to live at number five with your crazy mother and your dancing father. And I promise you, when I am done the new attitude will be no problem at all. You will not stink of failure; you will carry with you only the scent of fabulous womanly splendour! Come on. Come inside and the magic will begin."

"Ana Luisa, that is so kind, and really means a lot to me, but I need to be at home when Maggie gets back. Are you able to come over and sort me out there? I can wait, if you want to spend some time with..."

*With David, whose name I can't say. And is the real big, strapping, handsome reason why I don't want to go in the Big House.*

"Oh, those boys are ugly enough to look after themselves. Mr David's washing can wait. And if he has a problem with that he can do it himself. Now, go! I will be there in half an hour."

# Chapter Seven

"Ta da!" Two hours later, Ana Luisa spun me around, daytime television make-over style, and presented me with my new look in the living room mirror.

"No, no, no! You mustn't cry, Ruth. This will spoil it already. Here, quickly." She dabbed under my eyes with a tissue.

My frizzy, unkempt nest had been replaced with a sleek, choppy bob framing my face and softening pointy cheekbones. The colouring on my eyes and lips looked subtle, classy. The purple shadows had disappeared, along with the lines that told the story of a troubled year. The woman who stared back at me from the mirror appeared younger, happier, healthier and snazzy. She resembled a woman, not a thing. She was alive, and living.

I remembered this woman. From when she was a girl. I didn't know her well, but there had been many brief encounters. When I won my first art competition. When I sat my maths exam two years early and scored one hundred per cent. When I walked to school, in my floor-scraping navy skirt and black army boots, David's old denim jacket across my shoulders.

The last time I saw her was at a party, when the coolest boy on the maths course filled my glass with vodka and asked me to dance.

I gazed at her, this old acquaintance, and wondered if I could get to know her again. If by wearing her hair, her make-up, her shoes, she would stick around and become a part of me. Was I ready for that? To start living again? To find the potential me inside, the best me? I wasn't sure. Because embracing her meant acknowledging that she had been there all along. That I had wasted fifteen years allowing my brain to rot, my creative talents to fester and my beauty to hide under a thick, scratchy blanket of self-doubt, oppression and pathetic apathy.

The truth was, I had abandoned everything my mother had taught me and spent my entire adult life *settling* and *making do*. I had not strived, fought, adventured, embraced, journeyed, dared, been inspiring or inspired. I had barely laughed.

*Come on, Ruth. You can waste a whole load more years lamenting the lost ones, or suck it up, pick it up and make darn sure you don't waste another second of the ones you have left. For pity's sake. You've cried enough.*

Who'd have thought it? A minor epiphany brought on by a haircut and frosty nude lip gloss.

Maggie sauntered in. She raised one eyebrow. "You actually look all right."

"All right?" Ana Luisa smacked her on the head with the hair straighteners. "Your mother is gorgeous! Like an angel, or a beautiful mermaid come up from the sea to enchant a prince. You should be very proud of her."

And then Maggie said something that made all the rest of it – the letter, the willow tree, the fighting and the prospect of another ten seconds spent in the clenched jaws of Couture – seem like nothing but an annoying fly alighting briefly on my arm.

"I am."

Mum dug out her pasta machine and made crab ravioli with chilli and a saffron sauce to celebrate my new "finger snapping, hot and spicy hair with a saucy sultry complexion and fizz".

She baked hazelnut crème brûlée with frosted sparkles to honour Maggie's first day at school, because "You showed that Henderson girls have nuts and sparkle!"

I ate so much my jeans ceased teetering on the edge of my jagged hip bones. I drank a glass of wine with gusto. Gusto. Steady on, Ruth.

New Ruth was back at the dress shop at nine the following morning. It was hard to tell from her stiff face, but I gathered Vanessa was impressed as she let me stay on for an hour scrubbing grime off the back room window frames and skirting boards. Not an easy task in your mother's pencil skirt and borrowed heels, but a whole lot easier than trying to sit at a desk and type with Cramer Spence breathing his sour breath down the back of your neck. Eight pounds fifty ticked off the mammoth debt. Only four squillion, two hundred and seventeen to go.

After finishing at the shop, I stopped in at the Oak Hill Centre before going home to shower and change. Lois had phoned to say one of the cleaners had broken her ankle running away from an escaped tarantula, and they needed a quick replacement. I hated cleaning, but I hated secret debt and having to rely on my parents even more. I had an appointment with the senior manager, Martine McKinley. She beckoned me into her office.

"Hello, Ruth. Please take a seat. Make yourself at home. I'm Martine. M.A.R.T.I.N.E. Not Martin. It's a woman's name. I'm a woman. I've learned it's best to clear that up right at the start."

This may seem like a strange thing to point out upon meeting someone. Usually even very small children can figure out someone's gender, but although embarrassed, I was grateful for the heads up. Martine wasn't especially tall, maybe five foot four. Her hair floated in a wispy cloud somewhere above the top of her head. I didn't try to count the individual hairs during our thirty-minute meeting, but I maybe could have. The polite word for her build was "solid". She wore grey combat trousers and a black T-shirt. Several whiskers sprouted from random points on her face. A huge wooden cross – her only jewellery – hung from a leather thong over the top of her T-shirt. Her voice was gruff, her body language brisk and her hands were enormous. I could see how mistakes may have been made.

But what drew my attention, once we had introduced ourselves, was twofold. Martine had one green eye, surrounded by a ring of green eye shadow, and one blue eye, covered in blue. She also had the biggest, brightest, sunniest-day-on-a-white-sandy-beach-in-the-middle-of-the-ocean smile I had ever seen. It creased her face up so much her eyes were hidden, and only the eye shadow was left to remind observers which eye was blue and which was green.

During the course of my half-hour interview it became apparent that Martine was ferociously honest, highly opinionated and as mad as a hatter. I loved her.

"So, Ruth. How's your mother? Still running around trying to pretend she isn't sixty-nine?"

"She's keeping busy."

"Do you like cleaning, Ruth?" Martine held up her hands. "Think about it for a moment. Be honest. No point wasting each other's time with fudged answers we both know aren't true."

I thought about it for a moment.

"I like things being clean."

"I like tomato ketchup but I don't grow the tomatoes myself. Why do you want to be a cleaner?"

"I want to work somewhere that feels safe. At the moment I need a job that isn't going to be too intellectually challenging, or stressful, or emotional. I think the physical exercise will be good for me and the hours are right."

Martine frowned at me. She didn't look convinced. "Why not walk dogs or deliver newspapers? I want to know the truth about cleaning."

I took a deep breath. "Right now, Martine, my life is a mess. It contains dirt and rubbish and grimy secrets. I am a mess. I am working on that, but it's going to take a very long time. Meanwhile, I believe that eliminating other people's filth and straightening up after them will be like transference therapy. If that even is a type of therapy. I will get great satisfaction from knowing I've done something to make this world less grubby and more pleasant for someone else. It will give me hope. And I don't have to make small talk while I work, or be nice to people when I feel like biting their head off. I can work on my own, have space and time to think away from my mother and the ten thousand issues that live in her house, and when I scrub those toilets I will channel all the tension I've built up in longing to scrub away the dreadful mistakes of my past and wipe them clean instead."

Martine clicked her pen twice on the desk. "Only Jesus can do that, Ruth. You can scrub forever and you still won't undo what's done."

I shrugged. This was the type of place where people talked about Jesus. If you shrugged, they sometimes stopped.

"Some of that answer was doggy doo-doo. I don't like doggy doo-doo. I was expecting you to tell me you needed the money. But I think you need to be here more than you need money, Ruth. I think you'd better come and clean here. You are a lovely woman, but you need some peace."

That was that. I now had two jobs. Both low paid and totally unrelated to my skills, passions and personality. But they would do just fine until I managed to dust off my skills, rekindle my passions and work out whether I had a personality lurking somewhere under my new haircut or not.

I came home to find a plate of cookies cut into different shapes on the kitchen table: dark chocolate chip cookies in the shape of a dress; oat and raisin cookies in the shape of a bottle, with the word BLEACH written on in orange icing; and some plain circle biscuits with one blue and one green chocolate sweet on each cookie. I ate one of each type, with a cup of tea, shaking my head in wonder at my mother's unfounded confidence in my ability to come home from two job interviews victorious. There was a note with the cookies:

> *Taken Evelyn Scratt for a mammogram.*
> *Congratulations, my gorgeous girl! M xxx*

I was eating my third cookie, with one green and one blue sweet on it, when the doorbell rang.

A woman with greasy grey hair stood at the door, clutching a bottle of whisky.

"Hello?"

"Oh!" She was surprised – even disconcerted – to see me. "Where's Gil?"

"He's not here."

"Well, who are you?" She narrowed her eyes, which were small and watery.

"I'm his daughter. Who are you?"

"You are not!" The woman, who wore a pink anorak that strained against enormous breasts on top of saggy leggings, straightened up to her full height, which wasn't much. "I know Lydia and Esther and you are *nothing like them!*" She hissed these words out slowly, clearly implying that this was not a compliment. "And Miriam is in Australia!"

I briefly considered slamming the door in her face, but if she decided to keep banging on the door, or called the police to report an imposter in the Henderson house, it might give me indigestion, curdling those delicious cookies.

"I'm Ruth. Gil's youngest daughter."

"Well, he never mentioned you!"

"That doesn't make it any less true." I opened the door wider, revealing the photograph of me at Lydia's wedding on the wall in the hallway. "Now, do you have a message, or another insult for Gil's daughter, or can I close the door?"

The woman underwent a remarkable change in the few seconds it took me to finish speaking. Like steel melting in a hot furnace, she pooled into a plumpy, dimpled, fluffy middle-aged lady. The type of person who would be cast as a grandmother in a film.

"Oh, *Ruth*! I misheard, dear; it does happen at my age. I thought you said… something else. What a dreadful mistake. Yes, of *course* Gil has mentioned you. He talks about you all the time."

*No, he really doesn't.*

"Yes, he's so proud of his little Ruth."

*Nope.*

"Who shall I tell him called?"

"It's Ruby. We're bridge partners. From U3A. I'm trying to persuade him to join the amateur dramatics group I'm setting up. I think your father would make a fine actor. Such a commanding presence. You've either got it or you haven't. And he has so got it." She waggled the bottle of whisky. "This is a naughty bribe. Your dad loves a few wee drams. It really brings him out of himself."

"As I said, he isn't in. Or his *wife*. I'll tell them both you called."

I shut the door before she had a chance to say anything else. A naughty bribe. What on earth was Dad getting himself into?

I spent the next couple of hours waiting for Mum to come home, doodling pictures of smiling anacondas with greasy grey hair shedding their skin to reveal the evil, greedy, true snake hiding underneath. Then I felt guilty, so I screwed them up and drew a picture of a koala bear with one green eye and one blue eye instead.

Mum twirled in a few minutes after Maggie had stomped home and thrown herself in front of the television.

"Hello, hello, my marvellous girls. Isn't it a glorious day?" She swung six bulging carrier bags up onto the kitchen table, as if they were full of feathers, not flour and butter.

"Give me a hand unloading this lot and tell me all about it!"

I gave her a brief rundown of the day, which she found delightful. "You wowed Vanessa Jacobs with the impressiveness of your style and finesse. And Martine! Beneath that unusual visage is a woman of profound astuteness."

"Somebody called round. Looking for Dad. Ruby?"

Mum, filling up the kettle at the sink, went very still for a microsecond before turning around, a look of breezy unconcern on her face. "Really? Well, you can tell him when he gets home if you want. MAGGIE? DO YOU WANT A COOKIE?"

"Do you know her?"

"What, dear?"

"Ruby. Have you met her?"

Mum sniffed. "We bumped into her in the supermarket once buying processed cheese. She goes to the same Italian class as your dad. And maybe theatre. Or architecture. I don't know. I lose track of them all. You'd think he'd be too old to go back to school."

"She said they were bridge partners."

"Well, yes, that too then. Honestly, Ruth. Your father is allowed to have friends. Now pass me the milk and please stop going on about it."

Dad arrived home in time for dinner. Another celebration. Rainbow trout for "hope and a shiny future, full of colour and swimming to success".

I sent Maggie to do homework while I cleared up the kitchen with Dad.

"One of your friends came round today. Ruby."

I snuck a look out of the corner of my eye, and the expression on his face sent my heart juddering. A tiny smile crept over his wide mouth as a glimmer of lost light returned to his eyes.

"Oh yes? I'm helping her out with her photography project. She wanted to take some pictures of ballroom dancers."

*And is this any old ballroom dancers, or would it happen to be one in particular?*

Too overwrought about whatever was going on between Dad and the creepy grandma, I barely noted that he was actually making conversation with me.

"She said it was bridge. Or Italian? And theatre group?"

"Yes, we've ended up in quite a few groups together. She's a lovely lady, Ruby. Very friendly. A good listener. Did she say what she wanted?"

*How about your money, your body, your soul and preferably your hand in marriage, but if not, she'd settle for a wild affair?*

"It wasn't important. Something about amateur dramatics."

"Right. Well. I'd probably best give her a ring."

"Won't you see her tomorrow?"

Dad thought about it. His hands twitched towards the phone.

"It really didn't sound urgent. Mum's in tonight. Why don't you sit in the garden and I'll bring you both out a glass of wine?"

He thought some more. "No, I think I'd best phone."

I tried to earwig through the wall into his study, but couldn't make out the words. Was he deliberately keeping his voice down? How far had this gone? When had secrets and lies come to dwell in this house? How was I going to boot this man-stealer out of my parents' marriage?

# Chapter Eight

$\mathcal{A}$na Luisa came round the following evening to see how my first proper day at Couture had gone.

"Ruth! You look even better than I remembered. I am an excellent hairstylist, if I do say so for myself. She must have taken one look at you and gained a new wrinkle when she saw how beautiful you are. Did she give you all the stinky, back-breaking jobs to make herself feel prettier than you? I bet you aced them all!"

"It was fine, really. I did some cleaning and sorting. But I spent the afternoon going through her filing cabinets. Her paperwork is a shambles, so there's lots of nice, regular admin work to do as well. She sold me two outfits at a discount for me to wear in the shop, so I guess I'm staying. It sort of works."

"Not fun, though, working for a crow with a chip on her shoulder and a point to prove. I'll bet she is all power games and passive aggression. You stay smart and watch your back. Mr David told me about the orange puffa jacket. I think he is worried about you!"

"What?" I choked on my lemonade.

"Yes, I told him about your job, and the stinky failure, and how we transformed you into a butt-booting lady who booted Vanessa Jacobs right up her liposuctioned butt."

"What… what did he say?" David was worried about me? David had *thought* about me? *Talked* about me?

"Oh, nothing much. You know Mr David."

I did. I did know Mr David. And I wanted to crawl into the cupboard under the stairs when I considered he now knew Vanessa Jacobs, the woman he had chosen instead of me, said I stank of failure. Bury myself under the roll of carpet at the back when I realized he knew I had moved back in with my parents, despite all the times I swore I would get away as soon as I could, and was so desperate I allowed a virtual stranger to cut my hair and paint my face in order to grovel to Vanessa Jacobs for a job scrubbing floors in her shop.

I felt very, very grateful he hadn't seen me hiding in a miserable heap under his willow tree.

But now I thought about it… David could spot a harlequin ladybird at eighty paces. He would probably have noticed a grown woman sniffling in his own garden.

"Anyway, he is gone back to his grand job, saving the rainforest and protecting endangered species and rescuing kids from brain-rotting computer addiction with his amazing show. Oh, I will miss him. It is so quiet in the house when he is gone. It will be a long wait until Christmas."

He'd gone? But I wasn't ready to decide if I wanted to see him or not. I hadn't had time to think about it enough. I wasn't sure if I was avoiding him yet. But he'd gone. And he knew I was here. *He* had avoided *me*.

Yes, it would be a long wait until Christmas.

Two weeks later, Maggie's school called again. Busy vacuuming the church hall, I nearly didn't hear the phone. For another three rings I stared at the number ID and wrestled with the urge to pretend I hadn't. Of course, Maggie might not be in trouble again. She could be ill, or hurt, or upset.

Or not.

I grabbed a chocolate brownie from the Oak Hill café and ate it in the school car park. Slowly. This time the head, Mr Hay, was less sympathetic.

"A smashed-up iPhone was found in one of the girls' toilet bowls, and Maggie has been accused of stealing it and putting it there. We're hoping she will tell us who it belongs to."

"Is this true? You broke someone's phone and put it down the toilet?"

"Yes." Maggie sat in the plastic chair beside mine, her posture erect, face blank. I watched the rapid thump of the pulse in her neck.

"Why?"

"She annoyed me. I lost my temper."

Mr Hay leaned forward across his desk. "We have spoken about this several times, Maggie. Why didn't you talk to a teacher if someone was giving you a hard time?"

Maggie shrugged. "I didn't especially want a teacher – or my mother – to know about a picture going round school of me in my bra. For some reason, I also didn't want them to see it."

I sucked in a sharp breath of horror. *What?*

"You should have told us anyway." Mr Hay kept his face impassive.

"You wouldn't have believed me." Maggie scowled at the desk.

"You don't know that."

"The phone belongs to Annabel Wordsworth."

The head sat back. "That is a strong accusation, Maggie. Are you sure?"

Maggie looked at me and rolled her eyes. "Annabel is a prefect, gets straight A stars and is planning on playing netball in the Olympics."

"Now, Maggie. That has nothing to do with it. School policy says that –"

"Oh yes, and she's the assistant head's daughter."

"Are you going to question this girl?" I was seeing red. Sick with rage at the thought of a photograph of Maggie. She shouldn't have broken the phone, but right now I was mother lion fighting for her cub.

"I can assure you the situation will be dealt with appropriately, Ms Henderson. But that's not relevant here. Maggie stole an expensive item of property and wilfully destroyed it. That has serious consequences. If it was one of ninety-nine per cent of the other children in school sat here, I'd be calling the police."

"What's that supposed to mean?" Maggie flung her arms out, incredulous. "Poor, screwed-up Maggie, her dad's dead so we have to be extra nice to her in case she totally loses it or takes an overdose or something? She's all broken and doesn't know what she's doing? Don't give me special treatment, sir. And don't you dare pity me. Call the police and I'll tell them there were photos going around school for three days of girls in the changing rooms."

Mr Hay took a deep breath. "Were you the one who tripped Annabel down the stairs?"

"Maggie!"

"No. Not intentionally. We were wrestling for the phone and she lost her balance."

I resisted the urge to bury my head in my hands. I could see the headline in the *Southwell Bramley* newspaper: *Liverpool thug mugs star pupil, pushing her down stairs and shattering Olympic netball dream.*

"I'm not going to call the police. This time. But if this sort of behaviour continues, I will have to think very carefully about whether or not Southwell Minster is the right school for you, Maggie. In the meantime, I want you and your mum to have a look at this. If you decide to sign up, we can leave it at that. Providing you are prepared to compensate Mrs Wordsworth for the phone."

"How much?" My voice was a croak.

"Five-hundred and forty-nine pounds."

I looked at Maggie. She pulled a face. "You can take it out of my pocket money."

Maggie hadn't had pocket money in over a year. I would take it out of the precious pot called "new home, new life, sanity, independence, hope".

I was not looking forward to showing Maggie the details of Mr Hay's flyer when she came home from school. Tensions were already at boiling point. This would not be easy.

The front door banged open. I straightened my shoulders, perched on the stairs, ready to intercept.

Maggie saw me and threw the look of withering contempt that is every fourteen-year-old girl's speciality. "Can I at least get out of this hideous uniform and have something to eat first?"

"Ten minutes."

Twenty minutes later, we were sat at the kitchen table. Maggie was pretending to give all her attention to spreading a thick layer of chocolate spread on a piece of toast, but her shoulders hunched up in fear. She knew what the cost of replacing the phone meant. She knew how I would feel about the photograph.

"Did you know she'd taken this picture?"

"What?" Maggie screwed up her face, horrified. "You think I was posing for the cameras in the changing rooms?"

"No." I sunk lower into my chair. "Of course not. I just don't know what to think, Maggie. I have a job now. I can't keep dropping everything to come and deal with this stuff. Not when I need to somehow find five hundred and fifty pounds on top of everything else."

"Five hundred and forty-nine pounds."

"Seriously?" I lost it then. All the stress and despair and anger bubbled up and out, and I couldn't control it any more. "Well, that one pound makes all the difference! We'll be all right then, won't we? It's all right that you smash up people's phones, and trip them down stairs, and bang their heads into lockers. Do you think I give a flying fig about the money, Maggie, compared to watching you try your hardest to mess this up even more than it already is? I know you hate me right now, that you blame me for the move and the new school and having to bore you with our lack of money or anything else, but honestly, Maggie, I am doing my best. I did not crash that car. I did not leave us with a mountain of secret debt. I did not choose to be here either! So give us all a break and try and manage *one week* without making our situation a whole lot worse. I've got enough on my plate without dealing with all this."

She tried desperately hard to stop a tear from spilling out onto her face. It made a black streak of cheap eyeliner as it rolled down. I clenched my fists in my lap, took a few steadying breaths, tried to rein myself back in.

"Why didn't you talk to me about what was going on? You know I would have taken it seriously."

"And done what? Made it some massive thing? How do you think that would have gone for me? Don't you think I want to die already after this?"

Maggie's chin began to tremble. Her jaw clamped shut, and I watched my little girl fighting to hold herself together. I leaned forward slightly in my chair, desperate to pull her into my arms and offer her some sort of comfort, but she flinched away.

"I know this is really, really hard for you. I know your life feels rubbish right now. But things will get better, Maggie. Something else will happen, some new gossip, and the photo will be yesterday's news. The other kids will start to get to know you, and most of them will love you, because you are amazing, and kind, and so, so clever, and funny and cool. Now I'm working we can start to think about getting a new place to live, just us again, and make some plans for the future."

"Have you finished?"

I stopped talking.

"I mean, is the lecture over? Can I go?"

"We need to talk about this leaflet from Mr Hay."

"I've got homework to do. Can I look at it later?"

"I suppose so."

She got up and moved to the door into the hall. "You know nothing about my life, how I feel or what I want. And I don't know what made you think I would like to live somewhere *just us*."

The door banged shut behind her. I cleared away her plate and glass, screwed the lid back on the chocolate spread, cleaning the smears off the side of the jar. Putting it back in the cupboard, I then tucked the slices of bread that had spilled out back into Mum's homemade baguette bag and returned it to the pantry. I wiped the crumbs up off the table, and the chair where Maggie had been sitting, and flicked them into the bin, rinsing out the empty juice carton before dumping it into the recycling. I dried my eyes, wiped my nose and got on with preparing dinner.

I drove Maggie to school myself the next morning, determined to get the completed form that went with Mr Hay's leaflet handed in. Maggie was refusing to participate, but I was counting on finding a way to bribe her into changing her mind. Bribery. That wise and mature parenting technique.

Dropping her off discreetly in the furthest corner of the car park, I watched her scurry into the building, head down, shoulders up around her ears. My heart swelled up with so much pain, I couldn't help it: a tiny prayer slipped out before I could think. *Oh God, please do something. My girl needs a friend. One friend and all this becomes so much more bearable.*

And I almost heard God reply: *What about you, Ruth? Don't you need a friend?*

The following Friday was girls' night. This month we were at Emily's house in the centre of town. Ana Luisa walked with me. Emily's was not a dry house, and Ana Luisa carried an expensive-looking bottle of wine. She waved it off when I expressed my reservations about bringing a bag of party crisps and flavoured fizzy water.

"Pah – this is the cheapest wine in Mr Arnold's cellar. And the girls know I didn't pay for it myself. Mr David, he is so kind and generous. When I first came to the Big House he told me, 'Ana Luisa, you are part of this family now. This is your home. And please drink some of that crusty old wine, because my father never will.' Mr Arnold, he is not so up the front. He pretends not to be nice behind that gruff beard, but you cannot live with a man for two years and not know his heart. And look at how he raised his son alone after Mrs Carrington died. A world famous professor *and* a great dad? That is a rare type of man, to manage both things so well without a woman to partner with him."

I remembered the understated kindness he had shown me when I was a child. "One time he brought back an ancient Babylonian abacus. It was four thousand years old. He handed it over with that little frown he does behind his beard and said he knew I would treasure it with the honour it deserved. I'd just finished joint last in the county ballroom championships and he managed to wipe away every one of my sisters' smirks in one sentence. He always made me feel proud of myself. That didn't happen very often when I was growing up."

"This is Mr Arnold. He doesn't say much, but he makes it count."

We walked a little further along the road into the town centre, passing my old primary school and the cottage where a whole community of garden gnomes had taken up residence.

"You should call in sometime, have a coffee with Mr Arnold. I'm sure he would love to see you and hear all your news. Not many people understand what it is like to lose the other half of you and be left looking after a child alone. Mr Arnold knows this."

She was right. But how could I look Professor Carrington in the eye and talk about our grief, when the other half of me that I had lost was not the man who had died, and I suspected the woman who invited me was in love with that other half?

"God, I'm not going to ask you to bless this food. It contains a year's worth of saturated fat and more unnatural chemicals than a science lab, so that would take a miracle. I know you never intended that yellow colour to be eaten for dinner. But it tastes so darn delicious I thank you for it anyway, and I especially thank you for these five mighty women whose hips and thighs I get to share the zillion calories with. They are awesome. Big hearts and strapping souls.

Especially our newest friend, Ruth. What a gracious woman she is, working for Ms Vanessa Jacobs. You know what I mean by that, God. Please bless her with some extra patience."

It was Ellie's turn to say grace. Her tall frame balanced on Emily's bean bag in front of the fire as if she belonged here, which I suspected she pretty much did. The rest of us were either seated on armchairs or lounging on massive cushions in the well-ordered living room, clustered around a long, low coffee table covered in Indian take-away dishes and bottles of wine. Ellie was right: the food looked sinful. I could feel my clackety bones disappearing underneath curves of womanly flesh just inhaling it. Yum.

Everyone wanted to know about my new jobs. It was hard to find much that was nice to say about working at Couture, and this wasn't the type of girls' night where whining was indulged, so I kept it brief. They all knew Martine, and found it particularly hilarious that she had introduced herself as a woman.

"That was Ana Luisa!" Lois snorted fizzy water out of one nostril. "She called her *Mr Martin* for about two months before Martine finally snapped and spelled it out for her."

"Didn't she show you her boobs to prove it?" Rupa was folded in half, clutching a pillow to her middle as she guffawed. "In the middle of church?"

"No, no, no! That is not what happened at all. Nothing like that. You Christians are not supposed to bear false witness!"

"She was trying to set Mr Martin up with Carol Chambers, that piano teacher from the minster." Streams of tears were plopping onto Ellie's sweet-potato bhaji. "She thought Carol was so kind she would overlook Mr Martin's eye shadow."

"Only because she thought he was too old for you!" Emily put down her glass on the corner of the table. "Even I can tell Martine is a woman, and I'm *practically blind*!" She tipped over onto her side on the floor and wailed with laughter.

"If you could still see her properly then you would not be so sure!" Ana Luisa's eyes were bright, her hands on her hips, but she couldn't help smiling. "There is not a woman looking like this in the whole of Brazil. Not under the age of one hundred, anyway. I had never seen anything like it before! Where is her hair? Why is it all over her face and not on top of her head?" She looked over at me and waggled her fingers. "And you have to admit, Ruth, those hands are not a normal size for a woman."

"Did she really show you her breasts to prove it?"

"No! She came into the ladies' toilet and I politely" – the others let out bigger screams of delight – "POLITELY directed her to the gentleman's restroom. She then informed me that she did in fact qualify for the ladies' facilities and, not possessing the required apparatus, would struggle to use the urinals without making a mess."

"Tell us what she said then!" Lois cried.

Ana Luisa straightened her spine and lifted her chin an inch higher. "She said as it was Christmas in two weeks, she didn't think it fair to give her cleaners extra work to do just because my definition of a lady was a clown face and clothes suited to hanging around on street corners."

"She was really mad!" Rupa's beautiful doe eyes were round.

"Yes. But I apologized."

"Did she apologize?" I asked. "I know you offended her, but she shouldn't have said you dress like a prostitute. You always look gorgeous."

"Now I do. At the time she was right on my money."

"And you girls should have apologized too, letting her call Martine Mr Martin for two months and not saying anything. That wasn't fair to either of them."

"We didn't know!" Lois protested, waving a forkful of rice at me. "Her English wasn't as good then; we assumed it was a grammatical error. Or that we'd misheard. At least I did. And I knew nothing about Carol Chambers."

"Well, all is well that ends well. I taught her how to cook empanadas and now she loves me." Ana Luisa winked in my direction. "Everybody loves me in the end. They just can't help it."

The conversation moved on, and I sipped my wine quietly for a few minutes, thinking about Ana Luisa being brought to England by Mr David only two years before. Dressed like a street worker, barely speaking English, with a past that sounded difficult and unpleasant at best, and no doubt dangerous and horrifying. Maybe one day I would be able to ask about that story without it tearing my guts out. I so wanted to hate Ana Luisa, but she was right. I just couldn't help loving her. And I wouldn't begrudge her an ounce of happiness.

Once we had moved on to home-made ice-cream, courtesy of Lucie, Emily's eldest daughter, Lois showed us an identical leaflet to the one Mr Hay had given me.

"This is the latest buzz-technique to get kids to behave. Someone has decided suspending children gives them more opportunities to get into trouble, and less time to actually take in some education and self-worth, and apparently we aren't allowed to wallop kids any more. So this is the alternative. And with a foster son who's used up all his chances, we've got no option but to go along with it." She summed it up for us. "It's a befriending scheme. Kids have to spend four hours a week with an elderly person who could do with some support or company. They only choose adults who have something to offer, so the scheme works both ways."

"I've signed Maggie up, but she's refusing to consider it. Is Seth really going to give it a go?"

Lois grimaced. "It's either that or he doesn't get to finish the year. And now he's finally figured out what he wants to do with his life, he needs to get some decent exam results."

"What's that then?" Emily asked, with interest. Her twenty-year-old son still hadn't a clue.

"He wants to be a lawyer."

"Of course." Ana Luisa nodded her head, scraping the remaining ice-cream off her bowl with her finger. "He wants to put right the wrong that has been done to him. To defend the other little Seths."

"Actually, he wants to work for capitalist conglomerates, drive an Aston Martin, wear suits made out of hundred pound notes and shout a big 'so there' to his birth parents. But we're working on that. No child of mine is going to live their adult life trying to prove something to somebody else. I'm hoping his great-granddad, John, will sign up now he's sorted his life out a bit. Seth could do with spending some time with a family member who isn't a career criminal."

"I love Seth. Thank God he brought him to you and Matt. Have you managed to spend some decent time together yet?" Emily lazily flicked her shoulder length hair out of her eyes, which was difficult as her head was hanging upside down over the back of one of the chair arms.

"Without giving away any details that would make my husband blush – although he is pretty cute when he blushes, for a man called Meat – nothing anywhere close to what I'm dreaming about. But such is the life I have chosen. It would be easier if he wasn't so darn gorgeous."

"God uses handsome men to get women to go to church," Rupa mused. "I only went to Oak Hill because Harry invited me. I didn't want to go, I knew my mother would be furious, but I couldn't resist those teeth."

"That is ridiculous!" Ellie managed to find enough indignant rage to heave herself out of the beanbag. "Normal, intelligent women do not make life-committing decisions of faith based on a man's teeth! Or his eyes! Or his backside! There are, believe it or not, single women who are not actually desperate, hopeful or even bothered about finding a man, because we are far too busy enjoying life. Why do you feeble creatures always have to be defined by men? That's it! I'm so frustrated I have to go to the loo."

Emily stretched out her hand to meet Rupa's in a perfect high five. "Gets her every time."

"Just wind her up and watch her go."

I didn't know if God used handsome men to get women along to church. I had certainly made a life-altering decision under the influence of a charming man. But I reckoned a scowly, brooding guy in a battered black jacket might just get my daughter along to the Sherwood Court assisted living complex.

Ellie returned five minutes later, deliberately stepping on Rupa's foot as she sauntered past.

"Hey, Ellie. You could qualify for the adopt-a-granny scheme. You don't have to be a granny – just old and lonely and in need of help." Emily grinned in Ellie's direction.

"Hey, Emily. Your clothes don't match and they make your thighs look chunky."

"I love you, you mad old bat."

"Love you too, you wardrobe disaster."

Once we settled down with coffee and chilli flavoured chocolates, the spotlight swung back in my direction. Those girls were nosy, and after two girls' nights, they were no longer polite about it.

"Tell us about Fraser."

"Fraser?" I blew on my coffee, stalled for time, wondered if I could keep stalling until I had drunk it all and could go home. "What do you want to know?"

"How did you meet? Was it romantic? You must have been young," Rupa answered.

Okay. I could handle that. I could squish back the automatic prick of grief and anger that still accompanied my memories of the last few years. How we met was manageable.

"We were on the same course at uni. There were hardly any girls and only three of us showed up to this party. Fraser wore a leather jacket and faded Levis. He looked like Leonardo DiCaprio but tougher. When he asked me to dance I nearly fell off my chair. Then he persuaded me to drink four vodkas and I really did fall off. He walked me home, to 'sober me up', and then proceeded to charm the pants off me. Typical student seduction: a cheesy CD, lying on top of my single bed and playing with my hair, pretending to find my teddy cute and asking me about home."

Ana Luisa sighed. "You were young and crazy and in love."

"I was drunk, lonely, ridiculously flattered and feeling homesick because it was my birthday. He told me that when he saw me at the party every other person in the room disappeared. That his mates had been taking the mick because he couldn't stop staring at me in lectures and had to borrow their notes to fill in the bits he missed. I'd never had a boyfriend – how could I resist?"

"Aaah – but then you fell in love. The bad boy turned good!"

"Aaah – but then I fell pregnant. The bad boy turned responsible, at least." I stopped there, uncomfortable. The wine had loosened my tongue. I wouldn't usually be so flippant about Maggie's dad, or the man I had shared fifteen years with.

"He did an amazing thing, sticking with me. He never pressured me not to have the baby, and it was incredible how he put up with my swollen ankles and continual morning sickness when surrounded by non-pregnant eighteen-year-old girls who were constantly after him. He sacrificed as much as me to make it work – nights out, all that money, freedom. And his mother is a whole other story. I think that's why…"

I think that's why, and staggeringly this was the first time I had thought it, Fraser went on to spend so much time chasing fun, and freedom, and money. He was trying to reclaim those years when he should have been up all night painting the town, not winding a fractious baby. Something clicked into place in that moment lying on Emily's stripy cushion. Another level of forgiveness, of sorrow. Neither of us would have traded Maggie for the world. She was our joy, our song. A different adventure to the one we were expecting, but a better one. But maybe neither of us had ever felt safe enough to grieve with one another for what we had lost in becoming parents so unexpectedly and so young. Things were too fragile, too uncertain. Maybe that had become part of the thorny thicket growing between us. I knew Fraser made countless sacrifices for his daughter, for me. Not least of these being the approval of his mother.

We both shared the wounds of parental disappointment, but as I hid my wounds under a hard shell of bluster and indifference, I never realized Fraser was trying to earn that approval back with the heights of his success.

"Well" – Rupa swiped a tear from her cheek – "he sounds incredible. You must miss him so much."

I couldn't reply. Because there it was, that lump of guilt that blocked up my chest and made it hard to breathe. I had missed him. I still did miss him. We shared something of a life for a decade and a half. But not *so much*. No, not *so much*.

Lois was giving Rupa a lift home, so we had to snatch a few fleeting seconds during the evening to catch up on the Surprising Sexy Yurt Adventure plans. Ellie had been researching yurt hire, and it looked as though it could work. A basic tent with carpets and a heater cost around five hundred pounds for the minimum three-night hire. For a thousand, we could get an "all-in" honeymoon package, including sumptuous Asian interior design, a wood-burning stove, lighting, a bed and loads of goodies like chocolates, strawberries and a breakfast kit.

"A thousand pounds?" Rupa shook her head, whispering in case Lois was on her way back from topping up the crisp bowls. We had sent Emily's son, Jackson, to wander into the kitchen and distract her by asking if she thought women with large families should stay at home instead of going out to work. We could hear the rant through the wall, so had a few more moments.

"They do look amazing, but that's two hundred pounds each." She kept her eyes on the picture, but we could see she was worried. "Maybe we could get the basic one, and add the extras ourselves?"

"Or we could pay two pounds fifty each."

Ellie looked at me. "We don't have time for you to be cryptic."

"Why don't we ask the Oak Hill members to contribute? Four hundred people only need to give two pounds fifty each. It would be a great way to help some of them realize Matt and Lois aren't superhuman – that they need a break sometimes. We could ask people to give a little bit, see how much we get and then decide what yurt we can afford."

"Has anyone ever mentioned you're a genius, Ruth?" Ana Luisa stretched her long arms over and gave me a hug. "It would mean so much to them if the whole church was involved."

"But the more people who know… it would be impossible to keep it a secret. This is church – the fastest grapevine known to man," Emily said.

"So we don't tell them; just say we're making a collection to bless Matt and Lois with a surprise. I'll ask Martine how best to manage it practically." Ellie quickly shoved the printouts into her bag as we heard Jackson's feet thumping up the stairs. "I'll check Matt's work calendar for a free weekend at the same time. It'd be best to do it before the weather gets too cold."

Rupa smiled, her eyes glowing in the firelight. "I'm so excited. This is going to be awesome."

I was excited too. I had forgotten what it felt like.

# Chapter Nine

Sunday morning I stayed in bed. Mum had woken me up with a cup of tea at eight-thirty, pretending to be thoughtful but really just trying to get me up. I drank the tea in bed, and ignored her.

By the time my parents came home from church, I had dug out my old *Anne of Green Gables* video from the bookcase and was curled up with a patchwork quilt, hot chocolate and toasted muffin, absentmindedly doodling a group of foxes in a forest clearing, chasing butterflies and having a whale of a time together.

"Oh, Ruth, honestly! Are you not up yet?"

"I'm here, Mum, in the living room. I quite clearly am up."

"Not even dressed! It's nearly one. And such a glorious day. You're wasting it all!"

"I'm enjoying myself."

"Alone in your pyjamas! You should be out there, a woman of your age, making memories, enjoying yourself."

"I said, I am enjoying myself." I turned the volume up louder.

Mum couldn't bear it. "EEK! Get some life into you, girl!" She grabbed hold of the quilt and started shaking it. "Blow out those cobwebs!"

I stood up and yanked the quilt back. "MUM! What is wrong with you? I worked all week, stayed out past midnight on Friday *having fun* and then got up at half-seven and spent Saturday hauling boxes of handbags up and down stairs before working my backside off cleaning up other people's mess. I am tired, and need a day of rest. Not that any of this is your business. It doesn't matter if you agree with my decisions or not. I don't care if you like them, or approve. I don't need your permission to do *whatever I like* on a Sunday morning, or any other morning. I'm not an addict. I don't need an intervention. And if I choose to waste my life, that's not your business!"

"*Not my business?*" Mum turned the colour of Thousand Island dressing. "We are family! Your business is my business. We share a house! We…"

Dad stepped out from behind her gesticulating arms and settled into the armchair in front of the window.

"Leave her alone, Harriet."

"What?"

"Stop taking your frustration out on Ruth."

"I don't know what you are talking about, Gilbert. Would you please explain yourself?" Her voice was ice. I gingerly lowered myself onto the sofa, resisting the urge to pull the quilt over my head. This was going to be a humdinger.

"You heard me. Leave Ruth alone. You nagging her all the time isn't helping her or anyone else. You're going to drive her away again. If she needs a rest, let her rest in peace, for goodness' sake."

*Oh, Dad. You've done it now…*

"Leave her alone?" she hissed. "Leave her alone? You mean, like you have been doing for the past fifteen years?"

Dad sighed.

"Drive her away again?" Mum's voice began to rise in volume. "You think I drove her away? *Me?* I LOST MY DAUGHTER FOR FIFTEEN YEARS BECAUSE OF YOUR STUBBORN…"

There was a bang on the window. Loud enough to make me drop my English muffin onto the cream sofa cushion, butter side down. Through the blinds the shadow of a figure hovered, waving and pointing in the direction of the front door.

Dad went to answer it.

"Hello, sweetheart. How are you then?" It was Ruby. "I tried the bell, but don't think you heard." Her voice dripped with sympathy. "I hope this isn't a bad time."

I doubted that somehow…

"No, no, it's fine. We just got back from church."

"Oh, dear! The less said about that the better! Well, that would put anyone in a bad temper, wouldn't it?"

Dad *laughed*. A polite chuckle, but still. This was Dad. Church was family. It's a universal taboo. You don't laugh when someone slags off your family.

"Anyway, you must be in need of some cheering up, and I happen to have a two for one voucher for the Pot and Penny. Jemima cancelled, her hip's playing up again, and I couldn't bear to eat alone. I thought: I know, I've been looking for a way to thank that wonderful man for helping me out with my project. I must take him out to lunch. And what a perfect opportunity! So, you will come, won't you?"

Mum still stood in the centre of the living room. The White Queen. Aloof, contained, frozen.

"Excuse me for one minute, Ruby, please."

I heard the door close, with Ruby on the inside of it, and Dad poked his head around the living room door.

"You haven't cooked anything for lunch yet, have you?"

Mum moved her head, a fraction of a millimetre, to indicate no.

"Yes!" I was off the sofa. "There's a lamb stew in the slow cooker. And the veg is all waiting in the steamer."

"Oh." Dad looked back, behind him. I could imagine Ruby doing a little finger wave and pouting her lips. "Well, I could always reheat it for tonight. I don't want to disappoint Ruby. I think I'd better go. She'll be eating alone otherwise."

Mum said nothing. She lifted one eyebrow.

"She could eat with us." I was garbling now. "Save the voucher for when her friend's better."

*Yes, Ruth. Great idea. Invite the woman who is after your dad to stay for Sunday lunch. Well done.*

"The voucher runs out today," Ruby called in from the hallway. "That's very kind of you, but I'll just go by myself. I didn't mean to cause any trouble."

"No, no! We can't have that. I'll grab my jacket."

"Dad."

He re-poked his head around the door, sensing something in the tone of my voice. "Don't do this. Not now." I gestured my head towards Mum. Two pink spots of colour bloomed on her lovely cheekbones. The rest of her face was stark white.

"You need to sort this out."

He looked over at his wife. She was staring at the opposite wall, chin up, posture defiant.

Ruby called out something indecipherable. He shook his head.

"See you later, Ruth."

The front door banged. I peeked around the side of the blind and saw Ruby clutching Dad's hand as she pretended to need help getting down the wet patches on the driveway. Was this it? A step too far? The moment everything fell apart?

Mum dropped her head an inch, to the perfect dancer's angle. She swallowed and paused for a second before reaching one hand up to pat her bun.

"Right. I'd better get on with those carrots. I think I can hear Maggie in the kitchen. I need to ask if she'll help me carry some ironing round to Mr Porter later on. He's not been the same since his wife left him."

"Mum."

She hurried out of the room. I listened to the sounds of her over-bright chatter as she talked to Maggie, and wondered how long she could keep whirling and twirling, faster and more frantically, trying to ignore the fact she danced alone.

The following weekend, Maggie had her first session of the befriending scheme with Hannah Beaumont at Sherwood Court. I insisted she try at least one session, having promised to listen if she really hated it – but you never did know, sometimes miracles happened.

Hannah lived in a ground floor flat, sandwiched between two others, with a short stretch of grass in front. A path led up to the utilitarian front door squatting beside a window clothed with heavy net curtains.

The weather had turned colder towards the middle of October. Maggie slouched in last year's coat, a dark green parka with a furry hood. She wore a woollen hat covering the back of her head, and I wondered if this was an attempt to hide her hair. Two nights earlier the dye she had ordered online finally arrived, and now her hair shone metallic grey, symbolizing that her "entire social life consists of hanging out with old people".

Now her bluster had worn itself out, I suspected she felt a little embarrassed. Maggie had her faults, but she did understand respect. I hoped.

We rang the bell and waited for what was probably thirty seconds, but from the twitching and fidgeting beside me, it may have been thirty minutes.

"There's no one here. Let's go." Maggie edged away, ready to scarper.

I grabbed her shoulder. "Try knocking. Maybe the bell's broken."

She knocked with all the force of a rag doll. We waited some more.

"There's nobody here! Or she's, like, asleep or something. I don't want to wake her up. Come on, let's go."

"It might be taking her a bit of time to get to the door. Calm down."

"Please, can we just go?"

I knocked louder. "We'd only have to come back another day. She probably didn't hear your feeble knock."

"Urgh! You are so annoying. There's nobody here!"

"We ought to at least make sure."

I tried the handle and found the door unlocked. Tentatively

pushing it open, I poked my head in and called hello. "Mrs Beaumont?"

Stepping inside, a tendril of apprehension wound around my spine. I could smell mildew, unwashed clothes and stale food mixed in with the faint medicinal odour found in surgeries.

"Mum, what are you doing? You can't go in. Come back. *Mum!*"

I ignored Maggie's frantic whispers, opening the first door leading off from the tiny hallway, having to ram it hard against a pile of old newspapers before I could squeeze through. The room looked like it smelt – old, decrepit, unloved. So did the figure of Hannah Beaumont, slumped on the sofa with her head lolling on her chest, her eyes closed and skin as grey as the October sky.

I felt something clutch my arm and almost screamed, managing to stifle it to a muffled shriek.

That made Maggie, who had followed me in, jump too, grasping me tighter. She looked at me, her eyes wild. "Oh no. Mum. Is she…?"

"I don't know. She might be."

"What do we do? Shouldn't you, like, try and take her pulse? Or, I know, hold a mirror over her mouth and check if it steams up. Then you'll know if she's breathing."

"I suppose so. I don't have a mirror, but we could look around for one. Let's watch her for a bit. See if she moves, or if her chest goes up and down."

"Okay." Maggie giggled with nerves. "Why are we whispering?"

"In case she isn't dead."

"If she isn't dead, shouldn't we make some noise to try and wake her up?"

"I don't know. It'd probably terrify her to wake up and find two strangers standing in her front room."

Maggie tugged on my arm. "Yes. She might die of fright! Which would be ironic."

We watched her for a couple of minutes, the only sound the relentless ticking of the clock on the mantelpiece. Hannah was wrapped up in a thick fur coat, making it difficult to see if she breathed or not.

"How long do we stand here for?"

"I don't know. I have to get to work."

Maggie giggled again, still in a whisper. "You can't tell them you were late because you were in a strange house staring at an old woman trying to figure out if she was still alive."

"Right. Let's make a bit of noise." I coughed, twice, and spoke a little louder. "Mrs Beaumont? Hello? Are you all right? It's Maggie Henderson from the befriending programme."

Nothing.

I leaned forward and gently touched her shoulder, repeating her name.

Not a flicker.

"Oh no, Mum. I really think she might be… had we better call an ambulance? Or the police? We need to do something."

"Right. I'm going to try to take her pulse." Trying to ignore both my own pulse thumping and the reality of the situation, I quickly reached down and took hold of the limp wrist.

*She's fine, just sleeping, right? This is fine, I'm fine, I'll find it in a minute. She's just a very heavy sleeper…*

"Well?" Maggie hissed.

"I can't feel anything."

"I think I might be sick."

"Not on my carpet, you won't!" A voice – very much alive – rasped out from the frail figure who now sat bolt upright in her chair.

Maggie and I shrieked, in symphony, and both stumbled back until we crashed into the fireplace, sending ornaments smashing onto the hearthstone and the poker clattering to the ground.

Hands pressed tightly to our ribcage in a vain attempt to calm our speeding hearts, we gasped desperately for air, and composure, as Hannah Beaumont shifted in her chair and glared at us with watery, yellowed eyes.

It took another half an hour to properly explain the situation, trying to avoid mentioning at any point that we had suspected she'd passed away. I swept up the broken pieces of china and made us all a cup of strong, sweet tea, trying not to notice the grime and grot in the stained kitchen. Hannah Beaumont, it soon became apparent, was about as far from the rosy-cheeked, scone-baking, grandmotherly type that Maggie had hoped for as it was possible to get.

We had been told she was seventy-six. Despite thick make-up and dyed daffodil-yellow hair, she appeared closer to a hundred. Not just because of the wrinkles and curved spine. Her face was pinched as if from permanently wincing. Underneath the fur coat she wore saggy tights and sandals. "So you're Maggie Henderson?"

She nodded. "Yes. From the befriending programme?"

"Well, yes. I know that. I am old, not stupid."

Maggie shifted on the sofa, looking to me with slight panic in her eyes.

"I'm Ruth, Maggie's mum."

"I can see that. You aren't staying, are you? I wasn't told her mother would be staying. I don't have enough biscuits."

"No, I'm on my way to work. I just wanted to check everything was all right."

"Well, now you've checked. I'm not senile, drunk or dead, so you can be on your way."

"Yes. Um. I had better go. I'll see you later, Maggie. Have a lovely time. And sorry again about, well, the…" *Standing there, staring at you, wondering if you were still alive…*

I got up to leave, Maggie throwing a look at me which managed to combine "help!" and "I hate you!" at the same time. I closed the door gently behind me, and hovered on the path for a few moments before turning to walk away. Something – a wish, a prayer – popped into my head and flew out to wherever they go. *Please don't let this be one more thing to make Maggie feel bad about herself. Let this woman be nice to her. Make it all work out. Please.*

When I arrived home from scouring toilet bowls, scraping grease off cookers and scrubbing bannisters, the initial signs didn't fill me with hope. Maggie was waiting for me in the kitchen. She made me a cup of coffee. An ominous sign.

"I'm not going back." She sat up straight in the high-backed chair, hands folded on the table, and smiled.

I drank my coffee. Resisted the urge to draw a picture of a turkey in a fur coat wearing a yellow wig.

"Firstly, her house stank. It made me nauseous. Secondly, her house stank because it's disgusting. It's crammed full of about one million old newspapers and vases and pictures and *things*. They're all covered in, like, an inch of dust that's grey or black or green. Bits of food were on the floor, and piles of dust balls in the corners of the rooms. The kitchen seemed clean from a distance, but when she ordered me to make her another cup of tea, I couldn't find one clean mug in the cupboard. The worktops were sticky. And the sink made me actually gag.

"Thirdly, she is weird and possibly senile. She wore that fur coat the whole time, and kept going on about deportment and seemingly behaviour. She told me all these mad stories about how she was a countess who used to live in a stately home with a butler and went to parties with Princess Margaret, who isn't even a real person.

"Fourthly. She's mean. She flipped out when I didn't make the tea right. How am I supposed to know about warming the pot first, and that you need a strainer thing for tea leaves? I don't even like tea. Which she didn't know because she didn't bother to ask me. I had to drink tea, which I hate, out of a filthy mug, and eat Battenberg cake, which I also detest. On a greasy, foul sofa in a room that smelt like the rats we dissected in biology.

"Then, she went mad at me again because I didn't do the washing up in the right order. Or rinse the glasses and cups before drying them."

I took another sip of coffee. "What else did you do?"

"Nothing! That, and then counting out her ten billion medicines, took the whole time. And she went on and on about how girls today are like boys, and have no manners or taste, and they might be able to work a computer but what's the point if they can't even look after their home? She is sexist against her own sex! And she hates teenagers, especially me."

"Oh dear."

"*Then*, after all that, she asked me when I was coming back, and said how nice it'd been." She flopped back in her chair.

"What did you say?"

"I said I'm supposed to go back on Wednesday after school. But I'm not! She is freaky. I'm Freaked Out. I can't get that smell out of my nose. It's followed me home." Maggie waved her hands around in front of her face as if swatting a fly.

"She must have liked you if she asked when you were coming back."

"She liked having a servant! She called me 'girl', like I was her slave."

"She probably couldn't remember your name. And if the place isn't clean it's because she can't see the dirt. Or can't get down to clean it. Does she have any help? A carer or something?" I got up and placed my empty mug in the dishwasher, turning round to lean on the counter top.

"She said the district nurse was coming on Thursday. About five times." Maggie rolled her eyes.

"Sometimes when people spend a lot of time by themselves they forget how to talk to people. She sounds very lonely."

"Very selfish and stuck-up. And delusional."

"Maybe. But also lonely and afraid, and I bet she hates the fact she's out of control and can't take care of herself. It must be pretty humiliating having a fourteen-year-old girl come round as a punishment, to wash up because you can't manage it properly any more. She might feel very awkward. And if she's ill and in pain, think how irritable that makes you."

Maggie picked at the corner of the coaster. "I don't care. I'm not going back. I'll get some hideous disease."

"I want you to try one more session. It's all right to be assertive, as long as you're respectful. Tell her you don't like tea, and gently remind her your name is Maggie. If we talk to Mr Hay he's going to say you need to stick at it for longer before giving up."

"I knew you'd take her side. I hate this!" Maggie kicked back from the table, sending her chair screeching across the tiles. She slammed the kitchen door behind her. A photograph rattled so hard it fell off the wall, cracking the glass on the hard floor. I picked it up and looked at the picture of the two of us, standing on the beach in Spain, arms around each other in a big squeeze, laughing and waving at the camera. The crack split right across the top of our chests. I pressed out the broken glass and dumped it in the bin, then hung the picture back up.

That evening, we ate my mother's homemade minced beef enchiladas, to celebrate Maggie surviving "two hours with an old boot who doesn't mince her words but should". We had wraps, as a symbol of how we should embrace our lives, and sour cream, to remind us that some people are sour, but there's always guacamole instead. And salsa! Of course. Which needed no explanation, as the magnificence of salsa had been drummed into me before I could walk.

Maggie had a question. "How old are you, Nanny?"

"I am sixty-nine, darling. Too old to give a monkey's tail what anybody else thinks of me or what I get up to. Old enough to have eight splendid grandchildren, young enough that they still want to ask me questions and eat my enchiladas and whip me at computer games. Too young to give up, too old to give in! I plan on reaching one hundred and eight." She stood up and picked up a serving dish to take back into the kitchen.

As Maggie moved to help clear up I could see her thinking about Hannah Beaumont, seven years older than her nanny yet in a retirement complex, with a walker and a smelly house and no one to talk to for days on end, nothing to do, nothing to live for.

"Life is what you make of it, Maggie. But some people get dealt a much harder blow than others. Don't judge too harshly on first appearances."

She was still not speaking to me. "You officially rock, Nanny."

Mum grabbed another plate and jitterbugged out of the room, calling back, "Stick with me, kid, and I'll show you how it's done."

# Chapter Ten

I picked up Maggie from school that Wednesday and drove her round to Sherwood Court. She kept up her angry protests the whole way there. I ignored her, choosing instead to concentrate on not crashing my parents' car. As we pulled up in front of Hannah's flat, Maggie stopped talking. She flipped down the passenger's sunshield and quickly fussed at her hair in the mirror.

I smiled. "Trying to impress Mrs Beaumont?"

"Shut up, Mum."

Maggie couldn't care less about impressing Hannah Beaumont. She was thinking about the young man in black jeans and a white T-shirt, pushing a lawnmower up and down the grass next door to Hannah's flat. His black jacket was hanging off a rake propped up against a tree. Maggie opened the car door and climbed out. Seth glanced up and flicked the floppy black fringe out of his eyes with a jerk of his head. His muscles tightened almost imperceptibly as he gripped the lawnmower handle and brought it to a stop. One corner of his mouth curled up in a hint of a smile.

"You here to see her?" He gestured with his chin towards Hannah's house.

Maggie nodded. "Yeah."

He raised one eyebrow and shook his head. "Good luck with that."

I didn't hear Maggie's reply, as the mower powered up again, but my stomach broke out into swallowtail butterflies. That boy scared me. I didn't know if I was more scared of him rejecting my precious daughter, or deciding he wanted her.

Maggie chose to carry on with the programme after all.

Life settled into something of a routine for us over the next couple of weeks. I worked most days, either at the shop or Oak Hill Centre, and spent any spare time reading or watching television, going for the odd walk if I could find the energy. I searched the job sites, counted my pennies, worried about the growing interest on my debts, gradually began to chip away at the scary numbers.

Maggie went to school, and Hannah's, and in between she ate and slept and played on her phone. Her head of year called a couple of times to discuss how she was getting on, which was not great. She had detentions for various offences, including, among other things, lateness, rudeness, disrupting lessons, throwing stuff, breaking stuff, forgetting stuff and tipping her chicken curry over the head of a boy who called her skanky. But she was going to school and getting some decent grades, and beginning to make friends with a few girls who seemed okay, so I had something to hold on to.

She also spent more and more time in Dad's study. He had offered her the use of his computer, which he rarely needed any more, and she couldn't seem to live more than a few hours without. It was a man cave, Dad's study. Shadowy, crammed full of dark, old furniture, a brown swivel chair made of cracked leather and rows and rows of books about manly things like battles, the history of cricket and boat building. On the wall hung a photograph of Dad as a young man, with wild dark hair and a grin that split his face in two, having just been crowned the cross-country county champion. Along the back of his desk, and crammed in between the books, were his souvenirs – a piece of shrapnel from the First World War, an old rugby ball, a box of nails and screws, dance trophies, sports medals, a compass, a decanter of whisky and an old metronome.

But what surprised me more as the days went on, was that instead of scurrying off when Dad arrived home, Maggie lingered in the study with him. They did bits of homework together or discussed the news. Dad lent Maggie some of his less boring books, and she showed him how to load pictures onto the computer and Skype Miriam. In the end, Dad brought a chair through from the kitchen and would sit and sort paperwork and read the newspaper while Maggie flicked through her social networking sites or read blogs. I realized she had been deprived of adult male company, save for a few teachers, for eighteen months. And, if I was honest, even prior to that the man in her life had been frequently absent, often distracted, and prone to replacing quality time with expensive gifts and occasional grand gestures.

When was the last time Maggie had enjoyed the quiet company of a male relative? I couldn't remember. This was an unexpected bonus of moving back home – a hole in Maggie's life I hadn't known existed now being filled. I wanted her to make positive choices when it came to welcoming men into her life. To recognize a real man, a good man, a man worth committing to and sacrificing for and sharing your heart with. And, underneath the hurt and rejection, I knew that despite making a gigantic mistake regarding his youngest daughter, my dad was a man worth spending some time with. I was pleased. Relieved. Jealous. Agonized. Baffled. Hopeful.

November began with a snap of cold weather, causing my breath to puff in clouds of steam as I tramped along the crispy paths to work and back. The bushes were draped with frozen spider webs that hung like the finest Nottingham lace. The leaves of the willow tree turned yellow and crisp before tumbling to the ground in a thick carpet across the Big House garden. By the time I walked home in the early evenings, grass verges were covered in children digging through the detritus of autumn, on the hunt for conkers. The air grew lusty with the scent of bonfires and rotting vegetation. I wrapped up in my old gloves, hat and furry boots, walking the long way round town, revelling in the freshness and the bright burst of colours. I had forgotten, living in a city for so long, how invigorating the vibrant reminders of the changing seasons are; how the berries and the starlings, the frosty pavements and bare branches stir a buoyant anticipation I find irresistible.

Change was a-comin'. And I sucked in great lungfuls of cold, clear air and suspected that it might not be all bad. After the past two years, things couldn't get much worse. Could they?

November girls' night had been pushed back a week, as both Emily and Rupa had fallen ill with autumn colds, but Ellie texted to say she'd booked the yurt for the first weekend in December. Two weeks earlier, when Matt had been invited to speak at another church, taking the family with him, Ellie had grasped the microphone in the middle of the morning service at Oak Hill and told the congregation to get their backsides moving and their wallets open. "Our minister and his wife give nearly all they've got to serve the lot of you, listening and preaching and setting up and organizing and trying to show you the grace of God in every which way they can. They've run themselves ragged rescuing six neglected children and loving them back to life, and on top of that they have to listen to you whining and criticizing while your fat bottoms grow even fatter. Not all of you. Most of you are actually pretty amazing. But enough of you. When was the last time you stopped Matt and thanked him for running Oak Hill with integrity and wisdom? Have you sent Lois a card this year to tell her 'Good job, thank you for noticing me, for encouraging me and smiling at me when you're so tired you could weep'? Dropped round some flowers? Took a few of the children out to give them a chance to have a meal together uninterrupted?

"I know lots of you do that. I know you look for ways to support and encourage our leaders. I know you don't want them to get burnt-out looking after you, or get ill, or run away to work in a sweat shop in India where they would probably do less work for better pay and more thanks. I know you want to bless them like they bless us. To help them keep being the best leaders they can be. So – a few of us are organizing a surprise for our minister and his wife. I'm not going to tell you what the surprise is because the sin of gossiping hasn't quite been eradicated in this church yet, and I don't want any of you to feel bad for blowing the secret. But the secret costs a bit of money. Which is a great opportunity for you to think about how much you love Matt and Lois and those six kids, and to give something accordingly. Give whatever you feel like, and are able to. That might be nothing, or a whole lot. But God loves a joyful giver, so make sure you only give what you want to. No pressure. There are baskets coming round now. We will accept IOUs. Thank you."

It took about five minutes for the baskets to be passed along the rows of chairs, Ellie told me. By the time they were all piled up at the front, the crowd finally stopped clapping. Every basket overflowed. Not with coins, but with notes and cheques. We made enough money for the romantic, all-in wedding yurt. And to send Matt, Lois, Seth, Poppy, Connor, Freya, Martha and baby Teagan to Disneyland Paris, with Matt's parents along for the ride to help them out. There were a lot of people in Southwell who had changed their minds about Meat Harris. Me included.

Mum organized a family bonfire party for the first Saturday of November. The subsequent list of jobs reflected her usual extravagance, and as she expected me to complete a large chunk of that list, I arranged to do my cleaning the Friday night before, on what would have been the girls' night before it was postponed.

Martine was in the office when I arrived. She strode out to meet me.

"Ruth. Good to see you. Just the usual today. Oh – and one of the toddlers missed her potty and hit the carpet in the small hall this morning. The team tried to clean it up, but you might want to check if it needs another go. And you can leave the back office. The money advice centre is open tonight, and there's a new client coming in to see me and Gregory. You'll be gone by the time we're finished, so I'll lock up."

"No problem. I can do the office on Monday."

Martine didn't reply.

"Martine? Are you all right?"

She didn't look all right. Her face was the colour of a dirty dishcloth, and she frowned at the wooden floor as if it wasn't where it was supposed to be.

"Martine?" I went over and stared into her blue and green eyes, placing one hand on her shoulder. She jerked her head up.

"What?"

"You don't seem yourself. Are you okay?"

"Yes, yes. Just a bit peaky. I think I ate a dodgy sausage at breakfast. I'll grab a glass of water and a biscuit, and I'll be fine."

"Are you sure?"

"I'm sure! This client has been waiting for nearly a month to see a debt counsellor. I will not allow a rancid chipolata to besiege the meeting. However bad I feel, she will be a whole lot worse. She'd be grateful if a battle in the bowels was her biggest problem. Gregory can take the lead. I'll sit back and try not to embarrass myself."

It was nearly eight. I was mopping the floor in the foyer when there was a shout, and a man I assumed must be Gregory burst out of the back office.

"Martine's collapsed. I've called for an ambulance, but they're coming from Mansfield. Do you know if we've got any blankets anywhere?"

I dropped the mop. "In the kids' club. I'll go."

I ran up the stairs to where the youngest children's group met, and grabbed both the blankets that they sat on during story time.

She lay on the floor in the office. Gregory tried to straighten out her limbs, to make her comfortable, but she flopped like a doll. Her breathing rasped, frighteningly rapid.

"Is she conscious?" I knelt down and tucked the blanket around her torso and legs. I had no idea what to do.

"She seems to be in and out. I've tried to take her pulse but can't find one. Do you know any first aid?"

I shook my head. "We should probably put her in the recovery position. On her side, at least. I don't know. I don't know anything. How long until the paramedics get here?"

Gregory glanced at his watch. "Seventeen minutes." His hand shook, and sweat glistened on his forehead. He looked barely out of his teens and totally out of his depth.

"Sit down, Gregory. Have a drink of water. I don't want you fainting too." I glanced over at the other person in the room, a middle-aged woman cowering on a chair in the corner. "Are you all right? I'm Ruth. I clean here. Do you want a glass of water?"

She shook her head. "No. I… I'll just stay out of the way."

"Gregory, why don't you take your client – I'm sorry, I don't know your name – into the foyer, and get yourselves something from the machine? I can stay with Martine."

Gregory led the woman, Dorothy, out of the room, and the door swung shut. The only sounds were Martine's hoarse, uneven gasps and the pounding of my blood bashing through my arteries. For the first five endless minutes, I wished Martine would wake up and tell me to stop making a fuss and get back to my mopping.

When her eyes did begin to flutter open, and I felt the faintest squeeze where her hand lay in mine, I wished she would go back to sleep. She tossed her head fretfully, eyes open but unseeing, unearthly groans rumbling from her throat, legs twitching underneath the blanket. I stroked her hair and muttered half-hearted promises that it was all right, the ambulance would be here soon, she would be all right and not to worry. I concentrated on keeping my own breathing steady, bit back the lump at the back of my mouth and tried to suppress the adrenaline racing through my system.

She mumbled something, causing a dribble of saliva to run down her cheek. I bent my face closer and asked her to say it again.

"Pray."

*Pray? I can't remember how. I don't know what I'm praying to. I don't think he listens to me any more.*

Martine tugged feebly at my hand. I looked at the streak of blue, the streak of green, smudged around each eye, and I prayed.

"God, I don't have the right to ask you for anything. But this isn't about me; it's about Martine. Please help her. Don't let this be anything bad. Oh, please help. And get those paramedics here quick."

Before I had a chance to utter an "amen", the door opened, and a man and woman in green uniforms stepped in. Within moments, they had equipment set up and were working on Martine. I didn't know the answers to most of their questions about her details or what had happened, so I switched places with Gregory and joined Dorothy on one of the sofas. She sat motionless, clutching her handbag and staring at the wall opposite, her tea cold on the table in front of us. I wondered if she was in shock.

"Do you know Martine?"

"I spoke to her on the phone to make the appointment."

"Did you drive here?"

"I don't drive. I only live up past the Burgage. I can walk back."

The Burgage is Southwell's village green. From Oak Hill this was a brisk twenty-five-minute walk through the town centre. In the dark, and the rain, by herself after a horrible shock. It was too far.

"I would give you a lift, but I've walked too. Can I call someone to pick you up?"

She shook her head. "No, you're all right. I'll be fine."

We sat for a few more minutes. Dorothy's hands trembled as she gripped on to her bag. After a while the paramedics wheeled Martine out on a stretcher. She lay wrapped in a blanket, an oxygen mask over her face. I got up to hold the outside door open for them. Gregory held the door on the other side.

"She's going to King's Mill hospital. They think it's her heart. I've called Matt. He's heading straight there."

"Is there anyone else we should contact? Any family?"

"She's got a sister living in Nottingham, I think. Matt'll know. Are you all right if I go with her? I don't have any keys or anything."

"You go. I'll lock up." I glanced over to the sofa, where Dorothy still sat staring at the wall. "I can look after Dorothy; it's fine. Go.

And give her my love when she wakes up." I smiled, ignoring the tears at the back of my eyes. "Tell her I prayed. She'll like that."

I made us both a fresh cup of tea, this time from the kitchen, once the ambulance had left. The sound of the kettle, the spoon rattling against the cups as I stirred in dollops of sugar, rang hollow and eerie in the near empty building. I often worked in the building alone, at least for part of my shift, but this evening it felt different. I hurried round closing blinds against the black windows, muffling the drumming of the rain, and shutting doors, blocking out the shadows from vacant rooms. I hastily emptied the mop bucket and tidied my work tools away, disturbing a thick, black spider that scuttled across the dark floor of the cupboard.

I called Mum, hoping for a lift, but Dad had driven to the theatre.

Back in the foyer, I said to Dorothy: "I really don't think you should walk home. Are you sure there's no one you could call?" The wind had picked up, and I feared a storm was breaking.

"I could call my son." Her brow furrowed. "But Carl's very busy. He's a doctor. I don't want to trouble him."

"If he's a doctor, then he'll agree you shouldn't be walking home."

Dorothy looked unsure.

"Shall I phone him? I can explain what happened."

In the end, Dorothy reluctantly muttered Carl's number as I reached for my phone.

"But you mustn't tell him why I'm here! He doesn't know. I don't want him to worry."

"Of course not."

Carl answered on my second try. "Yes?"

I explained what had happened, missing out the reasons for the meeting.

"Blast. I'm up to my eyeballs here. Is there no one else that can take her?"

"She could get a taxi, I suppose, but she's very shaken up. I don't really want to send her home alone at this time of night."

The doctor sighed. "I'll finish up here, then try and get over. But I'm on call, so if something urgent comes up, it might be a while. Maybe an hour."

"Sorry, if I had a car myself…"

"No, it's fine."

Ending the call, I said to Dorothy: "He'll be here when he can. I know it's none of my business, but don't you think you ought to tell Carl you're struggling? If he's a doctor, he must be able to help you out."

"No. He's had enough problems lately. And this is my mess. I got myself into it. I have to get myself out."

"Debt is a big, scary thing to deal with alone."

Dorothy wiped her hands over her eyes, and bent her head. There were two inches of grey roots topping the cheap red hair. "That's why I called the centre. One of the girls I used to work with came here. She said they were dead nice."

"But keeping it a secret from your family?"

"I don't want him to be disappointed in me." She began to cry. "I can't bear the shame of it."

I shuffled over on the sofa to put my arm around her, taking the cup of tea gently out of her hand and putting it on the table. We cried together, two women carrying the heavy burden of debt and disgrace, weak and tired from shouldering it alone. I told her my story, more than I had been willing to share with anyone, about the anguish of choosing between three meals a day or paying for my daughter's phone so she could maintain something of a normal life in the wake of her grief. I spoke of how the fear and despair had writhed in my guts like an angry emperor scorpion.

She explained about losing her temporary job at the leisure centre, only three days after paying for new windows because the old ones were rotten and splintered. Then her brother had died, and there was no one else to pay for the funeral or the headstone. So she took out a loan, and then another loan to cover the first one when she couldn't find a job. She became ill then, with depression, and couldn't face leaving the house for days at a time. The letters kept coming, and the phone calls. They took her benefits straight out of her bank account, leaving nothing with which to pay the gas bill. And now her cupboards were empty except for a few tins and a packet of soup.

"You have to tell your son. You have to let him help you."

"I can't, Ruth. I just can't."

I listened to the broken woman beside me. I felt her ribs through the flimsy cardigan she wore, saw the lines etched into her face, the desolation in her eyes, and I couldn't do nothing.

"Then you must let me."

I was no debt counsellor. Had no certificate, like the ten hung proudly on the back office wall, and no training. But I had experience, and a horribly first-hand knowledge of dealing with debt, and creditors, and the slimy snakes who slither about snapping at your heels for money you haven't got, have no way of getting, and they have no moral right to demand off you in the first place. And I had a heart, which could not walk away from this woman.

We moved into the office, much warmer than the foyer now the heating had clicked off for the night. I topped up our tea – the remedy for any and every ill – and got to work.

It was nearly ten by the time Carl arrived. I had worked through a fair wodge of the paperwork – mostly unopened letters – that Dorothy had brought, forming some sort of order into urgent, important and pointless. It was too late to make many calls, but I promised to pass on our progress to Gregory in the morning, and had done my best to offer what she needed most – reassurance, hope and a ten pound note to buy some essentials. I also gave her my phone number in case she wanted to talk about it another time. We were back on the sofa, exhausted but calm, when the door pushed open.

Carl wore a navy blue coat over grey trousers. He had spiky light brown hair and carefully managed stubble. Trendy glasses framed brilliant blue eyes. He was tall, well over six foot, and broad shouldered, but his mouth was full and wide, softening an otherwise imposing presence.

He held out one hand to shake mine. "Carl Barker. So sorry to keep you waiting. I hope Mum hasn't put you out too much."

"Not at all. It's been nice getting to know her. She saved me from a pile of ironing and rubbish on the telly."

He looked me up and down, deliberately, with those bright blue eyes. "Really? A woman like you has nowhere to be on a Friday night? I find that very hard to believe."

"Well…" I blushed. I couldn't help it. His gaze was *piercing*. He probably only wore the glasses to protect women he stared at from swooning. "I was planning on seeing some friends for a girls' night in, but two of them were ill, so…"

"You missed out on your evening with your friends?"

"Well." I shrugged, and rolled my eyes goofily. Was I flirting? I hoped I wasn't flirting.

"And instead you ended up stuck here waiting for me." He frowned. "I feel terrible. Let me make it up to you – and thank you for taking care of Mum. How about next Saturday? I'll repay you with an evening out."

"Urr. I'm not sure. You really don't need to do that."

Carl lowered his head, his face intent. "Please, Ruth. I'm not very good at being in someone's debt. Allow us to buy you dinner. You could bring your husband, or boyfriend? If you have one. Which would be gutting, but understandable."

I glanced at Dorothy, who was picking at a loose thread on her coat. She smiled at me tentatively and gave a tiny shrug.

"Come on, just say yes." He broke out into a grin, and his face transformed in an instant. "You can trust me, I'm a doctor."

Those eyes were making me increasingly flustered. My romantic experience with men to date: a terrible end of school dance that cost me my best friend; Fraser; and a drunken man at a Christmas work do. I wasn't equipped, even when not tired and emotionally spent, to deal with a sexy doctor who wouldn't give up.

"I'll think about it."

"Excellent! You've got my number." He briskly left with Dorothy, and I set the alarm and locked up the building. The rain plopped in fat splodges onto my coat and seeped through my hat. I had to lean into the wind as it tried to buffet me back through the empty streets. As I waited to cross the road in the centre of the town, a lorry rushed past, soaking me with dirty puddle water. I barely noticed. I was thinking about Martine, and Dorothy, and seeing the tiny flicker of relief in her eyes, and her powerful son, who scared me, and made my insides wobble, and might be taking me out for dinner.

I was thirty-three years old and single. Okay looking, if a little scrawny. I had swishy hair and remained in control of all my faculties. I wasn't a weirdo, or a shrew, or desperate. Yes, I lived with my parents, had a delinquent daughter and a pile of non-money. But that wouldn't be forever. And he had proposed dinner, not marriage. With his mother present. My conclusion to all this stormy late-night thinking? I might just say yes to that invitation from Carl Barker.

I had been bedazzled by those sharp, sapphire eyes. Blinded to the fact that they had looked so long at me and ignored the mother in distress. I should have worn sunglasses. I should have blinked. I should have turned away.

# Chapter Eleven

$\mathcal{F}$ed by Mum's frenzied compulsion to distract herself, the bonfire party had taken on a life of its own, growing out of all proportion. She had extended the invitation well beyond the realms of family, resulting in a blazing row with Dad that involved him carrying out several chairs from the house into the garden in order to demonstrate that half the guests would have to sit on the bonfire. Mum made an emergency run to the Big House.

She arrived back, breathless, half an hour later.

"Right. That's settled. We'll use the front gardens to observe the fireworks, and locate the bonfire at the side of the Big House, in the old fire pit. Tables of drinks on our drive, barbecue on the front pavement, other food warmed and served in the Big House kitchen. Bathroom facilities available to use in both houses, downstairs only, same goes for inner seating areas. Fabulous! What are you waiting for, Ruth? We have half a ton of firewood to shift before five o'clock."

I spent the afternoon following orders, teeth gritted, temper on edge. I was seventeen again, the naughty youngest daughter, requiring, it would seem, constant supervision and bossing about.

Mum, I could just about put up with. Once I saw the effigy she had made for the bonfire, with its grey curly hair, enormous breasts, pink anorak and saggy leggings, I would have gladly carried ten thousand twigs in my teeth in order to make her feel better. But Lydia – my closest sister in age, and furthest away in likeability – had swanned in from her mansion in Surrey straight after lunch, dragging her husband Grayson, twin boys and seven large suitcases of attitude with her.

Lydia was a minor celebrity. She had not necessarily been the most talented of the dancing Henderson sisters, but she had certainly been the most ambitious. Which translated into obsessively hardworking, self-promoting and cut-throat. She had left home at nineteen to pursue fame and fortune in the big city, then spent a decade accepting bit parts in music videos before taking a short cut and marrying a television producer. For three years she danced professionally on a prime time, top ratings ballroom dance show, until becoming pregnant with the twins, who were now four. I had seen my nephews only a couple of times, when Maggie and I visited them for uncomfortable weekends of showing off and passive aggression. Lydia had been in Portugal filming an advert when Fraser died, so this was the first time in nearly two years that I'd seen her.

I didn't hate my sister. I pitied her shallow, self-serving lifestyle, her constant chasing after popularity, and that she valued everyone and everything by such a pathetic set of criteria. She was lost and, I suspected, very lonely. Yes, I did see the irony in me pitying someone else's lost, lonely, pointless life. And this only made her dismissive condescension even more irritating.

I finished wheeling the last barrow load of firewood from our garden over to the Big House, and went back to our kitchen to grab a glass of water. Lydia was draped artfully over the butcher's block, watching Esther wash potatoes at the sink.

She burst out laughing when she saw me. "That's hilarious! I just had a flashback to 1990!"

Grabbing Esther, she gleefully pointed out my filthy jeans and baggy jumper covered in bits of twig and other debris. I knew I had dirt on my face, my hands were covered in scratches and there were the makings of a sparrow's nest caught in my hair.

"I would hug you, Ruth, but this outfit cost more than your car."

"You haven't changed either, Lyd. Except, is that a grey hair? I don't remember seeing that in 1990."

"She doesn't have a car. She's scrounging Mum and Dad's." Esther turned back to the potatoes.

Lydia smiled her fake magazine smile. "Well, underneath the rustic charm your body looks amazing. I know celebrities who would kill for that figure." She leaned forward conspiratorially. "But if you ever want a good man to sort your face, let me know. I'd swear by mine. All the stars use him."

"Ruth is a cleaner, Lyd. She can't afford Botox."

The smile froze in place. "What?"

"I am a part-time cleaner for the Oak Hill Centre. I also work three days a week as a dogsbody in Vanessa Jacobs' shop. You may not have picked this up, but I don't have a partner to support me any more, Lydia. He died. Did anyone mention that? And, before you ask, as I know you are *just* about to, I'm doing pretty good, thanks, all things considered. Life was seriously rough for a while. I dabbled in a minor emotional breakdown due to crippling debts, losing my home and my job, trying to raise my grief-stricken daughter alone, but hey-ho, the unfailing support of my wonderful family got me through it."

I walked out, forgetting the water. This was why I did not see my sisters more than once every two years. When I had regained my self-control and no longer hated the person I was when I was with them, that might change. I hid under the bare branches of the willow tree until I'd calmed down.

The family spent the rest of the afternoon tidying up and setting out chairs in little clusters around the gardens. Other neighbours joined us sweeping the leaves off the pavements and lawns, carrying tables and lining them up along the Big House driveway. My brothers-in-law, Grayson and Max, hung bunting Mum had made with orange, red and yellow flags between the treetops and the side of the houses. Lanterns were dotted around the flowerbeds, and Christmas lights strung over the larger bushes. More barbecues were brought out, and plastic plates and cups and cutlery stacked up beside a growing collection of various drinks bottles and cans.

My three nephews joined the other children on the street jumping in piles of swept-up leaves, picking up huge handfuls and throwing them like confetti, making leaf dens and leaf beds, and having leaf wars. Arianna sat in the kitchen and painstakingly decorated eighty cupcakes with stars and sprinkles to appear like fireworks.

"Are you looking forward to the fireworks, Arianna?" I asked, during a three-minute tea break (yes, I was being timed).

"No. I don't like the bang or the noise or the scary fire bits that go up in the sky and then come down again. I'm going to stay inside and read my book."

"You could watch out of the window."

"No. All the colours make my head wobble. I want to read instead."

"That's a shame. I'm sure if your daddy held your hand you would feel safe enough."

She shook her head, determined. "Being scared is yucky. I don't like it. It's stupid."

"I know what you mean. But some things are good scared – like excited scared, when it makes you jump, or seems dangerous but is actually safe. Like a fairground ride. Or an adventure story."

"No. I don't like them. I just want to stay inside so I don't get hurt."

I finished my tea. I had lived for thirteen years trying not to get hurt again. Staying inside. Hoping to be safe. If I had learned anything in the past eighteen months, it was that you can try and be as careful as you want, but as long as there are other people in your life, you run the risk of a rogue firework whizzing down the chimney and setting the house on fire. I pulled out my phone and scrolled through the numbers to find Carl's. If life was going to bring its share of pain anyway, then I might as well go outside and watch some fireworks.

"Ruth! Stop skiving! Mum's looking for you. She needs someone to tie the Catherine wheels to the fence," Lydia bellowed through the back door.

"And why can't you do it, lovely sister?"

"I've just spent more than your entire wardrobe cost on these nails. My contribution to the party is the sparkle of my personality and kudos of my presence. Get to work."

I put the phone away.

Maggie stomped home just after four. Her hair was flame red, burnt orange and yellow, her expression black. She found me chopping up vegetables for a coleslaw.

"Hi, Maggie. How'd it go today?"

"Fine."

"What did you and Hannah get up to?"

"I made us tea, which took about half an hour; did three days' washing up while she stood there breathing at me. Then I cleaned her windows. Except that, of course, I did them wrong, as my neglectful mother hasn't bothered to teach me the correct procedure for cleaning windows. Apparently opening the front door and handing a man with a ladder seven pounds fifty isn't good enough. I had a lovely time standing in the freezing cold slopping water over myself and using newspaper and *an old pair of Hannah's knickers* to wipe her windows while she rambled on with more fantasy stories from her pretend life as a countess. So, yes, it was a great afternoon."

"Seth wasn't there, then."

"What?" Maggie screwed up her face and squinted her eyes at me, as if I had spoken to her in Martian.

I raised my eyebrows, completely innocent. "Nothing. I meant absolutely nothing by that whatsoever. I have not noticed at all that you come home from Hannah's singing with a secretive smile on your face on occasion. Or that on these occasions you happen to mention Seth, ooh, about twenty-seven times – how he happened to be around with John and maybe, coincidentally, you were walking home together at the same time or he knocked on the door with a random question about the supervisor or needed an extra pair of hands to move some furniture for his great-granddad. I had not noticed that at all. I am sure Seth being there has absolutely no reflection on your mood whatsoever."

She picked up a mug and banged it hard on the countertop. "*What are you talking about?* You are so embarrassing! This is why I never tell you anything. You want me to settle down here and make some friends, and when I do you go on about it like it's some big teenage romance. I can be friends with a guy without drooling over him and having a stupid crush."

"Who said anything about romance or a crush?" I widened my eyes and shrugged my shoulders.

"Shut up, Mum."

"Hey."

"Sorry. I'm in a bad mood, and no, it has nothing to do with Seth."

"What then?" I resumed chopping the cabbage.

"Nanny."

"Nanny?" I couldn't believe my ears. Had the perfect Nanny finally managed to annoy my daughter?

"Yes." She yanked open a cupboard door, and started forcefully searching for the jar of hot chocolate.

"Are you going to tell me what she did?"

"She drove me to Sherwood Court, pretending to be all kind and like she was doing me a favour. Then she insisted on coming to the door with me, and *invited Hannah to the party.*" Maggie pulled out the jar, slamming the cupboard door shut.

"Oh. And you don't want Hannah to come."

"Hello?" She grabbed a spoon before chucking about three too many spoonfuls of chocolate powder into her mug. "And stand behind me pointing out how I hold my sparkler wrong, or the correct way a lady should squirt ketchup on her hotdog? It's bad enough I have to spend four hours a week with her. I shouldn't have to spend my free time with the old bag as well."

"Maggie!" I pointed my finger at her over the top of the knife.

"Well, she is an old bag. She's not even that old. She just acts all weak and frail. I hate her. I hate having to go to her house and I hate the way she talks to me like I'm a piece of chewing gum stuck on her shoe and how she moves so slowly, shuffling that walker, and thinks I'm some sort of poor, deprived simpleton girl who doesn't know anything and can't do anything. She makes my skin itch and Nanny should have asked me before inviting her to the party!"

"Is she coming?"

Maggie turned on the cold water tap to fill up the kettle, so forcefully the water squirted back out and all over her top. "Look! I can't even fill a kettle properly. I'm obviously never going to amount to anything, destined to end up husbandless, flailing around in my own filth somewhere, alone. Oh no, that's not me, that's Hannah Beaumont. How dare she judge me?"

I removed the kettle, ushering her over to the table while I made her drink.

"You didn't answer my question," I prompted.

"I don't know if she's coming. As far as I can tell she never leaves the house. That doesn't make it all right though. Her or Nanny."

"No. It doesn't. I'll talk to Nanny. She's just got into a spin about the party."

I gave her the hot chocolate. Maggie blew on it a couple of times before replying, her eyes on the drink. "About the party, or about a fat, scary seductress chasing her man?"

"How do you know about that?"

"I'm not stupid. Despite what Hannah might think. He's with her today, isn't he?"

I nodded. "A trip to a museum or something. He'll be back later on."

"If he brings her with him, I'm going to burn a hole in the back of her anorak with my sparkler."

"Have you seen the guy Nanny made?"

Maggie looked at me. "No!" The clouds lifted and her face shone – one of those instantaneous mood changes unique to teenagers. "She didn't! I need a photo of this to show Seth."

She sloshed the remains of her drink in the sink, dumped her mug on the side and began to hurry out of the kitchen.

I called after her: "If you wait another hour he can see it for himself."

"What?" She turned back. "Seth's coming tonight?"

"Yes. Matt and Lois are bringing all the kids."

"Argh!" She spun round and barrelled out of the other door, thundering up the stairs. "You could have told me! How am I supposed to get ready in less than an hour?"

I picked up the empty mug and put it in the dishwasher, then wiped up the spray of hot chocolate drops splattered around the sink, relishing this moment of normal life with a grin. "I didn't think you were interested."

# Chapter Twelve

One of the reasons I spent most of the afternoon outside hauling wood, apart from the fact that once upon a time I was an outdoorsy, wood-chopping, fire-building type of gal, was because it kept me well away from the front door of the Big House. I hadn't been inside since the day of the school leavers' dance, afraid the memories it contained would be too potent, too vivid, too raw. That stepping over the threshold into the house would peel away another layer of the armour I had carefully constructed to protect my heart from the reminders of what I had loved, and who I had lost.

However, when Esther ordered me to carry a tray of spare cutlery over there, I wasn't about to explain that I was petrified the Big House would reduce me to a blob of weeping jelly. I saw no free hands to pass the tray on to on my way over. Even Lydia was occupied wiping her boys' runny noses. With great trepidation and a thumping heart, I entered the front door, the knives and forks rattling on the tray in time to my trembling hands.

Standing for a moment in the hallway, I let out the breath I had been holding with a whoosh. This was not the house from my childhood. The home where I'd spent hours at the dining room table whizzing through my homework before helping David with his trigonometry; where I'd lounged on the swirly rug in the drawing room sketching pictures while my best friend added notes underneath. I could find no trace of the place I had escaped to when the busyness, the sparkle and the dance-obsessed conversations all became too much.

For as long as I could remember, the Big House had been a museum. A mausoleum. A place where time had stopped, warmth and laughter had largely disappeared, and life went on in hushed tones and muted colours. When David's mother died, the professor retreated to his study, to the safety of books and history and theories. He hired a housekeeper to see to the basics: providing meals, cleaning, keeping an eye on David. But she was as cold and rigid as the antique dressers lining the rooms and the oil paintings hung upon the walls. I had never minded the Big House being gloomy, full of shadows and furniture that seemed imposing and dour. I felt soothed by the silence, and enchanted by the mystery of closed doors, dusty cupboards and strange ornaments from faraway places. I loved feeling welcome in a house that was gruff and severe. It gave me hope of a big world out there where I would fit in and find my place, and not feel judged or weird or like an alien.

But that house had gone.

I wandered through to the kitchen, taking in the bright, clean paint on the walls – white and duck-egg blue and buttercup yellow. The heavy drapes had been swapped for stripy curtains in red, green and navy, pulled back wide from the window frames, allowing the afternoon sunlight to shine through. The dark, oversized furniture had been largely replaced with light oak pieces, dotted with vases of colourful flowers and modern lamps. The depressing paintings were gone too. Instead, photographs in various frames had been scattered artfully along the walls. David on his travels in jungles or on mountaintops or sailing down rivers. Arnold on his research digs in a hard hat standing in front of a pyramid or underneath a waterfall. Some of them depicted Ana Luisa, and what must have been her family, smiling, waving, hugging, dancing.

I found one small photograph of a young girl, maybe five or six, standing beside a boy of a similar age. They wore matching camouflage outfits with streaks of mud painted across their faces and foreheads. The boy held up an enormous frog in one hand, the girl leaned towards him, all her attention on her companion, eyes bright and cheeks flushed. In an instant, I was back there. The day David Carrington said he would marry me.

Growing up, I had loved David with the pure, uncomplicated love of a girl for her best friend, and he loved me. At six years old we claimed the willow tree for our den. It had been a long, hot summer, and the untamed branches hung low enough to form a circular canopy underneath which we swore our unfailing loyalty.

I had brought a blanket. David had brought chocolate.

"My mum died."

Stretched out on the blanket, I watched the sun glinting through the top leaves of the willow. "I know."

"That means she can't come back ever."

I swallowed the last piece of my chocolate bar. "Do you miss her?"

David nodded. I closed my eyes because I thought he might cry and boys don't like girls to see them cry.

"My dad doesn't know how to cook Friday pasta or do the right voices for *Fantastic Mr Fox*. He didn't put the flannel on my forehead and the shampoo stung my eyes."

I thought about that. About what it would be like if my mum wasn't there, and it was left to Dad to cook dinner and tuck me in at night and find where my wellies were or make it better when I scraped my knee.

"If you like, I could be your mum. Not yet. But when I'm bigger I could make you Friday pasta."

David said nothing. I opened my eyes and looked at him. "Don't you want me to be your mum?"

He squinted at me, the shadows of the long, thin leaves flickering over his freckles. "Mrs Morris said you can't marry your mum, and we're going to get married and live in the house with the wonky dog."

"Are we?"

"Yes."

"Okay. Do you want to go to the pond and look for frogs?"

If anything could stop David missing his mum, it was looking for frogs. "I'll catch, you count?"

Of course. David always caught, I always counted. The perfect team. Isn't that the stuff lifelong friendships are made of?

I found Ana Luisa in the kitchen, dipping apples in toffee. Her hair was wound up on top of her head, a ray of sunshine glinting off the few wispy strands escaping the knot.

"Ruth, how good to see you. You can put the tray over there."

The old pine table, pushed up against the far wall, was covered in a vinyl cloth printed with autumn leaves. On the two back corners were vases filled with dried flowers. In front stood a grand pyramid of burger buns and finger rolls surrounded by three giant bottles of ketchup, mustard and barbecue sauce. A token salad bowl teetered on the edge.

"The house looks amazing, Ana Luisa. I'm guessing you're responsible."

She smiled, eyes focused on the apple dipping. "Mr David helped me paint the cupboards in here, but yes, I did the rest. I don't want to sound rude, but I couldn't breathe in this house before."

"You made a home."

"That was the plan. I have to earn my keep, you know?"

I wanted to ask her. To ask how she ended up here, in the Big House. Had love brought her here? Or did that come later? Where did the lines blur between her work and her relationship with David, and what dwelt on the other side of that line?

At that moment, the professor stepped in through the back door, his grey hair sticking on end like a cockerel's comb, one pair of glasses perched in the centre of it, another poking out of the pocket of his frayed shirt.

"Have we left any receptacles behind for a man on the brink of dehydration to trouble himself with a cup of water, Ana Luisa?"

Ana Luisa grinned, the sun bursting out from behind a cloud, and pointed her head towards me. Arnold furrowed his brow, deliberately taking the glasses from his pocket and putting them on.

He pulled his head back. "Well, I'll be pickled in perchloric acid. Here you are at last." He stepped forward and held out one hand to shake mine. He gripped me tightly, pumping my fist up and down. "Yes. Yes. Very good. Very good to see you, Ruth." Letting go of my hand, he pointed one finger up. "One moment, if you would be so kind."

He disappeared into the hallway. Ana Luisa had a strand of toffee running like a spider's thread from the apple in her hand to her hair. She pressed her free hand to her chest and let out a long, gentle sigh.

"Look at that. You have made him very happy. It is so good that you are here, Ruth."

Arnold came back into the room, carrying what looked to be an ancient protractor. "I thought you would, um, appreciate it."

"It's beautiful." I took the tool. It was made of brass, with careful engraved markings to depict the degrees. "I'm sorry I wasn't here to see it sooner."

He shrugged. "Well. When you're six hundred years old, time is relative. What about that water then, Ana Luisa? Any tumblers, goblets, beakers revealed themselves?"

"Of course, Mr Arnold. Here you are. Would you like an apple?"

Ana Luisa handed over a glass filled with water, ice and lemon. She smiled, ducking her head at the same time, the strand of toffee nowhere to be seen. Her eyes glanced at her boss, dark pools of melted chocolate, and I wondered how any man could stand a chance.

By six o'clock, the party was in full swing and every chair occupied. The night hung loaded with the scent of cooking meat, fried onions and wood smoke. Children flitted in and out of the shadows, waving sparklers; glasses chinked, neighbours laughed and the fire crackled. Mum came up behind me where I stood huddled against the cold, my fingers wrapped around a mug of mulled wine, and hissed into my neck, "It's time! Come and help me move the guy."

"Are you sure this is a good idea? Do you really want to do this?" I muttered out of the side of my mouth.

"I don't know what you are talking about, my brainiac child. Every bonfire party needs a guy. Preferably a wily, treasonous, appallingly attired loser. À la Guy Fawkes." She began dragging me over to where the guy had been propped up against the Big House's shed. "And if it is someone you think actually deserves a good roasting, so much the better. Come on, I'll take the legs, you grab the boobs. I'd ask your dad to help, but he's only just getting back from his busy day. I'm sure he'll be exhausted!"

Sure enough, to my horror, Dad pulled up into our driveway. To make things a million times worse, he wasn't alone. He opened the passenger door and offered his hand to the person inside. Out clambered a grey-haired, pink-anorak-clad woman with a smirk on her face and fluttering eyelashes.

I froze halfway across the Big House lawn. Some of the guests who had been watching us carry the guy now turned and looked at Ruby, then back at the guy again. Nobody uttered a sound. Esther and Lydia sidled over to block some of the view between Dad and where we stood. A few of Mum's oldest friends wandered over to join them.

Mum's eyes blazed hotter than the bonfire. Her jaw was clenched, her body poised for battle. "Is there a problem, Ruth? Shall I ask someone else to help me?"

I shook my head, careful that my pounding heart didn't pop out of my mouth, and moved with Mum across to the fire. Max and Grayson were waiting. They reached to help Mum toss the effigy onto the flames, but she had none of it.

"I'll do the honours, boys, if you don't mind. Although I very much appreciate your support."

Summoning all the passion and strength of a ballroom queen scorned, she heaved the guy onto the blaze. A cheer went up. Mum dusted her hands off, checked her French plait was still intact and marched into the darkness.

It took a full minute before Dad managed to close his mouth. By some miracle, Ruby trotted over to the dessert table, seemingly oblivious to the whole thing.

Boy, did that anorak burn.

Lydia and Esther cornered me a few minutes later by the drinks.

"What on earth is going on?" Lydia said, a tiny piece of spittle flying out from the corner of her mouth. "Who is that woman? Is Dad having an affair?"

"Her name's Ruby. I don't know what's going on. She's clearly after him, but I don't know how far it's gone."

"*Ruth!* You live here! How can you just let some *strumped-up old frump* come and steal Dad from under Mum's nose? What are you playing at?"

I turned to my sister, curled lip ready to fire my usual weapons of sarcasm and caustic comments. But then I saw the look in her eyes. The tear creeping down her cheek. Esther looked equally stunned. My own eyes, so leaky these days, filled up in sympathy.

"I've only met her a few times. I promise you, I made it clear Dad's married. He's with her all the time at these groups he goes to now. And when he speaks to her on the phone…" I let out a stifled sob. "He used to speak to Mum like that. It's the only time I've seen him smile since I came back."

"How could Mum let this happen?"

We shook our heads in mutual bewilderment. Mum: the toughest, craftiest, most loving, joyous, passionate woman any of us knew.

"She's terrified. She doesn't know how to fix this, so she's trying to fix everything else. And she feels so out of control, she's become a control freak. It all just moves her further and further away from him. They barely speak any more."

"Haven't you tried talking to them?"

"Have I tried having a conversation with Mum she doesn't want to have? How do you think that went? And you expect me to sit down and talk to Dad about this? Hello? Do you remember a minor Australian family incident? The one that ended up with me promising never to dance again and Dad disowning me?"

"Oh, come off it, Ruth. That was twenty years ago. You are such a drama queen."

I bit my tongue. We were heading off into old ground that was churned up enough.

"Maybe you could talk to them?" I looked at each of my sisters. Esther was still stricken. "Lydia?"

She snorted. "Well, somebody's got to. Not here, though. I'll check my diary with Marcia when I get back. In the meantime, Ruth, try not to let this family disintegrate any further. If you can't help, the least you can do is not make things any worse."

The fireworks began at eight. Some of the smaller children went inside to watch from the upstairs window of the Big House. Arianna stayed at ours, alone with her book. I spotted my daughter sitting in the crook of a silver birch tree in the garden of the house opposite, the shadowy shape of a young man on one of the branches above her. I saw a few whizzes and bangs, oohed and aahed with the rest of the crowd, but my gaze kept drifting off to that tree. I couldn't see Maggie's left hand, and I suspected it was nicely enclosed in the larger, stronger, hormone-riddled hand of the boy-man with her.

I knew what happened to lonely girls with self-esteem issues in the hands of charming boys. I went to find Lois.

Matt stood watching the show, Freya straddling his shoulders, Martha in one arm and baby Teagan in a pram by his side. He informed me that Lois had taken Poppy into the Big House away from the bangs. I used the front door, following the sound of women's voices towards the snug at the back. Pausing by the door for the briefest of seconds, I heard Ana Luisa. My hand hovered, still an inch away from the door handle.

"I don't know how much longer I can bear this, Lois. He has been so, so kind. Far kinder than I deserved. And in the beginning that was enough. You know how I was when he found me. I was a wreck. And for such a long time I burned with this shame. But his kindness... his patience and his *compassion* to me. I am whole again. I am ready now. I love to clean, and to cook for him, to make sure he has everything he needs and do my best to make him happy. But I think I need more than that now." Her voice broke. "Lois, I love him so much. I don't want to be his housekeeper any more. I want to be more than that. I want to do all this for free, from the love that is in my heart. To stand by his side, not in his kitchen. To go with him on his working travels. I am beside myself. I think my heart is really breaking!"

"You must tell him."

Oh, how I hated my treacherous, wicked feet that wouldn't move away from the door. My prying, jealous ears that listened to this confidence shared with someone far better than me. I darn well deserved to hear what Lois said next.

"Anyone can see he loves you, Ana. He just doesn't know how to show it. Given the circumstances of how you met, it would be very easy to seem like he was taking advantage. He's a proud man, and a good one. How can he tell you how he feels without putting you in an impossible situation if you don't feel the same, which I'm sure he would never imagine you did? At best, you leave, and he loses you. At worst, you stay out of fear, or pity, or obligation, and everybody loses."

"You really think he loves me?" Her voice trembled and cracked with a tiny thread of hope.

"I know he loves you. But you have to remember – it's been a heck of a long time since he had any romance in his life. And his heart was sorely broken then. He's probably as terrified as you are. I'm going to keep giving you the same advice, girl. Put on your best dress, light some candles, block all the escape routes, cook him a fabulous Brazilian dinner, and make it so bleepin' obvious that you want him he can't refuse."

They laughed, as the old, deep, deep wounds that riddled the surface of my heart burst open, and fresh pain and loss and longing gushed out. I gingerly turned around and crept back down the hallway of the beautiful house that Ana Luisa had brought to life, filling it with her warmth and her spirit and her radiant colours. She belonged here. This place was hers, not mine any longer. I had had my chance, and lost it. I was happy for her. Or at least I would be once I could breathe without feeling as though a wrench had been clamped around my vital organs and was squeezing so hard I thought I might die.

My plan was to go home, crawl into the back of my wardrobe and stay there until Ana Luisa and David were married and had at least ten children. But, dang and blast, I knew far too many people in this town, and they were all so chipper and friendly, wanting to chat and resurrect old stories and jokes, tell me how I hadn't changed a bit, but my, hadn't I grown up and what was I doing with myself these days? I was congratulated many times for having made the utterly sensible decision in coming back home, recognizing what everybody else in this town had known all along: that Southwell was just about the best place to live in the solar system. As the huge stock of fireworks gradually wore down, the flurries of sparks whizzing over our heads, I settled on a bench in a corner, found a sleepy nephew to snuggle on my lap, and scanned the crowd through the smoke and the flashing lights for any sign of my love-struck daughter.

It was the mulled wine. Or too much smoke inhalation. Maybe it was my snippy sisters entwined with their rich husbands. Or because a stray rocket landed in the middle of the willow tree and set it on fire, burning half of it to the ground before someone found a hose and saved the rest. Somewhere in all of this, my sorrow fizzled out. And from the ashes arose an angry, flippant, belligerent phoenix. The little boy in my lap roused himself and squiggled away. I may have squeezed him too hard. And at that point, oh dear, my phone rang.

It was Carl.

He hoped I didn't mind him ringing. Had I thought about his dinner offer? He'd managed to get hold of a table at Maggio's, a new Italian restaurant in Newark, for next Saturday. No strings, just a fantastic meal, and a chance for Dorothy and him to say thanks. What did I say?

I said, *Stuff it! I'm going out for dinner with a handsome doctor if I feel like it. I'm young, free and single, and bored half out of my brains with my own pathetic self.* Somebody was offering to do something nice for me, would probably even *be* nice to me; we would talk about normal things like culture and the news and travel, and I might even give him a goodnight kiss if I felt like it and his mother wasn't looking.

I said yes.

# Chapter Thirteen

Next Friday was the rescheduled girls' night. I had hardly slept, and considered cancelling the Sort of Date about every three minutes since the party. But whenever I picked up the phone, I remembered Arianna, sat on the sofa inside while the rockets whizzed and popped, the Catherine wheel careened and the rest of the children squealed and hopped about, their faces pink and ruddy in the glow of the fire. It was one dinner. I wasn't hoping for or expecting a second one, but it was time to get over myself, get over my fear and dip my toe in the river.

It took Emily – that awesome woman who sees the things most people don't – ooh, about twelve seconds to figure it out.

We were in Ellie's farmhouse, a short drive outside town, down a long, bumpy mud road and surrounded by sleek, state-of-the-art stables that only emphasized the neglected house slumped in the middle. Inside, the house was what one might kindly call practical. The rest of the girls, who weren't known for their flattery, called it stark.

"Like a robot's house," Ana Luisa told me as I drove her there.

Emily, Rupa and Lois were seated around a fold-up plastic camping table in what served as the dining room. As soon as I joined them, perching on a metal office chair, Emily said, "What's his name then, Ruth?"

"Pardon?"

"What's his name?"

"Urr... Whose name?"

"Wrong answer." Emily pointed at me, her nose wrinkled. "Spill."

"Please tell her something, otherwise she'll keep going on about it all night. I would like a chance to tell you my news." Rupa pressed her hands together like a prayer. "Besides, her women's intuition is never wrong. I'm curious now."

"I don't know what..."

Emily huffed. "Your voice is croaky from lack of sleep and you're wearing perfume. Something's keeping you awake at night. And suddenly you care about being attractive. So who's it for?"

"All right, Sherlock. If you must know –"

"Oh, we must."

"I'm going out for dinner."

There was a collective sucking in of breath.

"Don't say anything else."

Emily called out to Ellie, who was clattering about in the kitchen trying to find six plates that were for human beings rather than horses. "Get back here, Rodeo Jane. Ruth's got herself a date."

Ellie poked her head through the serving hatch. "Will paper do? It's only pizza and some bread. Is paper better than plastic?" She looked at us. Nobody said anything. "All right! I'm coming."

Thumping into the room, she tossed four mismatched china plates, a saucer, a heavily chipped cereal bowl and two plastic picnic plates on the table. "That's the best I can do. Last time I checked, pizza tastes the same irrespective of the plate it's eaten off. If you object to the cracks, you can finish off the crisps and use a crisp bowl. Either that or I've got a pie dish somewhere in the garage."

Emily sighed. "Are they clean?"

"Yes!"

"Then we can get back to Ruth's new boyfriend. To save us all a bunch of time, here is what we need to know, Ruth: who, what, why, where, when, how. Go."

I surrendered, secretly thrilled to have someone to tell this to apart from my mother. "It's not a date, not really. You know last week when Martine collapsed?"

"Martine!" Rupa squeaked. "I'd forgotten. How is she doing, Lois? I heard she was coming out on Tuesday."

"Yes, she had the test results back. She's going to be fine – nothing that the right medication can't sort out, apparently."

"Yes, yes, time for that later!" Emily barked. "Please continue, Ruth," she said with a smile like syrup.

"Well, this woman was at Oak Hill at the time, and I ended up sitting with her while she waited for a lift home. It was the night we had that big storm and she hadn't got a car." I glanced at Lois, aware that the debt centre was confidential regarding its clients.

"Anyway, her son came to pick her up. He asked me to go to dinner with them to say thanks. I thought about it, and decided why not? So we're going out tomorrow evening. But I haven't told Maggie yet. So please don't say anything."

"Ruth, darling. You know what's uttered on girls' night stays on girls' night," Emily replied. "What about the rest? Where, why, who, what does he look like? More details!"

"His name's Carl. He's a doctor. He's tall, quite trendy looking. Blue eyes. Glasses."

"Ooh – she noticed his eyes. She must like him," Rupa gushed.

"We're going to Maggio's."

"Maggio's?" Lois raised her eyebrows. "He's really trying to impress you. Unless that's where all the cool doctors eat these days. So where does he work? I don't know any Carls at the surgery."

"We didn't get on to that. But he worked Friday night, so it might be at one of the hospitals. His mum will be there. It isn't really a date."

"So what's the why?" Emily asked. "Last question, I promise. Then Rupa can tell us why she's wriggling about like a toddler with a secret."

At that point there was a knock on the door, heralding the arrival of the pizza. I had a good few minutes to think as we divvied up slices, helped ourselves to warm bread with dips and olives and topped up our glasses. It was Emily's turn to say grace.

"God. Thanks for take-away pizza. It may be slightly stodgy and have too much garlic, but it's a whole lot better than what my beloved friend Ellie would cook up. You gave her a lot of wonderful gifts, God, but you know better than anyone that cooking is not one of them. So cheers for the pizza, and the sharing, and the fact that even though I am a crotchety old cabbage, for reasons I cannot fathom, these incredible, magnificent, beautiful women have invited me to share in their food, and their friendship, and their lives. And please help Ruth, who is understandably still nervous of us all, as we can be unnerving at times, if not downright bizarre. Ta."

She paused long enough to wave at me. "Ruth? I don't think you got a chance to answer the question earlier. It would be rude not to let you finish. You were telling us why you said yes to a date with the hunky doctor."

"Honestly? Because he asked me. And I was vaguely attracted to him, which says a lot considering how long it's been. And… and… I haven't been out for dinner with a man in over four years. Unless you count a couple of Fraser's work dos, which I don't. I've never been out with anyone apart from him, either. I thought it might be nice to have done it just once. Why not? What's the worst that can happen? His mum'll be there."

I laughed, awkwardly.

"I am very pleased for you." Ana Luisa, who had been uncharacteristically quiet so far, raised her glass. "You deserve some happiness. And if you want to know what the worst that can happen is, ask Ellie to tell you about her date with Michael Hood."

We all swivelled round to face Ellie. The rest of the girls were grinning.

Ellie sighed, lowering her head onto the tabletop. From there, she stuffed another bite of pizza into her sideways mouth. "It was a roller disco."

There was another half an hour of bad date stories, accompanied by banter and gut-wrenching gales of laughter, before we finally got around to hearing Rupa's news. She began weeping even before she could get the words out, but the glow on her cheeks and the joy shining out of every pore said it all.

"You're pregnant!" we cried, smothering her with hugs and kisses and several toasts about how good old-fashioned sex had got there in the end. Lois cried out, "Tell us everything! Who, what, why, where, when and how!"

That Thursday, Maggie got invited to the cinema. After much poking, needling and downright nagging, I discovered she was going with another girl from school, the girl's boyfriend, and Seth.

"So, what's the situation here? Are you two going out? Is it a date?"

"Mum. I'm fourteen. I don't go on dates." She sliced off a tiny slither of the apple Mum had pressed into her hand, and nibbled it.

"Answer the first question, please."

"No, we aren't going out."

"He's not your boyfriend."

"No!"

"You aren't sort of seeing him."

"Mum! We're friends. What about that don't you get?"

"I don't get that when a couple go to the cinema, and another girl and boy go with them, the girl isn't smart enough to figure out that maybe some setting up is going on."

Maggie's eyes rolled so far I was surprised they came back. She sliced off another piece of apple.

"I'm so sorry, Maggie, that I happen, for some weird reason, to care about you, and your life, and who your friends are. I know it is bizarre that I might be interested in these things, but there you are. I am. So I'm going to ask you about them."

"How come if I'm sarcastic I get told off but you can do it whenever you like?"

"I don't know. That's just how it works. Have you decided what to do if Seth wants to be more than friends? He's had a pretty tough time of it lately. I want you to think carefully about whether a boyfriend would be a good idea right now before you give him the wrong impression." I knew this was as pointless as talking to the apple. But at least, for the record, I had said it.

"Okay then, I promise not to do it with him on the back row. Satisfied? Can I go now?"

"Um, actually. I had something I wanted to tell you. Speaking of dates."

"What?" Maggie went pale. She stared at me with huge round eyes, suddenly a child again. "I'm actually sort of hoping you're going to tell me Pop is going on a date with Booby Ruby rather than what I think you're going to say." She stuck her hands over her ears. "I really, really don't want to know. Can you just not tell me?"

I sucked in a big, deep breath and told her what she did not want to know, emphasizing the Dorothy part, the "saying thanks" part, and trying to disguise this as being no more than a friendly dinner.

Maggie threw her half-eaten apple in the direction of the compost bin, hurled the knife after it, where it clanged onto the work surface, and slammed out of the room. I put the apple in the bin, placed the knife in the dishwasher and wiped the splatter off the countertop. Taking out my phone, I began to dial Carl's number. Mum burst in, brandishing a rolled-up magazine like a scimitar.

"Don't you dare cancel that dinner. It's been over eighteen months! You are allowed to let a man buy you a nice meal if you feel ready for it. It could be twenty years and Maggie would still object. I'll talk to her, remind her she doesn't want a shrivelled-up prune for a mother. Goodness me. Don't you dare cancel that dinner! *Eighteen months* since a man treated you as special and you want to turn one down!"

*Eighteen months? Oh, Mum. It's been far, far longer than that.*

I asked Vanessa if I could have a staff discount to buy a dress. She routinely helped herself to stock, so I didn't think she would be too outraged.

"Really? I didn't think single mothers had that many opportunities to go out on the town. Not dressing up for one of the weird nights you have with those religious women, are you? What are you going to do – sacrifice a goat?"

"No. I'm not seeing my *friends*. I'm going out to dinner. To Maggio's." I used a pair of scissors to carefully slice open a box of accessories before ripping off the parcel tape.

"Ooh, la la! *Maggio's!* Very swanky. I've heard it's a rip off, but each to their own."

"So, can I have a staff discount?"

"You can have ten per cent if you tell me who you're going out with." She peered over my shoulder at the box, picking up a dark scarf wrapped in plastic.

"His name is Carl. He's a doctor. Enough information?"

"Is he fat?" She pretended to be engrossed in examining the scarf.

"No."

"Bald?"

"No."

"Hideously disfigured? Goatee? Freakily short?"

"What are you talking about?"

She sniffed, tossing the scarf back into the box before walking away. "Just wondering."

I waited until the last minute to get changed that evening. Mum dropped Maggie round at Seth's to watch a DVD. I had spoken at length to Lois about the wisdom of our respective children embarking on a relationship. Lois was pragmatic.

"They're both good kids at heart, Ruth. They have issues, sure, but who doesn't? At least throwing stuff and getting into trouble is in plain sight. In my experience, if two teenagers decide they want to spend time together there is little anyone can do to stop them. Matt is pretty open with Seth about relationships. As long as they operate within our boundaries, that's fine. We'll take it one day at a time, and if we can provide them with healthy ways to spend time together, it might help keep things from getting too intense."

Lois and Matt's boundaries were necessarily strict, given the nature of some of the children they had to deal with. Seth and Maggie were allowed to meet, for now, in the house as long as an adult was present somewhere in the building. Bearing in mind the relaxed, spontaneous nature of modern relationships, Seth and Maggie's first evening together was the cringiest, most awkward and embarrassing possible. A DVD with foster siblings and parents hanging around, arranged by his parents. That two teenagers were prepared to put up with these rules said a lot about how much they wanted to get together. I felt petrified about where this was leading. I so missed Fraser and his overprotective dad-ness to help me out here. I barely had time to worry about my own imminent foray into the world of Saturday nights out, so when Carl's black Audi pulled up outside I felt woefully unprepared.

One final quick look in the mirror. Simple navy blue dress zipped up and untucked from knickers – check. Subtle make-up covering black rings under eyes – check. Tights unladdered – check. Spare tights, comb, tissues, phone, money in blue clutch bag borrowed from my mother – check. List of normal, intelligent, not-too-serious questions to ask – check. Racing heart, sweaty hands and expression of desperate panic – check. Massive guilt – definitely check.

Anything else? The doorbell rang. I would have to do.

Carl greeted me with white roses, a kiss on the cheek and no Dorothy. She was in bed with a migraine. Apparently. It would have been a shame to cancel, wouldn't it? We could still have fun, couldn't we? I responded with an awkwardness he seemed to find amusingly endearing. During the thirty-minute drive to the restaurant I realized one thing with absolute certainty: I was not ready. Not ready for dinner, for conversation, for sitting alone in a car with a man I barely knew. The car felt disconcertingly intimate speeding through the darkness, warm and sleek, the faint sound of classical music covering up the hum of the engine. I was used to expensive cars, but ones that were large and loud and littered with old water bottles, forgotten hair clips and Maggie's discarded food wrappers. The skin prickled on the back of my legs. I felt trapped.

*This is a mistake.* I finally admitted it to myself just after the starters arrived. It had been a mistake to go out with this man. One I had spoken to for a grand total of three minutes before I agreed to waste an evening of my time with him.

What the heck were you thinking, Ruth?

The first indication that Dr Carl was not the man for me was that our table was seated for two, not three. Yes, he could have phoned ahead and let them know we would be one person short, but I didn't ask because I suspected something different.

The second indication was this:

When the waiter arrived to take our order, Carl said, "We'll have the crab to begin with." He winked at me. "Trust me, you'll love it. Then we'll have the veal, a dressed salad and a bottle of Barolo for the lady. Oh, and olives and bread for now."

I held back until the waiter had moved away.

"You're right, I do love crab. But I was going to order the aubergine."

He shook his head, the amused smile back. "In a restaurant of this quality, the crab is going to be better."

"Carl, my current circumstances may not be great, but I have dined in restaurants like this before."

He gazed at me with those blue eyes, which without his glasses now appeared slightly less sexy and possibly a tiny bit creepy, and said nothing. He continued to smile.

"And I really don't want more than a glass of wine. I'm not a big drinker." Not tonight, I'm not. I also want someone to check whether I mind eating veal, and for that someone not to refer to me as "the lady".

Carl snapped his fingers. Without taking his eyes off me, he called out to the waiter, who was currently at another table, "Scrap the crab. We'll have the aubergine, and a half-bottle of the wine."

"Excuse me, sir. One moment while I serve this table."

It took less than a minute for the waiter to come over. "I'm sorry, sir. How can I help you?"

"You can help me by listening the first time, so I don't have to keep repeating myself."

"Would it be possible for me to change my starter from the crab to the aubergine? We had a slight misunderstanding earlier. And if it's not too late, we'd like to cancel the wine, please. I'll just have a mineral water, thanks. Sorry about this." I grimaced at the young man, one customer service worker to another.

"No problem, madam. I'll inform the chef and be back with your mineral water in just a moment."

"And while you're at it, we ordered olives and bread."

"My apologies, sir. I will fetch that for you now," the waiter replied, with only the tiniest hint of annoyance. He nodded slightly before walking away.

Carl shook his head. "You just can't get decent service these days. So, Ruth. You said you have a daughter. How old is she?"

I didn't want to tell him about Maggie. Or living with my parents. Or my work, or Liverpool, or anything that involved sharing a part of my life with this man. I brushed off the question and asked him about his job. As we waited for the starters I heard about his incompetent colleagues, his dim-witted patients and the many times that he had saved the day at the hospital where he worked. I still had no clue where that was, or what he actually did.

I returned from the ladies' room to find two crabs on the table. No aubergine.

Carl grinned. "Don't throw a hissy fit. I know you lot can be jumpy about fish if it isn't in batter, but I really wanted you to try it. You'll love it if you take a chance. Go on, I dare you."

"Did you change my order back?"

He winked at me again. I gripped my dress under the table to stop myself from throwing the plate at him.

"And who do you mean by 'you lot'?"

He paused for a moment, then shrugged. "I didn't mean anything. Sorry. I talk drivel when I'm nervous. Beautiful women make me nervous. I apologize."

"Please excuse me." I got up and walked, in as dignified a manner as I could manage in Ana Luisa's heels, back to the ladies'. Lois answered her phone after two rings.

"Ruth? How's it going?"

"Are the kids okay?"

"Fine, fine. The others have gone to bed, so we're giving the lovebirds a few minutes alone. But what about you? Are you managing to keep your hands off Dr Sexy?"

I paced up and down in front of the row of sleek sinks. "Only just. But not in the way you think. I'm debating between slapping him in the face and kicking him in the shin."

"Oh dear. That bad?"

"Worse. His mum didn't come. He said she was ill but I think he's lying. He's turned it into a full-on date." I paused to grimace at my wild-eyed reflection in the mirror before resuming my pacing.

"Is that a bad thing?"

"Yes. Even if I was ready to date, which I discovered after about three seconds that I'm categorically not, it would not be with him. He's awful. Rude and chauvinistic and a total slime-ball." I clenched my hair with my free hand. "What do I do?"

"I don't know, Ruth. I'm not exactly experienced in the dating world either. Tell him you suddenly remembered you had somewhere better to be, like watching The X Factor. Or you don't feel very well. Make an excuse and leave."

"I came in his car."

"WHAT? You really haven't done this before, have you?"

"No. Please help!"

"Can you fit out the bathroom window? Or escape through the kitchen and call a taxi?"

I glanced over at the tiny window, set right into the top of the wall. "He's got my number, Lois. And knows where I live. I don't think he's the type to let that go without a follow-up. I think I might have to brazen it out."

I didn't know that two hours could last so long. I declined dessert, or coffee, but Carl had both, trying to tempt me with tiny morsels off his spoon. I was pretty sure you needed brains to be a doctor. How could this one be so clueless?

The drive back was quiet, at least. Carl pulled up a short distance away from the house. He switched on the interior light of the car, to maximize the impact of his stare.

"I had a wonderful time, Ruth. I'm actually pleased Mum couldn't be there, if you know what I mean. I really enjoyed introducing you to the high life."

I gritted my teeth, scrabbling with the seatbelt to get out.

"Well, thanks for dinner. The food was lovely." How could such an expensive car have such a rubbish seatbelt mechanism? Had Carl modified it to prevent poverty-stricken women from escaping his clutches?

"Especially the crab!" He laughed at our in-joke. "Here, let me get that."

He leaned across, his face coming about two feet closer to me than was necessary to click open the belt. I stiffened, not bothering to restrain my grimace. Without moving away, he murmured, "You don't have to be afraid of me, Ruth." He eased back, then reached one finger up to stroke my cheek. I flinched, groping to find the door handle. Carl chuckled, quietly this time. "So skittish."

*No, Carl. Not skittish. Try repulsed. Insulted. Hacked off. Fuming. Disgusted at myself.*

"I'm not afraid of you."

I found the handle, opened the door and tumbled out. Just in time to see a figure in thermal checked pyjama bottoms and a Liverpool hockey club sweatshirt with the hood pulled down over their face, hurl an egg at Carl's window. Was there some sort of condition that made you throw things? Was it called Angry and Fourteen?

As Carl shot out of the car, the perpetrator launched another egg, diving into the shadows before it landed with a wet, scrunching sound on the side of my head.

Carl scanned the darkness but failed to spot Maggie before she had slipped behind the side gate leading into our back garden. Champion thrower *and* sprinter. Forget the befriending scheme; I should get this girl into an athletics club.

I froze, still in the middle of the road. A blob of raw egg plopped off my hair onto the tarmac. Another gloop slipped down inside the collar of my dress.

Carl turned towards the sound of the banging back gate, but in the darkness seemed disorientated and unsure of where it had come from. "Did you see them? You must have seen where they went. Where did they go? I'm going to kill them!" He then began swearing profusely as egg dripped down his open car door.

"I'll get a cloth and some water." I hurried into the house, leaving Carl dodging up and down the road overturning wheelie bins and kicking bushes out of the way in an attempt to find whoever had egged his precious car.

Mum met me in the hallway with a bucket of warm soapy water. "Take this and clean up the mess. Whatever you do, don't tell him it was Maggie while he's like this. Honestly, Ruth. You have chosen to go on a date with a most bad-tempered man. You'd think a doctor would have learned to control his emotions a little better. Most undignified!"

"Where is she?"

"Locked in the bathroom. Don't be too hard on her."

"After the night I've had, I'm more tempted to give her a kiss than a punishment."

I tottered back down the drive, slopping water onto Ana Luisa's strappy shoes, and started wiping at the mess on the window. Carl quickly gave up his search and strode back over. "I'll do that."

"No, it's fine. It'll only take a couple of minutes."

"I said I'll do it." He reached forward and grabbed the cloth off me, tipping the bucket over so that the contents sprayed across the lower half of my dress. I stood there, wringing my hands, while he meticulously removed every last trace of raw egg from the side of the car, his teeth clenched in fury.

"Can I get you a drink or something to warm you up?"

"No." He stood up and stuck his chest out, lowered his chin like a bull preparing to charge.

"What are you going to do?"

Carl turned his head slowly to look at me. His eyes glittered like a laser gun. "I'm going to knock on every door in this street until I find the weasel who did this. And then I'm going to teach them what happens to overgrown rodents who mess up my car."

My stomach dropped out of the bottom of my dress and splattered onto the ground between my feet. "It's a bit late to be knocking on people's doors."

His face was a stiff mask. He paused for a moment. "If it makes you feel better I'll come back tomorrow. Thanks for a great night, Ruth. I'll call you."

He picked up the empty bucket and smashed it against the nearest lamppost, cursing the weasel as the handle broke off, cracking the plastic sides. He then drop kicked the remains into the garden of one of the houses opposite and flung back his head. "I'm coming for you, weasel! You can run but you can't hide!"

Yanking open his car door, my very first date ever slammed it shut and revved away into the night. Speechless, egged, dripping wet from the waist down, numb from a lot more than the cold, I turned to go and find Maggie.

"Sounds like someone's had a bad night."

I stopped in my tracks. That voice. It was cinnamon and honey. A long, hot shower at the end of an exhausting journey. A light flicking on after fifteen years of shadow. I turned around. Now I had come home.

David stepped out from beneath the shadows of the willow tree. He nodded with his head towards the charred trunk. "Inspecting the damage. I just got back." He looked at me sideways and narrowed his eyes. "It wasn't you, was it?"

I shook my head. My legs were water, my chest so tight I couldn't breathe. My body ice, my face on fire. He took a few steps closer towards me, only six feet away now, and my hands fumbled in the dark for something to clutch hold of, finding nothing but the chill night air. I wanted to run to him. To run away. To tell him everything that had ever happened to me. All the secrets in my heart. To beat him with my fists until my fingers broke.

He looked at me for a long, long time. His face serious, eyes in shadow. So much was different – the stubble on his jaw, the creases around his eyes and lining his forehead beneath the tangled fringe. The softer edges of youth had been replaced with sharp angles and high, strong cheekbones. His shoulders and chest had broadened, the lanky awkwardness gone, strength and surety in its place.

Yet everything was the same. The way he tilted his chin as he assessed me, every muscle in his body still. His hands tucked into the back pockets of worn jeans. Posture straight, feet slightly apart. That indefinable something – call it charisma, or the X-factor – that drew people in, got him noticed by the producers of *Whole Wild World*, and had me smitten before I even knew what love was.

"Hello, Ruth." That smile in his voice. My heart sang. *Be careful, heart!*

I tried to swallow the pineapple shaped lump that had lodged itself in my throat.

"Hi, David."

"Long time."

I nodded. Light years. An age. Millennia.

"How are you?"

*Darn it, David. Don't ask me that. Don't ask me.*

I took a deep breath. Blinked away the ache pressing at the back of my eyeballs.

"I'm wet. And sticky. And so cold I can't feel my legs." I paused. "How are you?"

"Right now, this very second? I'm pretty much perfect."

We stood there, in the dark, the faint rumble of cars from the main road a few hundred yards away the only sound. I could sense the warmth of him; feel the strong, steady beating of his heart. *Me too. Right now, this very second. Me too.*

"Well, you're probably exhausted. I'll let you get in."

"Come and have a drink with me. You can clean the egg up and dry out by the fire."

"I ought to get back. Maggie… my daughter. She… did you see who threw them?"

David grinned. The sun rose, birds sang and a symphony of whales leapt from the ocean and dived through a rainbow. "An excellent shot. Shame the window wasn't open."

"I think things are bad enough as it is."

"Please tell me you aren't in some sort of relationship with that Steroidasaurus."

"No." I shook my head. "It's a long story. I don't plan on seeing him again."

"Good to know."

I said nothing, still in shock that I stood on the pavement talking to David about me and Carl Barker. About anything.

"You'd better get back to her then."

"Yes." I started walking towards the house.

David called after me. "And don't worry. If the dinosaur comes knocking I'll tell him it was a wandering vagrant with an irrational hatred of successful men. Maggie's secret is safe with me."

I looked back over my shoulder. He was still standing there, unmoving. I lifted one hand in acknowledgment and he nodded.

"Goodnight, David." I spoke softly, so he couldn't catch my words, or the longing, the pain and the wonder they carried with them. He didn't need to hear. He knew. *Be careful, heart!*

Maggie was in bed, face turned towards the wall, pretending to be asleep.

"Come on. Let's do this now, otherwise neither of us will get much rest."

No response.

"Maggie."

She knew that tone of voice. Rolling over, Maggie opened her eyes and stared at the ceiling, her bored mask on.

"You're not supposed to come in my room without my permission."

"Would that rule still apply if you were dying of some terrible disease? Or if your wardrobe had toppled over and you were trapped underneath it? What about if the room was on fire?"

"Yes."

"Throwing eggs at cars forfeits that right."

"I'm not sorry."

"Will you be sorry if the police come round? Or do you expect me to lie to them?"

She shrugged.

"That was a really, really stupid thing to do, Maggie. I get that you're mad at me; that it was a shock and you think it's too soon for me to go out with someone. But that is between you and me, not him. You should have talked to me about it."

"And that would have stopped you going out with him?"

"Maybe. Quite possibly. But you have to understand. This was a thank you dinner, not a date, or the start of a relationship. His mother was supposed to be there. I wouldn't have gone, otherwise. And it won't be happening again, believe me."

"So you aren't going to get a boyfriend."

"I'm not looking for a boyfriend. But I'm thirty-three. I've got a long time to be on my own while you're off enjoying the world. I can't promise I won't ever meet someone."

Maggie let the tears roll down the sides of her face. "I know I'm being selfish. I know you haven't forgotten Dad, and you aren't going to meet some loser and go off and start a new family I'm not really part of. I know all that. But I'm scared. Every single thing in my life has changed, and that's not your fault, and not all of it is even bad, but I feel like I'm just starting to get my head together and now this. I can't cope with it. I'm sorry. I can't."

"Oh, Maggie. I'm the one who should be sorry. You're not selfish. I'm an idiot. Come here."

She sat up, and for the first time in a long time, she let me hold my baby girl.

"I'm still trying to figure out how to do this – be a responsible adult, and a mum, without Dad here to tell me when I'm being stupid. I'm sorry. And I promise you, I will not be going out on any more evenings like that one. I won't do anything you aren't comfortable with."

We talked some more, wiped each other's faces, and laughed at what an awful man Carl was. But there was a serious issue to be dealt with. Honestly? I didn't want Maggie to know how concerned I felt about Carl's reaction to the mess on his car. I had no idea what to do if he came around knocking on people's doors in the morning. I'd been brought up to believe you owned up to your mistakes, and tried to put them right where you could. But what if that meant putting a child in a harmful situation? Carl hadn't been specific about how he would teach the weasel a lesson, and I couldn't believe he would hurt Maggie physically, but I had a horrible picture in my head of the way he'd wrecked the bucket. The uncontrolled fury was unnerving. I did not want to subject my fragile daughter to that.

It was another restless night. Trying to convince myself Carl would have calmed down by the morning, probably see the funny side of the whole thing or brush it off as not worth bothering about. Remembering the look on his face. Worrying about what to do.

Thinking about David.

I didn't know which man scared me the most.

One thing was clear. For now, my heart belonged to Maggie.

# Chapter Fourteen

The following morning, I woke to find the house quiet. Discovering Maggie's bed empty at ten o'clock on a Sunday morning would have sent me into a panic had I not seen the note from Mum:

> *Seth is playing the drums at Oak Hill this morning*
> *and has promised to give Maggie a twiddle of his*
> *drumsticks if she comes along. There is a pumpkin*
> *waiting to be peeled, diced and roasted, once you*
> *have caught up on your sleep.*
> *M xxx*

My sneaky mother had removed Maggie from potential trouble this morning. No doubt she would find her somewhere else to be for the rest of the day. Possibly until the egg situation had been resolved. I showered and poured half a cup of coffee onto the ants' nest in my stomach. I was hacking at the pumpkin when the doorbell rang.

I freaked out for a couple of minutes, vegetable knife in hand, hoping that by the time I'd decided whether to answer the door whoever it was would have already gone.

"Aah!" Gasping, I skidded back six feet as a head appeared at the kitchen window. The window at the side of the house, *behind* the locked garden gate.

Backed up against the dishwasher, still brandishing the knife, I looked again.

It was Carl. He smiled and waved, pointing at my oh-so-funny reaction to his creepy face.

Accidentally forgetting to put the knife down, I opened the back door, not quite wide enough for him to enter.

"Hi, Ruth." He whipped one arm out from behind his back, awkwardly because it was holding a fruit basket. A large fruit basket. I could see, at first glance, two pineapples and a melon in among the rest of the items. "An apology."

"Um. There's no need, really." I leaned out to take the basket, but Carl moved it out of reach.

"It's actually incredibly heavy. Who knew fruit could weigh so much? I'll put it straight down on your table."

In the light of day, it seemed ridiculous not to let this lovely looking man wearing smart chinos and a neatly ironed shirt come in to put a gift on the kitchen table. What is it about a doctor that makes it hard to disagree with whatever they say? I stepped back, opening the door wide, and he followed me in.

"Looks like you're busy. It smells fantastic." He paused and looked around, a wistful look in his blue eyes. "It's been ages since I had a proper Sunday dinner. Not worth doing, really, when you're on your own, is it? Especially when I've been on call the night before."

"You could always invite your mum."

"Nah. She's not much of a cook, to be honest."

I didn't bother pointing out what I actually meant.

"Anyway. I really am sorry for losing it last night. I fully admit I'm completely over the top when it comes to the car. Not a great way to end our first evening together." He grimaced. "Maybe an apple can make it up to you?"

He picked out an apple from the side of the basket, and handed it to me. Tied on to the stalk was an envelope. Very hesitantly, I took the apple.

"Go on, open it."

Slowly – hoping my parents would arrive back before finishing – I opened the envelope and took out the contents. Two theatre tickets. To see *Romeo and Juliet* performed in a village hall a few miles away.

Carl waggled his eyebrows at me. "Thursday night. Best seats in the house."

"That's very thoughtful of you. But I can't. I'm sorry."

"Are you busy?" He frowned. "What about if I could get a different day? It's only running for a week, and Friday and Saturday are sold out. I could try the matinee."

"No. It's not that." This was horrible. Enough reason in itself to never go on a date again. Why did nobody warn me about this?

*Right. Be assertive, Ruth. Be clear as well as kind. Leave no room for doubt.*

"It was very nice of you to take me out for dinner, to thank me for looking after your mum, but that's all it was. I'm sorry if I gave you the impression it could become more than that. I'm really not in a position to start dating at the moment. Sorry."

Silence hung in the kitchen.

I tried to hand back the tickets. Carl held up his hands, playful now. "I understand. I came on too strong. I apologize – *again*. But it doesn't have to be an official date. I've got the tickets now. It's supposed to be a great production. We might as well go along as friends. Come on. I'll even let you drive."

"I don't think…"

"When's the last time you went to the theatre, Ruth, with a friend?" Serious, intense starey Carl now. I was getting edgy again.

"No. I'm sorry. My daughter isn't ready for me to go out with a man. Even as friends."

"Then don't tell her. You can't let a kid rule your life, Ruth. You deserve to be happy too. Have some fun."

"That may be true, but I don't hide things from her. And the truth is, I can't be happy if she's not. That's not her fault; it's called being a parent. Thank you for the fruit. I have some things I need to do now."

In the end, I got him to leave by agreeing to keep the tickets. Maybe I could persuade my parents to go together. I chopped at the remains of the pumpkin with hot, flustered cheeks. Sheesh.

Mum waltzed in a minute later.

"Was that him? He does look a lot juicier in the daylight – a lot less like a bull with a bee up his nose. Did you run him off?"

"Eventually. It took some doing. He's over the egg, and gave me these." I nodded at the fruit and the tickets.

"Goodness gracious! Still, that'll be the last of him, hopefully. I liked that bucket!"

I was indulging in a sorely needed Sunday afternoon snooze, face down in my own dribble, dreaming of watermelons, when Mum rapped on my bedroom door. "RUTH!" she mock-whispered. "Another young man is here to see you."

"What?" I rubbed the sleep off my face and tried to heave myself upwards.

Mum opened the door and came in. "A good one this time! David Carrington is on the doorstep. Isn't that superb?"

Yanking my curtains open, she handed me a hairbrush and clapped a few times in glee.

"You never liked me being friends with David." I tugged, half-heartedly, at the bush on top of my head.

"Poppycock! I always loved David. A fine young man. It wasn't his fault his father had to hand him off to those stony housekeepers. All things considered, he's turned out splendidly."

"You banned me from playing with him at least every other month."

She snorted. "It's not good for a girl to only have one friend. Especially when that takes her away from spending time with her family."

"Spending time dancing in her family's shows, you mean."

"I feared he would break your heart. And I was right. But that's all in the past. It would be rude not to say hello. And, incidentally, he's looking pretty darn scrummy. And single."

Single? I wondered what Ana Luisa thought about that.

"Mum, I've promised Maggie I won't get involved with anyone yet. She got really upset about Carl. It would make things a lot easier for both of us if you shelved this topic for a few decades. Please."

"Oh, stop waffling, Ruth. Come on downstairs. You can't leave an award-winning children's television presenter lingering in the hall!"

Seeing him this time, I was prepared, so the punch to my guts was therefore that much less forceful. He grinned. "Hi, Ruth. Are you coming out to play?"

"My mum won't let me play with stinky boys. They mess up my clothes and get my knees all dirty."

He raised his eyebrows at me. "Been out to play already, then?"

Oh, man. My shirt was buttoned up wrong, leaving three inches of bare skin at the top of my jeans on one side. I felt my cheeks flood with colour.

"Well?"

"Well what?"

"Are you coming out? I'm going hunting for conkers in the Spinney."

Go out. With David. Would he notice how my hands trembled when I pulled on my boots? Could he hear the fireworks exploding in my stomach? It would be ten billion times easier to say no. To pull down the shutter and shove him away, back into the soft, dark place deep inside where he couldn't hurt me again. But he was here. And he was real. And it was too late.

"Can you hang on a minute?"

He smiled. "Take as long as you need."

I found Maggie in the study, her bonfire-streaked head bent close to my dad's silver one as they puzzled over a math's problem on the school website.

"Maggie. Arnold's son, who I used to be good friends with, has called round, asking if I want to go for a walk. We used to hang around a lot together and…"

"David?" She glanced up at me, unconcerned.

"Yes. He —"

"Lois told me all about you two. It's cool. I get it. You've made a promise and I trust you."

"Thanks, Maggie. I love you."

"Whatever."

We began our walk in silence. There was too much to say, to explain, to ask. I thrummed with the unsaid words I didn't know how to express. David just strode along, arms swinging, face relaxed, as if merely out on a Sunday afternoon stroll with an old friend.

"Any word from the dinosaur?"

"Words, an overly extravagant fruit basket and two tickets to *Romeo and Juliet* at Averham. But he does seem to have let the egg thing go. I don't think he'll be knocking on your door demanding to search your pantry."

"So he's keen, then?"

"Maybe. I've told him I'm not interested in a relationship right now."

We turned off the main street, heading along a footpath that cut between the houses and up some concrete steps onto the track into the Spinney.

"Any relationship? Or a relationship with him?"

David paused at the edge of the narrow track to let me go first, holding back an overgrown bramble with his gloved hand. I waited until I could talk without seeing his face.

"Maggie was more upset than I'd thought about the date. She's only just beginning to cope with all the upheaval, and I have to put her first. I've promised I won't get involved with anyone until she's ready."

My heart wept; a hot, squeezing ache beneath my ribs.

The path widened as we entered the Spinney, no more than a small copse of trees tucked in among the 1970s housing estates, but large and sheltered enough to feel like its own secret world. David moved back to walk alongside me.

"That's understandable. It's been twenty-seven years and I'm still not sure I'd be ready for Dad to bring home a woman that wasn't Mum."

"But you must have reached a point when you were old enough to have accepted it for his sake."

"Probably. It's never been an issue though, as far as I know. I don't think he remembers what to do any more. If a woman showed any interest he'd probably lock himself in his study until she gave up and found someone else."

"Did you get to see him last night?"

"Yes. I'd called ahead to let him know I had a couple of days free."

"And Ana Luisa? She must have been pleased to see you."

He grinned. My heart wept a little harder.

"Ana Luisa is always pleased to see everybody. If Dad had found someone like that to look after me when I was a kid, my childhood would have been totally different."

"Yes, but without Mrs Macmillan to drive you out of the house every day you would have slobbed around watching TV and playing Super Mario. And without her wilful neglect, you'd never have learned how to survive in the whole wild world."

"Remember the time we left the injured stoat in the laundry room?"

"Only it wasn't quite as injured as we thought; just really, really scared and angry."

"In all my many travels, I have never seen anything as funny as watching Macmillan when that stoat ran up her trousers."

Ice broken, we spent close to an hour reminiscing, laughing, joshing, as we picked through the orange and brown leaves for conkers. The past up to, ooh, 12 July 1998 was safe territory.

David didn't want to play safe.

"What happened, Ruth? You never answered my letters. Or my calls."

I straightened up, tossing another conker into his open rucksack on the ground beside me, unable to meet his gaze.

"I saw you, that night. With Vanessa Jacobs."

"What?" He shook his head like he was dodging a fly. "That was nothing. She turned up bladdered and threw herself at me. I pulled her off like the awkward eighteen-year-old science geek I was and spent over an hour trying to get her to stop crying."

"So the fairy lights, the candles, the blanket and the picnic hamper. The CD playing the sappy love song. That was all a coincidence? You happened to be hanging around under the tree, enjoying a romantic evening for one? Had an extra champagne glass in case one broke?" My voice was beginning to rise. A cork had been unpopped.

"Ruth, what on earth has this got to do with anything, anyway? You were at the dance with that gorilla, Charlie. Which I had to drag out of Lois after you disappeared for the rest of the summer without even telling me. I thought he'd done something to you."

"I only went with him because you didn't ask me!"

"You said about a thousand times that you hated school dances. You'd rather sit in the dark under the willow eating stale cheese sandwiches than dress up and have to pretend you were having a good time in front of all the other kids."

"Well, of course I didn't mean it!"

"So if you were with Charlie, having such a good time, how did you see me and Vanessa?"

"Because I didn't have a good time. I had a rubbish time. Charlie only asked me to make Kate jealous. They ended up snogging on the dance floor, leaving me sat by myself like an idiot in Lydia's old salsa dress. So I came to find you. I just didn't expect to see you with her. Under *our* tree."

David was watching me again, the only movement the rise and fall of his chest. "So you were jealous that someone else was under the tree with me, and decided as a punishment to never speak to me again. I don't get it, Ruth. You were never petty or vindictive."

"No, I wasn't. I was heartbroken. I needed time to get over myself and figure out how to be friends with you without it killing me. I had waited twelve years for you to realize I was more than just a frog counter in holey jeans and wellies. My dad had practically disowned me, and now my best friend had chosen a horrible, shallow tart with fake tan and fake nails to match her personality instead of me. I'd seen the films, read the books. That night was when everything was supposed to turn out all right at the last minute. The happy ever after. You see me in my blue dress, my hair all done up, the hours of make-up, and realize you want to be more than just friends."

Angry I could still feel so worked up about it after all this time, I swiped at the tears on my face. "I didn't know how to say it in a letter. Or on the phone. And by the time I came home from Lydia's, you'd gone. I thought if I waited until the Christmas break, I could pretend it was fine. We could go back to how we were. But by then everything had changed."

David took three quick strides over to where I was standing. He leaned forward, his eyes boring deep into mine. I could feel the contained power in his body and backed away, hitting the trunk of the tree behind me.

"How could you be so stupid?"

"What?" That stopped my tears.

"The lights, the blanket, the champagne, the picnic hamper full of cheese sandwiches, the CD of that song you liked from *Dawson's Creek*? They were all for you, Ruth. I had been waiting for you for three hours underneath the willow tree. They were all for you. It was always you."

He span around and walked away, making it about fifty yards before turning back and marching right up to me again.

"I didn't think anything could hurt as much as not being able to talk to you, to see you any more, make you smile. Then I heard you'd moved in with some bloke you'd known for five minutes, in

Liverpool. That you were pregnant. And I found out I was wrong."

I couldn't speak. His words were a cannonball fired straight through my middle.

David let out a long, shuddering sigh. He ran his hands through his hair, tarnished gold in the deepening dusk. "You should have answered my calls, Ruth."

A long moment passed. I steadied my breathing and wiped my nose.

"You're right. I should have. I'm sorry. But I was eighteen, and messed up, and then I was slightly distracted by the whole teenage mother thing. That and throwing up every day for thirteen weeks straight. It's hard to write a nice letter when everything ends up splattered in vomit."

He picked up the rucksack, zipping it up and throwing it onto one shoulder.

"I'm sorry too. My plan was not to lure you up here and then interrogate you about something that happened when we were kids. Honestly, I just wanted some conkers, and to catch up with an old friend."

"Well, it's probably good to get it out in the open."

"It's nice to know we were equal in our romantic patheticness, at least."

"Were? I think last night proved I'm still as equally pathetic when it comes to the opposite sex."

"Hey, at least you managed a long-term relationship. You're still the only girl I've ever loved."

His voice was light, the ever present humour downplaying the potential of those words. But nevertheless my heart stuttered, threatened to stall altogether.

*Oh, David. If only you knew.*

We ended our walk as we had set out: in silence. I thought about Maggie, and knew that in the end I could regret nothing – neither the years with David lost, nor forgoing any chance to be with him now. I would do it all again, for her, no contest.

But boy, it didn't seem to soften the sting when David left, innocently explaining that Ana Luisa was cooking a surprise for him that evening, as in the morning he would be back on a plane.

# Chapter Fifteen

Vanessa Jacobs was a cornered rat. Fangs bared, claws out, she did not respond well to the invasion of Couture.

It was impressive quite to what extent the addition of four confident, powerful women on a mission could fill the boutique. Vanessa found Ellie's cowboy hat particularly challenging.

"Can I help you?" she snarled.

"No, thanks," Emily barked back. "Not sure you'd quite grasp the look we're aiming for."

"I'm not sure we *stock* the look you're aiming for."

"Stop it," Ana Luisa bellowed. "Ladies, we should be championing each other, not using our words to scratch the other's eyes out." She smiled her full on, brilliant white smile at Vanessa. "But Ruth knows the person we are here to buy for this morning, and what it is for, so if you don't mind, perhaps she could assist us?"

"Suit yourself. Just don't let the cowgirl touch anything." She retreated behind the glass counter and started flicking through a magazine.

"Hi, Ruth." Rupa waved at me. "How was Saturday?"

"Hideous. I'll tell you about it another time. How are you doing, Rupa?"

"Sick as a dog," she beamed. "Exhausted, weepy and my ankles are swollen already."

"Great."

Ellie was standing in the middle of the shop, arms hanging awkwardly by her sides. Her six foot two inch frame, broad shoulders and pained expression gave her the appearance of a giant in a fairy castle. She looked as though she was trying not to breathe too hard.

"Let's get on with it. I've set some things aside in the back room I thought might suit Lois. See what you think."

I had learned something in my few weeks in the world of high-class fashion. Vanessa's business thrived despite her scornful attitude (although some women seemed to find haughtiness reassuring). This was simply down to one thing. She knew fashion, and she knew women. And she was able to put the two together in ways that worked. I had been watching how she matched shapes, colours and styles to the different customers who came in the shop, and, having taken note of Lois's tiny frame, her pale complexion and the weekend of romance we were hoping to dress her up for, I had chosen some outfits I thought the girls would approve of.

After twenty minutes of bickering over whether we chose comfort (Ellie's choice: who can relax in itchy clothes you can't sit down in properly?) or texture (Emily declared that we needed something worth running your hands over), prettiness (Rupa loved a swirly, lacy buttoned dress) versus passion (Ana Luisa insisted that Lois required a slithery zip, not fiddly buttons), Vanessa was near screaming point.

"Here." She stomped out to the back and whipped through a rack of new arrivals waiting to be sorted before bringing out two dresses. "First night. Second night. Get the blue and the red shoes, Ruth."

"I'm not sure she'll be needing shoes," Ellie said.

Vanessa shot a withering look that told us what she thought about a woman who would buy a new dress and not bother to coordinate shoes with it. "Here, Ruth. Ring these up."

She added underwear, a pale blue chemise with matching robe and a cashmere shawl.

"Ruth gets ten per cent off, staff discount." Rupa pointed at the prices appearing on the till.

"They aren't for Ruth."

"Ruth is buying them. As a present! Do you check with all your customers if they're buying something for themselves or as a gift?"

"The rest of my customers don't get a staff discount. Only my paid members of staff. And that's always subject to change. Where does it end? Is she going to start buying the rest of you clothes and knocking ten per cent off? What about her mad mother? Or her gaggle of sisters? I haven't built up the most successful shop in the town by offering freebies to my employee's friends."

Emily moved over to the counter. Leaning down low across it she stuck her face right up close to Vanessa. "How about offering a discount as a gesture of kindness to a woman who spends her life serving other people, saving the lives of broken children and giving selflessly to the hundreds of people in this town who have the privilege of knowing her? Hundreds of people. All with friends and families. Who donated a lot of money to give Matt and Lois this gift. Who, I'm sure, would love to hear about how generous the owner of Couture was in her contribution to the special occasion."

"People don't spend money in my shop because I'm generous," Vanessa growled.

"No, but you might actually find those who do, think you're a tiny bit less of a cow."

"Hah! Do you think I care what the yokey-cokey, backward, inbred people in this nothing town think?"

Emily was steel. She had babysat Vanessa once upon a time. "Yes."

There was a long silence. Rupa, whose hormones were running riot through her bloodstream, let out a tiny squeak. Ellie stuck her hands on her hips, knocking a hat stand draped with Italian scarves with her elbow. Ana Luisa held up one of the more expensive necklaces to her chest, and checked it out in the mirror. My finger hovered over the computerized till button, waiting to see if Vanessa would break.

"Fine. Whatever." She rolled her eyeballs, flicking her hair over one shoulder. "Just make sure it's worth my while."

We paid for Lois's Surprising Sexy Yurt Adventure outfits ourselves, having covered all the other costs from the Oak Hill collection. My share was enough to make my eyes water, with or without staff discount. But I was glad to pay it. Lois deserved every beautiful, hand-sewn stitch.

Ana Luisa was planting tulip bulbs underneath the ruin of the willow tree when I got back from work. I wandered over to join her. Even though I knew David had returned overseas, I couldn't seem to stop my eyes from jumping over to the front of the house anyway.

"Hi, Ruth. Did Vanessa make the rest of your day a misery?"

"No worse than usual. Well, a little bit worse, but I can handle it. How are you?"

"Oh, you know. I'm doing fine, thanks. Nothing to complain about. How can we not feel joy when the sun is shining and the sky is blue?"

Ana Luisa did not sound joyful. Her white smile was tinged with sorrow. I wondered if her sadness was because she hadn't told Mr David how she felt about him before he left. I tried not to linger on the thought that maybe she had, and he didn't return those feelings. I wanted David to be happy; to have someone to love, to come home to. That couldn't be me, not for a long time. Probably not ever. And I refused to stand in his way, everywhere but in the secret recesses of my wild imaginings.

Another letter arrived, forwarded to me from Fraser's office. It informed me about the rising interest on my debt. Unless I paid off the minimum amount in the next thirty days, scary things would happen involving debt recovery agents, courts, even bigger fines and possibly handcuffs (the letter didn't mention that one, but the image was stuck in my frantic mind). If I wrote a cheque, which would surely then bounce anyway, would that be seen as acknowledging the debt as really mine? If I stuffed the letter in the back of my wardrobe, or burnt it in the stove, would the problem disappear up the chimney with a puff of smoke? Would showing the letter to my mother cause my stress levels to rise to the point where I had a stroke? Did I have any ideas that didn't make my insides clench up like a fist?

Yes, I had one. I made an appointment with the now fiercely healthy Martine before my shift started.

"Ruth." She bowed in the doorway to her office and beckoned me in. "Take a seat. What do you want to drink?"

"Whisky? Tequila?"

"Even better: extra thick and creamy hot chocolate. And if you promise to tell the truth and nothing but the truth, I'll throw in a fondant fancy."

She deftly prepared me the drink before taking a seat on the sofa opposite me. "How are you, Ruth? I've been praying for you."

Every single time I saw Martine, which was at least twice a week depending on her schedule and mine, she asked if she could pray for me. Since our moment together on the debt centre office floor, she considered me fair game. I knew my polite refusals were pointless, that she prayed for me anyway, but at least for now she didn't do it within earshot.

"I appreciate your offer, as always. But my mother has prayed for me every single day of my life, Martine. Look where that got me."

Martine looked around. Her blue eye twinkled like the sky in springtime. Her green eye sparkled like a leaf in the summer breeze. "Looks like it worked!"

I told Martine about the credit card Fraser had taken out in my name. She confirmed what I already knew – call it fraud or identity theft, he had broken the law.

Here was my dilemma: Fraser had committed himself to providing for me and our unborn child from the age of nineteen. He worked part-time jobs while studying for his degree, then paid for pretty much every single penny we had spent as a family since. As he crept up the career ladder, he took me on luxury holidays, bought me designer clothes, jewellery and a cool car. He had never once checked up on my spending, or complained, or told me I needed to make more of a contribution to the family bank balance.

Whatever had gone awry in Fraser's financial life over the past few years, however wrong it was for him to keep me in the dark about the reality of our situation, I knew that when it came down to hard cash, I owed Fraser a whole lot more than the twenty-one thousand pounds he had spent using my name. Add to this the role I played in the deterioration of our relationship by holding back that part of my heart I secretly kept for another man, and the pain and the shock it would cause Maggie to know I was pursuing criminal proceedings against her late father, and my decision was made.

"I'm going to pay the debt."

Martine clicked the end of her pen in and out a few times. "This is not your debt. You don't have to pay it, you shouldn't pay it and you can't pay it. How and why are you going to pay it?"

"I'll use some of the money I was saving to buy a house. I can stay with Mum and Dad a bit longer. It's not so bad."

Hah! Grand total saved so far: fifty-three pounds and six pence.

"I could probably find a few more hours' work now I've got a bit of experience. Southwell's full of rich commuters who need a cleaner."

"Ruth. As a cleaner you earn eight pounds fifty an hour. Your debt is twenty-one thousand, eight hundred and ninety-seven pounds. This month. At your current rate of interest, you'll need to work, let me see now…" She started clicking on her calculator. I didn't need a calculator. I had one implanted in my head.

"Eighteen and a half hours."

"Hang on a moment." Click, click. "Just need to divide by the… add in the interest rate…" Click click. "Eighteen and a half hours every single week just to make the minimum payment."

Martine looked at me. Her brained click clicked like the calculator.

"POW! You worked that out in your head. In about zero point five seconds. You are a genius, Ruth Henderson! What are you doing wasting a brain the size of a barn scrubbing my toilets?! It is a sin, and in my opinion should be a crime, to squander and squish the unique and amazing gifts you have been blessed with. If I had known this information, I never would have given you a job."

"If you remember, when you offered me a job I was recovering from an extremely stressful financial meltdown and a minor emotional one. I did carefully and honestly explain my reasons for taking the job."

"Well, praise the Lord that you are now firmly fixed on the road to recovery. I know a lot of people in this town, Ruth, who know a lot of other people. Surely one of them must be looking for a numerical whizz to be the solution to their problems! My mission is to find that prosperous yet mathematically challenged tycoon and then fire you as my cleaner. Let's pray!"

I was tidying my brushes and mops back into the store cupboard when Martine barrelled out of her office and yelled at me.

"Well, it looks as though Jesus has got your back, Ruth Henderson. How many nappy bins are you going to have to empty before you accept there is a wonderful life waiting for you if you have the courage and good sense to grab it?"

I leaned the broom against the back wall of the store room, briefly considering whether or not I should join it and close the door. "What are you talking about, Martine?" Could heart medication affect someone's brain?

"Answer one question and I'll tell you what I'm talking about. Take a look around, Ruth. Do you like what you see?"

I looked around, as instructed. I saw through the crack in a door a bunch of toddlers banging instruments and trying to sing along to a nursery rhyme. Half of the mums, the one dad and the child-minders who were with them were singing too, bouncing the babies on their knees. The other half were chatting, laughing, sharing and in one case crying while one of the toddler team gave her a bear hug.

Through the glass doors into the café, I saw the staff getting ready to serve hot meals to over sixty pensioners who would gather for the lunch club later on. The team leader, an eighty-six-year-old woman who had buried her daughter six months previously, stopped to give a word of encouragement and a pat on the back to her newest recruit: a man who had spent twelve years living on the streets overcome with drug and alcohol addiction.

I saw the animal pictures I helped the children do at the holiday club up on one wall. The late morning sunlight burst in through the large windows, bouncing around off the different shiny surfaces, creating tiny rainbows. I saw open arms and big hearts, and honest to goodness, genuine, nitty-gritty, in-for-the-long-haul *love*.

Martine scrutinized me with her blue and green eyes squinched up in their twin circles of make-up.

"Yes. I like it."

She waited, knowing there was more.

"I love what you do here, all right?"

"Yes. It is one hundred per cent all right. Gregory is leaving us to go and fight human trafficking in Eastern Europe. I've spoken to Matt. The mega-rich employer looking for a willing assistant appears to be the Lord himself, Ruth. He's a lot better at maths than you, but for some reason he likes using messed up, lily-livered, puny human beings to do his work. Gregory worked three days a week in the office, mainly doing finance stuff, and the other two as a debt advisor for the centre. Thirty-five hours a week. Here's an application form. What do you say?"

"I don't know what to say. I feel a bit bewildered and bulldozed, if I'm being honest."

"Be honest, Ruth. You know I don't work any other way. We'll be advertising for a couple of weeks, so you have time to think it over. Talk to Maggie. But I for one am hoping that no one else applies. Having someone I can work with is just as important as someone who can do the job. I like you, Ruth. You talk my language and hardly ever stare at my eyes. You never once accidently referred to me as male and you make a rollicking good cup of coffee."

"Thanks. I think."

"Plus, Dorothy has been on the phone asking if you can attend her next appointment. As a friend, not a counsellor, until you've been vetted and trained. It's next Monday evening. I hope you can make it. You made a big impression the other week. She said she found you a calming presence and you managed to explain things so that they didn't whizz around her head like a remote control aeroplane piloted by a small boy. Apparently, I didn't do that."

"I'll check my diary, but if I'm free I'd love to help."

"Good." Martine left, giving my head a chance to stop spinning while I finished up and fetched my coat and bag from the staffroom. I scanned the job description. Better pay, more hours, stuff I could actually do and enjoyed doing. But. A lot more responsibility. Martine wanting to pray for me every day and insisting on doo-doo free conversations. The weirdness of working full time for Meat Harris. Accepting that I would probably be staying in Southwell for a lot longer than I had originally planned.

The debt monster laughed. I told him to get lost, and scurried back home to a mug of soup, a new pad of drawing paper, sharpened pencils and serious escapism into a world of creatures who care nothing for money, jobs or whether the windows are free of smears.

# Chapter Sixteen

$\mathcal{I}$n the three weeks that Maggie had been mooning about since the bonfire party, glued to her mobile phone and blushing copiously, I heard nothing from school about her behaviour. It appeared that the lovebirds were smart enough to discern that the prize for staying out of trouble was time together. I briefly tried explaining to Maggie that her being allowed a certain measure of freedom when it came to her boyfriend was about trust, not reward... I might as well have told the wood pigeons who roosted in the oak tree behind the shed.

Then one Thursday afternoon I had the pleasure of hearing Mr Hay's voice on the end of my phone. I was transferring washing to the drier when he called.

"Ruth." We had started using first names somewhere around half-term.

"Hi, Ken. Long time no speak. I can't say I'm happy to hear your voice. Unless... are you phoning to let me know how hard Maggie's been working? She's won a prize for her exemplary behaviour? Ooh – I know. You want to make her a prefect."

"I wish I were. And we're getting there. She's coming on much better at school – started to hang around with some of Seth Callahan's new friends. I never thought I'd say this, but that boy is actually becoming something of a positive influence. Matt and Lois Harris are miracle workers."

"So what's the problem?"

The headmaster turned grave, using his oh-dear-I-am-very-sorry-for-your-awful-child voice. "Hannah Beaumont has been in touch. Three times. She's been having some issues with Maggie."

"Oh dear." I shut the door of the drier, and slid down onto the tiled floor. I had been half expecting this.

"Apparently, Maggie has been increasingly late for her visits. Last Saturday she didn't turn up at all. A couple of times she has hung around in the garden talking and, ahem, *interacting* with Seth for quite some time, instead of being with Mrs Beaumont. She's –"

"Hang on a minute. Interacting? You mean kissing? And how long is quite some time?"

"Um, yes. Kissing. According to Mrs Beaumont's records, the first occasion was for thirteen minutes, the second twenty-five."

"She keeps records? Of two teenagers interacting in her front garden?"

"It was her neighbour's garden."

"I don't know what to say to that. You'd better go on."

"Mrs Beaumont also complained that Maggie was, and I quote, 'discourteous, disrespectful, disengaged and dismissive'."

"Do you think she got stuck on the letter D in her dictionary of insults?"

"I have to ask that you take this seriously, Ms Henderson. Maggie is on probation here. If she fails to complete the placement…"

Whoa. I was back to being Ms Henderson again. Not a great sign.

"I know. I'll speak to her. Thanks for giving me the heads up."

"I'm not sure that will be enough."

"What?"

"Mrs Beaumont has asked to be removed from the programme. If it was for any other reason, for example illness, we could transfer Maggie to someone else, but under the circumstances that wouldn't be appropriate. This will constitute a fail."

"Can't it be put down to a personality clash? You said yourself Maggie's doing much better. I've met Hannah Beaumont. She's a difficult character, putting it politely. Some would say she's miserable, self-absorbed, crotchety and condescending. She also seems to be seriously deluded about her past – either that or a compulsive liar. I'd struggle to spend four hours a week with her."

"On two of these occasions it was tonsils clashing, not personalities."

I leaned my head against the side of the drier, wiped the frustration off my face. "Can you give me a chance to change her mind? I'll talk to Maggie and go with her to see Hannah, take some flowers or something. Please, Ken. I think it would set Maggie right back to where we were in September if this didn't work out."

"I think that too. That's why I've spoken to Mrs Beaumont, and she has agreed to let Maggie try one more session on Saturday, if you stay with her the whole time. But this is her last chance, Ruth. She has no excuse for being late, or for being rude."

As I continued my chores, vacuuming the downstairs rooms and vigorously attacking the woodwork with my mother's favourite household item, a damp duster, an idea occurred to me. It was Thursday. I had two theatre tickets. Maggie and I were going to spend some quality mother and daughter time together.

"I knew you would come."

I jolted in my theatre seat, sending the top dozen toffees in the packet I was holding skittering across the polished floor. Carl Barker laughed. "Steady on, Ruth. I don't normally have that extreme a reaction on women. Although… I kind of like it. And you can't deny chemistry."

I very slowly twisted around to find him leaning his arm on the back of my chair, boring into me with that now disturbingly intense gaze. Pulling back from the blast of hot breath on my face, I risked a glimpse at Maggie. Her expression appeared a smooth canvas, but dark clouds swirled in her eyes.

"Carl. If I'd known you still wanted to come I wouldn't have accepted the tickets. I thought the play sold out."

He shrugged. "I know the director. Saved his life once. No biggie." He winked at Maggie, who dropped her jaw slightly in horror and hurriedly turned away, burying her head in her phone.

"Your daughter's beautiful. She takes after her mother."

Yuck.

"Great hair." He raised one eyebrow at me. "I like a girl with spunk."

*Yuck!*

Maggie was still sporting her bonfire colours, having decided to leave her hair alone for a while and let the natural roots grow in. "Because Seth likes the real me – who I am underneath. He hates those fake girls who try too hard and pretend to be someone they're not. I can be myself with him." Spine-tingling words to hear from a fourteen-year-old daughter. How much of the real Maggie did he want to see? Being a fifteen-year-old boy, I suspected all of it. How much was she prepared to show him? Gulp.

"So, how are you, Ruth? Have a good week? Any more random incidents of hooliganism on that little cul-de-sac of yours?"

"No. And I'm fine, thank you. Thanks again for the tickets." I turned back around and pretended to read the programme, my blood buzzing in my ears.

Carl leaned even further forward. I couldn't imagine how he was still managing to stay on his seat. He moved his mouth about an inch from the back of my neck, sending chills across my skin, and murmured, "I think it was a mistake to wangle a seat right behind you. How will I be able to concentrate on the stage when I can't take my eyes off the vision in front of me?"

I felt the Veronese risotto Mum had cooked us curdle in my stomach. Carl employed smoother, less obviously rank tactics to my old boss Cramer Spence, but I was starting to suspect they were cut from the same piece of cloth. Cloth that was slippery black nylon with suspicious stains on it. I considered turning around and snapping out the inappropriateness of his comment, ordering him to back off. But I knew it would only engage him in further conversation and make no difference. I thought about asking Maggie if she would come with me to the toilet, so we could sneak out, but I didn't want to overreact and possibly scare her. Besides, I was frozen to my seat.

I should have done that. I should have left. Should have taken those silky, squirmy words more seriously.

The curtain rose and I pretended to lose myself in the star-crossed lovers, but all I could focus on was the unpleasant prickle that felt like a head louse clinging on to the hairs at the back of my neck.

How strange that bonding over a smarmy man who can't take a hint would allow me to persuade Maggie to give Hannah Beaumont one more try.


The following day was Lois and Matt's Surprising Sexy Yurt Adventure. Once the older kids were at school, and Lois had taken Martha and Teagan on the conveniently arranged toddlers' day trip to a nearby farm park, Rupa, Ana Luisa and Ellie broke into Bramley House using a key Rupa had pinched a few days earlier. Emily, who was at work counselling bereaved parents, planned on joining them that evening. By the time I managed to get away from the shop, the interior of the house had been transformed with manic cleaning, tidying, sorting and straightening. Ana Luisa was preparing two romantic dinners in the kitchen, one for each evening, and I found Ellie tossing various outside toys and clutter into a big pile behind the greenhouse.

In the far corner of the rambling garden, two men put the finishing touches to the construction of the yurt. Another couple ferried the various rugs and cushions, the bed and other pieces of furniture from the van. I helped Ellie tidy up the rest of the toys before sticking a path of garden lights into the lawn, leading up to the tent. By the time I then made the workmen the requisite cups of strong, sugary tea, they had put everything inside and in its proper place.

I nearly dropped the tray of tea.

It was stunning.

A bedchamber for a desert princess. Warm and cosy, and exotic and sumptuous all at once.

I left the men with their drinks and went to fetch the others. We gasped, and oohed and aahed a bit more, and waited for the men to drive away before bouncing on the bed a few times, rummaging through the food hampers and trying out our sultry Moroccan seduction dances. My phone whistled.

It was a text from Martine:

*PRINCE OF PERSIA ON THE MOVE EST TIME OF ARRIVAL AT RENDEZVOUS 16 MINUTES*

"So Matt's on his way home?" Rupa looked at her watch. "Eek! It's nearly three. Lois will be back soon. Ellie! Unwrap yourself from those drapes and help me unload the car."

While they carried in several vases of pink roses, Lois's favourites, and spread them around the tent, Ana Luisa and I quickly unpackaged the clothes we had bought, and slipped a Dean Martin CD into the portable player. Matt arrived three seconds later.

"What? Why? Has Lawrence of Arabia moved into my back garden?" He stood in the doorway to the yurt, wearing a scruffy fleece with stains on it, faded jeans and a patchy beard. The word that came to mind was "scraggly".

"You have fourteen minutes until Lois is home!" Ana Luisa flapped her hands in frustration. "Argh! No offence, Pastor Matt, but look at you! Oak Hill have bought you forty-eight uninterrupted hours with your gorgeous wife and you are going to ruin it all by looking like a man who cleans skips for a living. And – oh my golly – you smell like one too."

Matt looked at the rest of us. Ellie tried to adopt a casual position where she was sprawled on the bed. "Can someone please tell me what's going on, preferably without including any personal insults?"

"No time!" Ana Luisa grabbed Matt's arm and tried to muscle him out of the tent. "All will be explained once you are clean and presentable. Go, go, go! And wear that blue shirt with the green leaves on it. And your best suit. And smart shoes. And for all our sakes, get rid of that facial fluff – it is the worst passion assassin I have ever seen! Go!"

"Okay!" He held up his arms in surrender. "I'll trust you wild and crazy ladies and go and make myself irresistible. I wouldn't want to spoil whatever bonkers plan you've come up with this time. As long as someone makes me a cup of coffee and brings me a piece of that cake on the kitchen table."

By the time Lois arrived, Matt had been scrubbed up, revitalized with a cup of Brazilian strength coffee and filled in on the plan. Then Ana Luisa had to shout at him all over again. "What woman wants to step into that magnificent boudoir and see a blotchy man? Pull yourself together and remove those tears!"

He was waiting in the front garden when Lois pulled the minivan into the driveway, looking pretty darn hot for a priest-type person. He opened the car door and held out one hand to help his wife, handing her one of the roses. Meanwhile the rest of us had snuck over to the passenger side of the van, eased open the sliding door and were kidnapping the children out the other side. By the time Lois turned around to start sorting out Teagan, Martha, Freya and Connor, they had disappeared into the shadows.

We watched Matt lead a gobsmacked Lois round the side of the house, and then herded the kids in through the front door.

I left once Poppy had also arrived, dropped off by her school bus. Rupa and Ellie were manning the first shift, until Saturday mid-morning, along with Emily. Ana Luisa and I would then take over, carrying on until Sunday, when Matt's parents would arrive to help us get the kids ready for church.

At that point, we would tell the Harrises about the rest of the present, the trip to Disneyland. Providing, of course, they were all still in one piece, us included.

When I returned at ten the following day and saw the state of the babysitters, I wasn't sure about the likelihood of that outcome.

"How's it going?" I said, yelling to be heard above the combined noise of Teagan's wails, Poppy's toy harmonica, some cartoon about an evil supervillain Freya was watching, Connor's lightsaber war with Emily (who was using the Force), Martha repeating over and over "Where Mummy Daddy? Where Mummy Daddy?" and the washing machine, drier and dishwasher all rumbling simultaneously.

Ellie lifted her head off the kitchen table. A corner of toast was stuck to her cheek. She managed to crack open one bloodshot eye, briefly, before closing it and letting her head drop back down again.

Rupa jiggled Teagan up and down in front of the living room window, making desperate cooing noises, intermingled with what sounded dangerously close to sobs.

"Give her to me." I gently took the baby from her hands, increasing the volume of the wails by several decibels.

Rupa stared out of the window, her hair sticking out in a hundred different directions, her caramel complexion tinged with grey. "I've actually been trying to make myself one of those for the past four years. Like, spending all my life savings and jabbing myself in the backside on a regular basis. I let that greasy doctor examine me. For one of those." She shook her head, and peered directly into my eyes. "What the Jiminy Cricket have I done?"

"Go and make yourself a cup of tea. She won't stop crying while you're stressing her out."

"I can't drink tea. It makes me barf because I've got one of those crying things inside me."

"There's fruit tea. Or hot water. And have some toast." She looked as though someone had promised her a kitten and handed her a rattlesnake. "Go!"

I took Teagan upstairs and found her cot in Lois and Matt's bedroom. There was a well-worn comfort blanket in there, which I wrapped around her, tucking her firmly against my chest. I had a delicious fifteen minutes where Teagan decided that maybe I would do after all, before gradually reducing her cries to tired whimpers and then falling asleep. I gingerly laid her in the cot, and checked the baby monitor was on before creeping back downstairs to the chaos.

"RIGHT!" Growing up the youngest of four daughters, I had learned to make myself heard when necessary. "EVERYBODY STOP!"

Everybody stopped, except for the evil supervillain, but then what can you expect from someone whose sole mission in life is world annihilation? "What is Lois going to think if she comes in here to check on things and sees this going on?"

Nobody knew what Lois would think. The villain cackled.

"Well? Connor?"

Connor looked at me for a minute. "She's going to think you're rubbish babysitters."

"Is she going to think you deserve the party we've planned for you later on?"

Connor thought about that. Freya paused the TV. "I like parties. Wanna go to the party."

"You have thirty minutes to tidy up this mess, eat breakfast, get dressed and brush your teeth and hair. Everyone who is ready before the alarm goes off on my phone gets to come to the party. Wait! There are two teams. Connor and Martha are team one. Poppy and Freya are team two."

"What about me?" Emily asked.

"You're making things worse. You have five minutes to get your stuff together and go. Now, team one – are you ready?"

"YES!" Team one were ready.

"Team two, are you steady?"

"YES!" Team two were steady.

"GO!"

Ana Luisa dished up cereal, toast, more cereal, fruit and one last piece of toast while I dug out clean outfits for each of the children, flung duvets back onto beds and cheered them on as they got ready for the morning. Poppy needed more care, but her teammate knew exactly where everything was, and how to persuade her to sit still long enough to take her medication and get cleaned up while Ana Luisa did the rest.

By the time the thirty minutes were up, by some miracle we had five kids with full stomachs and clean faces, and a reasonably tidy house. Once they were assured of an invitation to the party, Freya and Martha disappeared to their bedroom before returning dressed as a lobster and a space alien, respectively. Connor tipped a box containing at least five million pieces of Lego down the stairs and Poppy was sick on "Daddy's chair", quite possibly in protest at him abandoning her to these strange women. But when I caught Lois tiptoeing into the shower room at eleven o'clock, I was able to reassure her with a straight face that all was under control.

She was dressed in the light blue dressing gown, her hair a bees' nest.

"Are you having a nice time? How are you doing?"

A slow smile spread across her face. "'Nice' is one word for it. How am I doing? I feel like a melted puddle of chocolate." She paused to wrap her arms around me in a massive squeeze. "Thank you. Thank you. Thank you."

A crash emanated from the kitchen behind us. Ana Luisa cried, "No, don't eat it! Or stick it there!"

Lois broke the hug, sticking her hands over both ears. "I didn't hear that."

I grinned. "Okay."

She looked at me pointedly. "But I think *you did*, Ruth."

"Oh, right. See you later."

By seven that evening, the party was on the wane. After a day of blowing up balloons, wiping noses, changing nappies, fetching drinks, clearing up spilt drinks, fetching new drinks, breaking up fights, kissing bumps, reading stories, bouncing babies, tidying up toys, fixing lunch, fetching more drinks... I was so tired my bones felt as though they were full of wet sand. A thirty-four-hour labour had been nothing to this. If Maggie and Seth hadn't arrived to supervise the games, I think I would have taken Ana Luisa up on her suggestion to hide under the stairs until it was all over.

All the children, particularly Poppy, settled down when Seth was there. They loved him as little siblings love big brothers who let them jump on him, kiss him, paint his nails and ask ten thousand questions, all of which he answered with utter confidence, patience and not a hint of patronization. My opinion of Seth Callahan grew to the size of the CN Tower that afternoon. Especially when, unasked, he brought Ana Luisa and me hot chocolate with giant slabs of coffee cake.

"How old are you, Seth?" Ana Luisa asked, her mouth full of cake.

"Nearly sixteen."

"Hmm. So nearly old enough to marry me."

"How old are you, Ana Luisa?"

"That's a rude question to ask a lady."

"Not if you're considering her proposal of marriage."

"I'm thirty-one."

"I'm no way near old enough to marry you. But I appreciate the offer."

She shrugged as he went back to judge the dancing competition.

We finished off the party with "Ruth's Amazing Art Animals", covering the entire conservatory with decorating sheets. The children wore my dad's old shirts with the sleeves rolled up. Ana Luisa and I donned boiler suits from the around-a-pound shop.

We made butterfly paintings, egg carton camels and reindeer with footprint noses and handprint antlers. There were origami jumping frogs painted in rainbow colours, pipe-cleaner snakes and spiders, and a turkey made from pine cones.

When the children were so exhausted their heads began nodding into the paint pots, we called it a night. Cleaning them up and getting them into pyjamas took another hour and a half, including a twenty-minute discussion with Martha about whether or not she could wear a plastic suit of armour to bed. We compromised with a breastplate, a sword tucked in beside her and a promise that if the baddies came we would give her time to get her helmet on.

I tucked Freya and Martha in, side by side in their one pink and one blue beds. "Right, then." I bent down to give Martha a kiss. "Go to sleep now. Granny and Granddad are coming in the morning, so you need lots of rest. Goodnight."

I went to switch off the light.

"You haven't finished!" Freya sat up in bed. I looked at her, steeling myself for another battle. "You haven't said a prayer."

Oh. That. I glanced out of the door, hoping to find Ana Luisa. She was still helping Poppy get changed. I could hear Seth reading Connor a bedtime story. I shuffled a couple of steps nearer to the bedroom door.

"Say a prayer, Ruth!" Freya demanded.

"Okay, right. Lie back down then." One of my parents had prayed with me every single night until I turned thirteen. I could do this. I could cobble something together.

"Thank you, God, for a lovely day. Please help Martha and Freya to sleep well, with lovely dreams. Amen."

"That was RUBBISH!" Freya sat up again.

"Ubbish!" Martha agreed with her. Sheesh. Having my prayers critiqued by a two-year-old.

"Well, why don't you pray then instead?"

"Thank you, God, for parties, and animals, and cake and balloons and yurts and slugs and rainbows and bedtime and morning time and dinner time and hammer time. You made a really amazing world full of nice things and I love it. Thank you for making me alive. Please help Mummy and Daddy have lots of fun on their secret holiday. I like holidays if I ever went on one, but I didn't. Please can I go on holiday one day. I would like to go to the seaside. Please can Martha come too? And thank you for Seth and Maggie and Poppy even though she can't talk and Connor and Teagan and Mummy and Daddy and Freya. And thank you, God, for Ruth.

She is really beautiful and kind and funny and good at animals and I love her. Please help her to talk to you better, because talking to you is nice. Bye."

She put her head back on the pillow and was asleep.

I went downstairs, sat on the sofa and wondered why I was crying, yet again. Twenty months and still so leaky!

Mum came round to pick up Maggie and drop Seth back at John's. She couldn't stop as she had one hundred mince pies to finish baking for the Oak Hill craft group.

Ana Luisa spent half an hour preparing a meal for Matt and Lois, then dished out the leftovers for us. We ate in front of the television, the faint sound of Teagan's snores rumbling through the baby monitor.

"Look at us, Ruth. We are like an old married couple."

"I can't believe I ever thought one child was hard work. How do they do this every single day?"

"Would you like any more children?"

I pretended to think about it. As if I didn't know. Took a deep breath. "I wouldn't want any more children unless I was married. And I can't see that happening. What about you? Would you like kids?"

Ana Luisa's eyes filled up. She reached across the sofa and grabbed my hand. "Yes. Yes, I would like kids. I would like at least four. But I have a very big mountain to overcome before that is possible. And I am starting to wonder if it will ever happen." She shook her head. "I am starting to think that maybe the only way to solve this problem is to go back to Brazil. Or to find a job somewhere else. Maybe Switzerland. Or New Zealand. Or Pluto."

It felt as though an invisible hippopotamus had climbed onto my chest.

"That sounds like a drastic solution. Do you want to talk about it?"

She smiled. "Thanks, Ruth. It's not really so bad. All hope is not lost. I'm just tired and we Brazilian women are prone to getting overly emotional about these things."

She stacked our plates and carried them out into the kitchen. I sank deeper into the sofa, acknowledging the beginnings of a migraine rumbling in the back of my head. Felt a moment's grief for the brothers and sisters that Maggie would never have. Growing up, I had always planned on having four children too. As a fourth child I hadn't wanted to deny a girl like me the chance of existing. Fraser and I had never had that conversation. The thread between us had been too tenuous, too uncertain for so long, and by the time we caught our breath and found some measure of stability, we had become house-mates, business partners, barely friends with benefits. If we were not able to commit to each other completely, give our hearts totally, love unreservedly, it felt like an unwise, even wrong, decision to bring another child into our fragile situation. The horrible truth was, both Fraser and I had one eye on the door. It was laziness, lack of opportunity and a downright miracle neither of us ended up walking into the arms of someone who could be that soul mate we were unable to be to each other. That, and the fact that I thought my soul mate was most probably somewhere up a tree in the middle of the jungle with Vanessa Jacobs.

But now, everything had changed. I used to spend Saturday nights sitting in my fancy suburban kitchen wittering over piles of paperwork, the television on to drown out the silence, calculating and recalculating as I tried to find a way to keep us in our home, keep me in my protective bubble, safe in my non-life pretending the gaping hole in my soul was the sudden loss of my partner, rather than the slow, steady drip-drip loss of myself. Now, I had ended up sitting in a ramshackle cottage surrounded by cardboard animals, looking after five children as a surprise for my friend – *a friend!* – while another friend held my hand and confessed her deepest fears – *two friends!* My weekends were bonfire parties, and bad dates, and curry nights. I had been offered a good job, on top of my two current jobs. I laughed sometimes. I was growing hips again. I was having an occasional conversation with my dad. He was getting to

know his granddaughter. I had not only seen David, I had gone
for a walk with him and managed to almost behave like a normal
person. I had actually gone whole hours at a time without thinking
about him, or fantasizing about life as Mrs Carrington.

I had spent eighteen months trying not to end up back in
Southwell. Fifteen years running from here. Expecting it to be a
microscope that showed up all my faults, my failings, my worst fears.

What an idiot.

After a frequently disturbed night, finished off with Martha on one
side of my airbed and Freya half off the other, I gave up somewhere
around five-thirty and put the kettle on. I could hear Ana Luisa
upstairs with Teagan fussing, so took up another tea and a bottle
of warm milk. We made it through until Matt's parents arrived, a
woman I vaguely remembered from my school days and a man who
had been largely absent from his son's upbringing. A rosy-cheeked,
doe-eyed, goofy-smiled Matt and Lois joined us as we began
bundling kids into coats, gloves, hats, scarves and, in Martha's case,
a Darth Vader helmet.

"Let's go then, troops. Apparently there is more of a surprise to
come at church." Matt grinned. "Although I'm not sure I can take
much more."

Freya clung on to my hand. "I'm going to sit with Ruth. Can I
go in your car, Ruth? Please? Please? Please?"

"Um, no. I'm actually not coming. I'm staying to tidy up, then
going home to get some rest. I'll see you soon, I'm sure."

Freya looked at me. Her little brow furrowed. Her cheeks turned
purple. "That is unacceptable, young lady!"

"Pardon?"

She wrapped herself around my leg, clinging on like a koala.
"Please come." Martha jumped up onto the other leg and joined
her. "Ruth, come!"

Connor then moved behind me and started trying to push me
out of the door. I looked at Matt and Lois, expecting them to step

in and tell their kids to knock it off. Matt grinned. "I'm a minister. I'm not going to stop someone inviting you to church."

Lois waggled her eyebrows at me. "Oh, stop being such a wuss, Henderson. Get in the van."

The last time I had been to a church service was Fraser's funeral. A bleak, dark, freezing cold chapel in Scotland, with oppressive ceilings and uncomfortable pews, it suited my mood perfectly. I had huddled on the front row, sandwiched between the stony Scottish Dragon and Maggie, the droning keen of the organ covering up the horrible silence.

Today I sat on a cushioned chair, a four-year-old leaning on one shoulder, her two-year-old sister playing with my hair on the other side. I had failed in my primary objective; that is, avoiding my mother. She had skipped over, clucking with glee, and given Lois the biggest hug. "Look what you dragged in! How was the weekend? Marvellous, if the bloom on your cheeks is anything to go by. Oh, Ruth, darling, you look like an introvert at a singles party. Stop huddling."

The best way to describe the next hour and a half was like a giant family gathering where most of the family actually not only loved but liked and treasured each other. The family were loud, fun, unrestrained, a bit mischievous, honest, serious, and boy did they know how to celebrate. I may have huddled a tiny bit less. I still felt like the black sheep of the family, but maybe slightly more grey than black.

After the last song had finished and the eight-piece band took their seats, the assistant minister, a Nigerian woman called Catherine with one of those deep, honey voices that can soothe all ills, took the stage. She called up Pastor Matt and Lois and each of the kids by name, including Seth, who was sat somewhere near the back with Maggie, and lined them up.

"Church, can I ask you to show your love and appreciation to our leader and his family?"

I had once watched a Liverpool football game, when Fraser was given some tickets by a grateful client. The noise when they scored was something like the sound that erupted across the hall for the next five minutes.

Catherine then shushed the congregation. "Can I also ask Ellie, Emily, Ana Luisa, Rupa and Ruth to come forward, please?"

The people cheered and clapped again. I tried to disappear under the seat, but it wasn't happening. The rest of the girls were making their way up. If I slid down low enough and let my hair flop in front of my face, perhaps no one would spot me.

"Ruth?" Catherine scanned the crowd. "Is she here? Can anybody see her?"

Mum stood up, from her position near the front, and waggled her long finger straight at me. "She's there, Catherine. Hiding."

Four hundred heads swivelled to stare at me. Now I was a thousand times more embarrassed than if I had just gone up there in the first place. I pictured clamping my hands over my mother's mouth until she actually stopped talking. She of all people, knowing what had happened the last time I stood on a stage, should have come to my rescue, not thrown me to the lions.

"Come on then, child," Catherine smiled at me. "There is nothing to be afraid of. This is not a place to hide."

I had been hiding from God, his church, the world, David, myself for a very long time. The last three months had been a gradual, inch-by-inch attempt to poke my nose out of my hidey-hole. Now, Oak Hill had taken a stick of dynamite and blown the roof right off it. I couldn't move. I felt naked. All I could think about was that I didn't belong here any more. I had failed. The shame I had carried for all those years was a manacle, chaining me to the floor. A weight too great to shift. I stared at my feet. Wanted to die. Angry at myself for even being here.

A warm bunch of tiny fingers grasped mine. Another hand pressed softly against my cheek. "Come on, Ruth. It's this way. Don't be scared. You can come with me."

I looked up and saw Freya's age old, ocean deep eyes on mine. Remembered stories about how two years ago she had come to

Bramley House a stone underweight, covered in scabs and bruises. Lost, wrecked, too numb to make a sound. The first time she cried, Lois and Matt had wept with joy. And I found I could. I could go with this girl whose life was a testimony to new starts, to hope and faith and courage. I held her hand, or rather she held mine, and walked with her to the stage, the debris of my shame falling off in glorious chunks behind me with every step. I didn't hear the applause, or Catherine's presentation speech, or the family's thanks. I couldn't see the faces of the people in front and below me. I felt a tiny hand in mine. Another on each shoulder, arms wrapped around my waist.

The yurt was due to stay for one more night. That evening, the doors opened up for a party, although we closed them tight once everyone squeezed in, as it was close to freezing outside. Someone ordered a dozen pizzas, and we drank fizzy grape juice and lounged about on cushions and rugs, listening to a couple of the men play guitars while the kids gradually dozed off, cuddled on the bed or in random guests' laps.

I had squished onto a giant beanbag with Lois. The warmth of all those bodies in the confined space caused my eyelids to droop. I felt a moment's gratitude that I had arranged to clean a couple of hours later than usual in the morning.

"How do you do it, Lois?"

She rolled her eyes over to me lazily and smiled. "You know, it's always far more exhausting looking after other people's children than your own. I don't attempt animal parties very often. And I have school, and nursery, and Matt. Honestly? I do a lot of closing my eyes and counting to ten, keep reminding myself that once a week I can go swimming for two hours by myself, and pray. Sometimes through clenched teeth into a pillow. I also pretend to need a lot more time in the toilet than I actually do. And I remember."

"Remember what?"

"I have a picture in my head of how every one of those kids looked the day I became their mother." She shook her head in exasperation. "I know it's fostering. They aren't legally mine. But that's a technicality my heart chooses to ignore. I remember how they were when they came to me. What life had done to them. And I remember what it feels like. To be a child who has no one to talk to, to turn to, when life is terrifying, and ugly, and wrong. What it's like when home is not a safe place, but a nightmare. To experience pain, and fear, and danger, and despair every single day."

"Lois, I never…"

"I know. I worked very hard at making sure you never suspected. I was good at being invisible, remember?"

"You were a ghost. I thought you were shy, or a bit strange."

"I know. You lived in a different world to me. And that's how it should have been. Don't be sorry that you were a child who didn't contemplate the idea that her friend could be suffering abuse."

"Oh, Lois." I didn't want to cry. It was a party. I was so done with crying.

She patted me on the knee. "Don't get too upset. It has a happy ending. Enough tears have been shed over it."

"How did you get past it? Become this incredible person? You're so strong now, and free and peaceful."

"I was partnered with Matt for that history coursework on the Cold War. He came round unannounced one time and suspected something was up. I tried everything to push him away. But he wouldn't give in. Then one Friday night, he called when Dad was drunk. Watched it through the window. So he phoned the police. I thought that was that, but he still wouldn't leave. It took me six years to accept he could actually love me. Another two before I dared to love him back. Gradually, we unmessed each other up."

"Wow. So that's why you foster."

"That, and Dad battering me until I couldn't get pregnant."

"Lois Harris, you are the most amazing woman I have ever met. What are you doing wasting your time being friends with me?"

"Oh, I don't actually like you. You're just another loser in need of rescuing. I thought you got that? As soon as you manage to sort your life out, I'm outta here." She winked at me. "Oh yes, and your mum bribed me to be friends with you. Fifty pence and a bag of lemon bonbons."

# Chapter Seventeen

Dorothy Barker's teacup rattled against the saucer. She hunched on the sagging sofa in her living room, nerves jangling. Martine was trying to explain some of the details regarding Dorothy's debt repayments, but her client was having a hard time keeping up. We had compiled a list of her paltry outgoings versus the benefits she received. It was grim reading. As Martine discussed consolidation, and the possibility of a debt relief order, I began scanning the bank statements that we had organized into a folder earlier.

"Hang on a minute, Martine. Can I interrupt?"

"It sounds as though you already have."

"Something isn't right here." I looked at Dorothy. "We asked you several times to tell us everything, all your bills and debts, and outgoings. Went over it all carefully. I'm sure Martine explained, Dorothy. We can't help you if you aren't honest with us. I know it's hard, but if you won't tell the truth, you're just wasting our time."

Dorothy paled. She quaked like a frightened mouse, but I wasn't in the mood to tread softly. This whole meeting was pointless if what I had seen on the statement was correct. And I had a thing about secret debts.

Her teacup rattled harder. Martine took it out of her hand and shoved some papers aside to make room for it on the coffee table. "I think you'd better explain, Ruth."

"All these bank statements have withdrawals — between twenty and fifty pounds at a time, at least once a week — that you haven't accounted for in your figures. It averages out at two hundred and sixteen pounds a month. Where's that money going?"

Dorothy shook her head. "I don't know. Just what I put on the list. It must be bits and bobs at the corner shop and that."

"Fifty quid a week? That's a lot of bits and bobs for a woman living on her own. Please try to think."

"Sometimes I buy a scratch card. Or one of those magazines: the ones with all the puzzles in. I might get the bus back from the shops if my back is bad. Apart from that, I don't know. I really don't know. I'm scatter-brained, Carl tells me. I lose things and he gets angry at me then because I've forgotten where I put my money."

"Do you ever give Carl money?" Martine asked.

She shrank back further into the cushions. "Only a lend – five pounds every now and again. Ten at the most. He's too busy to get to the bank machine, see? Usually works such long hours that he runs out of change for the hospital car park."

"Doctors don't have to pay for the hospital car park." Martine frowned, her blue and green eyes nearly disappearing in her suspicion.

"And a five or ten pound note isn't change." I tried to keep my voice calm, but the acid in my stomach was beginning to bubble. "Do you give him the money yourself, or does he take it straight out of your purse?"

Dorothy baulked at that. She sat up straighter in her chair. "What are you suggesting? That my own son is stealing from me? He's a doctor! How dare you!"

I put the bank statement on the table, where Martine could see it. "How soon does he remember to pay you back?"

"Well. I don't know. We're family. Families don't keep records of things like that. It's only a bit of change every now and then."

We tried discussing this some more, suggesting that fifty pounds a week was a lot more than a bit of change, especially in her current circumstances, and she must keep a more careful record of where this extra money was going, but Dorothy was hurt and angry, and we were getting nowhere.

Martine suggested meeting up in a week's time, once she had spoken to some creditors, and asked Dorothy to keep a very close eye on whatever she was spending. Frustrated and disappointed, I was the first to leave. I opened the front door and screamed.

"Woah! Steady on!" The lean frame of Carl Barker, looking every inch the professional in his pea coat and snazzy scarf, stood on the doorstep. He grabbed hold of both my arms, as if to steady me.

"Take a deep breath, Ruth. That's it. Breathe with me, in… and out."

I couldn't meet his piercing eyes, even with the glasses back in place. Stepping back, I tried to wriggle out of his clutches. "I'm fine. Honestly. You can let go of me."

"I can't though. I can't let go of you." A tiny murmur, but the icy wind whipped those words across to me, sending an arctic blast right through my bones.

"What?"

"Hmmm?" He shrugged, feigning incomprehension. The chill burrowed a little deeper. "Shall we step inside? Keep the cold air out of the house?"

"Actually, I'm leaving."

"Oh, right. Even better, I'll give you a lift. We can catch up in the car. You never told me what you thought of *Romeo and Juliet*."

"No, thanks. I'm getting a lift with my friend Martine. She's right behind me."

"Well, we can save her going out of her way, then. Good timing."

"You aren't used to people saying no to you, are you?"

He turned up one side of his mouth in a smirk. "I like to think I'm persistent."

"I wouldn't want your car to get egged again."

"I'll take the risk. Or drop you at the corner. One or the other."

Eugh. Why couldn't he tell the difference between playing hard to get and actually not wanting to be got?

"Carl? Is that you?" Dorothy appeared in the corridor behind me. She looked flustered. Martine barrelled out from behind her.

"We'll see you next week, then. And remember what I told you." Pushing me out of the door in front of her, so that I bumped uncomfortably into Carl leaning on the door frame like a catalogue model, Martine paused. She stared up at Carl, craning her neck in the confined space of the doorway. "You must be Carl."

Carl blinked a few times.

"Your mother tells us that you, a doctor, have been borrowing money off her, who is currently out of work."

His eyes narrowed. "What happens between me and my mother is none of your business. I suggest you stay out of it."

Martine tipped her head to one side as if considering this. "Possibly. Except that she's decided to make it my business by engaging my professional services."

"Oh?" he sneered. "Perhaps I'll have to speak to her about spending her precious money hiring busybodies to dictate how she lives."

"Go ahead. Makes no difference to me. She doesn't pay me a penny." She beamed, crinkling up her eyes. "Anyway. Very nice to meet you at last, Dr Carl. And I'll look forward to hearing how you are supporting Dorothy's attempts to get her finances back on track."

She held out one hand, as if to shake his, but when the slightly baffled Carl warily returned the gesture, she suddenly pulled her hand back. "Ah! Let me give you my card before I go. Then if you have any questions or concerns you can call me."

She opened up her briefcase, rummaging through the contents right under Carl's nose. "Here we go. I knew I had one in here somewhere. So much stuff in here. You never know what might end up being necessary."

Handing Carl a card, she snapped her case shut and smiled at him again. His eyes glittered like those of a snake in a cage. He appeared to be speechless.

"Is there anything you'd like to ask me now, or is it all perfectly clear?"

To my amazement, instead of grabbing Martine around the throat and throttling her, he simply shook his head and closed the front door on us.

She marched straight past me and beeped open the car parked at the bottom of the drive. "I would laugh if I wasn't so hopping mad."

Once we were safely inside the car, with the doors shut, she allowed me a peek into the briefcase. Alongside the case files was a shiny black gun.

"I confiscated it off Jobber Jones at youth group last Thursday."

"It's not…?"

"This is no more a real gun than Jobber Jones is a real gangster. It's not a bad imitation, though, from a distance."

"I can't believe you just threatened a client's son with a fake gun. Is this usual debt counsellor behaviour?"

"Men who steal money from their impoverished mothers do not play by the usual rules. And for the record, I gave him a business card not a threat. But stay away from that man, Ruth. He has a rotting cyst of rancid pus where his heart should be."

I tried. I tried to stay away.

The following Saturday, another meeting. This time, I accompanied Maggie. I had insisted on a rational mother–daughter conversation before we left in exchange for the money to go ice-skating that weekend. We managed, ooh, a miraculous twenty minutes before she threw a shoe at me. It was just about long enough. I had made some phone calls and prepared my plan of attack.

Hannah Beaumont greeted us as always with a face that could curdle milk. Saying nothing, she shuffled back into the living room on her walker, and lowered her bent body onto the high-backed chair.

"Hello, Mrs Beaumont. How are you?" I forced a smile.

She pursed her mouth, where red lipstick bled into the wrinkles either side. "Do you really want to know?"

Maggie looked at me. *See what I have to put up with?*

"Not if you don't want to tell me. Have you been up to much this week?"

"No." Hannah flicked her hand at Maggie. "Are you going to make tea, or do I have to beg?"

"That was rude." Maggie's voice trembled. For all her bravado at home, she was not used to standing up to this grouchy old woman.

"I beg your pardon?"

"You don't speak to me very nicely. All you have to say is 'Please could you make some tea.'"

Hannah looked bewildered. "What are you talking about? I did say that. For goodness' sake, girl. Are you going to stand there all day dithering, or put the kettle on?"

"Her name is Maggie." I was bristling now.

"Yes, I know that. I'm not senile," she snapped. My temper snapped too.

"Maggie has given up her free time this afternoon to provide you with some company and a younger pair of hands. And all you have done is bark orders, snap at and insult her. You don't even refer to her by name! This is a befriending scheme, Mrs Beaumont, but with all due respect you are not being friendly at all. Can you even remember how to be a friend?"

Halfway through this rant, Maggie vanished into the kitchen. Hannah Beaumont and I sat there, in the aftermath of my speech, and blinked at the wall in surprise. After a long, stunned silence, Maggie crept back in with the tea tray. She placed it onto the table, poured out milk and hot tea into three fine bone china cups and used a pair of silver tweezers to plop a sugar cube into one of the cups. Stirring it, she sat it carefully on top of a doily on the edge of the table.

Hannah lifted the cup, took a slurp, and set it back down again. She looked at me and said, "I don't know if I do."

She heaved herself up then, and limped out of the room. We heard the slow thump-shuffle of her walker down the hall corridor, followed by the slamming of a bedroom door.

"What have you done?" Maggie whispered.

I gnawed my lip. "Has she disappeared before? Do you think she's coming back?"

She shook her head. We sat there for a few minutes, sipping our tea.

"This tea is really good."

"Why are you talking about tea? Go and speak to her, Mum! You were really harsh. If I get dumped off the scheme now, it'll be your fault."

"I'll go in a few minutes, if she hasn't come back."

I had finished my tea and was dallying at the end of the corridor when Hannah reopened her bedroom door.

"Fetch the box off my bed. Bring it in... please."

I lifted it, a hexagonal hat box in faded cream and gold stripes. It was the weight of a small child, and I couldn't think how Hannah had got it onto the bed in the first place. She indicated that I should put the box onto the table in front of her.

"Maggie, go ahead," she said, gesturing at the box.

Maggie opened up the lid to reveal an interior squashed full of papers, thick brown envelopes and smaller containers. Glancing at Hannah, who nodded in confirmation, Maggie carefully lifted out the uppermost packet.

Inside, it contained photographs. Five black and white shots of a bride on her wedding day. In two of them she was alone. The other three also contained her groom, a slender man with thick, dark hair and a confident smile. The bride was radiant, her dress exquisite, her countenance pure grace.

"Hannah, is this you? You were enchanting. Simply beautiful." I picked up a photograph and took a closer look.

She nodded. "We were a handsome couple. The match of the county. It was in all the papers and society magazines. Five hundred guests. And a honeymoon in Europe."

"What was your husband's name? He looks charming."

"Charles," she snickered. "Yes. Charming. That's one way to put it."

"How long were you married for?" I handed the photo to Maggie, picking up another picture of Hannah gazing into her groom's eyes.

"Thirty-seven years."

"You must miss him."

"Hah! I must not." She paused, fists clenched in her lap. "I didn't miss him when he ran off with the housekeeper, or when he turned my children against me. I certainly didn't pine for him when he squirrelled all his money away in secret foreign investments and screwed me out of my divorce settlement. I laughed when he died. Laughed even louder when I heard he left that traitorous floosy with nothing either. If I knew where he was buried I'd tap dance on his grave."

Beneath the bitter bravado Hannah's words were wracked with pain. Maggie stared, mouth hanging open.

I tried to ease the tension. "You have children?"

"Two. Two sons. But they don't bother with me. Followed the money to their father. Started calling that tramp 'Mother'. I was disowned." She sniffed. "I'm better off without them."

"When was the last time you had contact with them?"

"A blinking long time ago. So you're right. I have forgotten how to be nice. What's the point when they all end up betraying you anyway?"

What could I say to that? There is nothing sorrier or more pitiful than a human being who has lost hope. I looked at Maggie, her face stricken. She was staring at the wedding pictures of that bride, resplendent in her loveliness, glowing with the certainty that the world and all its wonders were hers for the taking. Maggie knew that life could be hard, agonizing even. But to see the bitter remains of all that despair and resentment, the harsh reality of what someone who chooses to let herself be conquered by life's struggles could become – it was a sober lesson for her.

I was itching to grab my daughter's hand, fling wide the doors and sprint out into the sunshine before a single drop of this oppression could mark a stain on either of us. To shake it off like water from a dog's coat. But we had another twenty minutes before our time was up. I did the next best thing – changed the subject.

"This is a beautiful box. May I open it?"

Hannah nodded, and I picked out the slender velvet case, maybe eight inches by four. Inside was a pair of silk gloves, in the palest pink, three tiny pearls dotted along each trim.

"The pearls are real," Hannah said.

"Wow," I remarked, fingering the delicate material.

"I wore them for my presentation at court. I was a debutante."

"Really? I didn't think they still did that." I passed a glove to Maggie.

"I was one of the last."

"One of the last what?" Maggie asked. "Why were you in court?"

"To be presented to the queen!" Hannah unbent herself by about two inches in the chair. "The finest, most desirable young women in the country were presented to the monarch at the start of the season."

"What season?"

"The coming out season."

"Coming out? Are you trying to wind me up?" Maggie looked up momentarily, her eyes wide.

"Certainly not!" Hannah huffed.

"It was a young woman's introduction to the social season," I interjected, hiding my smile at Maggie's confusion. "Like a debutante's ball. A chance for them to meet suitable husbands."

"The ignorance of young ladies today is staggering." Hannah reached out and took the gloves back from me and Maggie, then snapped the lid shut on the velvet case. "When you come back on Wednesday I will instruct you in the procedures and etiquette of coming out."

Maggie shrugged. "Can't really see me needing to know those anytime soon, but whatever."

We tidied up the tea things, washed a sink full of dishes and left. Disaster averted, for now. Maggie was pensive on the drive back home.

"So. It looks like Hannah wasn't making it up. Or deluded. She married a count and lived in a stately home. There might be some interesting stories in that box. And it beats polishing the silver with her knickers," I said.

"I know. It's not that." She drummed on the car door for a few moments with her fingers. "How long have Nanny and Pop been married?"

"Nanny was twenty-one… Forty-eight years."

"Do you think that's too long to get a divorce?"

"Theoretically, you're never too old… but Nanny and Pop have had a great marriage. Their roots are deeply intertwined," I said, perhaps too forcefully. "Every relationship goes through blips, difficult times. You only stay together for nearly five decades by learning how to overcome them. I'm sure they'll get through this, Maggie. I don't think Nanny and Pop know how to exist without each other. And they take their marriage vows very seriously. Till death do them part… Although if Pop does anything stupid with Ruby that might come sooner than he thinks," I added, turning onto our road. "Nanny and Pop love each other."

"They don't act like it."

"Maybe not right now."

I remembered my mother's words on the subject of love and marriage and divorce as I was growing up: "What's love got to do with it anyway? Marriage is commitment, and trust, and respect. We made a vow and we meant it. Every decision we make is on the foundation of that vow. Love is the custard on the crumble. Delicious, oozy and yummy. But without it you still have a pudding. Custard on its own? That ain't going to satisfy you for very long."

"They'll work it out."

If I said it enough, maybe I would manage to convince myself as well as Maggie.

I pulled into the cul-de-sac, watching out for ice on the smaller roads. As the car crunched to a stop, I was still musing about love. Thinking about Fraser, wondering how many other couples ended up staying together out of convenience, habit, for the sake of the children.

What was love anyway? Was it all a myth? A mean joke? An invention to pay for Hollywood moguls' swimming pools and made-to-measure suits? I knew the love a mother has for her child.

The stomach-clenching, heart-exploding, every breath I-would-gladly-die-to-spare-you-pain mother's love. But romantic, sexy, flowers, empty the bin for you, no eyes for anyone else, ever, when you are nothing but a bag of saggy wrinkles I still choose you love? Really?

Then I saw him. Standing in the shadow of our burnt-out willow tree. Working with a rake to gather the last of the fallen leaves. He was coatless, the sleeves of his dark grey sweater pushed up to reveal the flex of arm muscles as he pulled the rake. Hair, even longer now, flopping over his face.

Oh boy. Love slapped me round the cheeks, whooshed up from the bottom of my belly and ricocheted a million times against the walls of my rib cage.

That was love. It was him. My love was him. Unbowed or dimmed or dulled by the passing of time or the weathering of my heart. I would love that man until death did us part.

Maggie grabbed hold of my arm, popping my love balloon thoughts. "Is that David *Carrington*? Your David is *that* David? I can't believe you never told me you were best friends with a famous person! You have to introduce me. Now. No. Hold on." She pulled down the sun visor, flipped open the little mirror and frantically tugged at her hair. "Okay, it'll have to do. Come on, Mum!"

I followed her out of the car, picking my way through the ice to stand beside her on the pavement nearest the willow tree. David had earphones in, but he caught the movement in his peripheral vision, pulling the phones out of his ears before propping the rake up against the tree trunk and smiling his hello.

"Ruth." He nodded at me. "And this must be the champion egg-chucker. Maggie? Pleased to meet you."

He stepped forward and shook Maggie's hand. She blushed and stammered, shuffling from foot to foot.

"Wow." David stared at her for a few seconds. "You look just like your mum would have done if she'd dwelt in a parallel universe where she was actually cool."

"Hey! I was cool!"

Maggie and David both looked at me.

"I was so not cool."

"How are you settling in? Finding plenty of ways to express yourself via food-related hooliganism?" David grinned, and rocked back on his heels, hands in his back pockets.

"Um." Maggie was genuinely star-struck. I couldn't blame her.

"I'm joking. Are you at the Minster?"

"Yes."

"Still Mr Hay?"

She nodded.

"I've met him a couple of times. He seems okay. A lot better than the donkey who used to be there. Who've you got for biology?"

"Mr Harrigan."

"Harrigan officially rules. Does he still have that old sweet tub full of maggots on the window-sill?"

"Yeah."

"Your mum once cut a hole in the plastic at the back with a craft knife. We were watching a film that lesson with the lights off. By the time anyone noticed, they were everywhere. Including trouser pockets, school bags, one girl's hair…"

Maggie squinted at me.

"I'm not proud of it." Okay, I felt really proud of it, especially when Jayne Tate found three maggots wiggling about in her bra during a geography test.

Mouth agape, Maggie said, "It's not that. I just can't imagine you doing anything that… fun. Or rebellious. Or interesting."

"Well, I wasn't always a boring old shrivelled-up play-it-safe non-entity of a person."

"Weren't you?"

"I was best friends with David Carrington, BAFTA award-winning film-maker and all round fun guy, remember? I couldn't have been a complete saddo loser."

Maggie looked doubtful.

"You should both come round for dinner sometime. I've got loads more stories about Ruth Henderson's childhood exploits. Many of them involving insect larvae and other assorted wildlife. My favourite includes a bag of fermenting peaches, a box of matches and the year seven recorder group."

Maggie looked at me, wide eyed, begging me to say yes.

"I suppose that would be all right." Weird, gut-wrenching, jittery, but all right.

"What about Sunday lunch tomorrow? I'll see what Ana Luisa has planned. But I'm officially home for Christmas now, so if not we can sort something else out."

"Can I bring my boyfriend?"

"Maggie!"

"No, it's fine. The more the merrier. Perhaps your mum would like to invite Dr Carl Jackass? Or would you launch the main course at him?"

Maggie, Seth, David, Ana Luisa, me, Carl. Cosy.

"I would." Maggie beamed, delighted that David thought my date was a jackass. "But she won't bring him. She's not going to be dating anyone else either for, like, forever."

David looked at me. His face was serious, but his eyes crinkled up at the corners.

"That's a shame," he said.

"No, it isn't. Mum dating is totally gross," Maggie added, kicking the leaves at her feet.

"After my mum died, I used to wish Dad would find some woman to make me birthday cakes and tuck me in at night. But at the same time, the thought of any actual living person being able to fill the crater she'd left behind, trying to come even close to replacing her, made me ill." He locked eyes with Maggie.

She returned his stare, her eyes welling up. "Parents dying is a heap of manure."

"It is. But you get used to the smell."

I think the non-politically correct term for Maggie's mood over the next twenty-four hours is "hyper". Many friends in Liverpool were messaged, as were boyfriend, new friends in Southwell and anyone else in cyberspace who happened to be listening. She bounced into my bedroom at around eleven-thirty that night.

"Mum? Are you asleep?"

"Yes."

She climbed onto the bed, phone in hand. "David has discovered three new species of plant."

"In the rainforest?"

"Yes. And one new type of centipede." She held up her phone for me to see.

"I'm sure that information will be fascinating tomorrow morning."

"Don't you want to know what they're called?"

Ah, the wonders of the information age. Everyone an expert.

"Will they still have the same name in eight hours' time?" I turned over on my pillow, closed my eyes.

"He called the plants scientificy names, but the centipede is called *Luto Puellae*."

My eyes popped open. "What?"

"*Luto Puellae*. Is that Spanish?"

No. It was Latin. *Luto Puellae*. Mud girl. In the spirit of a naturalist adventurer and discoverer, David gave most people and things a Latin nickname. *Luto Puellae* was mine.

Was I insulted he named a centipede after me? That I crossed his mind in the depths of the jungle, a million miles and a million years away?

I pressed that name like a soft, sweet flower into the folds of my heart.

"Can you go to bed now, Maggie?"

"I like David. He's not what I expected. He's normal. I mean, not all celebrityish."

"That's probably because he never wanted to be a celebrity. He just happens to be brilliant at what he does."

"Does he have a thing with Ana Luisa?" she asked, still scrolling through insect pictures on her phone.

"I don't think they're officially together, but they obviously mean a lot to each other. I wouldn't be surprised if a thing happens." My insides crumpled up a little bit.

"Did he ever have a thing with you? I mean he's, like, dead old and everything but he is still pretty hot. He won bachelor of the year once."

*Define thing…*

"No. We were always just friends."

"Good." She paused, feigning indifference. "So you're not going to end up together or anything."

"Haven't we had a conversation about this? I'm off the romantic market for the next five thousand years, aren't I?"

"Yes. But you did go out with a man who smelt your hair at the theatre."

I sat up, fully awake now. "He did what? You mean Carl?"

She nodded. "He leaned forward and smelt it. About three times. Didn't you notice?"

"Of course not! If I had, we would have moved seats. Back to the sofa at home!"

"How could you not notice? Anyway, given your cripplingly woeful starting point, I wouldn't be surprised if you fell for Hot David. But if he's got something going with Ana Luisa, and is way in your friendship zone, I'll stop worrying."

"You have absolutely no need to worry. And please don't call him Hot David."

"Okay. Just checking. I'm going to bed now."

"He smelt my hair?"

"Night, Mum."

# Chapter Eighteen

So lunch was weird: sat around the Big House table surrounded by Ana Luisa's exuberant Christmas decorations, eating roast beef and trying to ignore the tension. David appeared relaxed – playful even. But Ana Luisa dropped things, knocked over the gravy boat, was flustered and distracted, and a sorrowful sickly grey.

With Maggie and Seth loved up at one end of the table, and Arnold making random comments about ancient Egyptian courtship rituals the other (I didn't especially want the lovebirds to hear that Tutankhamun got married at nine, although they may have been put off by his wife also being his sister), it made Henderson Sunday lunches seem almost functional. As soon as we had finished the main course I jumped up, following Ana Luisa into the kitchen with a pile of dirty plates.

"Where shall I put these?"

"What? Oh, anywhere. Dump them on the side here. I don't usually make such a mess cooking dinner."

"Are you okay?"

"I'm fine." She began stacking plates into the dishwasher, but her face crumpled up and she had to stop and close her eyes. I reached over and put my hand on her arm.

"Want to talk about it?"

Ana Luisa straightened up. She dabbed at the corners of her eyes with the edge of a tea towel and smoothed her hair. "No, thank you. Not now. Not when we have pudding still to come." Her smile was tired and trembly. "I am honestly fine."

"Take five minutes. I know where everything is; I can serve pudding. I'll tell them you had a ladder in your tights and went to change them. But you can't go on like this, Ana. You have to tell him how you feel."

"I am not sure he even sees me, Ruth." She sighed.

"How can he not see you?" I replied. "That man sees everybody. And you know he cares about you."

"Maybe. But how can I expect him to love me like a man should love a woman? I have done terrible things, Ruth. The kind of things women in desperate circumstances are sometimes forced to do in order to survive. When he found me, I was not like this. There was a nasty, sticky darkness in me that took a long time, and amazing grace, to wash away. I fear he will always see that ugliness." Ana paused, took a deep breath. "But I've tried. I've really tried. And I don't think I can pretend it is enough any more." She opened the fridge and took out a lemon tart. "Here. And thank you. You are a good friend, Ruth. I am so blessed you came to live near the Big House again."

She gave me a quick hug on her way out. I felt the desperation in her squeeze.

"Ana Luisa?"

"Yes?"

"You do actually have a ladder in your tights."

"I'm glad. I have seen you try to lie before, and you are quite spectacularly bad at it," she said, the sparkle returning to her eyes.

"Go."

She went. Ana Luisa had grown up in violence and poverty, hoisted herself out of a life of degradation and despair, and found the courage and the strength to start again in a strange land. She had survived so much, and now a man was proving her undoing. She had to tell him. How could I not hope he loved her back?

Maggie announced she had homework to do and left with Seth as soon as we had finished eating. Arnold disappeared into his study with the same excuse and Ana Luisa went to lie down, leaving David and me to face the detritus of the table-top.

"Can I help you clear up?" I collected the bowls within reaching distance and stacked them in a clumsy pile.

David thought for a moment, then glanced outside at the December sunshine. "How about a walk instead?"

"Hmm, I don't know. It's freezing out there today."

He squinted at me. "Really? Ruth Henderson wimping out on a walk because it's a bit nippy? You want to come with me to the Antarctic sometime. That's cold."

*Yes, please!*

"Fine." I tried to hide my smile. "But I'm stopping off to change shoes and get my hat. And you have to tell Ana Luisa I wanted to help clear up but you forced me on a walk instead."

We turned left at the bottom of the road, towards the open fields. A route we knew well. After a few minutes of casual conversation, David slowed his pace and put his hand on my arm. His voice was gentle.

"I was gutted when I heard about Fraser," he said, stopping to wait for me to navigate an icy puddle in the centre of the footpath. "It's not the same, of course, but I understand how it feels to lose someone..." His voice trailed off.

"Thanks, David." I remembered the thin, serious boy without a mother.

"What was he like?"

"Fraser?" I paused and took a deep breath. "He worked a lot. Had this super-quick brain that needed to be kept occupied. He liked eating out and old westerns and nice cars." I shrugged. "He tried his best to be a good dad, even working away so much."

"I'm glad he stuck by you. He must have been a really good bloke." He grinned. "Even if I did want to hunt him down and punch his lights out at the time."

"Excuse me, but wouldn't you have been better off shaking his hand, all things considered?" The path widened now, and we walked side by side.

"Well, yeah, but I didn't know how things would turn out then, did I? Chances were high he'd run for the hills."

"I might be a little bit offended by that comment."

"Don't be. It was wishful thinking more than anything. I was young, foolish and heartbroken."

We walked in silence for a while before I replied. "Well, I'm glad you didn't show up and cause trouble. Things were tough enough right then."

He stopped as we reached the end of the field, turning to me as he opened the gate. "Would you mind telling me about it?"

If it had been anyone else, yes, I would have minded. But as we continued our walk, the starlings soaring in the clear sky above, the wood pigeons cooing in the trees, I told him. Not everything, but enough. And by the time we strode back towards the houses, the cars crawling through the frost, the pile of dirty plates and leftovers, for the first time in forever I no longer felt alone.

That evening was the Oak Hill carol service. Excuse me, did I say carol service? Make that crazy family party, with six hundred over-excited guests drunk on Christmas spirit (and possibly, in some cases, a different type of spirit), a carol sing-off between the dads' 'n' lads' choir and the over-sixties lunch club (the overs rocked da house), a pantomime nativity including twenty-five "sheep" from the toddler group pumped full of orange squash, a three-day-old baby with excessive wind and Ellie's horse in a donkey costume (I didn't know what a horse dressed up as a donkey looked like either).

I laughed so hard at Martine's angel costume I snorted. She had an angel throng consisting of twelve bald men, all wearing lashings of glittery blue eye-shadow on one eye, and green on the other. Meat Harris reminded us all what a bully looks like as evil King Herod, and to my secret pride and public embarrassment, my sixty-nine-year-old mother, playing the role of the star in silver chiffon, danced.

She didn't need a costume. For the first time in five months I saw my mother shine. She glowed, sparkled, shimmered and did whatever else it is that stars were created to do. Dad, sat straight as a rod three rows from the back, couldn't take his eyes off her. He had forgotten, I think, the woman he was married to. When she moved, it was no longer arms and legs and muscles and joints and steps and spins. It was beauty, grace, life, light and *passion*. I saw people's mouths drop open. They clutched their hands to their chest as the emotion swelled. Somehow, my fabulous mother expressed the jubilation and the joy of this incredible story better than any words could have done. As the final chords of music faded away, she stood alone in the spotlight and began to speak: "A light thrives in the depths of darkness. It cannot and will not be quenched."

My goodness, those Oak Hillians like to clap.

But the highlight, the absolute highlight, was when Mary-who-was-really-Maggie (if you want a major part in the carol service, try dating the minister's son) clambered off the donkey-who-was-really-a-horse and plonked her bare foot straight into the pile of stinky mess deposited by the donkey/horse during a moment of stage fright two minutes earlier. Maggie not only stepped in it; she skidded, fell and landed in it. On her face.

My heart leapt up my throat and tried to scrabble out of my mouth to get out there and rescue her. To my utter shock and amazement, my troubled, angry daughter did not swear, cry, kick the horse or pick up one of the offending balls of donkey doo-doo and hurl it at someone. She laughed. She picked herself up, aided by her handsome Joseph-who-was-really-Seth, and turned to the congregation. With the perfect balance of wry humour, she flicked at the smear on her cheek and said, "What can you do? I'm fourteen years old and pregnant. My pre-frontal cortex is in bits and my centre of gravity's knocked sideways due to the whole other person growing inside me. Not to mention the conflicting armies of rampaging adolescent versus antenatal hormones. It's incredible I managed not to fall off the donkey. Yet God trusted me, a teenager, to parent the most important person who's ever lived. You might be surprised about that.

"Don't be. I'm not. My mum had me when she was a teenager, and I tell you what, she was awesome then and is even better now. So, if someone can hand me something to wipe this poo off my face, perhaps we can get on with it? I think when I climbed off the donkey my waters broke."

I had become a mother at nineteen years old. Determined to swipe the patronizing smiles off my health visitor's bony face, I had been the most hardworking, well-read, consistent, downright fantastic teenage mum in the whole of Liverpool, if not the universe. I loved fiercely, disciplined fairly and worked my backside off to do right by Maggie. Then my darling daughter's world imploded and at the same time I dropped the motherhood ball. The result was not great. I had been stressed for nearly two years about the possibility that I had helped screw up my daughter forever; that it would take half a lifetime of therapy for her to be able to let go of the poor deal life had thrown her and move on; that at some point during said therapy she would come to appreciate just how much I failed her when she needed me most.

In that moment, with horse manure sliding down her face, wearing her nanny's spare pillow case on her head and a crooked smile, I looked at my beautiful girl and I knew that she would be okay. She was so much more than okay.

I had never been prouder. Sitting next to me, dragged along by threats, bribes and what must surely be a Christmas miracle, Hannah Beaumont said, "I didn't know you were allowed to say poo in church."

I had joined the end of the refreshments queue, humming the tune of "Hark the Herald", when a pair of hands clamped over my eyes from behind. I froze, a great burst of adrenaline whooshing out.

Several names and faces flashed through my brain. I didn't know a single person who would think this was amusing, or an appropriate way to say hello. Wait. Perhaps I did know one.

"Guess who?"

Yep, I recognized that sour, intense breath on my neck. I yanked myself away before he could sniff my hair again.

"Carl."

"Hi, Ruth. Fancy seeing you here."

"I work here, Carl. The chances were quite high I would be at the carol service."

"Here, I got you this." He picked up a cup of coffee from the window-sill beside us. "Black, no sugar. Just how you like it."

Those words slithered down my back. Not in a good way. How did he know how I took my coffee?

"Thanks, that's very kind of you, but I only drink decaf."

He smirked. "You're lively enough, right?"

Bleugh.

He held out the mug, bumping my fist so I was obliged to take hold of it.

"So, are you ready for your first Christmas in Southwell? Got many plans?"

"I don't mean to be rude, Carl. And thank you for the coffee, but I need to find my daughter. Excuse me."

Carl smiled, showing his perfect white teeth. His eyes were blue steel.

"I saved you a five-minute wait in the queue, Ruth. I think you can spare a moment to chat."

The line had shuffled forward, leaving us in a vacuum. Carl planted himself about six inches into my personal space, but I was backed up against the window and couldn't move away without physically pushing past him.

"I have to check my friend. She's elderly and infirm, and hasn't been here before."

"She'll be fine. Someone'll sort her out. You see, this is your problem, Ruth." I wished he would stop saying my name. "Always putting everyone else first, looking after their needs and wants. What about you, Ruth? Who's looking after you? Who's taking care of your needs? Your wants?"

*Help*.

"I wish you would let me take care of you." He murmured this. I felt as though a rattlesnake was coiling itself around my ribs. I was too stricken to reply.

"You didn't answer my question. About Christmas. When are you free?"

"I did say that I wouldn't be spending any more time with you. That still applies. Indefinitely."

"No one has to know." He winked. "It's more fun that way."

"No." I took a deep breath, wished my voice wasn't quaking. "I don't want to see you again, Carl. I'm sorry."

"Excuse me?" His smile became twisted, as though viewed through a broken camera lens. He bent his head really close to mine, and I felt a prickle of genuine fear. "Not even to tell me how sorry you are that your daughter vandalized my car? I hear she's been in a lot of trouble lately. How do you think she would like the police to come knocking on her door on Christmas Eve? You can squeeze me in sometime before then, Ruth. Help to take my mind off how upset I am about it."

I said nothing. For a hideous, horrible moment I thought he was going to move his face that tiny bit closer and kiss me. Instead he burst out laughing.

"Happy Christmas, Ruth."

I became aware of another presence beside me.

"Ruth. Harriet's looking for you. She wants to know if you need a lift home."

"David." I let out his name in a rush of relief.

Carl stepped back, and I was able to switch my gaze to David, holding on to the sight of his face like an anchor in a hurricane. He looked at me for a beat, before turning to Carl.

"We haven't met." He held out his hand. Carl shook the proffered hand, and for a few moments there appeared to be an actual hand-shaking man-tussle of strength. I'm assuming David won. Jungle explorer and all that.

"*Doctor* Carl Barker."

"Carl. I'm…"

"I know who you are." His eyes flickered between David and me, and I could see conclusions forming behind the icy blue. "I didn't know Ruth was friends with the nation's favourite bug lover. Anyway. I need to get on. A ton of paperwork before theatre tomorrow. I'll call you, Ruth."

He slithered away. I leaned back, a little weakly, against the window-sill and let out a shaky sigh.

"Thank you."

David took the mug of undrunk coffee out of my hands and set it on the sill. "You're welcome. Do we need to be worried about him?"

I shook my head. "I don't know. He knows Maggie threw the egg. Threatened to send the police round on Christmas Eve if I didn't go out with him again."

"Nice pulling technique. He must wow the ladies with his charm and finesse."

"Well, hopefully you scared him off. No surgeon wants their fingers crushed in your handshake of intimidation."

"Let me know if he bothers you again," he said, looking me square in the face.

"Right, so you can beat him up for me?" I laughed, unable to meet his eye.

"I'm serious. There's something off about that guy."

"I'm sure another tragic victim will grab the attention of his hero complex soon enough. I can't be the only pathetic female in need of rescuing in town."

David had moved to lean his solid frame against the window-sill next to me. He took hold of my hand – and my heart, lungs and liver did a triple back-flip. Pow!

"Ruth Henderson." I loved it when *he* said my name. "You are one of the least pathetic females I know. That is not the reason Dr Steroid is pursuing you."

"Pursuing. That's a reassuring word. Thanks for that."

*Why?* my heart shouted. *Why do you think I'm worth pursuing, David?*

My hand began to sweat, so I pulled it away. My thoughts careened about like a four-year-old boy at a wedding, so I pulled them away too.

"Where's Ana Luisa? Didn't you sit together?" I craned my neck past the queue of people still lining up for drinks.

"Yep. Which would have been fine, except that Dad decided to join us at the last minute. It was, to put it mildly, awkward."

"Three's company."

"Something like that. I was hoping you might walk home with us, diffuse the tension?"

"I think I probably owe you some tension diffusing. I'll find Mum and let her know. I think Maggie's going back to Seth's, so I'll have to make sure someone can take Hannah."

"Hmmm. Your mother performing an act of kindness to a person in need? What are the chances of that?" He rubbed his chin.

"Don't mock my mother," I said, nudging him gently with my elbow.

"Never."

"I still need to let her know."

"Do you want me to stick with you?" he asked, nudging me back.

*Yes. Hold my hand again. Stick with me forever.*

"No. I'll be fine. I won't go into any empty rooms alone, or take a detour into the spooky basement. You find Ana Luisa." *The woman you actually love, who is currently free to have an actual relationship with you.* "I'll meet you out the front."

It was a clear night. The stars twinkled above us, putting the artificial Christmas lights adorning the houses to shame. The air was crisp, the frost beginning to form a silvery layer on every surface, and behind us the echoes of laughter and badly sung carols drifted through the night. David insisted I link arms with him after my feet skidded out from under me for the third time, and we huddled in each other's body warmth, taking our time, chatting and telling old stories and swapping banter. It was magical. Heartbreaking. My pesky, rebellious feelings so enjoyed his arm in mine; inhaled, too deeply, the faint scent of him – earth and trees and the hint of almonds.

In front of us, I could see Ana Luisa striding along beside Arnold. Behind us Maggie called out goodnight as she turned off the main road towards Seth's. I resolved again to love David as a friend, a brother, as he had always been.

Pah! Who was I kidding? Would somebody please tell that to my feminine urges?

The following day was the Monday before Christmas. I started work at seven, cleaning up the expansive post-carol service mess with the rest of the cleaning team. Martine found me in the upstairs kitchen. She had a blue bauble earring dangling from one ear and a green one from the other. Her stocky frame was covered in a jumper with a nativity design knitted into it: stable, shepherds, wise men, the whole story. Jesus was a pom-pom.

"Here you are, Ruth. Scrubbing sinks."

"Hi, Martine. You were brilliant last night. You and the Martinettes."

"Thank you. That's because I know my strengths and skills, and I use them accordingly to bless those around me. Now, tell me, how many mathematical calculations are required to clean a kitchen?"

"I had to dilute one part bleach in four parts water."

"Don't be smart. Why haven't you handed in that job application yet? The closing date is today. If you choose to blow this opportunity off you'd better have a reason that is piffle-, waffle- and nonsense-free."

I sighed. "Are you just here to badger me, or do you really want to know?"

"What do you think?"

I finished scrubbing the tea stains off the draining board while collecting my thoughts. Martine huffed and hummed impatiently behind me until I told her that if she wanted the truth she needed to give me a moment to figure out what that was. When I was done, I took a seat on a stool and tried to explain.

"I didn't want to move to Southwell. It was a desperate last resort. To me, it was full of unpleasant memories I wanted to keep buried. It felt like I had failed. Because I had. I especially didn't want to live with my parents again. Coming home was a temporary, emergency measure. Not a long-term thing. Applying for the job is like accepting I'm building a life here; that we're staying. I don't want to let you down by packing it in in sixth months' time when I've saved enough to move away or back to Liverpool."

"Hogwash! If you really wanted to leave you'd take the job and get saving. We've been over this."

"I'm not sure about the church bit. I'm not exactly a good Christian, Martine," I said, staring at my feet.

"That's what grace is for." Martine pointed one finger at me. Her voice was uncharacteristically soft. "Have you stopped running yet?"

I squirmed. That question made me want to run.

"That's what this is about. Running away. For fifteen years. Maybe longer. Aren't you tired of running, Ruth? Aren't you exhausted to your very bones?"

I was. I was exhausted to my very bones.

"Isn't it impossible to think, to dream, to be free, when you are running so hard?"

It was. I wasn't free. I didn't dream.

"Is it time to stop?"

I was too tired to think. But I didn't need to any more. Right there, in a half-cleaned kitchen, in a pair of rubber gloves and a disposable apron, I decided to stop running.

My eyes and nose stopped running sometime later.

I applied for a new job.

Then I phoned up Vanessa Jacobs and handed in my resignation. She said, "Suit yourself."

# Chapter Nineteen

Five o'clock, Christmas Eve. I sat peeling potatoes in the kitchen, job number one hundred and forty-two on the list of three thousand and ten jobs Mum had left me to complete while she zipped around town, like Santa on speed, dropping off Christmas hampers to struggling families. Maggie was slobbing in front of a Christmas film. Dad was out. Nobody asked where.

The doorbell rang. I yelled at Maggie a couple of times to answer it before giving up, wiping my hands on a tea-towel and hurrying to open the door. On the porch sat a small box. Now, it was Christmas Eve, a night when all manner of magical happenings was possible, but I strongly suspected that the box, even had it managed to work its own way to our front doorstep, had neither the cognitive function nor the required digits to ring the bell.

Scanning the dark driveway, the shadowy garden reflecting dim flickers of the television through the bay window, the inky street cast in a faint, multi-coloured glow from the Christmas lights strung up on every other house and various trees along the roadside, I saw no fleeting figure scurrying away in a red and white suit. The sky, though clear, carried no rushing reindeer pulling a supernatural sleigh.

The world outside the warmth of the house was cold and ominously silent. Empty, save for this uninvited visitor on the doorstep.

I picked it up and carried it into the living room. Maggie paused the film.

"Is that for me?"

"I don't know yet. I found it in the porch."

"Ooh. Open it, then! No, wait! What does the label say?"

The box was about the size of a small book. It had been professionally wrapped – as in, wrapped up by someone in a shop. A silver ribbon tied in a curly bow secured a matching label in place. I held it out to Maggie.

"You open it."

"No chance. It might be a bomb or something."

"Yes, that's very likely. It was probably one of the Southwell terrorists campaigning against non-organic vegetables, track-suits in the town centre and incoming scallie-hooligans with offensive haircuts."

As I spoke, a shudder rippled through me. Christmas Eve: my deadline to accept a date from Dr Carl. I dropped the parcel as though it really was a bomb.

"What?" Maggie jumped, catching my jitters.

"Nothing. It's fine. I'm sure it's fine." Reaching down, I flicked over the label to find it covered in small writing. I had to kneel down on the carpet to read it properly. It said:

> *Ruth – to let you know I am thinking about you,*
> *and make sure you think about me. You deserve*
> *something special xxx*

The box contained a slinky gold bracelet. Some stones looking suspiciously like diamonds twinkled along one side. Maybe I did deserve something special, but without meaning to sound ungrateful, that bracelet was not it.

I knew who had given me this hideous piece of jewellery. It smelt of creepiness and anger, and the need to dominate.

I put it back on the doorstep. Perhaps a hungry vagrant would trade it in for a slap-up Christmas dinner.

Perhaps a magpie would swoop down and take it away.

Perhaps he was watching, and would get the hint.

Ho ho ho. This was not a merry Christmas.

It was the pink jumper.

The previous Christmas had slipped past almost unnoticed in our haze of grief. Maggie and I felt a little like naughty schoolgirls as we stayed at home rather than make the annual trek to the icy Dragon's lair. We spent the whole day in our pyjamas, ate chocolate for breakfast, bacon cobs for lunch and nachos for dinner. We read, watched girlie films, pretended we were having a day created out of indulgence not scarcity, Skyped Mum, phoned my sisters and left a message on my ex-not-quite-mother-in-law's phone. We cried, of course, and lit a candle to remember Fraser. It was quiet, lazy, and oh so gentle to our frail and fragile emotions.

Fast forward a year and Christmas had gulped down six double espressos. A noisy, overstuffed whoosh of family and food and frenzy, clamour and clatter and the clash of all those issues which simmered under the surface for three hundred and sixty-four days of the year but suddenly found the time and the tension to make themselves heard.

Esther and her family had lunch with us, planning to whizz off to Max's parents in Derbyshire in time for tea. It was a ridiculous, over-the-top, headache-inducing lunch; including nine different vegetables and six desserts no one had any room for. The whole kitchen felt like an oven, and having washed up four zillion plates and bowls and serving dishes, Dad and Maggie declared that they needed to get changed. Maggie returned in her pyjamas. Dad wore the pink jumper.

My dad was a ballroom champion. He spent many years in pastels, usually combined with sparkles, satin and occasionally feathers. He could handle pink. So I knew something was up when Mum turned as white as the fake snow sprayed across the living room windows. She sat bolt upright in her chair, eyes round and wild.

"What is that, Gilbert?" Her voice, crisp and clipped.

"What?" Dad looked behind him, feigning confusion.

"Don't. Play. The fool. With. Me."

Everybody froze. Even Timothy stopped bashing his new spaceship into the enemy base.

Dad looked his wife right in the eyes. "It's a present. I thought I'd wear my new Christmas jumper on Christmas Day. Do you have a problem with that?"

Mum let out a bark of hysterical laughter. "Do I have a problem? That you chose to wear a jumper given to you by another woman? In our house, in front of our family, on Christmas Day?" She stood up. "YES, I HAVE A PROBLEM! Why aren't you wearing the jumper I gave you? You could at least have had the decency to save that one for another day!"

"I like this one." Dad narrowed his eyes. He was hopping mad. "You can't control me, Harriet. I am a grown man. I will wear whatever jumper I like."

"Even if it hurts and humiliates me, your wife? Even if it dishonours our marriage?"

"What are you talking about? It's a jumper, for pity's sake!"

"It is not just a jumper, Gilbert, and you know it!"

"So? What – I'm not allowed to have any friends now? Or only friends that you've picked out for me? Ruby is a lovely woman."

"DON'T SAY HER NAME IN THIS HOUSE! She is an intruder. A wedge between us, and a home-wrecker! An ugly old floosy in a pink anorak to match your inappropriate jumper!"

Dad took a deep breath, then let it out slowly. He shook his head. "That was mean, Harriet, and totally uncalled for. In the fifty years I've known you, you have never been mean. Did it cross your mind that I might want to wear a jumper given to me by someone who actually appreciates me and, amazingly, thinks I'm doing all right as I am?"

He left the room, pulling his coat off the rack before striding out of the house, slamming the front door behind him. Mum collapsed onto the chair behind her, both hands clutching her head. She gasped. "He's gone to her. We haven't had the cake yet. What will I say when Lydia phones?" She looked up at us. *What if he doesn't come back?*

At some point during the wee small hours, he did come back. The following morning Dad was at the breakfast table, the atmosphere as thick as his cinnamon marmalade. He and Mum set off soon after to visit Lydia for three days, leaving Maggie and me fraught and anxious and hoping desperately that three days together, without pink jumpers or the giver of pink jumpers, might offer the breathing room they needed to remember how much they loved each other.

Maggie walked round to spend the day with Seth, leaving me to clear up the remaining seasonal detritus and enjoy the luxury of the house to myself. My phone rang, just as I prepared to step into the bath – an unrecognized number. I went into the bedroom to answer it.

"Hello?"

"Didn't you like your present?"

My insides turned to water. I couldn't think of a single thing to say.

Carl laughed. "It's all right – I'm joking. I should have checked if Maggie was in. I do respect that you want us to be a secret for now. Anyway, it's cool, no hard feelings. I'll keep it safe."

"There is no us."

"It's okay, Ruth. I'm a patient man. I can wait."

"Don't. I don't want you to wait. I don't want to have a relationship with you, Carl. Not now, not ever. Please stop calling, and buying me presents."

Silence.

"Do you understand? This has nothing to do with Maggie. There is never going to be anything between us. I want to be clear." All I heard was the blood thundering in my ears. It seemed easier standing up to him on the phone, but I still had to grit my teeth to prevent them from clacking together in time to my fear.

"Perfectly." He hung up.

I stared at my phone, unable to move. The bath water went tepid.

New Year's Eve. My parents had returned from Lydia's in a state of uneasy truce, involving pointed, polite comments and frosty glances. So, when Mum asked me to accompany them to "Southwell's Got Talent" I saw the anguish behind her eyes and said yes. We walked down to the Minster school building with Arnold, Ana Luisa and David. Maggie spent the whole time peppering David with questions about the fantastical celebrity lifestyle she was convinced he led, despite the fact that all his time off had clearly been spent in Southwell, hanging out with his dad and old school friends. This allowed Ana Luisa to scuttle up beside me, her eyes gleaming, cheeks glowing in the snap of the winter air.

"I have made my decision, Ruth." She glanced backwards at the rest of the party before clutching my arm with her stripy mitten. "I cannot endure to set one foot into another year without telling him how I feel."

"Wow. You're going to say something?"

"I am going to sing something. I have entered the competition. It is time! One way or another, tonight I will know if my feelings are requited."

"That's incredibly brave. Are you sure you want to do it like this – in front of all those people?"

"It is the perfect opportunity. I cannot change my mind or back out at the last second. And I refuse to any longer be ashamed of my love!"

I pressed my hand on top of hers, where it still gripped my arm. "Well, I wish you all the luck in the world, Ana. I really hope it goes well."

The school hall was buzzing. Fifteen round banqueting tables dressed in green and gold surrounded a square dance floor. A huge pine tree twinkled in the corner, fairy lights crisscrossing the walls and ceiling. Four judges' chairs and a table sat waiting to one side of the stage, and over a hundred festive men, women and children topped up their drinks and bagsied the best seats in preparation to discover if Southwell did in fact possess any talent.

My parents, brittle smiles in place, chose a table near the back, gesturing for me to take the empty seat between them. The lights dimmed, the introductory music started and our hosts for the evening, two young teachers I hadn't seen before, bounded onto the stage. We welcomed the judges, who ranged in age from eleven to eighty, and the show got underway.

Did Southwell have talent? Some did. Some not so much, but what they lacked in skill they made up for in enthusiasm. After an hour of dance groups, singers and musicians, a hilarious stand-up comedian and a magic trick that nearly ended up in A&E, Ana Luisa took her place centre stage.

All eyes were fixed on this gorgeous woman wearing a figure-hugging purple dress, as she scanned the audience. "My name is Ana Luisa, and I am going to perform a love song." She stuck her chin in the air and spread her arms wide. It was time.

"And what made you choose this particular song, Ana Luisa?" the youngest judge asked.

"It was inspired by a very special person. A person who gave me a new start when I was not doing so good. I am choosing this song because it tells how I am really feeling, deep inside me."

Half the heads in the room swivelled over to the table where David sat. The other half, who may not have known Ana Luisa or the man who saved her but still thought this was the most exciting thing to happen so far, tried to figure out who they were looking at. I was too far back to see David's face, but I did see him take a long drink from his beer bottle as the music began to play.

Ana Luisa did not have a great singing voice. But – wow. She sang Bob Dylan's "Feel My Love", and not a single person listening doubted the fact that she would crawl down the avenue and go to the ends of the earth for you, whoever "you" was. We did, indeed, feel her love. Nobody cared that she was crying by the end of the first line. By the end of the song we all cried with her.

The applause was rapturous. Most of the room were on their feet. I looked for David. His seat was empty. I hoped this was not what it looked like. Ana Luisa bowed, and punched the air, before running off the stage. I went to find her, but seeing Lois hurrying on in front of me, took a detour to the ladies' instead, hoping to gather my wits and calm down a little.

I splashed cold water on my face a few times, and blotted it with a towel. The door swung open and Mum walked in. In the harsh strip lighting she looked older, her eyes rimmed with purple shadow, her skin dry and dull.

"Are you all right, Mum?"

She rummaged through her clutch-bag for a lipstick. "This is the first year your father and I haven't danced."

I moved two steps closer to give her a hug. "I'm so sorry. I wish I could help."

"I feel blue, Ruth. Blue like a tiny boat bobbing around in the middle of a vast, empty ocean. All I can see is blue." She let out a long, shuddering sigh. "And Dad has sailed away and left me here."

"You have to remember, Dad is not the enemy," I said, with all the conviction I could muster. "The ocean between you is." My tone softened and I reached out for my mum. "Your anger is only pushing him further and further away, and you know where he'll end up going."

"I know that," she said, pressing her hand over her eyes. "But I am so very cross and sore I can barely control myself. I never expected this. I never for one second imagined we could end up like this. Maybe that's the problem. We should have seen the signs, protected our love better."

"You haven't ended up anywhere yet. You can still get through this if you work together."

We held each other for a long time, my mum and me. For the first time in forever, I gave her comfort, words of wisdom;

offered strength and hope. Mother and daughter switched roles inside that embrace.

"I love you, Mum. You are amazing."

"I love you too, Ruth. Will you take me home?"

"No. I think Dad should do it. Go and see in the New Year with your man."

I struggled to regain my party spirit after watching them shuffle out of the door. Once the last act had finished, the winner was announced and the dancing began, I decided to walk home. I bumped into Ana Luisa and Lois in the car-park.

Not a good sign.

"What's happened?"

Ana Luisa shook her fist at the sky. "Pah! Nothing happened – that's what! He…he…he…"

Lois grimaced. "He told her what a lovely song, and whoever it was for was a very lucky man."

"What?" I didn't believe this. There was no way in a zillion years, in any way, shape or form, that David would not have known who that song was for. Even if he did not, after all, feel – or want to feel – Ana Luisa's love, he should have told her, with as much kindness, grace and tact as the situation deserved. Why wasn't he out here, in the car-park, with the woman who had just bared her soul before him so publicly? I felt a rustle of anger, confusion and frustration that this wasn't all sewn up and sorted.

"You have to confront him then," I said. "Be even more obvious. Tell it to his face. Give him no option to misunderstand."

"Exactly what I said." Lois clutched Ana Luisa's hand. "It will be *unbearable* to leave things like this – it's worse than before. Go for it, girl. I'm right behind you."

"Are you coming, Ruth? I need as many friends as possible to catch me when I fall on my face."

I shook my head. "Lois'll be more than enough for you. I'm not feeling great. I'm going to walk home, clear my head. Lois, can you bring Maggie home later?"

"No problem. Feel better, Ruth. And Happy New Year!"

I walked up Nottingham Road, turning the long way home onto Westgate. Passing the glow of floodlights illuminating the striking Minster, I reached the centre of town. Here the pub on the corner thumped out seventies disco as various revellers swayed along the pavements. As I waited to cross the road onto Queen Street, a slick, sleek, sinister black car pulled up alongside me. Before it had reached a complete stop, I began hurrying down the main road in the opposite direction. Despite being the town centre, it was a narrow road with no room to park, and the car already held up a taxi behind it. The driver had no choice but to keep on moving away from me. I waited until it disappeared around the corner, and ran across the road up an alleyway that led into a car-park. Sprinting, grateful for the strength produced during four months' hard graft with a mop and bucket, I ducked between the rows of cars, making for the footpath at the far side. That would lead me up past the primary school field and to the top of the hill only two streets away from home.

I didn't make it. The last car in the row sat idling, engine on, weird jazz music blaring. As I scurried past, the window hummed open. I tried to ignore it, head down, moving forward. Behind me, I heard the door close. Too frightened to turn left onto the footpath, where I would be flanked by overgrown trees and the empty field, I instead moved right, back onto the main road. It felt like only a second before the car pulled up beside me again. Carl crawled along, keeping pace with my frantic strides.

"Ruth, it's me. Didn't you recognize the car?"

I said nothing. Kept moving. It was a five-minute brisk walk back home. Thank goodness Mum and Dad would be waiting for me.

"Ruth? Get in. I'll give you a lift."

He wasn't going to go away. Against my better judgment, I looked across at him. "I'd rather walk."

"I can't let you walk home alone. Let me give you a lift."

"No. Thanks."

My eyes were back on the road, but I could hear the smile in his voice. "Suit yourself. But I'm not leaving you out here on your own."

The window hummed back up, but Carl continued crawling along at walking pace next to me. If I sped up, he increased his speed to match mine. I knew if I turned around, he would loop back again and find me. Three minutes to home. If I tried something else – running off, hiding somewhere – he might get out of the car and come after me. I kept walking, head down, lungs heaving, mind racing. It didn't feel like a coincidence that he had spotted me walking home. Even though, as I hurried into the cul-de-sac, already fishing in my pocket for my key, he beeped his horn twice and sped away, I knew something for certain, with a cold dread that wrapped around my windpipe and stole my breath.

Carl Barker was not going anywhere.

# Chapter Twenty

New Year's Day, Ana Luisa came round to cut Maggie's hair. A strange day to do it, but Maggie had a statement to make, and when fourteen-year-old girls have something to say, it's now, yesterday or never, and the world had better stop what they're doing and listen.

I found them in the kitchen. One glance and I knew.

"You told him."

"I did." She looked up from her snipping, and I swear a thousand peacock butterflies flew out of her smile and did a lap around the kitchen.

"At the party?"

"Yes. At the party, walking home from the party, after the party. We brought the party home with us!"

I filled the kettle and switched it on. Took three mugs out of the cupboard and carefully measured out scoops of coffee into the cafetiere. Lifted Mum's best jug off the dresser and poured milk into it. Found the sugar bowl and a spoon. Sucked in a deep breath. Patted the top of my chest a few times.

"So? Tell us everything."

"It was nearly midnight, and I knew it was now or never. I asked him to dance. He said no, about four times, but I was a woman on a mission! I dragged him onto that dance floor. I could not be stopped. And, Ruth, I *danced*. As if my life depended on it, which I think it almost did. The last time I danced for a man, hmmm, my life depended on it that time also. But in a different way. I have danced many times for oily men with sweaty hair, bad breath and worse morals. I tell you, many times I thought I would never want to dance with a man again.

"But this time, girls, I was not dancing for my life, my livelihood. I danced for love! And I told him that when he found me I did not know what a woman was. But he gave me a safe place to heal and to forget, and he makes me happy to be a woman for the first time. To be a woman who is loved by a man."

Maggie's eyes were wide. "You told him that?"

"I did."

"What did he say?"

"Not a lot. He was very shocked, I think. And a little intimidated by my sexy moves. But then the clock struck midnight, and while everybody cheered and hugged, I grabbed his face between my two hands and kissed him."

"And he kissed you back."

"Oh, yes, Maggie. Once he had remembered what to do, he kissed me back."

Ana Luisa had to stop cutting to twirl about the kitchen in rapturous delight.

"And then he walked me home, and we talked and talked, and he held my hand the whole way. A man has never, ever held my hand before. It made me feel like that old, degraded, cheapened husk of Ana Luisa was finally, really dead. She has been dying for two years now, getting weaker and fainter, but last night she breathed her last." She resumed snipping, no doubt itching to get finished and back to her new man.

"And this morning, when I got up, there were flowers on the kitchen table. We made breakfast together and watched the sunrise, and the whole time he never let go of my hand. I tell you, Ruth, you need to get yourself a man like this someday."

"Maybe someday."

Maybe not.

"Ta-da!"

Maggie was finished. Gone were her red, orange and yellow autumn streaks. Left behind was a head covered in one-inch spikes of mid-brown.

I tried to mumble something about how it made her eyes look bigger.

"Chill, Mum. I look like I sold my hair to pay for the upkeep of my secret love child. It'll grow. And it'll get better. It's time to embrace my new start. No more hiding, or wishing I was somewhere else or someone else. No more crying in the bathroom because I'm so sick and tired of being me."

She did that?

"Sometimes we have bad hair days. Or bad days. Or bad years. But hair grows again. I'm over it. Bad hair won't decide my life. Or stop me deciding that I'm going to be happy. And it could be worse."

Could it? And, incidentally, who was this wise woman and what had she done with my daughter?

"Some people don't have hair," Maggie continued.

"That's true," I nodded.

Ana Luisa frowned. "Do you hate my haircut, Maggie?"

"It's not pretty, Ana Luisa. But that's the whole point. I love it. You can go back to the Big House and hold hands with your new boyfriend now."

I spent the next few days as a robot: wading through piles of information on debt advice and administration, helping Mum help everybody else, watching endless repeats of cheesy American sitcoms. Anything to stop thinking about the romance unfolding next door. I avoided windows, stayed inside, took my animal posters off the bedroom wall and replaced them with photographs of Maggie.

The first Saturday of the New Year, I woke in the middle of the night to the sound of my phone ringing. Lurching out of bed, knocking the lamp on my chest of drawers to the floor, I fumbled through the pockets of discarded clothes until I found it. A ringing phone at three o'clock in the morning was one of two possibilities. Either my sister Miriam calling from Australia, who after twelve years is still seemingly incapable of working out the time difference, or an emergency.

"Hello?"

No answer.

"Hello? Miriam?"

I waited another few seconds; was about to hang up when I heard a rustle down the line.

"Hello?"

I hung up. Registered that the caller had blocked their number. Sat on my bed for a few minutes as the coil of dread in my stomach uncurled itself a little, stretched and settled back down again.

I added a third possibility to the list of middle-of-the-night callers. A sick, scary man who did not take rejection well.

The next night, my phone rang at one-thirty, three-fifteen, three-twenty and five. I should have turned it off, but I needed to know.

Monday, Tuesday – I lay in bed awake for hours waiting, but no more calls.

Wednesday afternoon, the day before I started my new job, someone knocked at the door. I answered it in holey jeans and a saggy sweater. David stood grinning on the doorstep.

"Hi."

"Hi, David," I answered, forcing myself to look at him.

"I'm off again in a couple of days, so I need to store up some calories and reckoned a few slices of your mum's cake should do it. Are you busy?"

"Um… I'm trying to slog through a six-inch file on church procedure and policy before tomorrow."

*What are you doing here?*

"Sounds like you could do with a break, then."

*This can't be a good idea. Where's Ana Luisa?*

He ran his hands over his hair – neatly cropped. I hated that it stabbed me in the gut to know who had carefully cut it.

"Okay. The truth is, I needed to get out of the love nest for a few hours. It's driving me crazy."

"What?"

"Way too much holding hands and soppy grins and darling and sweetheart and I love yous. It's all very nice, don't get me wrong, but I'm beginning to feel slightly nauseous."

Oh no. Poor Ana Luisa. He felt nauseous?

"Oh. Right, well I suppose…"

"And my dad? I know we're both adults and all that, but it's still weird." David shook his head.

"Yes. It must be."

"Still, forty-eight hours and they can have the place to themselves, run about playing kiss-chase as much as they like."

"Sorry?" I was now slightly confused. "Who can play kiss-chase?"

David furrowed his brow. "Ana and Dad. Who else would I be talking about?"

"Ana and Arnold? Ana and *Arnold*!"

Leaning onto the doorframe in order to remain upright, I tried to catch my breath, but the clanging in my ears got in the way. As I fought to regain control of my vital functions, David stood and watched me, hands in back pockets, his face neutral. Standing up straight again, I decided that, in these exceptional circumstances, dishonesty was the best policy.

"Sorry. I haven't eaten yet today. I came over all dizzy for a moment." I tried a quirky, duh-what-a-silly-mare-I-am smile. He didn't return it.

"Coffee then, and cake. I'll make it, you sit down." He strode past me into the kitchen, providing a much needed minute to pull myself together. *Ana Luisa and Arnold! It was Arnold! Arnold loved Ana Luisa! David was nauseous!*

We sipped our coffee at the table, accompanied by white chocolate and hazelnut brownies.

"So, where are you off to this time?" I couldn't stop smiling. It was all I could do not to burst into song.

"South Africa. For eight weeks. Then possibly a stop-off in Egypt. I'll be back by Easter."

"Plenty of time for the honeymoon period to have cooled down in the Big House." *Arnold!*

He nodded. "You've lost weight again."

"Excuse me?"

"What's up?"

I pondered the flower pattern on the tablecloth for a moment. Figured out whether to feign offence, outrage or denial. If anybody else had asked, I might have given it a go. But David knew me. He knew the classic symptoms of me being stressed out. And besides, I was basking in the soft glow of him having noticed.

"Apart from the joy of living with my parents and having front row seats to the floundering of their marriage, my – shall we say *challenging* – daughter and tenuous financial circumstances?"

"You had all those problems a month ago. Since then, you've got a new job and Maggie is doing much better. What's really up?"

I picked at the last few crumbs on my plate. "Carl Barker."

David went very still. I saw the muscles tense in his forearm as he gripped the mug.

"He's still bothering you?"

"I don't know." I told him, briefly, about the present on the doorstep, the kerb-crawling and the phone calls. David swore under his breath.

"I have no proof the calls are from him. And really, buying me a gift and making sure I get home safe are hardly crimes."

"He's stalking you, Ruth. Why are you making excuses for him?"

"Uh – because I'm terrified?" My jaw began trembling uncontrollably, my eyes filling with tears.

"Okay, it's all right." David reached over and took hold of my hand. "You're taking this seriously. That's good. Have you told your parents?"

I shook my head.

"You need to do that. In case they see him lurking around. Keep a record of any hang-up phone calls, or other contact. And for goodness' sake, Ruth, try not to go walking about by yourself after dark, will you?"

He pushed the chair back and reached over, wrapping me up inside his big, broad chest as I cried. I clutched on to the folds of his T-shirt and inhaled great lungfuls of his earthy, woody, almond smell. He stroked my hair, resting his chin on the top of my head, and I was seventeen again. Full of secret yearnings and whizzing hormones. Was it wrong to pretend to cry a bit longer and prolong the hug?

A door slammed above us, and Maggie's Dr Marten boots thudded down the stairs. She crashed into the kitchen just as I pulled myself up out of David's arms. She stopped for a moment, then laughed with relief.

"For a hideous second there I thought you were with a bloke! Hi, David."

"Duly noted: Maggie does not consider me a bloke."

"Oh – you know what I mean. You don't count. You're not after my mum." She grabbed a bag of crisps and an apple, and stuffed them into her rucksack. "I'm off to Hannah's. We're going to sort through the rest of the jewellery in her box, see if anything's worth donating to a museum. Bye. Bye, David. Bring me something mysterious back from Africa."

She left, and David swigged back the rest of his coffee. Maggie's entrance had been a sharp slap back to reality. I was not seventeen; I was a mother with a damaged child. Two months without David suddenly seemed like a very good idea. Maybe he would come home married to a stunning South African naturalist. Maybe by then a miracle would have occurred and I would be living on the other side of town. Maybe. I hoped so. I tried to hope so, anyway.

We said goodbye on the doorstep. David looked carefully at me. "So you thought Ana Luisa and me, then?"

"What?" A big, juicy blush flooded my face.

"You thought Ana Luisa and I had got together. And when you realized the truth you nearly fell over."

"No. That's not what happened! I was surprised. Arnold must be twice her age, at least."

He leaned in close to me. I felt the warmth of his gentle breath on my burning cheek. "Because I care about both you and your daughter, I am not after you, Ruth Henderson, right at this very moment. I have been waiting for you most of my life, and I can wait a little longer. However, know this: I will think about you every hour of every day for the next two months, and picturing your face when you realized I was not in love with Ana Luisa will bring me back here as fast as is humanly possible. I'm going to be here the second you are ready. I'm not messing it up this time."

With that, he turned and walked back down the path. I sat on my doorstep, too stunned to do anything but laugh and tremble and marvel and pinch myself until I saw Mum's car skidding around the corner of the cul-de-sac.

Things were beginning to turn a very gradual corner between Maggie and Hannah. The hat box had proved to be a treasure trove of a life that Maggie found fascinating and hideous at the same time. Boarding school, polo matches, winter balls. The hat-box world had revolved around catching the right husband. Hannah had never worked, even after the count left her, instead spending all her time managing the household, organizing social events and trying to keep herself as attractive as possible.

Maggie, horrified that someone actually still thought a woman belonged in the home, resolved to prove that she could hold her own with any male. I could not have dreamt up a better way to get her head in her books, homework done, if I tried.

That Wednesday, she came home and stomped into the living room, plonking herself on the sofa next to me.

"I can't stand it!"

Oh dear. I closed the document I was reading and straightened my spine.

"I thought things were going better."

"Not that!"

I raised my eyebrows.

Maggie waved her hands about. "The whole thing. Hannah. Her awful life. She does *nothing*, Mum. And I mean nothing. Her life is pointless, and unbelievably boring and sad. All she does is watch TV and read the paper and wait for the district nurse or home help to come, or sit and feel depressed about her past. She has no friends. One of her sons phoned her up at Christmas and she told me the *entire conversation* about six times. I can't stand it!" She got up and began pacing around, waving her hands about some more. "Look at Nanny and Pop! Look at the difference. It's like Hannah has given up on life and is waiting for it to end. Her whole existence has been so meaningless and shallow she doesn't even know how bad it is." She stopped prowling and looked at me.

"And what will they say at her funeral? Stories about when she was a teenager and went to some posh parties? Or won a beauty competition? How she snagged an impressive husband? You could sum up her last fifty years in one sentence: husband left, got old and ill. We have to do something!"

Maggie wanted Hannah to join U3A like Dad. I could see why, and agreed it could benefit Hannah tremendously, but getting her along to anything involving people, activities, going outside... it would take some doing. And I wasn't sure if U3A could handle Hannah Beaumont.

"What about the lunch club at Oak Hill? That might be a better place to start. I'll see if I'm free to pick her up. If not, I'm sure Nanny would give her a lift."

"I'll ask her on Saturday. It's not like she's going to have anything better to do."

That Friday was the first girls' night of the new year, postponed a week due to the holidays. It was the Big House's turn to host, and the huge old dining-room table groaned under the weight of Ana Luisa's Mexican take-away.

The evening was, of course, dominated by talk of the new romance. Ana Luisa floated about on a cloud of dreamy rapture, and it took a severe reprimand from Emily to stop her making excuses to knock on the study door.

We didn't mind. We were thrilled for her.

The Big House felt strangely empty. I stole secret peeks at the photographs of David and let my heart flutter. He was thinking of me. I thought about him too.

I started to settle into my new job – completing a day's formal debt counselling training and getting stuck into a new software package designed to simplify the church finances. However, Monday morning Martine asked if I would show the replacement cleaner the ropes.

"Dorothy!"

"Hello, Ruth." Dorothy looked like a different woman. The boulder of shame and worry had fallen off her shoulders. She was still wan and worn, but there was a steel in her eye that surprised me.

"How fantastic to see you! How are things?"

"Things are going good, thanks, Ruth. Not great, but good. I've got my budget sorted and all those bills and letters – Martine took them away and fixed them. I'll be debt free in two years! And what with all the stress gone, I started to feel so much better Martine asked me to apply for this job. And I got it! I can't tell you how good it feels to be working again."

"I'm so pleased for you, Dorothy. You look great." I meant it. I was thrilled for her. But it felt as though a baby crocodile had hatched in my guts when I considered what unpleasant opportunities this might present to her son.

I was on my lunch break, eating apple and parsnip soup in the café, when she came to find me again.

"I'm done then, Ruth. I'll stick this lot in the outside bin and I'm off."

"Okay, see you soon."

She disappeared down the back corridor just before the glass door to the café opened and Carl swung in. His eyes scanned the half-empty room, and short of scrambling under the table, there was no way to avoid them landing on me. He grinned, and ambled over.

"Ruth. Fancy seeing you here. Happy New Year." Mr Normal.

"Hi, Carl." I pretended to study the sheet of paper in front of me, hoping he couldn't hear the hammering in my chest.

"I heard about the new job. Congratulations! You're moving up in the world."

"Thanks." I didn't look up.

"So, how's it going? How are you? Seems like ages since we've talked."

*Really? Is that because all your phone calls are silent ones?*

"I have to get back to work."

I cleared the half-finished soup over to the serving hatch, and shoved the paper and my water bottle into my bag with quaking fingers, my appetite vanished. I felt discomfited being rude to what appeared to be a polite man making friendly conversation. But as I hurried out of the door into the foyer, he moved right behind me.

"What a happy coincidence, Mum getting a job at the same place as you. I'll be picking her up most days from now on – you know, supporting her efforts to get back on her feet. So we'll be seeing a lot more of each other. It'll be like we're dating again."

I couldn't help it. Running into the office I slammed the door shut behind me and leaned against it, scrunching my eyes closed, trying to shake off the prickly feeling that squirmed across my skin like a plated millipede. And now he had invaded my wonderful new job – tainted it with his poisonous promise. I would have been angry, if only I wasn't so darn afraid.

Over the next few weeks, a pattern began to emerge. Dorothy worked Mondays, Wednesdays and Fridays. On those mornings, my blood pressure would start to rise as the clock ticked towards lunchtime. I hid in my office, found errands to run, took extended toilet breaks. But Carl was an expert stalker. He would show up early to "grab a drink", or be "held up at work" and turn up late. He popped in at the end of the day, as Dorothy had mislaid her purse again, or to double check the date of an event he'd spotted on the notice-board. Most of the other people in the building were bowled over by this charming, thoughtful young man. Only Martine kept a dubious distance. Perhaps in memory of the fake gun, Carl made no effort to convince her to do otherwise.

Maybe three or four times a week, the silent calls returned. There could be six calls one after the other in the middle of the day, or three staggered at hourly intervals through the night. I changed my number after the first week, but two days later they started again. I turned my phone off during the night, but the daytime calls intensified as a result, and it didn't stop the number of missed calls showing up in the morning when I switched it on again.

I could sense myself becoming jittery, paranoid. I saw flashy black cars everywhere, glimpses of spiky-haired men out of the corner of my eye when I did my shopping, heard footsteps on the pavement only to turn and find no one there. I felt safe nowhere, half out of my mind, doubting myself when I did bump into Carl and he came across as so respectful and pleasant. The worry whittled me back to a bag of bones in only a month. I considered resigning, going back to Liverpool, taking Maggie out of school and visiting Miriam in Australia. But the debt monster still reigned, trapping me in my present circumstances. And besides, I felt terrified that moving job, house or even continent would not be enough to shake this predator off my tail. I was being hunted.

Maggie had failed in her efforts so far to get Hannah "a life". The excuses for avoiding any sort of group, club or activity aimed at older people ranged from being too tired, too young, too ill, having too many appointments and the meetings being too boring.

It became a personal challenge to find Hannah an activity she couldn't refuse. "She won't go to groups involving food because of her dodgy intestines, or anything without men because it reminds her of boarding school. And now she says she won't go unless I go too, so it can't be a U3A group or one for retired people. As if anything could be worse than sitting at home all day! It's like she's mummified in her own misery."

I shrugged. "You need to stop thinking of her as a project, and remember she's a woman under all that stubborn bluster. Once upon a time Hannah Beaumont knew how to be sociable, to let go and have fun. Just because she's elderly doesn't mean she suddenly likes knitting or bridge. What did she love when she was younger? What made her feel alive and beautiful? That's what you need to find. Then, make it so irresistible she can't refuse."

"Mum. You're a genius."

"So my mother tells me."

The next Saturday, she had it.

"Where's Nanny?" She hurtled into the living room, where I sat huddled on the sofa with a book, trying to hide from the world and all its stalkers.

"Shopping. Did it go all right today?"

"Yes," she yelled back at me, already halfway out of the door. "Pop. POP!"

"He's out too. Can I help?"

"No. Urgh! This is so annoying. Why are people always in your face bothering you, then when you actually want them they're out doing shopping or – where's Pop? Not with Booby Ruby?"

"No. Not on a Saturday. He's agreed to no one-on-one meeting up with female friends. And you really shouldn't call her that," I added, a picture of self-restraint.

"Oh. So that's why he's been moping around the house like a kicked cat."

"Yes. Today he's fixing Esther's leaky pipes." I went back to my book.

"When will he be back?"

"When the pipes are mended."

"Thanks, that's really helpful." Maggie crossed her arms.

I sighed loudly, put my book down and looked up. "So what is it you're so desperate to tell Nanny and Pop that you can't tell me?"

"I've found an activity Hannah Beaumont cannot refuse," Maggie said, her face glowing.

"Sky-diving? Pot-holing? No – I know – drag racing."

"Dancing."

I let out a burst of laughter at the thought of grumpy Hannah Beaumont dancing hunched over her Zimmer frame, then quickly swallowed it back at the look on my daughter's face.

"Not disco dancing. A tea dance. In a fifties style, like Hannah's heyday. With cakes and sandwiches, and proper, Hannah-standard tea with real leaves and fine china. We can decorate the hall –"

"What hall?"

"Oak Hill hall, of course. You work there. You can book it for us for a special price." She started pacing up and down in front of me. "Anyway, stop interrupting. We'll have a swing band, hire a proper dance floor – you can do that; Misha did it for her party – and Hannah can wear her coming-out gloves and the pearl necklace her dad gave her on her sweet sixteenth. If she doesn't want to dance, she can sit and enjoy the music and think about all her happy memories. It'll be awesome!"

"It sounds like a lot of work for one dance," I said.

"But that's the whole point – it won't be just one! That's why I need Nanny and Pop. They can start a group teaching the old people – well, whoever wants to come, they don't have to be old – to dance. Like, really simple easy dancing if you can't move very well. Zimmercise! And then when Hannah's a bit stronger, and her stiffened-up old muscles have remembered how to move again, we'll have the party. With, like, really slow music that even Hannah can keep up with. She was a brilliant dancer, a proper ballroom one. She'll love showing off her steps."

I looked at my daughter, her eyes shining under her spiky, brown, non-creative hair. I remembered a girl who spent her life inside her headphones, head down, face pinched.

"You know, I don't think you've thrown a single object in the whole of this year so far."

"Mum! What's that got to do with anything?"

"I think it's a fabulous idea. I'm proud of you, Maggie. And if you can get Nanny and Pop dancing together again, I think you'll have stolen the title of family genius."

"Hah. A Henderson girl's plan never fails."

"Amen to that."

Maggie used all her granddaughter's charm to persuade Mum and Dad to run an initial tea-dance taster session. She printed out a load of flyers, distributing them around Sherwood Court and the Oak Hill lunch club, Dad posted it as an event on the U3A Facebook page, and Mum badgered a few of her old dancing friends to come along. Hannah agreed to go on the condition that she didn't have to dance, Maggie made the tea and they played some Fats Domino.

It was a Thursday towards the end of January, and I had hired the smaller hall at Oak Hill. We needed twenty dancers to cover the costs. Five minutes in, the people in the hall consisted of Maggie, Seth and four of their friends, Hannah, Seth's great-granddad John, another couple from the retirement complex who had both arrived on mobility scooters, and me. Mum made some last-minute calls while Dad talked us through a warm-up. The mobility-scooter couple gave up after two minutes and sat back down on their chairs next to Hannah, wondering out loud when the tea was coming.

We quickly rearranged the programme, serving tea and cakes while three more people, guilt tripped by my mother, dug out their dancing shoes.

By the time they arrived and were served refreshments, we had twenty minutes left to dance. It felt like three hours. My parents, shiny smiles in place, managed to avoid touching or speaking to each other for the whole hour. The teenagers giggled and flopped about and flirted in the corner. Hannah point blank refused to get out of her chair. The mobility-scooter woman started getting chest pains and had to lie down on a sofa in the foyer. Mum's friends played along, but danced with all the enthusiasm of kids in a school country dancing lesson (we had those in Southwell – holding a boy's hand while stripping the willow – yuck!).

I danced with John. He was pretty smooth – I could see where Seth got his charm from. I was pretty smooth too. It felt beyond weird, being back in my parents' dance class. I was rubbish by Henderson standards, but after all those years I could still pull off a merengue.

And at the end, Dad beckoned me over and held out his hands in invitation.

Woah. I swallowed back the boulder in my throat, shook off a hundred screaming arguments that all ended with "I'm never going to dance again. Especially with you – ever!" and danced with my father, trying not to slip in the waterfall of tears that gushed from our pathetic eyes and formed a lake of wasted time and stupid regrets on the wooden floor between our feet.

Sometimes a big moment, a crunch conversation, is not required. Past transgressions aired, apologies offered and forgiveness accepted is not always necessary. As we swayed, twizzled and stepped together, we said it all. I had been a difficult, stubborn daughter who uttered some terrible stuff, hurting my dad in countless different ways. I had scorned his whole way of life – his passion, his business, the way he chose to build his family. In getting pregnant by a near stranger at a party, I also rejected the values and principles he raised me with. But I had been a kid. Angry, hurting and so very unwise, as most kids are.

Yes, he had handled it dreadfully. Accepted my rejection, instead of fighting it. Failed to understand his strange, bewildering youngest daughter. Made no room for me to be myself, and still a valued, vital part of his family. But he was only human. Flawed, and proud and stubborn, as so many are.

There was no great reckoning. Just the power of dance, of moving in time to each other, holding hands, locking eyes, sharing that rush of joy and adrenaline as the music takes control. The girl – the Ruth who had sworn never to dance with her dad again – kept her promise. A different Ruth, a whole lot older and wiser and less complicated, danced with him instead. It was a rubbish tea dance. A near-total failure. It was the best hour I had spent since coming home.

Mum, exhilarated by the challenge, bouncing on a flicker of hope sparked by an hour working with her husband again, booked the hall for the following week. Dad, still smiling at me, agreed to give it one more go. The rest of the class mumbled and shuffled their feet; all except for Hannah, who, it turned out, found the whole débâcle hilarious. She booked her place for next time. John agreed to bring her, if she would consider giving him a twirl around the floor. Hannah flapped her gloves in front of her face, coyly ducking her head. "I'll think about it. As long as you know where to put those hulking great feet. I don't want any broken toes."

"Oh yes, Mrs Beaumont. I know what to do."

"My friends call me Hannah."

# Chapter Twenty-One

A few days later, the temperature plummeted. We woke up to a town transformed. A thick, crisp layer of snow like royal icing coated every surface. Usual morning sounds of dogs barking and children on their way to school were swallowed up by a strange new world. The willow tree, comically lopsided from the firework damage, bent down even lower under the added weight.

I crunched my way to work and back in old walking boots, the bitter wind whipping my scarf back and forth as I battled through the snowdrifts. Only a couple of cars crawled past, churning up the roads to a dirty grey. My two clients cancelled their debt-advice appointments, and Martine sent me home at four to avoid having to walk the journey in darkness. Halfway home, the hum of a car joined me. I hunkered down into my scarf and kept moving. The car pulled ahead, stopping several yards in front. Carl got out and jogged around the car to the pavement.

"Hi Ruth."

I nodded my head and carried on walking.

"I went to pick up Mum, but she's not been in today. They told me you'd just set off."

I glanced at him, now only a few yards away, without slowing.

"Come on, it's freezing. Hop in."

"No, thanks. I'm enjoying the snow."

There was a short pause. I held my breath as I walked on.

"Not celebrity enough for you, Ruth?" The words were a sneer, sending my pulse careening. "Not won enough BAFTAs? Ruth the secretary too good to be seen in the car of a small-town doctor? Who do think you are?" He spat this out. I flinched, trying to pick up my pace. "Well, look around you, Ruth. I can't see your famous boyfriend coming out to make sure you get home safe in the snow, or checking up on you, making sure you're taking care of yourself: sleeping enough, eating properly. You look scrawny, Ruth. He's obviously not taking care of you. Because he doesn't love you, not really. He can have any woman he wants. Be honest, Ruth: why would he pick you? I'm the one here every day, looking out for you, thinking about you. And you have the audacity to throw it back in my face."

I stumbled, skidding along the packed snow, gasping in air that froze my chest and made my eyes sting. Carl still stood behind me, by his car, but I knew he could catch up with me in a moment if he chose.

"Don't walk away from me, Ruth!" He shouted now, the words echoing along the snow-muffled street. "Come back and get in the car, you stupid woman! I said I'm giving you a lift home!"

I realized that the strange mewling noises were coming from me. On this stretch of road the houses were far apart and set back behind security gates and privacy fences. It was growing dark beneath the sheet of heavy cloud, and fresh flurries of snowflakes were beginning to fall.

I glanced up from the path in front of me, muttering a faithless prayer that God would get me out of this. But he answered me before I spoke the words. There, in the gloom ahead, I spotted the lithe figure of my father, striding over the treacherous ground as though the snow didn't exist. He reached me half a minute later. Only then, with my arm safely linked through his, did I turn to see Carl standing in the shadows like something out of a horror movie. He reversed backwards towards his car, and although his face was a mere silhouette, I could feel those laser eyes boring into me. Climbing in, he skidded the car around in a three-point turn and revved away.

Dad frowned. "Some people shouldn't be allowed a driving licence. Is he a friend of yours, Ruth? He looked familiar."

"No. He's not a friend." We began making our way home again. If Dad noticed how heavily I leaned on his arm, he didn't say anything. "Were you on your way somewhere, Dad? You don't have to walk me back."

"I came to find you. Make sure you got home safe."

"You were worried about me." I gripped his arm a little tighter.

"I've been worrying about you since the day you were born."

"Thanks, Dad." I felt the breath coming back to me, my pulse slowing.

"You're very welcome. Are you going to tell me now or when we get home what he did to make you tremble like this?"

"I'm fine," I lied. "In case you hadn't noticed, it's freezing."

"In case you hadn't noticed, this is your dad you're talking to. I know the difference between my girl being cold and being terrified."

I stopped there, at the corner of our little cul-de-sac, as snowflakes settled on our eyelashes and sprinkled our coats like lace, and threw my arms around him.

"I missed you, Dad," I breathed into his damp chest.

"I love you," he said.

"I love you. And I *am* freezing."

"Come on. Your mother's got the kettle on."

Over steaming mugs of tea I gave Mum and Dad a watery, half-hearted, sanitized version of the situation with Carl, omitting the gift, the phone calls and the hair-sniffing. Mum launched herself up from the table and began bashing pans about as she channelled her anxious anger into a "heart-warming, soul-strengthening, snowy stew".

"Do you want me to speak to him?" Dad was papa bear, brow furrowed, knuckles white. "Or knock some sense into him?" he murmured under his breath, causing me to shake my head and place one hand over his.

"No, I can handle it for now. He's got a horrible temper. I don't want to provoke him if we can help it. He'll get the hint, eventually. I'll let you know if I change my mind."

"Well!" Mum started hacking at a pile of potatoes with noisy thunks. "It's understandable, Ruth. You are *completely* gorgeous. I'm sure the only reason more men aren't following you about, half crazy, is because you intimidate them. If Dr Carl feels the need to make every last effort to win you over, who can blame him?" She scooped up the potato chunks and tossed them in a pan. "The problem is, he's quite clearly punching well above his weight. He thinks he can change your mind by prowling about the town after you, gunning his engines and ordering you into his leather man-lair. How utterly tiresome and ridiculous! Men like that need to be flicked off and squished like a mosquito."

Dad glanced across at her, a rueful half-grin on his face, saying to me, "I always said I was just another one of her stalkers. But she happened to love me back, so nobody realized."

"Gilbert Henderson! You never beat your chest at me like those prehistoric gorillas. You courted me. With style and panache!"

If I had even an ounce of the Henderson grace, I would have snuck away, slipping out of the room like a dandelion puff without breaking the moment. However, I have never once entered or exited a room silently, so I kept still, kept quiet and watched what might have been, quite possibly, another tiny flutter of life in my parents' critically ill marriage.

Over the next few days, it kept on snowing. Along with the rest of the county, Southwell ground to a halt. Schools were cancelled as buses failed to bring in the kids from the villages, and most of the teachers were snowed in. The shops began to run out of basic essentials like bread and milk as panicked buyers stockpiled and lorries failed to deliver fresh supplies. A couple of main roads were cleared by the snowplough, but the council, as always, focused on the larger towns, and within hours fresh flurries wiped out all their efforts.

I spent the mornings at work, enjoying the atmosphere of camaraderie as the staff and volunteers rallied round to keep things running as smoothly as possible. A rota was organized to deliver groceries, medicines and other help to those who might struggle to get out in the bad weather, and most afternoons I took my turn dragging a sledge loaded with goodies to various elderly or otherwise housebound members of the town.

One advantage of this was that we visited in pairs, and I could move through the streets with relative confidence. The roads were completely empty of vehicles, so I was fairly sure Carl wouldn't be able to trail me in his car. However, if he chose to "run into" me on foot, I felt happier with the reassurance of Catherine, Oak Hill's formidable assistant pastor, beside me.

Wednesday lunchtime, as I chose a jacket potato from the café's increasingly sparse menu, the woman behind the counter chatted to me about the weather.

"Still," she said, "you get some fools who think their job is so important they insist on trying to drive, despite the fact the roads are an ice-rink. My cousin, the one who works for the police, says they've had ten times the usual number of traffic accidents. Four fatalities. Just trying to get to work!"

I nodded my head and picked up a bottle of orange juice from the chiller.

"Not to mention that couple from Fiskerton who were found half frozen to death in the ditch. They were going to the cinema. Taking a fifteen-mile drive in a blizzard! It's not like there aren't enough things to watch on the television these days…"

She carried on, decrying the stupidity of the English in bad weather. I listened with half an ear as I helped myself to cutlery and a paper napkin, nodding and murmuring my agreement at appropriate moments, until, as I walked towards a free table, she said something that nearly made me drop my tray.

"It's all very pretty and all that, nice for the kids to have a day off school to build a snowman, but your fella must be run off his feet, what with the cars crashing and old folks slipping over. Not to mention hypothermia. That drunk man who nearly died."

I put the tray down carefully on the table and turned back to her.

"Excuse me?"

"Didn't you hear? The man that used to work at the garage, with the moustache."

"No," I continued. "You said something about my fella."

"Well, it's a lot of work for him, isn't it, the snow?"

"I'm not sure who you mean." Only I did. I knew exactly who she meant.

"Your boyfriend, Dorothy's lad – he's a doctor, isn't he?"

"Yes. But he's not my boyfriend."

She coloured slightly, tugging at her cap. "Well, I don't know what you young people call it these days. That one you're seeing."

"No. I don't mean that. I'm not seeing him. We don't have any sort of relationship. We aren't even friends." I tried to keep the strain from showing in my voice. "Who told you we were seeing each other; that he was my boyfriend?"

"He did."

I was momentarily speechless.

"I think you'd better put him straight, love. He seemed to think it was pretty serious, from what I gathered."

"Yes, I will. Thank you."

I gave my potato to the caretaker. My stomach was full of black-bellied hornets.


At the second tea-dance lesson, things got worse. A total of eighteen students came, including an additional three of Maggie's friends. The mobility-scooter couple couldn't manage the snow but had sent four neighbours in their place, along with a message saying they would be back next week. John braved the ice to bring Hannah in his truck, there was a slightly strange young man in a teddy-boy outfit, and me. Oh yes, and one late arrival in a pink anorak, saggy leggings and glittery silver leg-warmers.

Ruby removed her anorak and shook the snow from her hair. Every man in the room's jaw dropped open at the sight of her leopard print leotard straining to contain that enormous chest. A bra might have helped. Mum practically sprinted over to where Ruby stood, preening, by the doorway.

"Ruby."

"Harriet."

"How excellent to see you! We were just wondering who Frank here would have as a partner."

Nobody had been wondering that. By default, I would have danced with the teddy-boy. Now I would have to either partner with Maggie's friend Misha or stick with Dad. Mum thrust Frank at Ruby, and stormed back across to where Dad fiddled about with the CD player, his face stricken.

"We had an agreement, Gil. You have broken that in the *worst possible way!*"

Oh dear. Mum whispering. Might as well have used a megaphone.

Ruby called out, "Is there a problem with me being here, Harriet? Gilbert did invite me."

Mum ignored this. Dad tried to put a calming hand on her arm, but it was swiped off.

"I didn't invite her, specifically," he said softly. "I told you I put it up on the U3A website. She must have seen it there."

"Must she?"

"Harriet. Remember you are a professional. We don't veto members of our classes."

Mum snorted. She stamped out a pasodoble on the parquet floor.

"I'm not the one who needs to remember, Gilbert."

Mum wasn't merely professional, she was sweetness and light, grace and serenity as she guided us through the Viennese waltz, using every male in the room except Dad as a partner. In choosing not to compete with Ruby, but to simply be her very best self – not hard, considering the context – she outshone her in every way. How could a six-foot, elegant swan in a flowing ball gown compare to a jealous, desperately dressed duck out of water?

A tiny bit of my seething rage towards Ruby actually melted into pity as I watched her floundering to elicit anything beyond the minimum courtesy from Dad. Ruby turning up at the tea-dance class might end up being a blessing in disguise.

Two of the new students, Viv and Eddie, expressed their surprise that my nice handsome boyfriend wasn't there to dance with me.

"Ooh!" Viv winked at me. "I bet he's got some moves."

"And he trusts you with all these other men!" Eddie laughed, and then broke into a fit of coughing.

"If you mean Carl Barker –"

"Him with the eyes – the doctor."

"Yes. Him. He is not my boyfriend. I'm not seeing him. I just know his mum. That's all."

"Whatever you say, love." Viv, absentmindedly patting Eddie on the back, winked at me again.

I swallowed hard, determined not to throw up.

Frazzled, frayed, frustrated and frantic with fear, I was in dire need of a girls' night. It was my turn, which meant it was Mum's turn, to cook, clean and bark orders while I mentally counted my tiny stack of new-house savings and willed it to grow faster.

She cooked tapas – "food to share". She prepared mussels: "all good mussels open when ready, just like good friends – if they refuse to open, chuck 'em away!" and stocked up on fizzy white wine, as "girls' nights should bubble and sparkle". Dessert was key lime pie "to add zest and zip".

Ellie called to say she couldn't make it. Although she would happily have braved the two-mile slog through the snow, she didn't want to risk leaving her horses, in case she couldn't get back. The others all walked together, accompanied by Rupa's husband Harry, terrified she would slip on the ice and hurt herself or the baby. We didn't let Harry stay.

The tapas ready, Mum dragged Dad off to babysit for Esther and Max. It was Ana Luisa's turn to say grace.

"Thank you, God, for bringing us safely here. We are a little bit cross with you about all this snow, to be honest. It was fun to begin with, having snowball fights and sledging down the school field. We even liked the way it brought everybody together and made a, what do you call it, war time feeling everywhere. But we think it is enough now. Especially because Ellie can't be here. We miss her. Please bless her and those horses. And bless this evening and Harriet, who so kindly made this feast when all the take-aways cannot be taking anything away in this terrible snow. She rocks. Thank you for my wonderful girls. They kept me sane in all my romantic suffering, and never told me to shut up and get over it. They gave me the courage to share my heart, and now my dream has come true. May all their dreams come true too, God. And please make the snow melt. Seriously – enough already! Amen."

We dug in. I asked them if they knew of any rumours about me and Carl. Lois and Emily had heard a couple, but quashed them as best they could. I described a little of what had been happening, but those women were such good listeners that before I knew it I was blubbering the whole story.

Emily leaned over and put her arm around me – strong, like a fortress. "We've got your back, sister. However you want to play this, we're with you."

"As long as it's legal," Lois added, with a shaky smile.

"Speak for yourself! I'm not a pastor's wife."

"Thanks." I looked at my friends and felt the colossal weight I carried shift and settle more comfortably across my shoulders. "I don't know what to do. I haven't seen him all week, though. Maybe he's getting bored or going off me."

Emily frowned. "This isn't about what he feels for you any more. It's about power and winning. I don't think he's going to give up until he gets what he wants. Or somebody stops him."

I took a big sip of my sparkling wine. "What does he want?"

"To control you? To have you do whatever he says? Or to love him? He's crazy. Who can guess what he really wants from you?"

"You're not really making me feel better here, Emily."

"I'm not trying to make you feel better. I want you to be safe and happy. I want you to take this seriously, and deal with it, not learn to live with it."

She was right. I had spent long enough living with situations I should have dealt with.

Ana Luisa tossed back her hair. "In Brazil, my brothers would shoot him for you. But in this country we have a police force that actually works every day and listens to normal people, and you don't even have to bribe them first or anything like that. Can't you call the police?"

"And say what? That a man stopped me a couple of times to offer me a lift, and told a few people we're going out? That's not a crime."

"The phone calls are," Lois said. "Matt and I've had to deal with all sorts of rubbish like that, Ruth. It's horrible. It lurks over you like a hideous black cloud of acid rain, and you watch for it to burst all the time, like a nervous wreck. If you contact the police they'll get a trace put on the calls."

Right on cue, my phone rang. Withheld number. I rejected the call.

There were three more calls before we finished eating. It was hard to talk about anything else. I could see worry and anger in my friends' faces, but I didn't want to ruin the whole evening.

"How are you feeling, Rupa? You don't seem yourself." That was an understatement. She had hardly eaten, or said a word, all night.

"I'm not great, to be honest. Sick and tired of being sick and tired. I'm twenty-six weeks now. All the books say I should be blooming."

"It'll be worth it, Rups." Emily patted her knee in sympathy. "Hang on in there."

"Thanks, Emily. Help me up, would you? My bladder's uncontrollable. Literally."

She left to go to the bathroom, and we chatted about ways we could help her out a bit, until she staggered back in, her face grey like the dirty snow lining the gutters.

"I think my waters broke." Her knees gave way as Ana Luisa, who was nearest, jumped up to catch her. We carefully lowered her onto the sofa, and hurriedly cleared some of the food out of the way. And then the nightmare started.

Rupa began to keen, like a lost kitten, her arms wrapping around her stomach as she felt her first contractions. Lois called for an ambulance, but another fierce blizzard raged outside and half the roads were blocked. We wrapped Rupa up in a blanket. She gripped on to Emily's hand tight, crying for Harry, who battled through the storm as fast as he could.

Her entire body shook. There was nothing we could do save offer her painkillers, and pray as if her life depended on it, while wondering if the life of the precious child she carried might.

We called the emergency services back, begged them to hurry. They promised to be there as soon as they could.

The surreal calm that accompanies such moments soon settled, our minds in survival mode, temporarily numb to the tumbling emotions that would drown us if we took our focus off the here and now. I made tea. Emily and Lois let their families know they would be late home, if at all, that night. We called Ellie. Maggie came downstairs and helped us clear away the dinner as quietly as possible – as if noise would somehow make Rupa's condition worse.

Harry arrived. Still no sign of the ambulance.

In the midst of all this, our hushed vigil, my phone rang. Withheld number. Before I could think twice, I answered it.

"Carl!"

Silence.

"Carl, you don't have to say anything, but please listen for a minute. I really, really need your help. My friend's in trouble and the ambulance is taking forever. If you're anywhere nearby, please come. Please help."

The line went dead. I looked up to see the others staring at me, their expressions inscrutable.

Five minutes later – *five minutes! In a blizzard!* – the doorbell rang. Dr Carl, bag in hand. I nearly wept with relief. What a difference a day makes.

He shooed us out, deftly striding over towards Rupa. Harry stayed, refusing to move further away from his wife and unborn child than absolutely necessary. We hovered outside the living room door, too overwhelmed to do anything but grip each other's hands and wait. There were murmurings, a brief moan from Rupa, and – at last – the distant wail of a siren. We dashed out to greet it.

As the ambulance chugged up the cul-de-sac, half skidding to a stop on a fresh patch of snow, the front door opened and Carl stepped out, shrugging back into his coat. He paused by me, his face grave, gaze steady. "I'm sorry to rush off; I've had another call. A child's gone through the ice at the park pond. Don't worry, though. The paramedics will soon have everything under control. Their van has a lot more equipment than my bag. I'm sure she'll be fine. Thank you for trusting me with this, Ruth. It means a lot. I'll call you to see how she's getting on."

He slipped and slid down the drive, jogging towards his car. In the silver moonlight, the whole world gleaming white, for a second I almost believed again that he was merely a handsome young doctor, trying to save the world – and me. Lois soon put me right.

"Where on earth is he going?"

"Another emergency. Said a child fell into a pond."

Lois peered at me. "At ten o'clock at night?"

I shrugged. Stranger things happened.

"And he couldn't wait five minutes to fill in the paramedics, tell them the situation?" she added, her voice incredulous.

"That does seem a bit unprofessional."

"He didn't even say hello to them."

In what seemed like seconds the amazing paramedics had loaded Rupa into the ambulance, hooked up a drip and done numerous other medical-type things I knew nothing about. They eased off into the darkness, blue light flashing through the straggly remains of the blizzard. We fell back into the warmth of the living room. Waited. Hoped. Wept. Prayed. It was a long night.

Five o'clock that morning baby Hope was born. She weighed two pounds, one ounce. It had been touch and go, but she was fighting. The doctors were fighting with her. Girls' night officially ended with bacon sandwiches and strong black coffee. I called Dorothy and asked her to pass on the news to Carl. She didn't ask why I hadn't called him myself.

Monday, Lois caught up with me at the centre.

"Hi, Ruth. You look like I feel."

"Tell me about it. Are you going to the hospital later?"

"Not today. Rupa's parents have driven down from Manchester. But I wanted to talk to you about Carl."

I let out a long sigh. "I've been thinking a lot about that. Now he knows I know it was him making the silent calls, I'm not sure what that means – if he might stop. Unless, of course, I've just pushed him into being stalker Carl all the time. But I had to do it. Do you think it was stupid? Have I made things loads worse?"

Lois put her hand on my shoulder. "Stop."

I managed to stop.

Lois said, "I've been making some enquiries about Dr Carl Barker. Or should I say ex-Dr Carl Barker."

"What?" A feeling of dread pulsed through my body, crashing into every organ as it went.

"Let's go into your office."

We closed the door, shutting out the noisy chatter of the craft group. I collapsed into my desk chair. Lois sat on the sofa.

"I spent most of yesterday afternoon searching for Dr Carl Barker on the internet."

"And?" A chill crept up my spine.

"I found a few, but none of them were him. So I asked Dorothy if he ever used another name. Barker is Dorothy's maiden name. Up until his dad divorced her, when Carl was five, their surname was Coombes. "

"So you tried Coombes?"

"Yes." Lois looked at me, her eyes grave. "A Dr Carl Coombes had his medical licence taken away two years ago. In the States."

"Why?" The chill had spread to my lungs. I couldn't breathe properly.

"He began an inappropriate relationship with one of his patients."

"I don't want to hear this."

"Apparently, they dated for a few weeks. She claimed that when she broke it off, he started to pursue her. Aggressively. Follow her to work, bombard her with phone calls, send her things in the post, turn up at her gym, stuff like that. He always kept things just inside the border of the law, but when she complained, there was an investigation and the relationship on its own was enough to get him fired."

"What happened? Did he leave her alone after that?"

Lois took a deep breath. She looked me straight in the eye. "She committed suicide three months later."

The buzzing in my head increased. I couldn't think, let alone say anything.

"But – listen to me, Ruth. Moira Bourdin had been suffering from depression long before Carl came along. She had chronic health problems, including crippling arthritis. That's how they met. She lived alone, had no family to speak of and couldn't work. Carl may have been the final straw, but he didn't drive her to suicide. She was a very troubled woman."

"That's why he picked her." My voice sounded as though it was the other side of a pane of glass. "He likes troubled women. Weak women. Hopeless screw-ups he can control and manipulate and eventually break."

"Yes. But you aren't one of those women any more, Ruth."

Then why did I feel like one?

# Chapter Twenty-Two

*I* showed my parents the information Lois had found online. I also had a very difficult conversation with Maggie. I didn't want her to be afraid, but I did want her to be aware of the situation, so she could be careful. Lois spoke to Martine, and Matt arranged a meeting with Dorothy. I absolutely insisted on being present.

Dorothy claimed to know nothing about Carl having been struck off and subsequently deported. She thought he had returned to the UK to be nearer his family, and work at a private hospital in Sheffield. Matt asked her the name of the hospital, the name of any colleagues we could speak to, any friends. She knew nothing. I asked her where he lived. She confessed that four months ago he moved back in with her, as his place was being remodelled, but had asked her not to tell anyone, as it didn't look good for a doctor of his status to be bunking at his mum's. She had never seen his house.

Yes, she knew Carl and I were seeing each other, but had promised to keep it a secret, as Maggie hadn't been told.

We had several questions. What did he do all day when he went off to work? How did he pay for petrol, phone calls, swanky meals out and diamond bracelets, especially now Dorothy guarded her purse more carefully? Where was he now?

Dorothy fell apart when she saw the articles describing the scandal in America. Bewildered by his behaviour over the past few months, too upset to be humiliated, she sat bent over an untouched bowl of red pepper soup and wondered what on earth to do when Carl picked her up that evening.

The police were wonderful. A serious young officer came to the house, listened, made detailed notes, got straight on to my phone company to trace my call records and promised to pay Carl a visit.

Except that Carl Barker, ex-Dr Carl Coombes, had disappeared. The phone calls stopped.

A weak February sun appeared, and the snow began to melt.

I went to work, administrated, filed, sorted, visited desperate clients in dire straits, wrangled with debt companies and whizzed through important, life-saving numbers with the calculator inside my brain. I spoke to Rupa, dropped round my mother's fortifying fish pie and joined with several other women (and three men) in knitting a square for a patchwork quilt that we sewed together in hope, for baby Hope. Enough knitters joined in to give all the premature babies in the two Nottingham hospitals Hope blankets. The craft shop in Southwell ran out of wool.

One Saturday, my fingers feeling itchy, I dug out a pencil and a piece of Mum's best writing paper, thick and slightly coarse in texture, and I sketched a boat, riding on a choppy ocean. I gave the boat two storeys, depicted by two rows of round windows, and a sloping roof. Peeking through the windows I added two elephants, two monkeys, two racoons, a pair of lizards, some stripy snakes, a sheep, a reindeer and several smaller animals like rabbits and hedgehogs. Crawling up the side of the roof were snails, ants, a pair of chameleons with curly tongues and some furry caterpillars. Bats hung under the eaves of the roof, and a toucan and a wood pigeon nested on the top. In the central window I drew a man and his wife. They looked like Harry and Rupa. I drew in the name of the boat. It was "Hope". I then dug out a Bible from Dad's study. It took me two hours to find the words I wanted to say to Harry and Rupa – and to Hope. I inscribed them in tiny letters on the side of the boat, along the rooftop, around the portals. I wrote them in the rainclouds and weaved them in between the fish swimming under the sea: *I have made you and will care for you. I will carry you along and save you. Do not be afraid, for I am with you. I will strengthen you and help you. When you go through deep waters, I will be with you.*

I heard those words as I wrote them. They prodded and poked at my soul. I had been in deep waters – drowning, flailing, up to my neck, no land in sight. Had he been with me – God? That question felt uncomfortable and comfortable at the same time.

I gave Rupa and Harry the picture, having spent another morning adding some bright colours and a few final flourishes. They cried. I blushed. Then I cried too.

I went to tea-dance classes with Maggie and a growing bunch of older and younger members, wondering how long my parents could run the group together without actually dancing with each other. Wondering how long Ruby would keep coming, and at what point she would concede defeat. Wondering if Hannah Beaumont would ever get up and dance.

I scuttled through the town, head down, ignoring the urgent need to scan the roads for black cars or bright-eyed men, trying to believe Carl had gone, and that if he hadn't, somebody else would spot him before I had to. Determined to carry on life as normal, having tasted freedom on the tip of my tongue, I did everything I could to find it again. I watched my tiny pile of saved pennies grow and my humongous pile of debts shrink, laughed with my friends, ate with my fractured family, tried, tried, tried to breathe deeply and enjoy my surprising new life.

Valentine's Day came and went, I held my breath, barely slept. No card, no flowers, no Carl. I breathed a little easier.

The last day of February an envelope addressed to me landed on the doorstep. The handwriting stirred up delicious, forbidden treacly feelings in my stomach. I closed my bedroom door and read the postcard inside.

*Ruth*
*Still thinking about you... counting the hours*
*Yours (when you want me)*
*D*

I used the postcard to fan my burning face a few times before hiding it in my underwear drawer. I tried to get cross about my wayward feelings, to focus on Maggie, who had enough to deal with watching out for a potential crazy stalker after her mum, let alone the man who lived next door. I couldn't. I couldn't get cross about them. I felt ridiculously happy just at the thought that David would be back soon, that he thought about me, that I could pass him on the road and say good morning, or walk down a country lane with him, or share a pot of tea. *A pot of tea! Together!*

I would count my blessings, be grateful for what I had, refuse to hope or dream of more. Well, I would try.

Three days later, my old friend Mr Hay the headmaster called to ask why Maggie had not turned up for registration. It wasn't school policy for the head to follow up on every absent child, but given the concurrent non-attendance of Seth, and Maggie's history, he was taking a personal interest.

"Oh dear." I managed not to swear.

"So you thought she was in school?"

"Yes. She left at the usual time in her uniform. I'll try her mobile."

"I'd appreciate that. Let the receptionist know when you hear anything, please. I'll speak to Mrs Harris."

Maggie's phone went straight to voicemail. I wracked my brain trying to recall any suspicious behaviour. She'd been out the night before, supposedly watching a film at Seth's house. He had walked her home in time for her ten o'clock curfew and she had gone straight to bed. That morning she got up late, rushed about, grunted when spoken to and slammed the front door so hard the hinges rattled when she left. A typical Monday morning. A tendril of Carl-fear began coiling around my neck. I rang Lois.

"Ruth. I've just spoken to Ken Hay. I'm furious, disappointed and baffled enough to feel slightly anxious. They've done such a good job of earning our trust – I can't believe they'd chuck that away without good reason."

"Maggie was an expert skiver in Liverpool. If she'd wanted to sneak a day off, she would have been a lot cleverer than this about it."

"So it was spur of the moment. Or else she wanted you to find out."

"Why would she want that?"

"In my vast experience of kids bunking off, because she's either mad at you or has a problem and wants you to find out but can't tell you."

Some scary thoughts rattled around my head like a pinball machine. Pregnant. Being bullied. Flunking her exams. Pregnant. Carl.

"What about Carl?" I asked, near frantic with fear.

"What – you think he's kidnapped them? It would be a big stretch to imagine he'd done something to Maggie – but Seth? That boy has learned the hard way how to protect himself."

Lois had a point. "What do you think then? Has Seth given any clues?"

"No. He seemed fine this morning when he left. Even smiled a couple of times. I'm flummoxed. We might have to sit tight, remember how well they've been doing, and try not to burst a blood vessel when they come home."

"I'm not that bothered about the skipping school. It's the reason *why* that fills me with dread."

There was a crash followed by a howl on the end of the phone. "Sorry. That's Martha. I have to go."

"I'll speak to you later."

"Stay cool, Ruth."

"You too," I replied, feeling anything but.

As the clock crept past four and on towards evening, I did not stay cool. I left another message on Maggie's phone, tried a couple of her friends to ask if they knew where she was, paced up and down the living room and fretted about how long I could leave it before contacting the police, bearing in mind that I had discovered her missing backpack and toothbrush.

Sometime around nine, Lois phoned. "Don't freak out."

"Okay, that has me freaking."

"Seth texted."

I stood up quickly from the sofa. "What did he say?"

"'Sorry, but Maggie had to get away. Don't worry.'"

"Did you reply?" I pressed one hand to my forehead, trying to steady the pounding.

"I rang and texted but he's turned his phone off. Then I got smart."

"And?"

"I rang his half-sister, Cheryl. The one in Mansfield."

"The one who works as a lap-dancer to fund her drug habit?" My hand slipped down over my eyes.

"Yeah, that one. Anyway, they turned up there a couple of hours ago. She's going to let them stay tonight and Matt'll go and fetch them in the morning. We figured racing over to Mansfield at this time probably wouldn't help the situation, whatever that is."

"So they're spending the night together. At a lap-dancer's house. With drugs. And Maggie is too mad at me to let me know."

Lois blew out a sigh. "If you want to go and haul her out, we can drive you over. But, for the record, we trust Seth not to do anything stupid."

"Like bunk off school with his girlfriend and take her to *Cheryl's house*?" My voice had gone supersonic.

Lois, who had spent eight years dealing with troubled teens and their associated adventures, remained calm. "It'll be fine, Ruth. One night in that house and Maggie'll be itching to come home."

"She's fourteen, Lois. I don't want her staying there. I don't understand why she's gone. We've been getting on so much better. I'm terrified she's in trouble."

"She's a good kid, Ruth. You're a great mum. Whatever it is, we'll get through it."

When I dragged myself up to bed, having driven my parents half crazy with my wittering and worry, I discovered in my underwear drawer a postcard ripped into quarters. Ah. I called Maggie's phone. As expected, it went straight to voicemail, but I knew she wouldn't be able to resist listening to her messages at some point.

"Maggie. It's not what you think. There is nothing going on between me and David. Nothing. I've kept my promise. There is *nothing* going on. It's just a postcard. Please be careful. I love you. Bye."

Did she sleep that night thinking her mother had betrayed her? Or did she lie awake, like me, feeling sick, empty, like a human pile of refuse? Guilt, my old friend, slunk back into bed with me. I gazed at where the pictures of Maggie hung shadowed on my bedroom wall. I did not think about David.

I don't know who was more angry: me or my daughter.

Matt picked up the kids straight after breakfast. I waited on the front step, a bag of jumbling emotions, as Maggie slowly heaved herself out of the back seat of Matt's car and stomped up the drive towards me. Pushing past, she flung open the door and went inside, running up the stairs with me three steps behind her.

I had pre-emptively wedged open her bedroom door with a flip-flop, thwarting her attempt to slam it in my face. This did not ease her temper.

"Get lost!" she screamed at me, the tremble in her voice betraying her. "I have nothing to say to you."

"Well, maybe I have something to say to you."

"I don't care what you have to say! It's all lies!"

*Deep breath. Count to ten. Remember I am the adult.*

"Are you all right? It was okay at Cheryl's?"

"What do you care?"

"Can we talk about the postcard?"

"Ungh!" She took off her boot and threw it at me. "Go. Away!"

"I'm not going away until we've talked about what happened. I understand you're mad at me, Maggie, but skipping school, running off to that dangerous house and refusing to let me even try to explain is not an acceptable way to deal with this. If I found something of yours – something private, a letter – and read it, then jumped to conclusions and refused to talk to you about it, you would consider that hugely unfair. I've done my best to be open and honest with you since we moved here. To respect you with the truth, and trust you in return. Don't you trust me enough to at least hear my explanation?"

Maggie was still, holding the other boot down by her side, her shoulders hunched up to her ears and her face glowing red. She stared at the floor for a long time.

"I need a shower. My hair stinks of weed. And some breakfast. But if we're being honest, I can't think of a single explanation that excuses you keeping a postcard like that from David."

Half an hour later, we were in the living room. It felt more like a courtroom.

"So." Maggie shrugged her shoulders, angry. "Explain."

"There is nothing going on between me and David, like I said. We were best friends for a long time. Just before he left, David indicated that he had, um, feelings for me. But he knows I've made you a promise not to get romantically involved with anyone, and he respects that."

She snorted. "*Yours when you want me. Thinking about you.* How is that respecting your promise? Tell me exactly what he said."

"He said he'll wait until you're ready."

"So, what, he assumes you like him back?"

"I suppose he might." I shifted position on the armchair.

"Why would he think that? What did you say to make him think that?"

"Nothing!"

"So why would he think that then?" She continued to glare at me, arms crossed.

"I don't know, Maggie. It was a brief conversation. I was very uncomfortable," I said.

"So?"

"So what?"

"Do you like him back?" she asked through gritted teeth.

"You know I like David, Maggie. He's my oldest friend."

"You know what I mean! Do you have feelings for him?"

What could I say? I had a thousand, million, squillion feelings for David Carrington. None of them welcome, or wanted.

"How I feel about David is irrelevant. I made you a promise and will keep it. I'm not going to enter into any sort of relationship with a man until you're ready."

She just stared at me, eyes narrowed, until I answered her question.

"Yes." I looked down, hugged a cushion to my knees.

"Are you in love with him?"

"Maybe. Possibly. I don't know. But it makes no difference. I will always, always love you more."

A concrete statue sat in my daughter's place. "You can't be friends with him then. Not if you feel like that about each other. Can you?"

The statue's face cracked, and I saw the hurt and the loss and the confusion inside. I got up and moved across to sit beside her on the sofa, wrapping my arms around her.

"Oh Maggie, I'm so glad you're safe. Promise you'll talk to me next time before running away with a boy to an exotic dancer's drug den."

"She offered me a job."

"What?"

Maggie burst out in a shaky laugh. "Relax, Mum. I said no. And before you ask, we didn't have sex."

"Good to hear."

"No way I'm losing my virginity on a dodgy stained mattress

with a load of stoners in the next room." She leaned her head onto my shoulder and I rested mine on hers.

"Like I said, good to hear. Now go and get changed. You've got an appointment with Mr Hay."

"Good to hear."

"And by the way, you're grounded. Indefinitely."

# Chapter Twenty-Three

The meeting included much grovelling, many apologies and warnings, and a liberal sprinkling of the fact that it was a tricky time of year for Maggie and me, being only four days before the anniversary of Fraser's car crash. Although little had been said, the date still hovered in our minds. I had been dreaming about the night a policeman knocked on my door, weird twists of my imagination involving Fraser's mother, bailiffs and the weighty feeling of blackness that shrouded our family for a season. We both found ourselves mournful, more fragile than usual. On the day itself, we caught the train to Liverpool.

We didn't visit Fraser's grave – that lay in Scotland, alongside his father's. Instead, we went to the places that reminded us of him the most, where our family had been happiest, and we could celebrate having known him, rather than grieve his loss. We didn't go anywhere near our old house – that would have been pointlessly painful – but we walked in Croxteth park, took the bus into town and strolled along the regenerated docks, splashed out more money than was sensible at Fraser's favourite restaurant, and eventually ended up being blown about Wallasey beach.

Maggie flung back the hood of her parka, letting the salt spray and biting wind whip her hair about and turn her cheeks pink. "Liverpool!" she squealed. "I love you! I miss you and your freezing coldness and your awesome accent and big, tall buildings and old drunk Irish guys and abundance of tracksuits! I yearn for -

massive bridges and the smell of the sea and the superlambanana and a way less creepy number of trees! Yay Beatles! You are far better than Robin Hood. And you actually existed. You'll never walk alone!"

I hoped the few other people on the beach wouldn't be offended by a fourteen-year-old's memory of Liverpool and muttered an apology to the ghost of Robin Hood for my daughter's lack of faith. I liked Liverpool, a lot, but it had never been home.

We allowed the gale to buffet us down the sand parallel to the steel-coloured waves. Every few strides one of us bent down and picked up a stone, hurling it into the water while speaking out a memory of Fraser.

"He was the world's best tickler," Maggie grinned.

"He cooked fantastic omelettes."

"He always came to tuck me in at night, even when it was really late and he thought I was asleep."

"He worked really hard to give us lovely things."

"I never saw anyone so bad at dancing the robot."

"True. But slow dancing? *That* he could do."

"I loved your impressions of all my different teachers, Dad!"

"You were the sexiest boy on the maths course!"

"Eew! Keep it clean. You pretty much hardly ever embarrassed me in front of my friends!"

"You put up with my crazy mother!"

"You were an amazing dad." Maggie spoke this so softly the wind snatched the words away. She stopped walking, and folded herself into me. "I miss you, my daddy. I love you and I wish you were here every day. I miss you."

Our tears mingled with the Irish Sea spray as we gazed out towards the horizon, and wondered and remembered and held each other tight. I missed him too, the man who had shared my life and my bed and the young woman beside me. Life was safe with Fraser, and oh so dangerously wide open without him.

It was a good day. I watched Maggie on the train journey home reading the latest John Green book and marvelled at the difference between this young woman and the angry, mixed-up girl hiding behind liquid eyeliner and blue hair I had dragged kicking and screaming from the same city only seven months earlier.

She turned the page and, without glancing up, said, "Stop staring at me, please."

"I'm just thinking how much I love you."

She rolled her eyes, still reading, if that's possible.

"Are you happy, Maggie?"

"It's the anniversary of Dad's untimely death. I've spent half the afternoon crying, or trying not to cry. I'm grounded, on probation at school and my boyfriend is forbidden from seeing me unsupervised after taking me to a crack-house. My mum is being stalked by a madman, my grandparents are on the brink of marital breakdown and my best friend is a bitter, lonely old woman who treats me like a servant. Oh, and I have terrible hair." She looked up at me, a smile in her eyes. "Yes, I'm pretty happy."

"Do you still want to move back to Liverpool?"

"Is that ever going to happen?"

"Probably not."

"Then I'll live with it."

"I'm unbelievably proud of you – you know that?"

"Yes." She resumed reading for a few more minutes. "Can I go to Sam's party on Friday?"

"Still grounded."

"No longer happy."

"You can live with it."

I got a phone call from Rupa's mother-in-law, who lived in Leicester. Could I do three more of the Noah's ark pictures for her other grandchildren? Only her eldest grandson, Daniel, loved the Bible story about Daniel in the lions' den. Could I draw lions? And her other granddaughter loved butterflies, so could I do a picture with some butterflies in it? She would pay me, of course.

I ummed and ahhed, doubtful that my amateur artwork was actually worth paying for.

Mistaking my modesty for haggling, she upped the price. One hundred pounds for three pictures.

I shrugged my shoulders, hung up the phone and dug out my pencils. I could almost hear God chuckle as I buried myself in the Bible for the second time that month.

That Friday was girls' night. Rupa's turn. We brought lasagne and freshly baked Italian bread from the deli, leafy salad and carrot cake with extra-thick lime and mascarpone icing. Ana Luisa and I arrived an hour early, planning to spend it vacuuming, scrubbing, sorting and ironing while Rupa soaked in the bath.

Instead of being greeted by Rupa's pretty smile at the door, we found ourselves face to face with Vanessa Jacobs, of all people. She looked us up and down, a faint smirk lurking at the corners of her squishy lips.

"Yes?"

"We're here to see Rupa. She's expecting us."

"She's resting."

Vanessa crossed her arms defensively. A duster dangled from one hand. Ana Luisa thrust the cake tin she carried in through the doorway until it nearly rammed into Vanessa's rigid chest.

"Not a problem. We won't disturb her. We came to do her ironing."

"Done."

"Vacuuming, then."

"I've done it."

"Washing-up? Tidying? Changed her bed? Hah! What about her kitchen cupboards?"

Vanessa rolled her eyes. "Whatever." She stepped back to let us in. "And don't worry, I won't be hanging around for your little party. I've got better things to do on a Friday night than giggle and gossip like twelve-year-olds at a sleepover."

"Something better than laughing with your friends? I have to know what that could be," Ana Luisa asked oh so sweetly. Vanessa dropped the duster on the hall table and yanked on her jacket.

"Let's put it this way. I'll be having a sleepover of my own. And there aren't any girls invited."

She opened the front door and called over her shoulder as she left, "Say bye to Rups for me. Tell her I'll bring that shopping over in the morning."

We stood and watched Vanessa's sports car screech away.

"Well."

"My thoughts exactly. I suppose we should clean some cupboards."

The others arrived an hour later, laden down with groceries, magazines and teeny-tiny baby clothes.

We settled in Rupa's small living room, packed even tighter now it was filled with bunches of flowers and about a thousand cards.

"How are you doing, Mum?" Emily asked Rupa, curled up on the sofa in her pyjamas.

"I'm fine, thanks."

"I'll ask again. How are you, Rupa?"

She sighed, allowing her chin to tremble. "Wrung out. Like an empty sack. When Hope got that infection last week – I honestly didn't know how I would bear it. But I did. And she's okay, and I know I have to choose between feeling angry this happened, my whole life becoming hospitals and tubes and waiting and worrying, and feeling so very grateful she's made it this far, and is doing well, and everyone's been so wonderful... it's like the worst, horrible, scariest times only give more opportunities for people to show love and kindness. Honestly, every time I think I can't do another day, like when I hear mums with their big, fat, healthy babies complaining about them crying all night, or having sore boobs from breastfeeding, when I feel like that, I look at Hope's blanket and I think about all those people who are standing with us. And I, I don't know, I feel strong. I feel carried. I feel blessed."

Ana Luisa asked the question we were both thinking: "So, speaking of people being kind – Vanessa Jacobs?"

Rupa smiled, and wagged her finger at Ana. "Vanessa has been amazing. I will not hear a bad word said about her in this house. I've cried on her shoulder so many times in the past few weeks she could have charged me rent."

The girls bristled. What was wrong with their nice, soft, friendly, less fashionable shoulders?

Ellie shook her head in wonderment. "I don't understand. Since when did you and her become best buddies?" She gasped. "Is that who drove you to the doctor's last week when you turned down my offer of a lift? Did Vanessa Jacobs take you?"

Rupa sighed. "I can't believe you're jealous."

"We're not jealous!"

We were, a teensy bit. Vanessa had long, silken ringlets, a blemish-free complexion, a killer body and bad girl attitude. And now she was muscling in on being kind and generous too?

"Vanessa gets it. And it's, I don't know, *soothing*, to be with a person you don't have to explain it to; they just understand what to do and what not to say and all that."

"Oh." Ellie was taking this hard.

"Can you remember when Vanessa moved away for a couple of years? About a month before I met Harry? Well, she left Southwell to get married. They had a baby, twelve weeks prem. He didn't make it; her marriage fell apart a few months later. It's not a secret, but it isn't common knowledge either. She might come across as abrasive and mean, but really underneath Vanessa's just wounded. She lashes out because she's terrified that someone'll see beneath her stylish exterior and find a worthless reject inside. I don't think she has any real friends."

Emily raised her eyebrows. "Sounds like she needs to come to the clinic for a few sessions. I knew about her marriage, but not the baby."

"Actually" – Rupa wriggled on her seat and mustered up a

surprisingly determined look on her face for someone so sweet-natured – "I wanted to ask her along to girls' night next time."

Awkward silence.

"I mean, she's not Ruth's boss any more, so there's no conflict there. And really, if you get to know her, then, well…" Rupa petered out, shrugging her shoulders at the floor.

"I think it's great that you're friends and she's been there for you. But the rest of us have some catching up to do. I'm not sure we're ready to trust Vanessa yet at a girls' night." Lois smiled to soften her words. "How about we invite her along to some other stuff, get to know her a bit better first? Give Ruth a bit of distance – Vanessa wasn't exactly a pleasant boss. Does that sound okay?" She looked around, gauging our opinion.

We shrugged, mumbled, fiddled with our cups. No, it was not really okay, but hey-ho, these Christian women didn't half go in for giving people fresh starts.

It was my turn to say grace. I had been stressing all day, trying to wangle my way out of it, remembering Freya and Martha's withering assessment of my praying abilities on the yurt weekend.

The girls were having none of it. "Don't be an idiot, Ruth. It's just talking."

I sighed. "You women have no idea how incredible you are, do you? And that it might actually be intimidating for people like me."

"People like you?" Emily scoffed. "What – brave, beautiful, compassionate, wise, artistic, funny people?"

"I was thinking of messed-up, clueless, guilt-ridden, broke, homeless people, actually."

Ana Luisa was horrified. "Is this how you see yourself, *still?*"

I thought about it. "Okay. I'll say grace. No teasing."

"Get on with it then! The lasagne'll go cold."

"Right. God. Hello. Um. Thanks for tonight; that we can be together. Thanks for friends who see us differently to how we see ourselves, and aren't afraid to tell us when we're being pitiful. Thanks for love in dark places, for hope – and Hope – and for keeping her safe so far. Please help Rupa to relax this evening; may our love and laughter recharge her batteries, restore her strength and refresh her soul. Help us keep girls' night real. It is a rare thing to find people you can be utterly honest with. I can't believe these women call me their friend. And that carrot cake looks like it came straight from heaven. Thank you. Amen."

We toasted friendship, and being excellent women, and Hope. Then Lois told us a story about how Martha had tried to set a roast chicken free in the garden, and we laughed so hard we almost felt our ribs crack.

# Chapter Twenty-Four

David was back. I could feel it in my bones. The atmosphere had shifted. I felt restless, scatter-brained. The crocuses under the wreck of the willow tree were blossoming; the branches above that had escaped the fire sprouted tiny, fisted-up leaves, reminding me of baby Hope.

My mother's daughter, I busied myself with work and motherhood and nail biting and stomach clenching and smacking myself about the head in frustration at my deep and desperate feelings.

I found him sitting on the kerb at the bottom of my drive when I returned home from work one Tuesday evening. His hair was lighter, and long again, the beginnings of a beard emphasizing his exquisite jaw-line. He wore a grey-blue cotton sweater, with the sleeves pushed up above his elbows. Even his forearms were gorgeous.

"Hey, Ruth."

"Hi." I paused, unable to meet his smiling eyes.

"Want to join me?"

My shoulders sagged. I closed my eyes momentarily, and when I opened them again, prepared to speak, David had risen to stand beside me.

"Did you get my postcard?"

"Yes." I flicked my gaze to the house, hoping Maggie wasn't watching.

"And?"

"And. And nothing, David. Nothing's changed. Please stop pressuring me."

He nodded. "Okay. Sorry, no pressure. I'll behave myself. And try to be content with us being friends. For now." He grinned, and it cut through me like a scalpel.

I shook my head tightly. "I can't. I'm sorry."

He pulled his head back – the grin had vanished. "You can't be friends? Why not?"

"Maggie found the postcard. Right before the anniversary of the car crash. She didn't take it well. I'm sorry."

"So she decides who you can be friends with as well as your love life?"

"No! It's not like that. But you have to see she wouldn't want me hanging around with someone who's got feelings for me. She'd be constantly wondering what's really going on."

"Doesn't she trust you?"

"Yes, but –"

"But what? You can't have a male friend in case he finds you attractive? What about Matt or my dad? There are a lot of men in this world who probably find you attractive, Ruth, but, unbelievably, can actually manage to control themselves."

"It's not that!"

"What, then? Why are you letting her decide who your friends are, instead of asking her to trust you?"

"Because I don't trust me!" I turned away, angry and riddled with pain. "*I don't trust me to be friends with you, David!*" I lowered my voice, aware that we were standing in the open. "And, quite frankly, it hurts too much to think about you, let alone spend time with you. Can you imagine how much it kills me to know I never loved Maggie's dad as I should have – as she and he deserved – because my heart was still stuck with you under that willow tree? I gave Maggie a pathetic, sub-standard, lifeless example of what it is to love a man, because the only way to stop thinking about you *every hour of every day* was to stop thinking altogether. I was half mad with love for you, David. Reckless. Foolish. *Untrustworthy.* But I blew it. We blew it. And life happened anyway. I made a promise to my daughter, and the only way I can be certain I keep that is to stay away."

David stared at me, his body completely still.

I tried to pull myself together, to get out what I needed to say.

"So, I'm asking you, please don't call round, or send letters, or wait for me to come home from work. Don't wait for me at all."

"Ruth —" He reached one hand out towards me, and I did the only thing I could do. I ran away from David Carrington for the second time – not as far, but an ocean, a desert, a galaxy away nevertheless.

Three days later, he flouted my request, and was once again sitting on the pavement outside my house when I came home. I pretended to ignore him, as I had been trying to ignore the gaping wound in my chest, and strode past him up the drive.

"I've been offered another job. With an open-ended contract. The producers want to make *Whole Wild World* into a show marketed for adults as well as kids. It'll mean staying away indefinitely."

I paused by the front door, half turned away, head down.

"Last week I told them I wasn't interested. I had no reason to leave Southwell and a very good reason to stay. But they called again, made me a better offer." I heard him moving closer. "So. If there is even the slightest shred of hope, the tiniest chance, that I may still have that reason, that things might change, just say the word and I'll turn it down. Is there any reason at all I should stay?"

My heart hammered in my chest, pounding out the reason with every beat. All the moisture had left my mouth, but my voice sounded loud and clear as I replied, "I think you should take the job."

I got all the way up the stairs and into my room, closed the door and shattered into a million pieces.

By the time the rest of the family returned home, I had stuck myself back together again. Cracked, probably a little bit wonky, but without looking closely it would be hard to tell the difference.

Thankfully, talk at the dinner table was all about the dance classes. Maggie was keen to book a date for the big party, to get things moving. My parents, those pinnacles of perfection, shuddered at the prospect of releasing their fledgling dancers on the general public. Hannah still hadn't even got out of her chair to try the warm-up. Maggie, smirking at me over her stir-fry, had a whale of a time listening to her grandparents united in their views for once.

Things had temporarily plateaued regarding the state of their relationship. Yes, Dad had cut down the number of U3A groups he attended to two or three a week, and as far as we knew he hadn't seen Ruby again on a social basis. Mum had also kept her promise to slow down her rescue-the-downtrodden-of Southwell campaign, and consequently they brushed shoulders from time to time in the house, as well as at the dance class. But. It was a mere peephole in the towering wall between them; the barricade still stood strong. The wild, deep-spirited, beautiful lovers they had once been – bone of my bone, flesh of my flesh – remained elusive. Maggie and I, my sisters, their oldest and wisest friends suggested counselling, a second honeymoon, date-nights; at the very least a good long hard conversation or a bunch of flowers.

But so far, pride won out, the path of least resistance beckoned, and Ruby hovered hopefully in the wings.

The Oak Hill administrator – Ms Ruth Henderson – found a convenient space in the diary for the tea dance during the first week in July. Did the fact that the date coincided with her parents' forty-ninth wedding anniversary have anything to do with the availability of the hall? Absolutely.

When I told her at dinner that evening, Maggie was thrilled. "I've been thinking. We need to liven things up a bit. Make it more exciting. Up the ante. Give the dance class something to work for."

The colour drained from Dad's face. He paused, a forkful of rice halfway to his mouth. "Please no. Not a show. Not this lot. It'd take decades to get them up to show standards."

"No. Even better. A competition."

Mum threw her arms up in the air, accidentally hurling a chunk of naan bread over one shoulder in alarm. "Compete for what? The creakiest knees? Slowest turn about the floor? How do you expect the geriatric members of the class to stand a chance against your hoody-clad compadres?"

Maggie smiled. "I don't. That's the whole point. They aren't going to be competing *against* each other. But on the same team. An intergenerational dance competition. One member of each couple has to be at least fifty years older than their partner."

"*Fifty?*"

"All right. Thirty."

Dad frowned, thoughtfully. "Twenty-five. That's more like a generation. Do you really think your friends are going to want to dance with the older lot?"

"Depends who it is. And what prize is at stake. And if we can stir up some competition between them, they'll end up fighting for the best biddies."

"They might not appreciate being called biddies." I tried to hide my smile, waiting for my parents to explain to Maggie the foolishness of her idea. But those two loved a competition. And then Maggie made one final suggestion and the deal was sealed.

"I thought I'd dance with you, Pop. If you think I'm good enough."

Dad widened his eyes in surprise. A smile broke out across his face that was so broad I worried his jaw would dislocate. He suddenly appeared to have something in his eye. Both eyes.

"That... Well. You would be perfect."

I ignored the stab of pain: something like jealously, something like rejection. It wasn't as though I wanted to dance with him, was it?

I plodded through most of April, enjoying my job, getting to know a few new people, feeling more comfortable with those I already knew. I stuck a bandage over the big hole in my heart, and counted my blessings.

Three women from Oak Hill phoned. They had seen Hope's

Noah's ark picture. Could I do one for their niece/granddaughter/
son, only with a zebra/giraffe/slow loris? I could. I named each boat
the name of the child it was for. Someone asked if I could draw a
barge instead of a boat, as her best friend was moving into a house
boat. I did, changing the messages accordingly. It all went into my
new house fund.

The shadow of Carl receded enough for me to start striding my
new, decidedly un-stick-like body along the footpaths that meandered
their way through the fields surrounding Southwell. I avoided my
childhood haunts – the places David and I would hunt out wildlife
in reed-rimmed ponds and murky thickets – instead choosing busier
routes through the strawberry fields, along the edge of the golf course
or down winding lanes lined with trees dripping with blossom.

I walked and looked and listened to the abundance of life
buzzing and bleating and barking all around me, losing myself in
the pattern of lichen upon a tree stump, or the dance of a dragonfly,
or the smell of a bluebell carpet, heady and lush with the promise
of summer. I felt alive, like Sleeping Beauty awoken after a hundred
years of slumbering. And glad to be so.

One Sunday afternoon, I climbed the rickety stepladder up
to the attic. Digging through the cobwebs and tickly layers of
dust and grime, I found a wooden crate. Jimmying the lid off
with one of Dad's screwdrivers, I gazed at the contents with
unbridled delight. A carefully ordered, perfectly sharpened set
of drawing pencils, three varying sized sketchbooks – a little less
crisp than they were, but still useable. A slightly bashed-in tin
of charcoal, miniature easel and a clipboard for leaning on in
awkward positions (like under a bush, or balancing on a bouncy
tree branch). A set of pastels, the green and brown worn down to
stubs, and a wooden box, about eight inches square, containing
watercolour paint tubes, brushes and a mixing palette. I carefully
lifted out the pencils, the smallest sketchbook and clipboard,
bashing the box lid back into place before clambering back down
onto the landing.

I packed the equipment into a rucksack, along with a picnic blanket, bottle of water and bag of apples, and dug out Mum's straw hat. Maggie found me fiddling with the angle of the brim in the cloakroom mirror.

"Nice hat."

"Thanks. It's Nanny's."

"I was joking. You look embarrassing."

"You're fourteen – I always look embarrassing. In about five years' time, that will miraculously change. It's a law of nature."

"Where are you going?"

"Out into the middle of nowhere, where my terrible taste in headwear can't offend anybody."

"Irritating! Can you answer my question?"

"I'm going to a tiny clearing in the woods about a mile down the old railway line. I may be some time."

"What?"

"There's the most incredible cluster of wood anemone. I'm going to draw it."

"Have you got your phone?" Maggie frowned.

"Yes."

"Is there a decent reception out there?"

"Yes. Reception, and dog walkers, and ramblers, and kids racing up and down on bikes. I'll be fine. If I see a creepy ex-doctor with weird, toilet cleaner coloured eyes, I'll make a run for it."

"It's not funny, Mum."

"No. He is not funny. But what's even less funny is letting him control where I go and what I do, and making me afraid to walk in the countryside where I spent about ninety per cent of my childhood. I refuse to allow him any power over me. He's gone."

If I said it enough, it might even be true. I left her working on some maths revision with Dad, and hiked along the trail, pushing myself hard until I outran the grey shadow of foreboding that Maggie's anxiety had cast.

The rest of the afternoon was bliss. Me, the occasional passer-by, the gentle scratch of graphite on thick, lovely paper and the rich splendour of creation: birds, butterflies, two rabbits and glorious spring sunshine. The pencils settled in my fingers like old friends. My hand flowed over the paper. I stayed until the light began to dim, whole and happy. And for those precious hours, the sharp, empty ache inside lessened a little, the air in my lungs found enough room, my head cleared and my spirit sat at peace.

Five days later, on my way to work, humming the latest tune from Maggie's favourite band, I saw a black car creeping down one of the side-streets.

*It's nothing. There are tons of black cars in Southwell. It's moving slowly because it's looking for a house number.*

I shot my eyes forward, away from the street, picked up my pace and tried to shut off the siren clanging in my ears. A discreet enquiry later on reassured me that Dorothy, still confused and in partial denial, had heard nothing from her son.

I didn't feel like walking that weekend. I drew the fat, drunken bees clambering over the honeysuckle in the garden instead.

That Wednesday, while alone in the house, the phone rang. The caller display said withheld number. As soon as I picked it up, the line clicked dead. I wrote it down in the logbook the police officer had advised me to keep, then ate a piece of Mum's fudge cake to squish the dread in my stomach. He was gone.

The first week in May, baby Hope came home. Due to her vulnerable immune system, she wasn't allowed out of the house yet, or to see too many visitors, but the many well-wishers and quilt-knitters and meal-providers needed to celebrate, so we gave her a Skype party.

On the May Day holiday, over a hundred of us gathered in the sunny back hall at Oak Hill. Afternoon tea was served: an assortment of dainty sandwiches cut into fingers; raisin, coconut or cinnamon scones with cream and locally produced jams, and every type of cake known to man, including pink and blue miniature macaroons, cupcakes decorated with baby booties, and cookies in the shape of old-fashioned prams. Pink and blue balloons bobbed above our heads, spring flowers decorated every spare surface and on the giant wall-screen in the corner a tired-looking, beaming Rupa and Harry held up their baby girl to show her just how much fuss we thought she was worth.

When she conveniently fell asleep, which premature babies are inclined to do for about twenty-three and a half hours of the day, they handed her over to her enchanted grandma, swapped the Skype for a Hope-themed slide-show and sped around to personally thank everyone for all their support over the past three months. Vanessa Jacobs hovered a little sheepishly at the top of the list. I girded up my loins and made an effort.

"Hi, Vanessa."

"Ruth." She flicked her hair over one shoulder. For the first time I detected a whiff of bravado in the gesture. It was amazing what you spotted when looking properly.

"It's a lovely party, isn't it?"

"Not bad. Someone certainly likes bubblegum pink."

"How's the shop? Busy?"

"Yes, thanks. I've hired a new assistant. A fashion graduate from Nottingham Trent. She practically runs the place; the customers love her."

"That's great."

Vanessa frowned. "She's useless at maths, though. The accounts are a mess."

I let slip a grin, accepting the compliment. "Rupa told us you've been brilliant."

"Yes, well. You and the sobriety sisters don't have the monopoly on friendship, you know."

An awkward silence strolled up and inserted itself into the gap between us. It whispered to me out of the corner of its mouth: *go on then. Invite her to the tea dance. What's the worst that can happen?*

"So. There's this tea dance Maggie's organizing."

"Maggie?"

"My daughter."

"Oh, right."

"Rupa probably won't be able to make it, but Lois and Ana Luisa are definitely coming. And Emily. If you fancied it. I mean, coming along."

She tossed her hair again, like a very shiny, irritated horse. "Sounds... interesting. I could drop in I suppose, if I've nothing else on. I'm pretty busy at the moment."

I took a deep breath. "That would be fantastic. I really hope you can make it."

Startled, Vanessa shot a look at me, checking for sarcasm.

I put on my best friendly smile.

"Right." She marched away, swanky heels clicking.

I turned around to see Ana Luisa and Arnold on the far side of the room, heads bent close to one another. Arthur laid his hand on Ana Luisa's arm, and she smiled, brushing the cake crumbs from his jumper. Maybe the Big House would soon be filled with pink or blue balloons.

Having avoided the Big House since David had left for his new job, I wandered over to say hello.

"Ruth! It is so good to see you – your mother tells me you are working all the time, too tired to come and visit. This is no good."

"What can I say? For the first time ever I like my job. I haven't just been working, though. I'm helping Maggie plan her tea dance, which includes dance lessons once a week. Despite the fact I vowed never to set foot in a ballroom after the last time. It's like being a kid again; I'm being sucked back into this world of streamers and sequins and high heels."

"You vowed never to dance again? Ruth! What terrible thing could make you do that? Tell me!"

"It's a long story."

Arnold coughed. "I'll go and fetch some more tea. You take your time. Would you like another scone, Ana?"

"No, thank you, darling. But tea would be lovely."

Ana Luisa watched Arnold walk across to the refreshments table, her eyes glazing over. She let out a delicate sigh, sinking her chin onto one hand.

"Whew, Ana. You've got it bad."

Shaking out her long hair, she straightened up again, one side of her mouth curling into a smile. "Oh no, Ruth. I've finally got it good."

"It's going well?"

"It is more than I ever dreamt of. Once he got over his nerves!" She laughed. "He is attentive, and patient, and kind. He doesn't only take care of me, and remember all these thoughtful little things like picking me a flower from the garden, or noticing a new dress. He *talks* to me and asks my opinion. Like I am his equal, not a pet or a piece of meat or a thing to be ogled and used and tossed away. He makes me feel I can do anything, like I am treasure. Like he is honoured to be my boyfriend! I never knew this before!"

"Stop. You're making me cry. I am so happy for you. You deserve it. And you are treasure. He should be honoured. I'd kick his butt if he wasn't."

"Yes, yes. But you are changing the subject. You were telling me why you vowed never to dance the ballroom ever again."

"Do I have to?"

"Hmm. I suppose I could ask your mother. Or – hang on – didn't I see your sister over there?"

"That's blackmail."

"Why? What dreadful things will they tell me?"

"Um – the truth?"

"I like the truth."

Preferring my version of the truth to my mother's – or, please no, my sister's – I took a fortifying bite of smoked salmon sandwich and told Ana Luisa the whole story.

# Chapter Twenty-Five

When I was fifteen, my parents entered a team from the dance school into an exclusive, highly prestigious dance competition in Australia. We fundraised for nearly a year to raise the money to take the team of six girls and four boys on the trip. Cake sales, sponsored bike rides, and a plethora of raffles and ticketed shows eventually enabled us to reach our target. One of the girls' dads owned a construction company that agreed to sponsor us, providing the funds we needed for costumes. For a whole year, the Henderson household ate, slept and breathed the Australian Dancesport Open. As the trip drew closer, rehearsal time tripled to every night after school and four hours every Saturday. Lifts were perfected, music chosen and discarded and re-chosen; Mum spent hours embellishing our outfits.

It was my idea of hell.

Years of enforced lessons had moulded me into a competent dancer. I could pick up steps and was fearless when lifted, flung and thrown about by Luke, my dance partner. But I was not Australian Dancesport Open material. And everybody except for my doting dad knew it, said it and – in the case of my sisters – screamed it.

If only I spent my time practising, instead of plotting ways to disappear off into the woods with David Carrington, I might stand a chance, my mother told me. If I only concentrated, put more effort in, got my head out of the clouds, worked harder, ate better, behaved more like my sisters.

They had lost all perspective, all reason, all sensibility. I soon lost the bedraggled remains of my self-confidence, self-respect and any belief that my family actually wanted, loved or liked me.

The month of the trip arrived, and it became apparent nothing was going to make Dad drop me from the team. (I considered jumping off a wall to break my leg, but then someone would have had to stay behind to look after me, and whoever it ended up being might literally have killed me.) I couldn't sleep, my appetite vanished, I couldn't focus at school. And as I boarded the plane along with the excited, hopeful gaggle of fellow dancers, I had never felt so alone.

Lying on my lumpy hotel mattress the night before the show, I stared at the blackness and begged God to give me food poisoning, or send a freak tornado. Unable to sleep, I eventually got up, pulled on my jeans and a jumper, and tiptoed past Lydia in the bed next to mine out into the corridor to see if I could find anyone else awake.

When the unmistakable boom of Mum's voice rose up the hotel staircase, no doubt the rest of her following straight after, I scampered back to a discarded room-service trolley and hid behind it. Her words soon drifted into earshot.

"Well, Gilbert. It's too late now! You should have listened to us months ago."

I held my breath, trying to catch Dad's mumble.

Mum hissed back, "Of course she's not up to it! She's a girl of many talents, but the Henderson genes just aren't there, Gilbert. She can't dance."

Now, I knew my mother meant the Henderson *dancing* genes weren't there – the ones including grace, rhythm, style. And I knew I could dance perfectly adequately for most situations. It was the Australian Dancesport Open that reached beyond me.

But, oh boy, at fifteen, stressed out and lonely, those words ripped through me like the claws of a spiny cheek crayfish.

Dad coughed, drawing level with the trolley. I pressed one hand over my mouth to try to quiet my heaving lungs.

"If she tries hard enough, manages to keep it together and lets Luke do the work, it might not be a complete disaster."

"Well, that's what we were hoping for when we raised thousands of pounds to bring our brightest students halfway round the world on the trip of a lifetime. As long as it's not a complete disaster, it'll all have been worth it!"

I heard them pause outside their room, Mum unzipping her bag.

"She had to be a part of this," said Dad. "Dancing is what the Hendersons do. Who my girls are."

A metallic clunk, and the door creaked open. I caught my mother's last words as she stepped inside. "You can't make her something she's not, Gilbert. And she is not a dancer."

So I was not a dancer. And not a Henderson, apparently. Not one of Dad's girls. Fine. I would dance in the stupid competition tomorrow, because poor Luke had been forced to practise with me forever and I owed it to him. And that would be it. Stuff the dance school, the ridiculous costumes and the echoey floors and shows and tedious old music and applause. Stuff the Hendersons. After tomorrow night, I wasn't going to dance another choreographed step. And if that meant I was no longer a Henderson girl, so be it.

Bluff and bluster is easy enough when sneaking back to a darkened room in the middle of the night. About to walk out in front of five thousand strangers, your family and teammates staring anxiously at you, knowing you are going to humiliate yourself and let everyone down, is another matter. Jet-lagged, seriously sleep-deprived, the apple juice I forced down for breakfast sloshing in my stomach, I stood there in the wings of the Australian Dancesport Open stage. Sweat dripped down my forehead as I waited for the judge to call my name. Head spinning, paralysed with fear, all I could hear was my father's words from the night before.

I felt a push from behind. Mum hissed at me, "Get out there, Ruth! Everybody's waiting."

She pushed again, and the momentum carried my shaking legs out onto the stage and up towards Luke, who took one look at me and turned green beneath his fake tan. I bumped into him, allowing him to grab my hands in his, ready for the opening bars of music. As the first beats pumped into the auditorium, he frowned at me. "Pull yourself together, Ruth. You're a Henderson girl. You can do this."

*No. No. No no no no no no no.*

Something in me snapped. I wrenched my hands out of Luke's grasp, and shoved my way past him, clattering to the far side of the stage where nobody stood except for one of the technical guys. Stumbling, careening off scaffolding and old scenery, ducking my way underneath a clothes rail full of costumes, I slammed into the emergency exit, and fell, tumbling, into the back alley beyond. As I dragged myself back up and began sprinting for the far corner of the building, I heard my mother's voice behind me, pleading with me to calm down, get back inside, it wasn't too late.

But it was. It was far too late. As I reached the main street, full of noisy traffic, I glanced back and saw the confused, distressed figures of Mum and Luke. But what made me pause, for the tiniest of moments, was Dad's face. A mixture of thunderous rage and disgust. I turned and ran.

For the rest of the evening I wandered the streets, ignoring my dance-shoe blisters, eventually ending up at a bus station. Huddling in one corner of a bench I attracted curious glances from the few travellers boarding or leaving buses, and as the night wore on I grew frightened of the groups of men who slowed down to stare at me or make bawdy comments about my outfit. I went into the furthest ladies' toilet I could find, locked myself in a cubicle, kicked off my stupid shoes and curled up on the sticky, stinking floor until I drifted off to sleep.

A woman with two small children came in to use the facilities that morning, waking me up. Uncurling stiff limbs, I climbed up and squatted on the toilet lid until they left. I washed myself and tidied up my hair as best I could, then marched out into the station as if I had no care in the world.

It was just two minutes before a bus driver, having been informed to keep an eye out for a fifteen-year-old girl in a ballroom dancing outfit, clamped one hand on my shoulder and solved my problem of how to find our hotel.

Needless to say, I spent the rest of the trip in bed hoping I might die while the Henderson family proper enjoyed the sights, along with their adopted dance troupe. Miriam in particular enjoyed the sight of the policeman who had taken the missing girl report, already hatching plans to get herself back to Australia as soon as possible and stay there. My other sisters, without the distraction of a holiday romance, were spitting lava. Mum clucked, patted my head through the bed-sheet and told me to pull myself together.

Not a single word passed between Dad and me until we returned home. The following week, when he asked me to get changed ready for dance class, I told him exactly what I thought about his precious dance school, the Henderson family I considered myself no longer part of, and him.

It did not go down well.

He accepted my unofficial resignation from the family, if not in words, then in action. Years of misunderstandings, rebellion and disappointment reached a crashing crescendo. Dad didn't know what to do with me, so did nothing. I pretended I hated him, buried the pain of my failure and rejection under slamming doors, scowls and spending every spare moment out of the house. What a pathetic mess.

Ana Luisa, no stranger to family struggles, pursed her lips at me. "Well, it is no surprise you ran off to a strange city and jumped into the arms of the first man who was nice to you."

Maybe not. Maybe it was no surprise that I stayed with him, clinging to our shambles of a partnership, finding neither the courage to fix it nor the confidence to walk away either.

Harry grabbed me before he left the party. He had managed a whole fifty minutes away from Hope, an impressive forty minutes longer than Rupa.

"Hey, Ruth. How are you doing?" Brimming with emotional energy, he clasped me in a bear hug.

"I'm good, Harry. How are you?"

"Brilliant! Knackered, but brilliant. So, I wanted to thank you again for looking after Rupa that night."

"It's okay, Harry. I think the first six thank yous covered it. I didn't do anything really, apart from not throw her out in the snowstorm."

He frowned at me. "Rupa mentioned about that doctor pestering you. You asking him to help means a lot."

We hadn't told Rupa the discoveries since that night. She had enough to deal with.

"No, it's fine. Please stop thanking me. It's getting awkward." I smiled at him, rolling my eyes a little bit, wondering how grateful he would be when he found out I placed his wife in the hands of a struck-off, disgraced doctor.

"Okay, but I need to tell you something. I didn't think much of it at the time, with everything going on, but when the guy was examining Rupa, he opened his bag. He had binoculars in there. High tech ones – like night vision goggles."

I quickly sat down in the nearest chair before I fell down. "Are you sure?" I managed to croak.

"I'm sorry, Ruth. Do you need some of us to pay this guy a visit?"

I shook my head feebly. "No. It's okay. I've spoken to the police. He's disappeared, anyway. No one's seen him for months. Thanks for telling me."

The party came to an end early evening, with one last ogle at Hope via the big screen. I had taken six more orders for pictures: three for new babies, two for wedding presents and one for a woman who simply liked animal pictures. I stayed to help clear up along with a bunch of other people, Lois and Matt included. Bumping into Lois by the outside bin, I hurriedly relayed what Harry had told me.

"Eew. That's horrible."

"I feel so bad for letting him near Rupa. What if the ambulance hadn't got there so quickly? Who knows what he might have done to her."

"Woah, Ruth. Calm down. Carl was struck off for an inappropriate relationship, not incompetence. And the ambulance did get there. Let it go."

"Binoculars. Night vision goggles!" I yanked at my hair in frustration.

"I know."

"He was watching me! I knew he was – the whole Christmas present thing and how he kept turning up all the time. He watched me. In my own house. It makes me want to throw up."

"Me too. And it didn't even happen to me. But he's gone, Ruth. You calling on him to help Rupa turned out to be a good thing. You scared him off."

Maybe. But I had an ugly feeling Carl Barker could not be scared off so easily. There were five cars remaining in the car-park when I left. None of them black. I ducked my head and marched the twenty-minute journey home, eyes down, heart pounding, fear nipping at my heels.

Later on that week, another withheld number. I disconnected without answering, got up and closed every blind and curtain in the house despite the fact the sun blazed outside.

On a drizzly morning near the end of the month, I picked up Lois in the car and set off towards the motorway. She had armoured up in a pair of elegant brown trousers and white top trimmed with lace. Her hair freshly styled, nails brown to match her trousers, Lois hid behind her classy exterior.

"Okay?" I flicked down the radio a notch, glancing over at her chewing on a nail.

"I'll do. It means a lot to me, you doing this."

"No problem. I have to use my holidays up sometime. I told Martine we were having a day out."

Lois grimaced. "That's one way of putting it."

"So how are you really feeling about this?"

She stared out of the passenger window for a moment, hands knotting and unknotting in her lap. "Apprehensive. Guilty. Sort of numb. It beats how I used to feel."

"Scared?"

"Terrified. And filthy. Worthless and broken beyond repair. Resentful. And the anger? It ate at me like I was knocking back battery acid," Lois said.

"You don't feel angry any more?"

"Not about him. Virtually never. I have more important things to channel my anger into. You know – justice, fighting the flaws in our social care system, people who insist on making bad choices on behalf of my kids… evil drug lords, the slave trade, the poverty crises, my continuing lack of a romantic life. I'm not sure quite when or how it happened, but I forgave my dad. Not for his benefit, if I'm honest, but for mine. And Matt's. I just needed to be done with it."

"And this is the final step," I added.

"More like the beginning of the end. You know how messy the aftermath can get."

"Well, if it's any help, I'm pretty good at sorting through all that complicated stuff."

"Thanks."

We drove in silence for a few miles. The truth was, I felt nervous on Lois's behalf. She had called the day before, uncharacteristically fretful, and asked if I would go with her to visit her dad in hospital in Birmingham. Having not seen him for more than a decade, during which time he'd gone into prison and come out again, he'd named Lois as next of kin and asked the hospital to get in touch. He had liver failure. He wanted to see his daughter before he died.

She asked if it could wait a few days – her husband was in bed with stomach flu. Apparently there were no days to wait. So, here we were.

# CHAPTER TWENTY-FIVE

"Will your mum want to see him?"

Lois shook her head. Her mum had remarried sixth months after her divorce came through. She now lived in Spain with her husband and his children. "No. She barely sees *me* because it reminds her of her old life."

"That must be hard."

"Yep. But Matt's parents fill in some of the gap." She looked across at me and grinned. "And I have some awesome friends. And a massive Oak Hill family who do stuff like send my kids to Paris. I have more blessings than I can count. I'm at peace with it. Mum's doing her best to survive. I get that."

We drove some more.

"Do you still feel angry, Ruth? About losing Fraser?"

I considered that. "No. I'm not angry he died. I felt angry he left with no will, no life insurance and a pile of secret debts. Furious I had to uproot Maggie from her home and her school and come back to Southwell and cope with my parents. I really didn't want to have to face those memories. But if I'm still angry, it's at myself. Looking back, I can't believe my laziness. I had given up. I had no friends, Lois. No hopes, no plans, no energy, no confidence. I refuse to feel sorry for myself any longer. This is my life now, and all I can do is choose to make the most of it."

"I'm proud of you, sister. Amen to that."

"You know, when you pretend to be a pastor's wife I get an overwhelming urge to tell a dirty joke."

"You don't know any dirty jokes."

"I could probably make one up if I tried."

We parked the car and made our way through the hospital corridors to the ward. A nurse buzzed us in, and directed us to the right bed. Lois gripped tight to my arm as we made our way along the bays.

My memories of Rupert Finch were of a powerfully built man with a red face, who used to clap people on the back a lot, point his finger and make loud jokes that weren't funny but people laughed anyway. Looking back there was nothing to distinguish him as a monster. Even less so now.

A withered, yellowed, unkempt old man wearing a hospital gown and several days of grey stubble cowered in the bed furthest along the bay. He slowly rolled jaundiced eyes over to see who approached, and growled out, "Nurse?"

Lois clutched my arm tighter. I felt her take in a deep breath, hold it for a second before slowly exhaling. I touched her hand and stepped back. She responded with a tiny nod, and walked across to stand a couple of paces from the bed.

"Dad. It's me. It's Lois."

I found a nook set out for visitors with a couple of comfy chairs and a rack of magazines. Still only halfway through discovering the style bloops of the recent red carpet event, as described by a publication whose copy read like that of a jealous school girl, I looked up to see Lois waiting for me.

She looked tired, but her shoulders were straight and her mascara was intact.

"How was it?"

She shrugged. "I didn't need the tissues. Shall we get a sandwich or something before you drive back?"

"I'm happy to do whatever you want."

"Honestly, I just want to go home and hug my children, then my husband, and blob on the sofa with a box set of something brainless and cheesy."

"I didn't think you got any blobbing time in your house."

"I'm making time. We can survive on fish and chips for once. And if the kids have no ironed uniform for school tomorrow, boo hoo. They'll get over it."

I stood up, reaching to give her a hug, but she held up her hands to block me.

"Don't. Not here. I'm a whisker away from causing a scene."

Her chin wobbled, and I took hold of her hand instead. "I knew it was all a show. Underneath you're a total wimp. Come on, I wouldn't want you to embarrass me in public with an overly dramatic display of emotion."

I took my strong friend home, back to the guilt-free, resentment-free, self-pity-free, incredible life she had created despite every excuse not to.

That afternoon I walked down to the bank and deposited the most recent cheque for five thousand pounds that Dad had given me following my failure to cash the first two. A punch in the face of the debt monster. Pow! On my way back, in an empty alleyway, I danced a little rhumba and then a few steps of the tango. I was a Henderson girl. Well, look at that. I was dancing after all.

That is, until I sashayed out of the alleyway. Just down the road in front of me crouched a sleek black car. I stumbled to a halt, and the car slowly accelerated away from the side of the road. As it turned the corner, I swear its lights flashed. Either that or it was a vein exploding behind my eyes.

I stomped home on quaking legs, furious I hadn't kept enough presence of mind to read the number plate, frustrated I had no idea whether I was being paranoid or not. I drew the blinds in the living room and the kitchen, and got out the evil-stalker logbook, all the time listening for the sound of an expensive engine crawling down the cul-de-sac.

My head said not to panic at the calls, the sightings, the white rose I found on the doormat the following morning. There could be any number of rational non-Carl related explanations. My guts, my instincts, my womanly intuition agreed – no need to panic, but don't for a second try to convince yourself this is anything other than ex-Dr Carl Coombes-Barker. Mum or Dad started giving me a lift to work. I finally gave in and bought another phone, telling no one but Maggie and my parents the number. Nobody complained when I drew the curtains any more. He was winning. The fear was winning. But I was darned if I was going to let him see it.

Lois's father died a few days later. There were half a dozen mourners at the crematorium. After the brief ceremony, I went with Lois and Matt to visit his old flat. We stood, appalled, in the skeleton of one man's life. A couple of shabby, mismatched pieces of furniture, empty cupboards, bare beige walls. A few worn out items of clothing in the wardrobe. Nothing in the bathroom except a used-up toilet roll. Dirt, dust, grime. Too many empty bottles of gin to count.

Matt called a company who would clear everything out and clean it up. We locked up and left, driving home through bright sunshine, each with the same thought stark in our minds: there wasn't a single person on the planet who would miss Rupert Finch, one-time property entrepreneur, husband and father. What a terrible, shocking, heartbreaking waste of a life. What a sharp reminder to get up, get out, love, laugh and live while we can. To take life by the hand and, by golly, to dance every step.

By June I was beside myself. The silent calls had transferred to the landline. Whether it was once a week or five times in one afternoon, what scared me most was that they only happened when I was home alone. I took to bolting all the doors, turning up the television loud and holing up in the living room until someone else arrived back. My life had become a sick game, and the stress was taking its toll on the whole family. In front of them I smiled and made jokes about it, neglecting to tell them the frequency or timing of the calls, pretending I was being a bit of a silly billy really. But they weren't fooled for a second. I wasn't the only one with pinched lines around my eyes, jumping when the phone rang or a shadow passed in front of the door.

Something had to give. This couldn't go on much longer.

Carl Barker agreed with me on that, if nothing else.

# Chapter Twenty-Six

It was a sunny Saturday lunchtime. I found Maggie mooching about in cut-off shorts and a T-shirt, killing time until her visit to Hannah's. Things had improved somewhat as the befriending scheme came towards its end. With one of the sessions now taking place at the dance class, it had the added bonus of giving them something to talk about during the Saturday session too. Hannah had been helping Maggie plan decorations, digging out faded recipes for cakes, compiling a list of her favourite songs from the fifties. They had even, on a few occasions, ventured out into the garden. Instead of barking gardening-related orders from the window, Hannah had taken to sitting on a plastic sun lounger borrowed from John next door, underneath a saggy brimmed hat. Maggie even caught her walking unaided a couple of times.

"I reckon she's grown a good four inches. It's because she doesn't stoop over that frame any more, unless someone's looking. She's stopped wobbling so much too. I knew she couldn't really be that frail."

"You've given her something to live for. She's standing tall because she's happier. And she's wobbling less because she's starting to feel strong."

"Well, whatever the reason, I wish she'd admit it so she can iron her own face cloths."

"Nobody irons their face cloths!" I exclaimed.

"No. They just get child slaves to do it for them as punishment instead."

"The befriending scheme wasn't a punishment."

"Really? You try ironing someone else's unmentionables in a dark, dirty flat while your friends are all out sunbathing."

"Are you out with Seth this afternoon?" Seth and Maggie were now on probation. One evening and one weekend date per week, with a ten o'clock curfew.

"Hello? I'm at Hannah's. She's showing me how to make napkin swans."

"Don't be rude. I meant afterwards."

"No."

"No? Are you seeing him this evening instead?"

"I'm revising."

"You used to revise together."

"What is this? An interrogation? I didn't think you wanted me spending time with him anyway." She flung herself off the sofa and left the room. I followed her into the kitchen – I couldn't help it. I'm her mum; it's what I do.

"The two of you spent months trying to convince me you can be trusted to go out together. It's understandable I'd be curious when you aren't making the most of it."

"He's busy. All right?"

I raised my eyebrows. Had Seth Callahan had the audacity to brush off my daughter? Where was a shotgun when you wanted one?

"As long as you're sure that's all it is."

"I told you, I trust him! When are you going to accept that we actually love each other?"

"I'm sorry. I just want you to be careful." I made a mental note to speak to Lois.

Maggie stared at her half-made sandwich for a minute.

"Why didn't you and Dad get married?"

I could have fobbed this question off as I'd done a thousand times before. Or pretended I didn't know. Pretended I hadn't really thought about it. Did I tell the truth? Maybe a selective, filtered version.

"That's not an easy question to answer. If you'd asked Dad, he probably would've given you a different reason."

"Didn't you even talk about it?"

"We had a conversation when I found out I was pregnant. But, honey, we were students. We weren't ready, we barely knew each other. It was scary enough trying to figure out how to be parents. Husband and wife felt too much right then."

"But what about later on? When you were older, and knew you loved each other?"

Oh, boy. I could not tell the whole truth here.

"I don't know – we honestly never really discussed it. I used to wonder, when you were little, if at Christmas or Valentine's Day Dad would surprise me with a ring, but he was never really into all that. There was always something – a house move, or looking for a new job, a different car. And you know Grandma Margaret would have hated it. She'd have turned our wedding day into a nightmare. It didn't really matter that much. We were a family, weren't we?"

What a big, fat lie. Some women, and fair play to them, don't give a fig about a wedding, a white dress, a first dance. A man who is prepared to commit himself legally to one woman, making public vows to honour, care for her and all the rest of it for as long as they both shall live.

I had never been one of those women.

I still thought about Maggie's marriage question an hour later, staring at the half-completed Oak Hill newsletter on my laptop. That's not quite true. My daydreams about marriage did not include Fraser. Shutting the computer down I sighed and went into the kitchen to put the kettle on. In every imagined wedding scenario, I tried to picture gliding down the aisle in my antique-lace dress towards an anonymous husband to be – one I had met at some unspecified time in the distant future. So why did he stand at the front of Oak Hill church with his hands in his back pockets, a grin that warmed me down to my toes and eyes like pools of silver?

David had gone from my life again. But the brief time we spent together confirmed what I knew all along: I would always love him. Not as a friend or a brother, or because he happened to want me. I didn't primarily love the way he made me feel, or the memories he stirred, or the idea of being truly loved. I loved him. That man. Everything about him. So, how he felt, or where he was, or even if –

The kitchen door swung open.

"Hello, Ruth."

The coffee cup slid out of my grasp and smashed onto the tiles at my feet.

# Chapter Twenty-Seven

"What are you doing here?" I could hear the tremor in my voice. Time stopped as I tried to recall where my phone was. Think, Ruth. In the living room? No. Not had it this afternoon. Still by my bed? Don't think so. In my bag? Maybe. Think!

Carl Barker carefully closed the door behind him, turned the key and pocketed it. Ignoring the broken cup, he smiled at me. "Looking for this?" He held up my phone then, never taking his eerie blue eyes off mine, dropped it onto the floor and crunched it underfoot.

"There you go, Ruth. I know you like to buy yourself new phones."

I darted towards the hallway, but Carl anticipated me, slamming the door before I reached it and blocking the exit. His presence seemed to fill the kitchen – with horror and dark, demented insanity.

As I ducked back he grabbed me from behind, wrapping both his arms around me in a vice-like grip. He reeked – of stale sweat and evil.

"We're going upstairs. You're going to show me how much you missed me."

"The police know everything."

He laughed. "Oh, I doubt that."

"They know about that other woman – in the States – and the phone calls, and you following me about."

"Phone calls? Following you? Sounds like wishful thinking to me. Sounds like you've been dreaming about me. You never got over me, did you, Ruth? Couldn't handle the fact we broke up?"

I said nothing, desperately scanning the kitchen for some way to get him off me, anticipating the moment he might relax his grip, hoping I would be strong enough to get away. I wished I had shoes on so I could kick. Or a pen in my hand to jab him with.

He began to stroke one hand up and down my cheek.

"I heard Tarzan left. Couldn't handle you being with me. Sending me secret messages. Encouraging me. Begging me to come back. So here I am. I forgive you, Ruth. I'm prepared to give us another chance. But you have to show me I can trust you again. How committed you are."

Blood pounding through my veins, I assessed my options. Bending my head as far forward as possible, I slammed it back as hard as I could into his face. But I was too short, and only succeeded in smacking into the hard bone of his chin. He didn't even loosen his grip.

"Your choice. We can do this the easy way. Or my way."

He flipped me around to face the door as though I was a cardboard cut-out, grabbing the back of my neck and bashing my skull into the wood a couple of times, until my head span and my knees began to give way. As I stumbled to catch my balance, he reached into his dishevelled coat pocket with his free hand and pulled out a syringe.

"This is what I prescribe for troublesome women who don't know any manners and need to learn respect." He pinned me to the door and I felt the sharp stab of the needle in my bare shoulder. That was the last thing I remembered.

I awoke in a heap of nausea and cramping muscles on my bed, slowly remembering the horrifying situation. Realizing that something had jolted me out of unconsciousness. The crashing of the front door. Beyond the thick haze I heard the random banging of cupboards in the kitchen below. One frantic, despairing thought pushed through the fog in my brain: *Maggie.*

As quickly as I could manage, which was about the same speed as wading through mud, I rolled off my bed, tumbling onto the carpet. Frantically, feverishly, I manoeuvred myself onto my front and used the side of the bed to heave to a kneeling position. I crawled through the fog and the pain and the mallet in my head towards the open bedroom door. Panic flooded my system as I heard the sound of feet thumping up the stairs. Collapsing in the doorway, I saw Carl step out of the bathroom, caught a flash of silver glinting in his hand. Maggie reached the top stair and paused, confused and angry. Before she could speak, Carl leaned forward. He smiled. "Hello, brat. I was hoping you might show up."

He kicked her down the stairs. I heard her bones bounce off every step. With the warrior strength of a mother I stumbled to my feet and out onto the landing as Carl, who had sprung down after her, jumped off the last step with both feet, landing beside her crooked legs.

He roared with laughter. The silver glinted in his hand again. A scalpel. My beautiful daughter, a twisted, lifeless rag doll, lay there at the mercy of a monster and I couldn't reach her. For the first time in my life, I knew what genuine fear felt like.

I must have moaned or wailed, or something. Carl glanced up at me and raised his eyebrows in delight. "Ruth! You're awake."

He kicked Maggie again, hard, and bounded up the stairs two at a time. I fell back towards the bedroom, half blind with rage and despair, my head still fighting whatever poison he had pumped into my bloodstream. Towering over me, he licked at the spittle in the corners of his lips. He carefully removed his glasses, placing them on the bedside table. Untied the laces of his grimy shoes, and lined them neatly by the side of the bed. Attacked by another wave of dizziness, I sank onto the carpet.

"Get on the bed."

I shook my head, no. He bent down, and I feebly batted a hand at his face. Giving me no more mind than he would a moth, he picked me up and tossed me onto the covers. I sprawled there, in the place where I had said my little girl goodnight prayers, read secret stories under the bedclothes, pinched myself to stay awake until Santa came.

Carl breathed heavily, licked his lips again, reached down and stroked the hair off my face. "You have no idea how much I've been looking forward to this."

I struggled to sit up, and he struck me across the side of my head, still smiling. "Come on now, Ruth. Play nice. The easy way, or my way."

I shook my head again, too messed up to speak. I would play nice. I couldn't take any more of that drug. I had to stay awake for Maggie. She needed me. I must get to Maggie. If it meant killing this evil monster, I would get to her.

I think I prayed. Is it ever okay to pray for a chance to kill someone?

I closed my eyes, tried to find a dark corner of my head where I could wait it out until all this was over, when suddenly I felt the shadow of Carl move away from me. Heard the sound of pounding flesh. A grunt. Turning to look, I saw in my semi-delirium what must have been an angel pinning Carl to the far wall, before throwing a punch to his head so hard he sagged to the ground, unconscious. The angel talked on a mobile phone. He took a roll of masking tape out of the doctor's bag sitting on my dressing table chair and deftly taped the monster's hands and feet behind his back. Moving to my bedside, he placed his strong, rough hands gently either side of my face. I knew those hands.

"Are you all right? Ruth? Are you hurt?"

*My body, not so much. My heart, soul and spirit? Crushed.* I managed one whispered word. "Maggie."

The angel nodded, bending down to kiss my wrist, my forehead, my mouth, before quickly leaving the room. I sank back down into the murky blackness.

I remember vague snatches from what happened next. The bump of the wheeled stretcher as it slid into the ambulance. My mother's stern instructions to keep calm, don't worry, hang on! A cool hand slipping on an oxygen mask. Drifting in and out of befuddled dreams to find myself in a different room in the hospital every time. One pervading thought clawed its way through the malevolent, agonizing mist that writhed inside my head, until I thought it would explode. *Maggie.*

In the end, after managing to keep my eyes open for more than a few seconds, sip an inch of water and cough it back up again, when I had confirmed that I did indeed know my name and the prime minister's, they gave in to my frantic protests and took me to her.

My parents sat either side of her bleeping, wire-encased, machine-controlled hospital bed. Buried under a tiny mound of blankets, sleeping, she looked about seven years old.

Mum stirred. "She's all right, Ruth. She will be all right."

Guilt, shame and excruciating remorse bubbled up from somewhere deep down inside me. I let out a cry that pierced the air with its sharpness. Mum looked right at me, her face granite, and took my fluttering hands in hers. "This is not your fault, Ruth. You did not do this. A wicked, damaged, dangerous man hurt your girl, and you could not have stopped him. He stuck you with enough sedative to fell a rhinoceros. Do not feel guilty about this! Feel angry, and sad and frustrated, and as if it was your heart that was kicked down the stairs, not Maggie. But do not take the blame! Not one speck! Now. Your father is wheeling you back to your bed before you collapse. Don't worry, I'm staying right here."

Dad wheeled me back through the maze of antiseptic-scented corridors to my ward. He helped me shuffle back into bed, then straightened the sheet.

"I won't tuck you in. I know you hate tight sheets."

My eyelids felt weighted down. I couldn't keep them open much longer.

"Your mum's right. Try not to feel too bad about what happened." The last thing I saw was Dad's shoulders slumping with sorrow. The last thing I heard, his broken words. "I'm sorry, Ruth. I'm so sorry."

Maggie had a broken ankle, a fractured pelvis, a thousand bumps and bruises, shattered innocence, haunted dreams, but – and I found myself thanking God for this – strength, determination and courage. She would recover. We would recover. I forgot to ask what happened to the person who did this. I found out later it involved lawyers, no bail, no lenience and a trail of damning evidence including a stash of stalker photographs, secret video footage that I cringe to think the police and lawyers watched, and a cache of illegal drugs.

My angel came to visit me. He didn't stay for long because I asked him not to. I didn't trust myself in my weakened, befuddled state not to grab him by the lapels and snog the oxygen out of him. He had seen Carl's car in a neighbour's driveway. Knowing they were away, he grew suspicious and came to check on me. He left a bunch of freesias, my favourite flowers. He didn't say much. Just stared at me, smiled and cried a little bit in a sexy, manly way, then kissed me on the forehead again before leaving. Oh yes – and he left a card. Inside it said:

> *I ripped up my new contract. Turns out everything I wanted in the Whole Wild World is here.*

By the next afternoon I was ready to transfer my aching bones to Maggie's bedside, relieving Mum to go home and shower and bake enough cookies for the entire hospital before returning with a bag of essentials to see us through the next few days. For the two weeks Maggie stayed in hospital, I lost count of the number of friends that came to visit. My sister Esther came three times with Arianna and painted everybody's nails. Hannah brought a pile of napkins and they sat and made swans until their fingers grew tired (about six minutes). Vanessa Jacobs brought an Italian scarf to decorate her cast with. Of course Seth. He arrived every day ten minutes before visiting hours started, blatantly flaunting the terms of the probation. I watched him with my daughter, patient when she snapped and grumbled, thoughtful when she grew tired or emotional. He made her laugh. He made her feel strong. He made her shine. I considered removing the probation. Then the nurses told me that twice he had hidden under Maggie's bed, once more behind a curtain, then snuck out after visiting hours were over and crept into bed with her. My growing soft-spot for Seth Callahan re-hardened slightly. I narrowed my eyes at his swarthy good-looking swagger and the probation remained intact.

Maggie wanted to talk about the tea dance, now only three weeks away.

"How many tickets have you sold? Who's doing the decorations? Hannah can't do everything. What about the food? You need to stop visiting me so often and start sorting it out, Mum!"

"It's fine. All under control. Nanny has organized a team to sort the food, and the Oak Hill craft group are following Hannah's instructions regarding the decorations. It's great – she's having to go along to the group to check they're doing it properly, for *your* sake, of course. She even walked there yesterday."

"Right. But what if nobody comes?"

"We've sold sixty tickets, Maggie."

"SIXTY?"

I grinned at her wonderment. She looked so young with her hair unstyled and no eyeliner.

"We've had to say no more entries for the intergenerational competition. Pop said there were twelve couples, and unless we decide to hold heats, we can't fit any more on the dance floor."

"Did he cross us off the list?" Her face fell glum again. "He was really looking forward to dancing. And we were bound to win."

"Well, you can give some poor disadvantaged non-professional a chance instead."

Maggie looked at me, her expression sly. "Or... you could do it."

"No."

"Why not? You used to dance. You could pick up the steps really quick. Oh, come on, Mum. You'd make Pop's day. I bet he'd love to dance with you. Please, Mum. Please, please, please."

"No."

"I'm grievously injured and, like, seriously emotionally traumatized, and my one and only wish is to see my mother dance with my grandfather, bringing home the first ever Oak Hill teadance intergenerational trophy and giving me something to smile about in a world that has become cruel and twisted and –"

"I'll think about it."

"Hah! That means you're going to do it. Hand me my phone. I'm texting Pop. You need to get learning the steps straight away. I know you've had years of training, but if your half-hearted attempts at class are anything to go by, you need all the practice you can get."

"That's it, Maggie. Insulting me is definitely the way to get me to agree to this. Perhaps you want to tell me how hideous I'll look in a ball-gown?"

"Nah. Now you've grown some boobs and hips you'll carry it off."

"Glad to hear you sounding like your old self again, my darling."

Oh, my goodness I was glad. Breathless with relief. Of course I would dance for her. Hopefully, no spending the night on a toilet floor this time.

So Maggie came home. Mum was delighted to have a full-time needy person to cluck and fuss over, although Dad chipped in, in his unobtrusive way. I balanced my time between catching up on a mountain of work, finishing off orders for eight more pictures, awkwardly, nervously learning dance steps while Dad and I tried not to tread on each other's toes and tearing my gaze away from the Big House.

David had called in at the hospital twice to see Maggie. The first time, I bolted to the restaurant, still too vulnerable and inside out and upside down to know how to deal with him. The second time, I walked in to find them playing black-jack. Maggie ordered me to join in. For a glorious thirty minutes I caught a glimpse of what life could be like if I managed to get a grip on my rampaging hormones and maintain a friendship with David without spending the whole time wanting to nuzzle his neck.

We bumped into each other once more, a week before the dance. I was strolling home from work, having been caught in a summer shower. My clothes and work bag were dripping wet, but the air was warm and clean in between the fat raindrops, and I was taking my time.

He came up behind me, calling my name from a few yards away. "Hey, Ruth."

I turned to see him striding through the rain, hair plastered to his head, the water glistening off his tanned arms.

"Hi," I smiled. I suspect it was a little goofy.

"Didn't want to sneak up on you."

"Thanks. I am still pretty jumpy. Mum surprised me in the bathroom the other day and I screamed so loud it must have reached the Big House."

"I learned to ignore screams coming from the direction of number five a long time ago," he said, grinning.

"Probably wise."

We walked through the rain for a few minutes. The air carried the scent of ozone and fresh grass. The street leading out of the town centre stood deserted, and it felt as though we were the only people alive.

"I can't remember if I thanked you. That day. I can't remember much of it, to be honest. But if I didn't, then, well…thanks."

David smiled. He kept looking straight ahead, but moved close enough to take hold of my hand. His hand felt strong and safe. My bones turned to treacle.

"Oh yes. You thanked me. I think the word was 'angel'. You said that, ooh, about two hundred and thirty-two times. And um, let me think… hero. That was another one. Amazing, wonderful…I'm pretty sure you called me gorgeous, and pledged your undying love to me not once, but three times. In fact, I think dinner was promised at some point, followed by marriage and many, many babies…"

"Very funny. Please do continue to make jokes about my harrowing hostage ordeal at the hands of a crazed madman."

"You did call me an angel."

"Let's remind ourselves I was under the influence of illegal drugs."

We walked a little longer.

"And you told me that you love me."

A fiery blaze of heat whooshed up through my body. I dropped David's hand, totally flustered. "I've always loved you. You're the brother I never had. You know that."

David turned to face me, drawing me to a stop. He looked at me for a few moments, his face intent. I watched a rivulet of water run down the side of his cheek, fearful of meeting his eyes.

"Is that how you want this to be?"

I shrugged, scuffed my feet on the ground. "It doesn't matter what I want."

"It doesn't matter what you want. Doesn't matter to who? It does to me!"

"What do you expect, David?" I raised my voice now, angry and hurting and so, so tired of this. "Do you think that three weeks after going through a living nightmare Maggie'll look more favourably on me getting involved with a man? Find it easier to trust a bloke? I told you to leave so we didn't have to keep going over this. So *I* didn't have to keep dealing with it. I can't do it any more. It's too much of a tangled mess. You're my past, David. And a lot of that past is not pleasant. We had our chance. It's stupid to think we can go back."

David continued to stare at me, his eyes burning. "Why can't you let yourself be happy, Ruth? You don't want Maggie to give her blessing because it gives you an excuse to continue punishing yourself for mistakes a teenage girl made a hundred years ago."

"That is not true!" That was so true. "You are so darn arrogant, David Carrington. What makes you assume I want a relationship with you anyway?"

I turned and fled, my lightweight pumps skidding on the soaking wet pavement. If I cried, then the tears blended with the rain so perfectly I couldn't tell.

# Chapter Twenty-Eight

The morning of the tea dance, two cards sat forlornly on the kitchen table. *Happy anniversary, love Harriet. Happy wedding anniversary, yours, Gil.* No flowers, no chocolates, no talk of one of Mum's themed dinners. I had a brainwave and rang Esther in the hope she could help me out. No problem, her baby sister might yet save the day – she was on it.

We spent the whole day at Oak Hill, getting everything ready. Mum bustled, Dad hung lights while Maggie directed him with her crutches, and I snuck off every chance I could get to practise my dance steps in the disabled toilet. We had sold every last ticket. A hundred. The morbid curiosity generated by the organizer having recently survived a gruesome incident with a psychopath helped, of course. Seth, who had been at his girlfriend's beck and call all morning, adjusting her cushions, fetching her drinks, calming her down, disappeared soon after lunch.

"Did Seth have something on this afternoon?" Surely not. This day had been planned for months.

"Yes."

"What's that then?"

"I don't know." Oh dear.

"Don't look like that, Mum. We've got loads of help. I said I didn't mind."

"I'm just surprised."

"Really? I thought this was exactly what you expected from Seth.

It gives you more reason to prolong this totally unfair probation."

It might have been what I expected, but Seth's secrets were not what I wanted for my daughter. Maggie was right: I couldn't keep this probation up forever. I muttered a silent prayer that Seth would either get his act together or increase his dodgy behaviour to the point where Maggie decided not to put up with it. *Just please, please don't let this boy break her heart.*

I joined Emily, folding napkins at the speed of light on one of the round corner tables.

"Hi, Ruth. How's it all looking?"

"Pretty good. I think it's going to be spectacular."

"Describe it to me."

"Well, we have white and midnight blue gossamer drapes hung in a circle across the ceiling, meeting in the middle like a tent. The blue drapes have white lights running along them, and the white ones have blue. There are more drapes covering the walls, and the rest of the round tables are like this one. White tablecloths and blue or silver runners."

Mum had dragged in huge leafy branches and weighted them down in buckets around the edge of the room, adorning the branches with fairy lights. The chairs had white covers, with blue or silver gossamer bows, and Maggie's friends were creating pretty centrepieces using silver plates covered in moss, tiny summer flowers and more sparkly lights.

"It looks like we'll be dancing in an enchanted forest clearing," I added.

"Sounds incredible." Emily's nimble fingers continued to fold napkins into swans without slowing down. She sighed. "I would like to take a good look at that."

I shuffled my chair closer and leaned my head on her shoulder. "I would like that too."

Emily rested her head on top of mine. "How are you, Ruth? Still having nightmares? Any more flashbacks? Cold sweats or crying for no reason? Anxious or unusually guilt-ridden?"

"Yes. All of that. But it's getting better."

"Give my secretary a call and set up some sessions. Mates' rates. Which in my case is nothing."

"If I decide I need professional help, I'll pay you for it. But I'm doing okay really."

"Okay. I thought so. Unfortunately, I don't consider okay a satisfactory state for any of my friends to be living in. And neither does your mother."

"Oh, here we go…" I sat back up again.

"Book the session, Ruth. You'll be doing me a favour," she said, in a tone that meant business.

"How?"

"I'm furious with myself!" Emily ripped up a napkin – made of pretty good quality paper and not easily torn – and threw the bits across the table. "I'm raging that I didn't see this coming. Didn't take this guy seriously enough. I should have spotted it."

"If it'll make you feel better, I'll think about it. But maybe you need to listen to your own advice."

We sat and folded napkins together for a few minutes.

"Mum's going to pay you for the sessions, isn't she?"

Emily smiled. "I couldn't possibly comment."

"Mates' rates? It's about time my mother stopped paying people to be nice to me."

"It's about time you stopped running away and let people be nice to you."

"Is she paying you for this conversation?"

"Remarks like that are exactly what I'm talking about."

"Oh, there's my lovely boss, Martine. I must go and say hello."

Emily shouted after me as I dashed off. "Running away!"

Later that afternoon, the Henderson family got the shock of their life when a voice boomed out, "Stone the crows! Would you cop a loada this?"

"Miriam!" My mother vaulted across the room, tossing the tablecloth in her hand over one shoulder as she ran. Throwing her arms around Miriam, she cried and laughed and stood back to look her up and down before clutching her tightly again. Dad followed close behind her.

After a few minutes, I prised my parents away long enough to give my favourite sister a hug. "What on earth are you doing here?"

"Heard there was going to be a Henderson reunion. Ya didn't think I was going to miss it, did ya?"

I must have looked confused. Mum whispered, "It's meant to be a secret! Lydia is one of our surprise celebrity judges!"

Lydia, a judge? Great. Maybe people would expect her to show bias towards me due to our sisterly status. I snorted at the very thought. At least dancing with Dad might reduce the temptation to mark me down.

Miriam, the exact image of Mum save for her dark brown hair and Sydney tan, peered around the room. "Well, where's that champion niece of mine? I want to sign her cast."

Introductions were made, tea was fetched and eyes were wiped. Miriam called her husband, Adam, in from the foyer, and the remaining preparations were put to one side.

Against all odds, despite past vows and by some sort of miracle, at seven o'clock that evening I found myself dressed up to the nines in a white ball-gown, hovering at the edge of a dance floor. The hall looked amazing, even better than we had hoped. Maggie, hopping in on crutches decorated with silk flowers, took in a slow sweep from one end of the room to the other and glowed. My Maggie, stunning in a simple black and white fifties-style dress, *glowing*. Ana Luisa and Ellie had agreed to man the door, checking tickets and pointing guests in the direction of the seating plan. Ana Luisa stood resplendent in a fiery red salsa costume, Ellie unbothered in her smartest blue jeans and a checked shirt.

I joined a table primarily made up of Oak Hill employees. Lois and Matt sat entwined on one side, enjoying a rare evening as a couple. Martine perched on my left, shimmering in an aqua tasselled flapper dress, complete with a blue and green feathered headdress and her usual make-up.

"Ruth! You've been avoiding me!"

I couldn't help smiling. It was true. I'd been feeling too emotional, too fragile for Martine's frank honesty these past few weeks. I thought I'd been pretty subtle about it, though.

"Maybe."

"You heard about Dorothy?"

I shook my head. I knew she had resigned from her cleaning job the day after Carl's arrest and gone to stay with a relative in Derby. I'm sure my face showed just how interested I was in hearing news about Dorothy.

"She's got a new job, working in a leisure centre again. It's going well, apparently. She's moving forward with her life."

"Good for her." *Ouch, Ruth. Sarcasm does not befit white ball-gowns.*

"Yes. It is good for her. But what about you, Ruth? Managing to move forward, or does the elastic of unforgiveness keep pinging you back to that dreadful day?"

"Can we talk about this some other time?"

"No. This discussion is long overdue. You've avoided me at all other times. And as long as you refuse to forgive all parties concerned, including yourself, you might as well be dragging a life-sized model of Carl Barker with you everywhere you go. Do you want to be free of him or not?"

"It's been a month, Martine. I'm doing my best."

Martine did a little growl of frustration. "I'm going to fire you if you don't do better."

"What? You can't do that!"

"Probably not. But go and see Emily anyway. She's a good counsellor. And maybe she'll be able to help you sort out your pile of issues while you're at it."

"My pile of issues?"

"Pile. Mountain. Heap. Rubbish dump. Issues!"

"Fair enough."

"So you'll go?"

"I've got nothing better to do with my evenings once this tea dance is over. At least on Emily's couch I might get some peace."

At that moment, Maggie tapped me on the shoulder.

"Mum!" Her face was white.

"What is it?"

"Hannah's not here."

Hannah was getting a lift to the dance with her neighbour, John. This whole dance had sprung from Maggie's attempt to help her reclaim a life for herself. Hannah had worked for weeks planning everything, even dusted off her old pearls and silk gloves to wear. I tried to hide my concern.

"Is John here yet?"

She shook her head.

"They'll be here. He would've let us know if there was a problem." Maggie didn't look convinced.

"Give it another half hour, then we'll start worrying, okay?"

At that moment, there was a fanfare of dramatic ballroom music. Dad glided onto the stage from behind a curtain. Dapper in top coat and tails, he stood in front of the microphone. Relating the story of how Maggie cajoled them into starting a tea-dance class, to help her friend Hannah, he described the early classes, with the rag-tag bunch of teenagers and residents from the care home. Explained what a privilege it was to see the two very different groups of people having fun together, and how it had borne the idea of the intergenerational dance-off.

"But you have to wait till later on to see the fabulous fruits of the tea-dance class efforts! We're going to begin the evening by giving you a taste of what they went through. On your feet, ladies and gentlemen, and please offer a very warm welcome to the best dance instructor in the country, if not the universe: the internationally acclaimed, twice UK champion, Harriet Henderson!"

Mum floated onto the stage, her full-length gown whooshing out in a blaze of shimmering sparkle as she twirled to join Dad.

The crowd broke out in spontaneous applause. Half the people here had been on the receiving end of Henderson compassion. Mum took her husband's hand as she curtseyed, and a thousand memories zipped through my mind: shows, parties, the heat of theatre lights, the smell of waxed floors and cheap foundation.

They coached everyone through a waltz, with a perfect balance of professionalism and light-heartedness. Mum demonstrated with one of Maggie's school mates, who blushed sheepishly as she insisted he hold her "like a man". Dad beckoned Martine to come and be his partner. She earned top marks for enthusiasm. I'm not sure who was leading who in that waltz. As the music played and two-thirds of the one hundred guests squeezed onto the dance floor, within moments everything descended into hilarity and chaos. The novice dancers muddled through, until a few minutes in someone turned the music off. All the lights dimmed, save one spotlight in the centre of the floor. Esther and Miriam, two tables away from me, began chanting, "Harriet and Gil! Harriet and Gil!" By the third chant, the couples around them had got the hint, retreating from the floor and joining in with the increasingly loud demand. Martine pushed Dad into the spotlight, and Maggie's friend dragged Mum "like a man" next to him.

I held my breath, too nervous to chant. For the first time ever, my parents looked uncomfortable to be in the spotlight. The chants died away and we waited, in silence, to see what would happen next. A lot of people knew all had not been well in the Henderson family of late. I prayed – a genuine, gut-wrenching, eager prayer – that they would take this opportunity, make our dreams come true and dance.

Esther did not let me down. Out of the empty, endless hush came the first few bars of "At Last" by Etta James. Mum lifted her head as Dad lowered his to meet his wife's gaze. A tiny smile twitched at the corner of each mouth, and Dad offered his hand. As Mum drew gently closer, into the perfect Viennese waltz hold, she could not have looked any less beautiful, less radiant, less *content* than she had when those same few notes played at the first dance of her wedding reception, exactly forty-nine years before.

At last, indeed.

Nobody breathed, or uttered a sound, or so much as rustled their tea dress as the music soared and the best two dancers in the country, if not the universe, performed a love story so exquisite it expressed everything needing to be said without a single word. Dad ended by dipping Mum to a couple of inches off the ground, before sweeping her up again. She tapped him on the backside and said, her voice bouncing off the rafters, "Well, Gil Henderson. Looks like you've still got it!"

Dad's face was serious as he replied, "Maybe. What matters is whether I've still got you." He walked over to the side of the stage and lifted up the microphone. "Ladies and gentlemen. I have a confession to make. I never really liked dancing all that much."

My sisters sucked in an audible breath.

"What I love – my passion, my calling, my dream – is dancing with Harriet Henderson. She makes me want to dance. And the reason I worked so hard at it all those years ago is because she was the best, and I had to be the best to deserve a chance at dancing with her. I forgot that, briefly, for a time. Never again. Happy anniversary, my darling. Thank you for the dance. And now it's someone else's turn. I need a sit down. Is there any whisky?"

The music was turned back on, and various couples, some from the classes, some not, began drifting onto the floor. There was still no sign of Hannah. Or Seth. I found Lois arranging cupcakes onto stands in the kitchen.

Standing next to her, I sliced up a lemon drizzle cake. "Seth isn't here yet. Is he all right?"

Lois glanced over at me out of the corner of her eye. "He's great, thanks."

"Oh." I loaded the cake onto a china plate. "Is he coming later?"

"I imagine so."

"Lois, he's not going to –"

Lois interrupted me. "Ruth, did you actually see Seth with Maggie in hospital? Or the cards he's sent every day he's not been allowed to be with her since? Not texts, or emails, or online posts. He walks round every day in between school and homework and babysitting his sisters and weeding his great-granddad's lawn and practising for his drum exam, and posts a card through your front door because he respects your ridiculous decision but still wants Maggie to know how much he's thinking about her. He's a great kid with a massive heart who made one stupid mistake months ago, with no harm done. How long are you going to keep punishing those two for being in love?"

I was speechless. Lois, however, hadn't finished.

"You know what this is really about?"

"Um. Your very troubled foster kid taking my equally troubled fourteen-year-old daughter to spend the night in a crack brothel?"

"No! It's not about that! It's about you trying to pretend two teenagers can't have a love that is genuine and honest and good for them both, and as deep and real and true as any adult feelings. Because then you have to accept that you and David did not have some childish crush but were actually the love of each other's life. How about you stop trying to work out your messed-up emotions on my kid and get yourself booked in for some therapy!"

Before I could splutter something along the lines of how, in fact, I had already agreed to therapy, Maggie spoke from the kitchen door behind us.

"The competition's about to start." The door banged shut as she left again.

I froze, cake knife in hand. "Did she hear that?"

"I don't know, Ruth. Why don't you ask her?" Lois grabbed a couple of cake plates and pushed through the door back towards the hall. Flummoxed and flustered, I followed.

Mum stood on the stage announcing the judges. Lydia already lounged elegantly behind the judges' table. A far cry from when she had been judged, by millions of viewers, every Saturday night. It was good of her to come. Matt Harris took his seat beside her, to a hearty round of applause, followed by a local performing arts teacher. Then Mum announced our second celebrity judge: "Someone who may not be an expert in the art of ballroom, but certainly knows a lot about the rhythm of life. And, golly, does he have the X-factor! Southwell's second-best celebrity, BAFTA-winning explorer, wildlife presenter and the person every woman would choose to be stuck on a desert island with: David Carrington!"

David emerged, grabbed Mum for a smacker on the lips, grinned and waved at the audience, and flopped into the last judge's chair.

Every other person in the room faded into black and white. I allowed myself a lingering moment to drink him in before trying to wrestle my adrenaline under control and taking my place on the dance floor.

There were twelve couples, ten of them from the class. The eleventh was Ana Luisa and Arnold, who due to having almost twenty-five years between them just scraped in. The twelfth couple had put their names down as Fred and Ginger. I suspected some kids messing about, but Mum just winked at me when I mentioned it. Each couple had two minutes to themselves on the dance floor. Dad and I were fourth.

My whole body trembled so hard as I positioned myself in the centre spot, I felt certain the spectators must see it. Dad wrapped one arm around my waist, his hand taking mine. He murmured, "Look at me, Ruth. Chin up." And I raised my eyes, expecting the familiar frown of impatience, the whisper to buck up, straighten my spine, firm up my arms. Instead, I got caught in a beam of utter joy radiating from every feature on his face. He mouthed, "I love you", and my soul embraced those words like a glass of water in the desert, which is indeed what they were. If only he had known, twenty years ago, that this was what I needed, craved, longed for. What would have got me through the most challenging routines, the most frustrating choreography, every troublesome move or lift or turn.

I twirled within the strength of my father's arms, let him lead me where I had for so long refused to go. When I stumbled, he caught me. When I felt unsure of the next step, he guided me. And for one minute, dancing was not my prison or my adversary. It was my saviour and the promise of redemption. The music stopped; people clapped as if they actually meant it. We scored thirty out of forty. My all-time personal best. Maybe I would do it again sometime. A quickstep or a jive. Something lively and energetic.

We retook our seats. I sneaked another glance at Southwell's second-best celebrity. He was sneaking a glance at me. Our eyes locked and his face hardened, jaw tight. All the oxygen left the room, along with my delight at the past few minutes. Mum announced the next couple, and I dragged my gaze back to the floor.

Ana Luisa and Arnold danced a rhumba. Arnold surprised everyone with some pretty slick moves. Ana Luisa, smokin' in her figure-hugging, backless red dress with a slit up to the hip, was sexy-sational. The man sitting next to me loosened his tie and said, "Is it just me, or did it suddenly get really hot in here?"

They scored thirty-four. However, as the whistles and cheers died down, Ana Luisa grabbed the microphone off the stage.

"Ladies and gentlemen! If I could please have your attention for one moment. I have a very important question to ask my partner." She turned to Arnold, who still looked utterly dazed and bewildered from the rhumba. "Arnold. You are my hero. My best friend. My heart " – she pulled a face – "but also my boss and my landlord, and this makes things kind of awkward. I don't want you to pay me to love you any longer."

Martine, two seats down, barked out, "This conversation could appear highly inappropriate for a church event. Especially considering that dress and that dance!"

There was a ripple of laughter. Ana Luisa rolled her eyes, mock-horrified. "I am his housekeeper! Don't you dare disparage this honourable man! Now, can I finish? Arnold, I want to... Oh – I have forgotten my speech!"

"Good!" Martine shouted. "Get on with it!"

"I read somewhere that it's better to marry than burn with passion. And Arnold – you make me burn! Will you marry me, Arnold Carrington, and make me happier than I ever believed possible?"

Arnold sighed. He frowned and shook his head. "Well, well." He pulled a ring out of his jacket pocket. "If you'd waited five minutes longer I could have asked you myself."

"I have waited long enough!" Ana Luisa yelled excitedly. "I could not wait a second longer!"

The ring went on, the guests clapped again and Mum reclaimed the microphone, tapping it a few times to recapture everyone's attention.

"Ladies and gentlemen, we have one last couple to take to the floor. Would you please welcome Fred and Ginger!"

Out from the shadows, where nobody had seen them creep in due to the distraction of the spectacle that was Ana Luisa, came the last couple in the competition. Walker-free, head held high and heels on, Hannah Beaumont stepped carefully into the spotlight, led by her partner, looking Hollywood-handsome with slicked-back hair and a tuxedo, Seth Callahan.

The opening bars of "Moon River" filled the stunned silence, and hesitantly, creakily, stiffly, Hannah began to waltz. Seth kept his expression professional, his head high, as he gently led her round the floor.

They scored forty points. And a standing ovation. They politely refused an encore.

Maggie raised her smug eyebrows at me from the next table, daring me not to scrap the probation now. What could I do? Seth understood pain and fear and loss. He had learned how to use it to make life better for him and those around him. I believed he loved Maggie. And that was going to turn out to be a good thing.

# Chapter Twenty-Nine

Competition over, trophy presented, the judges retired behind the curtain, the guests helping themselves to more cake before the next part of the evening. My sisters intercepted me on the way to the bar.

"Well done, sis. A respectable third place for the Hendersons."

I pulled a face. "Since when have any of you considered third place respectable?"

Lydia nudged Esther, who poked Miriam in the ribs.

"Okay. What do you want?"

Miriam spoke first. "We thought we'd do a routine. For old time's sake. Maggie said she'd like to see it."

"Well, it's Maggie's night. If she doesn't mind, go for it."

The circle tightened. "That's great, Ruth. But you see…"

Lydia interrupted. "If the Henderson girls are going to dance, we want you in it."

"Hah! You're hilarious. Do you want anything from the bar?"

"No." Miriam reached out and stroked my arm. "Really. We want you to dance with us. We're going to do the number from the Aladdin pantomime."

"The what?"

Esther reminded me. "Lydia wore that pink frilly cape and the purple knicker things."

"Oh. That one." I had been about eight when I danced in that pantomime, and my sisters had not quite given up on me at that point. "Thanks, but no thanks. I'll cheer you on from the sidelines."

They pressed even closer, like a flock of hungry pigeons, cooing and flapping and murmuring enticements at me, until I shouted, "Stop!"

They stopped.

"I am not going to dance. I hate performing. I hate dancing with three clearly far superior talents, and I haven't been able to do the splits in twenty years. I appreciate the gesture, but I don't need to dance with you to feel like a Henderson girl."

Esther thought about this for a moment before widening her eyes in comprehension. "You don't want to dance with us, but still want to be a Henderson girl? Like, just as much part of the family but without that part?"

Somehow I managed to restrain myself from replying with any of the dozen sarcastic remarks that jostled for space on my tongue.

"Yes. I love you. You are amazingly talented and I respect your determination and commitment to ballroom. But I don't share it, I don't want to share it and I'm happy with that." Lydia screwed up her face as much as Botox would allow. "You don't mind if we're honest about you being not that great a dancer? You won't feel left out?"

"I want to be left out! You don't have to understand me, just accept it. I like maths and sketching wildlife and helping people with debt problems. I might even enjoy an unchoreographed boogie to a cheesy song at a party. Now, go and do what you like doing."

They went. I stood in the queue at the bar and surveyed the evening. The dance floor was full, the sound of Tony Curtis barely discernible above the buzz of chatter. Ellie shuffled in one corner, performing the school-disco two-step. Emily swayed with her husband, tucked tightly into his chest. Vanessa, who had somehow been persuaded to give a five per cent discount to anyone buying their outfit for the evening from Couture, chatted stiffly to a couple from Oak Hill. I made a mental note to thank her later. She had ordered in dresses for Maggie and me without us even asking, correctly assuming that with everything going on neither of us would have got around to buying one. And it goes without saying, they were perfect. Rupa's influence had done something miraculous to my old boss. And it is amazing how hearing just a snippet of someone's story can help you to see them in a softer light.

I couldn't see Maggie or Seth. I chose not to worry about that. My parents were leading a small group of older women through the moves to the foxtrot. They each had their own partner, but every couple of seconds their eyes met and teeth flashed in a smile. I had no doubt that all the problems of the past year still existed, but just maybe they would now be faced together, rather than swept under separate carpets.

Lydia rushed over, hurrying as she had only five minutes until the pink-cape-andpurple-knicker-thing number.

"You're right."

I raised my eyebrows.

"You should stick to your own talents." She waved her phone at me. "This afternoon, at Esther's house, Arianna showed me the drawings you did for her and Timothy, so I put them up on Twitter."

Of course she did – Lydia belonged to that breed of twenty-first-century celebrity who found it impossible to fully appreciate anything unless sharing it with the world.

"Ruth, they're trending. Hashtag 'funkyanimalpictures'."

This was somewhat lost on me, as I didn't quite know what that meant.

"I've had dozens of replies asking where they can get hold of one."

"What? *Dozens?*"

She glanced back at her phone. "Eighty-one. No. Eighty-two."

"I don't have eighty-two. Each one is original... I don't..."

Her fingers flew across the screen. "Okay... hang on. I've tweeted 'in very high demand, huge waiting list'. What's your website address?"

"I don't have a website." I started to feel a little faint.

"Okay. Hang on. I've said they were a preview, no orders being taken at moment, stay tuned for further details... No – wait!" She looked at me, eyes gleaming, and named a very famous British pop star, currently splashed all over the tabloids. "She's going to be godmother at Sycamore Green's christening and wants a picture of a sycamore tree full of animals for next Saturday. Oh, and can you write the lyrics to her latest number one in the branches?"

From the snatches I had caught on the radio, before changing stations, these lyrics did include the word "baby" several times, which may have been appropriate had they not been surrounded with other words. Like "booty", "sweat" and "sexy".

"No chance."

"Hang on. No. She's happy to go with the other stuff."

"Does she realize it's Bible verses?"

"That's cool. It's for a christening."

"I can't do it. I've got two pictures already due before then. And it's the Oak Hill Centre AGM. I have a ton of paperwork to wade through."

Lydia's fingers raced across the touchscreen. She named a ridiculous figure, with four numbers in it. I swallowed, hard.

"I suppose I can squeeze it in."

As the night wore on, I wandered between tables, restless, my subconscious searching for the only person there I really wanted to see. David appeared to have left the party. I couldn't blame him for avoiding me. I remembered the steel in his eyes as he had glowered earlier, and tried to pretend it was all for the best. We simply could not be friends. Too much baggage. Nothing to do with my inability to look at him without imagining what it would be like to lean into his broad chest, bury my head in his shirt and –

"Mum!"

I snapped back to reality.

"Hi, Maggie. How are you doing? Not using that leg too much?"

"No." None of the usual teenage scorn at a suggestion I might care about her wellbeing. I decided to push my luck and put my arm around her in public.

"Look! What an amazing night. You did this. I am so proud of you."

"Hardly. Most of it was Nanny bossing other people into doing it." She allowed herself to smile, despite her words. "It did work pretty well, though."

"So – what about Seth Astaire? When I thought he might be skulking off with another woman I did not imagine Hannah."

Maggie said nothing, just continued to watch the party, her crutch digging into my thigh. That tipped me over – no wheedling, pleading, sulking, threatening or shouting about the flawed image I had constructed of her boyfriend.

"Maybe you'd like to invite him round for dinner sometime? We can pick a night Nanny's out if that's less daunting."

She didn't rise to the bait and ask me why she would want to waste one of her precious nights with Seth having dinner with me.

"And I'm going to book in a few sessions with Emily soon too. Seth could come round and keep you company. He can fetch you a drink, answer the door if anyone knocks."

Slowly, Maggie hobbled round until she faced me. She coiled the octopus arms all fourteen-year-old girls possess around my neck and leaned into my shoulder. "I get the message."

I patted her back. "You know I'm doing my best at this whole mum thing."

"I know. We won't let you down."

"You couldn't if you tried. Just be yourself, honey. Make mistakes, feel your way, keep your head, and do not ever let fear make your choices for you. Unless it's fear of getting pregnant or catching an STD."

We started to sway together with the music, jigging clumsily between Maggie's crutches.

"Why did you never teach me to dance?"

"I wanted you to find your own steps. Your own passion. And look, you found dancing all by yourself."

The song finished, and a slower one took over. Seth came up and tapped me on the shoulder. "Excuse me, Mrs Henderson. If Maggie can manage a dance, I'd really like to cut in."

I clenched her tighter, even as she tried to pull away. "On one condition. Don't you dare call me Mrs Henderson when you come for dinner this week. There's only one Mrs Henderson and I am not anywhere close to filling her shoes."

As they began to move away, Maggie turned back. "Oh yes – I came to tell you something and then you kept talking and I forgot. I have a message for you." She looked up at the ceiling, pretending to try and remember. "I think it was from David…"

I took a couple of deep breaths, blowing them out again.

"He asked me to ask you to meet him in your place. Or something cheesy like that."

"When did he give you this message?" My voice was faint, as if it came from a cave deep inside me.

"After the competition."

"Why didn't you tell me before?"

She shrugged. "I was thinking about it. He said only to pass it on if I was sure."

"Sure of what?" *Don't faint, Ruth. Not here, not now. Not when David is waiting.*

"That I was okay with you meeting him in *your place,* wherever that is, and then meeting him again, a lot, for a long time and maybe even forever."

"And you *are* sure?" I was staggered, gobsmacked, dumbfounded. "This isn't just because I dropped the probation?"

"Hello? I'd already come to tell you, hadn't I? We had a talk. Straightened out a few things."

"I don't know." I began to feel a rising wave of panic. "It's so soon, Maggie. You're still recovering, and everything's still up in the air with where we're going to live, and you're just starting to settle in at school. I don't know."

"Mum." Maggie shrugged her shoulders. "I can see the way he looks at you. Dad never looked at you like that. Like you're some beautiful, rare species of butterfly and he can't believe you've landed on his arm. He's going to stop everything and stay completely still in the hope that you stay for a few seconds longer. And even if you do fly away, it will still have been the most amazing thing that ever happened to him and totally worth it. Even if his dinner gets burnt in the oven, or he misses his train or has to give up the job opportunity of a lifetime, he would be grateful it happened. I will never love David like I love Dad. But David has loved you forever, and I'm not sure Dad ever did."

"I think you need to stop reading Nanny's paperback romance collection. Thank you for passing on the message. Now go and dance."

I turned away before Maggie saw the tears, and stepped outside. I cried that I had given my daughter such a pitiful example of a relationship between a man and a woman for so long. That my words to her to go after her dreams, that she deserved the best, to be loved and honoured and cherished, were drowned out by my actions, that said, "Settle, don't rock the boat, learn to live with it, be grateful he stayed with you. There is no Mr Right, no man who will still be blowing your socks off with his kindness and his sexiness and his strong love for you fifty years down the road. Men sneak, and ignore, and work late, and refuse to commit; they forget and get bored, and would rather watch golf on TV than bother to have a real conversation."

I cried because she had seen what I could not dare to believe: that David not only loved me, but wanted, waited, *fought* for me.

I cried for fifteen years spent with a man who made me feel a little smaller every day.

I cried for the wedding dress I never got to wear; that my mother never got to sew the lace of my veil; that my father never got to give me away to a good man.

I cried because I was sad, because I was overjoyed, because out of all this God had given me a daughter who took my breath away.

I cried. And then I stopped. I wiped my face, told Mum I was going home, and started out on the longest walk of my life. It took me to the willow tree. And to the rest of forever.

The sun was setting as I walked round the corner of the cul-de-sac. A few wispy clouds floating along the western edge of the sky sent streaks of pink and gold, amber and violet across the deepening darkness. I made my way straight over to the tree made up of one half long, bushy branches trailing down to the earth beneath, the other still a lopsided, spiky bristle of new growth poking out from the fire-damaged trunk.

I slipped my shoes off, my aching feet sinking into the deliciously cool grass of the Big House garden. As I approached the willow, the sound of "I Don't Want to Wait" – the song from that fateful summer; the one David had meant to play for me on the night of the school leavers' dance – drifted through the leaves. My heart pounded. My bare skin flushed despite the chill in the air. As I reached the tree, a thousand white fairy lights flicked on, bathing the branches in a soft shimmer. Gingerly pushing past them, through the canopy, I stepped off the grass and onto a very small plywood dance floor. Later I saw the table with champagne and two glasses, the hamper of cheese sandwiches – not stale – and the folding chairs. But I didn't notice them then. All I could see was David. Sticking his hands in his back pockets, a tiny frown creased his forehead. He coughed, then looked away, before shrugging his shoulders.

"A bit cheesy."

"I love cheesy."

"Took me ages to find the song."

"I love this song."

"I'm so sorry it's sixteen years late."

"I don't care."

"Ruth Henderson. I have loved you my whole life. Are you ready to dance with me now?"

I nodded, laughing in response to his widening grin. David stepped forward, one arm extended. I took his hand. And finally, we danced.

# Epilogue

It was girls' night at Lois's house. We lounged around the garden on various chairs, beanbags and children's play equipment while making our way through an Italian feast. Ana Luisa, balancing a bowl of gnocchi on a belly as round and ripe as a melon, shifted awkwardly in her camping chair.

"This is no good. Can somebody help me up? I have to empty my poor, squished bladder before something embarrassing happens."

Ellie leaned forward on her cushion and managed to pull Ana Luisa to a standing position without even getting up. "Are you sure you're going to last until after the weekend? I've delivered a few foals in my time, but I think whatever you're incubating in there is going to need more than some strokes on the nose and a bag of oats before it gets out."

"Tell me about it!" Ana Luisa stretched out her full magnificence in a dress that encased her glowing – and still growing – frame like a tent. "I cannot believe I have another six weeks of this to go. I can't even remember what my feet look like. And my nipples! My goodness, they look as if –"

"Too much information!" Maggie, one of the night's honorary guests, grimaced in horror.

"Keep going, Ana. Feel free not to hide the more unpleasant aspects of pregnancy with my loved-up daughter."

Maggie spluttered. To be honest, so did a few of the others. "ME? Loved up? Says the woman who *simpers* and *blushes* every time anyone mentions tomorrow. Or David. Or anything remotely, vaguely connected with either one of those things."

I smirked. I did do that. I was indeed utterly, deliciously loved up.

Ana Luisa waddled off to the bathroom.

"Where are your sisters tonight, Ruth?" Ellie asked. "Aren't they coming over?"

"They'll probably pop in later on, but first they need to get themselves beautified ready for tomorrow. Lydia's brought them the latest celebrity fad treatments. Including a face pack made of nightingale droppings."

"Nice." With that thought, we resumed eating.

Emily suddenly barked out, "Hand it over!" thrusting her arm out in Rupa's direction.

Rupa smiled sweetly. "I don't know what you're talking about." She surreptitiously folded her hands in her lap.

Emily waggled the fingers on her outstretched hand. "I told you if you couldn't keep it in your pocket, I'd confiscate it."

Ellie shook her head. "Seriously, Rupa. That's been, what, all of eight minutes."

"I know, but she's got a cold and –" She broke off into a squeal as Ellie launched out of her chair and made a dive for the phone. The two women wrestled briefly before Ellie's superior size and strength forced Rupa to give it up.

Puffing slightly, Ellie passed the phone to Emily, who tucked it into her jacket pocket. "There we go. If Harry calls, or texts, I will be sure to let you know."

"That's not fair!" Rupa looked at me for back-up. "You can't stop me texting my husband. Why do you care anyway? I'm still joining in with the evening. And I'll only get more stressed if I can't check she's okay."

I pulled out my phone, reading from the screen. "Please take R's phone if texts or calls me again. Hope asleep and new episode of *Whole Wild World* on."

Rupa gaped at me.

"She's fine, Rupa. Please try to relax and enjoy tonight. You really need it."

Her eyes flicked from Emily, now tossing an olive into her open mouth, across to my mum, who pulled a wry face, lifting up her glass in a toast.

"All right. I'll try. But you have to promise to tell me if Harry messages. And I'm going home at ten."

"Of course you are." Emily winked. "Here, have another glass of fizz in the meantime."

Ana came back, leading a last-minute guest. "Look who I found lingering on the doorstep."

Vanessa stepped into the garden, carrying a pretty gift bag tied with a cream bow. "I don't want to intrude. I just came to give you this."

She handed me the bag, hovering awkwardly until Mum propelled her into a seat, thrusting a cranberry and lemonade mocktail into her hand. I opened the bag, carefully taking out the silver tissue paper parcel. Inside the parcel was a set of ivory vintage lace lingerie, complete with garter.

"These are beautiful, Vanessa!" They were. A world away from the high street bra and knickers I had been going to wear.

"The garter's just a lend. It belonged to my grandmother. I thought it would do as your something old and borrowed. And, see the blue ribbon?"

"Well, there you go, Maggie." Mum tutted. "There was no need for the hair dye after all."

Maggie flicked her cobalt-coloured hair over her shoulder and shrugged.

I stood up to give Vanessa a hug. Who'd have thought it? Vanessa Jacobs at my hen night. Vanessa Jacobs *invited* to my hen night. Lois leaned over and had a closer look.

"They are sensational, Vanessa. Sexy and sophisticated all in one. You should stock them in the shop. I think I might be able to persuade Matt to get me some."

"You might. But don't let him see the price tag before he agrees to it."

"Oh, maybe I'll just surprise him one morning."

Emily grinned. "I take it you're both enjoying Teagan starting nursery."

"Enjoying? Relishing! This Wednesday was her first time staying for the whole day. Which of course, coincidentally, also happened to be Matt's day off."

"Oh, how lovely!" Mum boomed across the garden. "Did you have a day out together?"

A long, slow smile spread like hot fudge sauce across Lois's minister's-wife face. "We did not. We had a day in together. And yes, it was lovely."

Maggie stood up, flinging her drink onto the table. "That's it! I can't take any more! Is this what you do on girls' nights? Talk about sex and intimate body parts while ogling raunchy underwear? You're all obsessed. If you don't let me go in and watch TV with Seth and Matt I'm going to gag."

"Permission granted." I grabbed her as she slipped past me, and gave her a kiss on her cheek. "Don't stay up too late. Big day tomorrow."

"Really? I hadn't noticed."

A big day. Tomorrow I would wake up in the quirky cottage David and I had bought on the outskirts of town, half paid for with the earnings from my animal pictures. I would drink champagne and eat a smoked salmon bagel for breakfast. My hugely pregnant, about-to-be step-mother-in-law would style my hair and do my make-up, while my other friends faffed and laughed and helped keep my sisters under control. I would put on the exquisite silk wedding dress hand embroidered by my mum (no sequins), don my veil and take my father's arm as he led me down the aisle to meet the man – not of my dreams but of real life. My life. It had taken long enough, but I had actually, finally got myself a life worth living.

If you loved *I Hope You Dance*...
don't miss

# Making Marion

"A wonderfully warm-hearted story full of love and laughter."
– *Victoria Connelly*

Marion Miller comes to Sherwood Forest to uncover her father's mysterious past. She is looking for somewhere to stay, but instead finds herself on the wrong side of the reception desk at the Peace and Pigs campsite. Despite her horrible shyness, she promptly lands herself a job working for the big-hearted and irrepressible Scarlett.

It takes all of Marion's determination to come out of her shell and get to grips with life on a busy campsite, where even the chickens seem determined to thwart her. Then an unfortunate incident with a runaway bike throws her into the arms of the beautiful, but deeply unimpressed, Reuben...

Can Marion discover her father's secret? And will she find peace, and perhaps even love, among the pigs?

ISBN: 978-1-78264-099-8 | e-ISBN: 978-1-78264-100-1

£7.99